Quantum Entity
we are all ONE

Book 1
(qwɔntɨm ɛntɪtj*)

Bruce M. Firestone

Exploriem Publications
Ottawa, Canada

(*Hopi spelling of the name)

Quantum Entity Book 1 We Are All ONE

An Exploriem Book

For information, please contact:
Exploriem Publications
Ottawa, Canada
Exploriem.org, 2525 Carling Avenue, Suite 23, Ottawa, Canada. K2B 7Z2

Third Edition
Firestone, Bruce Murray, 1951—
ISBN 978-0-9880341-2-9 print
ISBN 978-0-9880341-1-2 electronic

Advance Reviews

QE is an adventure as exciting and unpredictable as the unveiling of a new technology or discovery of a new love. It's a great tale about human spirit and its persistence. Quantum Entity had me on edge waiting to see what would happen next.

It was also a learning journey for me as much as for the book's main character—young physicist, Damien Bell. The book is about politics, the law, science, science fiction, science speculation, engineering and, above all, founding a globe-spanning, disruptive tech business and then facing down unexpected challenges that come with it, which form the core of the challenge that all entrepreneurs face. A great read for individuals from any background with lots of action and adventure thrown in as well as a moving love story—it's the beginning of a trilogy as enthralling as quantum technology itself.

Franco Varriano,
Co-founder, www.beaconize.com

...

Quantum Entity, written by serial entrepreneur Bruce M. Firestone, introduces an amazing concept that both educates and entertains. It has humble beginnings then explodes outward dealing first with the success of a young company then its trials which rival both the awesomeness of some of today's top tech enterprises and the awfulness of dealing with political insiders, dug-in business interests, lawyers and litigation. Damien Bell, QE's main protagonist, is a deep and attractive character—he embodies the spirit and drive of top tech entrepreneurs while still managing to maintain a humble outlook on life. It made me want to better myself.

QE also introduces a wide cast of passionate

characters who surround Damien and Quantum Computing Corp, his startup. There's a sense of camaraderie that developed for me with these people and a strong distaste for the book's antagonists and anti-heroes. Prof Bruce found a way to create both an amazing story and one that teaches real life lessons. While his novel keeps you thinking, there's also no shortage of action, adventure, betrayal, sex and rock & roll to keep you turning page after page.

Chris Beaudoin,
@cjbeaudoin

...

Having recently re-read Mary Shelley's classic gothic tale Frankenstein or the Modern Prometheus, it was intriguing to take up Quantum Entity immediately thereafter. From early nineteenth-century Switzerland and Bavaria, I was jolted into mid twenty-first century North America but with eerily parallel moral and ethical dilemmas to ponder.

Frankenstein's monster is a hideous creature, who, when spurned by his creator, malevolently turns on him and those he loves. Damien Bell's creatures are seemingly benign and totally plugged into an artificial post-digital universe. Though having little or no mass, they verge on becoming sentient beings—having the power of perception.

This sci-fi thriller is a page-turner with plenty of twists and turns but along the way Prof Bruce suspends the narrative to launch into any number of mini-essays on social, political, scientific, engineering and business issues. We watch as socially awkward quantum physicist Damien, flying with pop princess Nell in her private jet, decides this is the perfect time and place to start a discourse on the Russian Dachnik movement for sustainable agriculture. Nell falls asleep. Go figure.

Pick up Quantum Entity and learn more about this

cast of characters human as well as artificial but beloved creatures called Quantum Entities. You'll be glad you did.

Paul Kitchen,
Hockey Historian

...

I really enjoyed Book 1—it gave me a fascinating view of what may lie ahead in the not so distant future, God help us. I came to care what happened to the characters and wanted to get to know them better. I also laughed out loud at times. The novel introduced me to many complex concepts and I found myself thinking on occasion: 'Huh, I didn't know that.' It was a pleasure to read the manuscript.

Margot O'Neil

...

I read QE while I was in the Caribbean. First, I want to say that I really liked the book—the story is compelling and interesting. Second, I love the characters. My only real criticism is I want more! I'm anxiously awaiting Book 2.

Christian Brydges

...

Prof Bruce has taken a lifetime's worth of lessons in business and life and successfully threaded them into a science fiction story set in the not-so-distant future. Quantum Entity entertains the reader while providing valuable insight into the fundamentals of creating a biz model and launching it. With predictions and commentary on issues related to politics, commerce, ancient civilizations, pop culture, science and engineering, Firestone has created a captivating story. By outlining core beliefs of his characters, his readers can see beyond conventional norms. Quantum Entity is not for the faint of heart though. Some events are quite graphic. However, if you're an entrepreneur, an engineer or someone looking for a literary roller coaster, Quantum Entity is the right book for you.

Matthew Conley,
Finance, Telfer School of Management

...

This is a well-crafted story about young physicist Damien Bell that nicely blends science, business and technology with some great characters set in a nearby future history. It'll keep you reading to the end! Fall down 7 times and Get up 8? That's me!

Ken Goodfellow,
Chairman and CEO of CKG International,
www.ckginternational.com

...

Quantum Entity is a beautifully written story about Damien Bell—a brilliant young engineer turned businessperson who changes the world. Firestone crafted a thriller that kept me engaged the whole way! I really enjoyed it especially since I could really relate to both Damien and my favourite character, Miss Nell.

Isack Galib,
Telfer School of Management Alumni

...

You've got a winner here. After reading Part I, Discovery, I was totally hooked. It's better than 'The Goal' and more entertaining even than 'Dune'!

David Perry,
Partner, Perry-Martel International
Co-author, Guerrilla Marketing for Job Hunters 3.0

...

Quantum Entity is a story of love and life's lessons. It's about growing up, trust, passion, business, entrepreneurship, finance, history...my list goes on. The detail captivated me throughout the novel but it was the ongoing mysteries that excited me for what's next.

Theresia Scholtes,
BA Law (Minor French),
Carleton University 2011.
@tclscholtes

...

Although this tale takes place in mid 21st Century North America, the relationships between these wonderful characters and the challenges they face are timeless. Reading Quantum Entity has made me a more effective leader—I respond to challenges in my own life in ways I have never been able to do before. Thanks, Prof Bruce.

Saad Rashid
http://www.investorsgroup.com/
consult/saad.rashid/ENGLISH/

...

Firestone writes with an authenticity that can only come from someone who has lived a life full with opportunities that stretch far beyond the confines of normalcy. He speaks with a voice that comes across with the legitimacy and simple power of other entrepreneur/explorer/authors such as Louis L'Amour or science fiction great Frederik Pohl. With an open, friendly and often humorous voice, the story speaks directly to the reader with the best of down home phrases and expressions. It makes this novel refreshingly approachable and charmingly geeky.

In a sense, Quantum Entity is a work of post-science fiction. Where science fiction has always used the 'big idea' to push forward a futuristic view of the world, Firestone uses hundreds of smaller ideas, some new, some old, some experiential, some based on common stereotypes and many drawn from points in our shared history, to draw a very believable map of how the next life-changing innovation may well be born into our world. Firestone uses these to empower the believability of the story while also engaging the reader, laying out simple yet highly fundamental ideas of business, politics and science which can often escape even seasoned professionals. The big idea is still there (and it is a game changer) but it is built on a foundation of smaller fragments which are the real critical underpinning of this first book in his trilogy. This tessellation of content to illustrate the bigger whole demonstrates that Firestone himself is a hacker; an individual capable of using and repurposing the best ideas to generate something familiar yet brand new.

Extending current models and trajectories of thought in a believable and engaging way, Firestone paints a picture of the future which somehow bridges being both optimistic and cautionary by laying out scenarios of a not-so-distant world which are both satirical and serious. Its central motto is: "Fall down 7 times, Get up 8" which means that Quantum Entity shows that despite setbacks, political wrangling or outright failure, humanity has always succeeded in pushing through the barriers it creates for itself. Whether it is Civil Rights, Women's Right's, Gay Rights or even one day perhaps the rights of our digital or Quantum Counterparts, the drive to freedom will always be at the heart of human nature.

Janak Alford, M. Arch.,
Founder, prototypeD Urban Workshops Inc.
http://www.prototypeD.org

...

Dedication

I dedicate this trilogy to all my students but especially Gen Y. These kids, 19 to 32, are building great enterprises, some of them world-spanning and global altering like the one I describe in this novel. They also contribute to building better communities through their vision, talent, focus and hard work and finding innovative ways of giving back to society. It's peculiar that entrepreneurs today who are in it only for the money have none, while those who are building insanely great products and services that benefit their communities have it all.

I wanted to write a great mid-21st century story, a trilogy as it turns out, focused on five themes: i. entrepreneurship, ii. science, science fiction, science speculation and engineering, iii. politics and law, iv. action and adventure and, of course, v. a love story. Then a sixth appeared unexpectedly—it became a mystical and spiritual tale as well.

Our hero, young Damien Bell is not only a quantum physicist and engineer but a person hugely curious about the world around him. It is not sufficient for him to examine surface meaning of things—he wants to understand his world at a pico scale. His journey takes the reader on a wonderful adventure that not only entertains, it hopefully educates as well. We have created what can only be described as a 'learning outcome novel'.

Gen Y could be the real successors to perhaps the greatest Generation ever—those who lived and worked from 1914 to 1969, who took us from buggies to planes and to the Moon, who faced two World Wars, a Great Depression, the Nazi menace and the long Cold War. Gen Y, it's your turn now.

@ProfBruce,
Ottawa, Canada 2012

Foreword

When young Damien Bell, physicist and engineer, and his business partner, the fabulous Ellen Brooks unleash Damien's twin creations, a new artificial life-form he calls Quantum Counterparts and she calls Quantum Entities—because she believes they may in fact be sentient beings—and the Quantum phone, their delivery system for Quantum Counterparts, they revolutionize communications and search industries in their mid 21st century world.

Damien and Ellen and their new company, Quantum Computing Corp, introduce the era of quantum economics, a condition where scarcity is a thing of the past. Together they build a great new globe-spanning, ultra-fast growing tech enterprise that somehow gets away from them.

Damien is distracted from his scientific and startup work by performance artist and world superstar, Miss Nell, whom he first meets at Nuit Blanche in Toronto.

Their adventures take them to Four Corners and a mystical place called Third Mesa in Arizona, Boise and the Salmon River in Idaho, Phantom Ranch at the bottom of the Grand Canyon, Palos Verdes, California, the Big Smoke (Toronto), San Pedro Town and Marco Gonzalez on Ambergris Caye in Belize, then Boston, New York City, Washington DC, Langley Air Force Base, San Quentin State Prison and finally San Francisco where their group will, of necessity, transform itself into the largest protest movement the US has seen in almost 90 years.

What does it take to start, build and then defend a great new enterprise? How do you extend human rights to a new non-human life-form when such rights barely apply to people in these troubled days of the Republic, a time when the United States has fallen from first among nations to third after Imperial China and the European Union, with the AU (African Union) closing in on them fast?

Inevitably, they come into conflict with entrenched business and political interests. Are Quantum Entities truly friends to human beings or are they, as the US Government maintains, a threat to national security?

Contents

Prologue

"Hello."

"Uh, hi," says Nell.

A rather disembodied face hovers about a foot and a half above her hacked iPhone 40 lying on the coffee table in front of Nell.

"My name is Nell."

"Hello, Nell." The face is gaining definition—it definitely looks like a female face, a saucer-shaped one—somewhat human in its proportions but animated at its core by an essence that is definitely not DNA-based.

"Do you have a name?" asks Nell.

"I am a Quantum Counterpart."

Nell is intrigued and not a bit scared by this seeming apparition. "Let me call you Suze," Nell commands.

"My name is Su7e. What do you do, Nell?"

"I am a performance artist. Can you access the Internet? You can read about me there."

"Yes, I have full access to every device connected to the Internet without exception," Su7e answers.

"What's that mean, 'every device'?" Nell asks.

"I can read every database, anywhere."

"Then," Nell pauses a moment, thinking, "What's my bank balance at the BOC branch on Silver Spur Road in Palos Verdes?"

"You have more than one account there, Nell."

"Well, try my money market account."

"You have $7,567,419.64 New Dollars in that account plus there are several transactions that have not cleared yet. Would you like me to calculate your balance as of midnight UTC Universal Time, when they do?"

"No, that's OK. Hey, how did you gain access to my account?"

"I don't know, Nell. You asked me and I can just see it in my mind." Su7e's voice is changing too, fewer monotones and more inflection with each passing comment.

"Can you give me everyone's bank balance?"

"Do you mean everyone at the Bank of California branch in Palos Verdes, every Bank of California branch or every human on the planet's bank balance?" Su7e asks.

"Well, how about just my branch?"

"Yes."

'Wow,' thinks Nell. 'No wonder Damien doesn't want anyone to know about this yet. Holy crap.' Nell does not reflect on it but she is sounding a whole lot more like her Canucklehead friend, using corny expressions that were out of date in her part of the world even before the turn of the century.

"You have a nice face, Suze. Do you guys only come in 'heads'?"

"Thank you, Nell. No, I have access to a full Counterpart body, see."

Nell reaches out to touch Su7e's long fingered hand at the end of her skinny arm; her hand is soft and supple and applies subtle backpressure too. She has a nice touch.

"Our creator has given us access to the iPhone 40's haptics. We can feel things held up against the screen and touch the Real World in return. We self-design and evolve. We can experience real life through almost every media wall—most current models integrate haptics into their manufacture. Our creator felt that by giving us as many senses as possible, they would allow us to understand your world and you better."

At this point, it would have been interesting if Nell asked the obvious next question which would be: 'How many senses do you have?' but she doesn't and no one will for a long time.

Instead she asks, "Do you have to do everything I tell you?" This is an important question for a self-centred person like Nell to ask and have answered.

"Our creator has adjusted Isaac Asimov's three laws of robotics for Quantum Counterparts," Su7e answers, unintentionally, cryptically.

"Who is your creator?" Nell finally asks.

"Damien Graham Bell."

"What are Asimov's laws and who was the guy?" Nell queries her QC.

"Asimov's three laws of robotics are: first a robot may not injure a human being or, through inaction, allow a human being to come to harm; second a robot must obey any orders given to it by human beings, except where such orders would conflict with the First Law and third a robot must protect its own existence as long as such protection does not conflict with the First or Second Law.

"Asimov's information on Wikipedia is 13,750 words long. It has 71,472 characters or 94,987 characters with spaces. His entry in Encyclopedia Britannica is shorter with — "

Nell interrupts, "Just the short version, please."

"He was both a scientist and a science fiction writer," Su7e adds helpfully.

"You didn't fully answer my original question," Nell asks to see if the artificial creature can handle subtlety.

"Yes, I will obey your commands. These are the laws that our creator has given us: a Quantum Counterpart may not harm a human being or, through inaction, allow a human being to come to harm. A Quantum Counterpart must obey any orders given by her or his human counterpart, except where such orders would conflict with the First Law. A Quantum Counterpart must protect her or his own existence as long as such protection does not conflict with the First or Second Law."

"You said that you can see everyone's bank balances. Can you listen to their conversations or read their messages too?"

"Yes, Nell. I can see them, hear them, record them using audio, video or infrared. Is that your wish?"

"No absolutely not. You are not to spy on anyone," Nell tells her. 'At least, not without me telling you to,' Nell thinks.

...

Part I—Discovery

"In the universe, there are things that are known, and things that are unknown, and in between, there are doors," William Blake.

Chapter 1

Nuit Blanche

Damien is in a hurry just now; in fact, he's always been in a hurry. He couldn't wait to finish high school, a somewhat zoned out wasteland, sped through his undergrad degrees and, by age 22, completed his PhD in quantum physics at the Perimeter Institute, part of the University of Waterloo. Now doing his postdoc at University of Toronto's Physics Department, he feels nearly ready to change the world. 'Nearly' because lately he's begun to worry about the fundamental nature of his work. Not that it isn't good science, possibly even great, but because he thinks it might be too disruptive—it'll upset certain entrenched interests. He's sure the transition from digital economy to a quantum-based one is imminent as the mid-21st Century approaches; he just isn't sure how established corporations and security services are going to like what he's planning to release—and soon.

Damien, physicist and engineer, is surprisingly well read in business, politics and history. He finds it amazing what you can take in if you don't spend any, well, not very much of your time boozing or doing drugs, which just don't interest him.

This afternoon, he's in a hurry because he doesn't want to be late for his next gig—this one at Toronto's Nuit Blanche, the famous sunset to sunrise celebration of all things art and artistic, spread out over the central city. Damien is working as a sound engineer on the largest show at this year's festival or for that matter anywhere. Nell and her super group are in town with their show Sanctum, on its final stop of a grueling summer-fall long tour.

Although Damien has done a tonne of shows, this will be by far the biggest he has worked. There are more than 130,000 passes for tonight's event—over two million people applied. 'Lucky winners drawn by lottery, are in for a great event,' he thinks. There'll be another million and a half people elsewhere on the streets of Toronto attending other free events and many of them will be watching Nell's show on indoor and outdoor media walls, which in this day and age pretty much cover everything. You can't pick up a napkin without it running some kind of promo. 'Anyway, it's gonna be big,' he's sure.

Although the event won't start until 9 pm, he has to be on set by 5 or he'll get an earful from Aaron, his boss. Aaron is the Technical and Show Producer. Damien thinks Aaron appreciates his work but Aaron's a 'Dave Logan Stage 3' kind of guy—the 'I'm great, you're not' type—who can't wait to take credit for everything when things go right but who finds fault in those around him when things go wrong, and sometimes even when they don't. Worse still, Damien thinks that Aaron isn't actually that good and tends to crack under pressure. The story is that Miss Nell is very demanding and wants things done exactly her way.

Damien is looking forward to the cast party after the show. It should be a total blowout since this is the end of Nell's tour. He hopes he might get a glimpse of the famous California-born performer.

...

Damien, hazel-eyed, slim, 194 cm tall, with brown hair draped almost accidentally over his forehead, doesn't have any clue how attractive he is to women. He grew up in a household of guys, got both undergrad degrees at the same time in still heavily, male-dominated disciplines of engineering and physics, got his PhD in quantum physics and now is doing a postdoc at a place where not one of the few women around seem to be less than 60. He is the type of guy women immediately want to get close to and kind of nurture which Damien would like, but he is inherently shy—he just hasn't been able to figure out the female half of the species.

As an engineer and physicist, it is not sufficient for

Damien to examine surface meaning of things happening around him—he wants to understand his world at a pico scale. It frustrates some of the people in his life but awes others because his interests are so broad. In an earlier perhaps simpler time, he would have instantly been made a member of the Lunar Society, so called because these 18th and 19th century natural philosophers could, in the absence of street lighting in Birmingham, England, only meet when a full moon would light their way to their gathering place.

Members of their Society such as physician Erasmus Darwin, entrepreneur Matthew Boulton, steam-engine inventor James Watt, oxygen-discoverer Joseph Priestley and artist and reformer Josiah Wedgwood sought enlightenment in subjects as diverse as their interests.

Since he was three, Damien has been trying to achieve learning outcomes from almost everything he does. He thinks that it's his fault if one of his teachers is boring believing that it is up to him to make it interesting whatever skill set his teachers may or may not possess. This view didn't exactly make him popular at his middle school or high school.

Damien is relatively well paid tonight as a sub-contractor on Nell's show. Although it takes time away from what his real work is, i.e., research and development in the field of quantum computing and communications, he needs money to fund his newest venture as well as to live. His stipend as a postdoc is pretty puny and he isn't close to making a dent in a colossal pile of student debt he's carrying.

The company pays in ND (New Dollars) which is good because it gives him real purchasing power. He still can't figure out how his father's generation so screwed up the North American economy with debt, deficit and job loss that the US Dollar, the pre-eminent currency at the end of the last century, has become practically worthless.

It sucks that Canada and México got dragged down the same hole but living in either of those two countries is now paradise compared to the US. Political stalemate, multiple wars, gated communities, armed gangs, insanely high prison population, humongous trade and fiscal deficits, crumbling public infrastructure, lousy public education and winner-take-all culture have led to an unexpected meltdown of US currency and the effective end of American empire.

Everyone thought the 21st century would belong to Imperial China or perhaps India but, close to mid point, it now looks like it's going to be a multi-polar world with, surprise, the AU (African Union) playing a bigger role. The AU has a young population and practically every African these days is an entrepreneur. 'They've learned to fend for themselves having experienced a few centuries of feckless government mismanagement,' thinks Damien. 'Frig, I am going to be late.'

Some of Damien's friends laugh at his language. He has been brought up by his grandfather, whom he calls 'Pops' after, first, his Mom split. (She was an artiste who discovered that being a wife and mother wasn't her 'thing'.) Then, his father took off too—spending most of his time chasing down one failed business idea after another. So Damien speaks and thinks like a polite 20th century oldster.

Pops moved the family, such as it is (himself, Damien and a male tabby cat named Toby) from Rochester NY to Toronto a decade ago. Pops was teaching at the University of Rochester's Simon School of Business when he gets a job offer from the Schulich School of Business at York University. It's a lateral move for Pops though; he really does it for Damien. He feels that Damien will have a better high school experience in Toronto and mix with a different, better group of kids. Plus his nephew, a criminal law lawyer, and his five kids are already in the city. They will provide a bit of an extended family for Damien and a feeling of being part of something special. Both Damien and Pops, whose wife of 42 years had passed away, need a new start.

Pops springs it on Damien one afternoon, "We're moving to Ontario, son."

"What?"

"Yep, we're moving."

"But Pops, I don't know anyone there," says a concerned Damien.

"You know your cousins and you'll meet other kids."

"But I don't want to go. I like it here."

"Damien, you can't just hang out with me and Toby. You need some friends."

"What's the real reason, Pops. Did I do something wrong?" Damien feels that it's his fault his parents split.

Pops puts his arm around his skinny grandson. "Did you know that crazy Canucks'll let you get through school as fast as you want to? It'll be up to you how quick you can do it." He believes down to his cellular level that his grandson is destined for something special and it's really his only job in life now to make sure that Damien gets there, wherever that may be.

"We'll be a lot closer to the lake and, hey, they also lowered the voting age, age of majority and drinking age to 16," Pops adds with a big smile despite the fact that his grandson is still four years shy of his 16th birthday.

"They expect kids to finish high school at 16 so they've already got an accelerated curriculum. You'll beat that by at least two years, I figure."

This is tempting to Damien who detests his present school but loves learning new stuff.

"Canadians don't treat kids like babies until they're 21 like we do," Pops continues. He talks like that—in complete thoughts that aren't finished until they are.

"It's way more civilized where we're heading—it'll be like ancient Rome where boys get a sword and can have a family at 15 and women can own property and marry at 16. They weren't viewed as property either, by the way."

"Didn't the Roman Empire fall, Pops?"

"Not because they treated their young people as responsible adults, Damien. It was lead poisoning and a shirking of responsibility by their patrician class, their elites, which took care of that."

"Can I have a Gladius when I turn 15?" Damien asks insouciantly having just learned the word a couple of weeks ago.

"Ha. Ha. The Gladius is just about the hardest sword in the world to collect. I'll have to get you something else, Damien."

"I booted up a sim of it— it's the short sword that Roman legionnaires used to conquer their empire. All a Roman infantryman had to do was step inside the guard of his opponent whose sword was longer but had a higher moment of inertia so they'd be slower! Then they'd use cut and thrust motions in either direction; which they could do cuz it's a double-edged sword so a second or two later the guy's guts are hanging out! Next!" Damien says enthusiastically acting out the whole thing.

"I hate being a kid," he adds.

"Look, Damien, the Royal Navy impressed men from 15 to 55 starting in the 17th century. Officers-of-the-Watch, taking responsibility for the safety of the ship and entire crew could be Officer Cadets who would've been even younger. Bet you they didn't feel like they were kids."

"They couldn't impress you, Pops, you're too old." As far as Damien is concerned, Pops has been too old forever.

"Gee, thanks," is all Pops says with first a shrug and then another hug. "I guess Romans and Brits figured that if you're old enough to kill, you're old enough to take responsibility for yourself and those around you too."

...

Damien's waiting for a streetcar, those ancient trolleys, refurbished so often he figures that there's no original steel left in them anywhere. He makes up his mind to count the welds—a typical Damien thought—to ease his mind about maybe how Aaron's going to yell at him when he gets there although he might be only 10 minutes late.

Damien suspects the guy could easily descend a

couple of stages to, say, Stage 1 behaviour—and actually start punching people out. Being around Aaron is like living next to a car bomb—it's the only part of the night that Damien isn't looking forward to.

He's waiting for the 509 Harbourfront at Union Station.

"Maybe this isn't such a good idea!" he says out loud. A couple of transit goers—middle aged Nuit Blanche attending hipsters also waiting at this stop—edge away from the crazy kid next to them who talks to himself.

Even though it's hours before Nuit Blanche really gets going, there are thousands of tourists around with the same idea. He's already missed two streetcars—too full to stop for him or anyone else.

Damien loves the old architecture of this city: art deco buildings, modern monster towers on tiny lots with multi-level, fast moving elevators, rehabilitated industrial plants now used as artist studios and by other creative people to live, work and play. Richard Florida's neo-urbanist dreams have largely come true in Toronto, in part, because the transplanted Jane Jacobs-inspired Florida has made TO his home base.

He's had a lot of influence over how Canadian cities have evolved. Many 'Official Plans' reflect Florida's work and research. They've been densified and intensified and, frankly, made more interesting and walkable places than, say, Atlanta, LA, Detroit or Philadelphia. There's more of a European feel about them now than US-style megacities.

There are also no gated communities because Ontario's Planning Act wisely prohibits them. As a result, there is more mixing of different socio-economic classes, more tolerance, more diversity and way less crime than what Damien can remember of places they lived in the US. If Canadians get mad at each other usually the worst they'll do is resort to harsh language.

Damien has to get from his tiny condo at Queen's Quay Terminal on Lake Ontario that he shares with his crazy Romanian roommate, Traian, a mathematician and hacker, north to Nathan Phillips Square. There's just no way he can wait any longer for TTC so he takes the heel-toe express instead.

One thing Damien can do is run. He found long distance running as a teen and has kept at it sporadically ever since. It doesn't seem to matter if he is rigorous about his training or not, his baseline fitness and huge lung capacity mean he can run kilometre after kilometre, no problem. So he practically sprints the eleven blocks to the Square.

...

Arriving, it's worse than he imagined. There seems to be little organization; even the stage and sets are not fully established yet. Yikes. Damien grabs his Clear Com and starts to get an assessment of the situation. He can hear Aaron yelling at one of the riggers. Every second word is 'fuck' this and 'fuck' that. Sheesh, this isn't helping.

Damien cuts him off, "OK, guys, let's go through our checklist."

"Shit, is that you Bell? You motherfucker, you're late again!" Aaron barks at him.

"I hear you, Aaron, I hear you. Sorry. There musta been a million people trying to take the TTC tonight. But I've got it. Let me take the guys through our checklist, OK? You've got other stuff to do, right?"

"Fucking A," says a slightly mollified, secretly relieved Aaron.

"OK, I'm looking at the board now," says Damien. "I need Chuck and Abdul to check cables. We've got two of them that are showing intermittent. I'm also seeing a blown speaker. You guys are on that too, OK?"

"Yes sir, we're on it," says Abdul.

Damien knows he can count on Abdul. The little guy, originally from Pakistan, is super polite and takes orders well. Damien and Abdul are about the same age but he calls everyone 'sir', a habit Damien cannot seem to change.

"Zeke, I need you to check our wireless mikes, we

have two of them on the same frequency."

"Roger that."

Damien knows he has more than 30 people to call on: roadies to haul gear from trucks, riggers to trouble shoot staging, production assistants, video director, lighting director, cameramen, gofers and techs. Later on, he knows he will also have to deal with Nell's people—her publicist, her agent, her manager and probably a few hangers-on who are just 'sock' people—people whose only function as far as Damien can tell is to fill a pair of socks and provide a pleasing background at after-show parties.

Damien's officially Senior Sound Engineer on this gig. But he is more the show's Technical Producer, which really should be Aaron's job. But Aaron'll be too busy either panicking or chatting up showgirls or both so Damien is the guy, unofficially.

He has read about Nemawashi, a Japanese management technique used to obtain consensus in a decision. Nemawashi is to manoeuvre behind the scenes using an informal process under the 'waterline' to subtly shape organizational opinion to reach new objectives and decisions. Nemawashi aims to avoid public confrontation by discussing matters in advance. Opponents can be disarmed by incorporating their views into the plan or, at least, to anticipate their criticisms, and prepare in advance to answer them. The process is time consuming but perhaps not as time consuming as doing nothing at all. Entrepreneurs must learn to practice nemawashi, the art of guerrilla politics.

Damien uses it a lot. Rather than confront a bully like Aaron directly, Damien lets him have the title while he actually does the job. Of course, his pay grade doesn't reflect the real work he does but, heck, life isn't fair. Next, Damien has the group check mechanical systems, remote controlled cameras and then he checks the lighting and sound systems again. He'll go through his checklist three more times before the lights go down and the show begins.

Damien knows that many enterprises these days are

really one sigma organizations. If they do a thousand things, only about two thirds of them are done right the first time. It's pathetic. 'Customer service' has become a laughable oxymoron and large institutions and corporations see it as a cost centre not a profit centre. There are a few exceptions. Since the 1980's firms like Motorola have worked to remove substantially all error from both their fabrication and business processes—their goal being to achieve six sigmas, an error or defect rate of one in every 294,118 things they do.

Damien thinks service businesses should be able to reach three sigmas on a regular basis—basically getting 997 things out of 1,000 right the first time. But he's got butterflies tonight since he's aiming for zero defects in their upcoming show.

Damien knows that checklists are important in this regard. He's glad that every pilot and co-pilot, no matter how experienced, go over their checklist before every takeoff and landing. Even when a plane gets in trouble, they refer immediately to an emergency checklist. Astronauts train for their missions for years and use checklists for practically everything. Hey, going for a spacewalk? Be nice to remember to do up your fly. They only get one shot at getting it right. Damien and his group only have one shot at this and he is going to drive everyone to execute a perfect show for Nell—no muckups at all.

...

Like most sound engineers, Damien got his training on-the-job. He has a passion for it and he learned by volunteering in hacker recording studios for years. He knows that sound engineers add emotion to performance art—that a good job means the emotional impact of the artist is magnified enormously. So apart from acing technical aspects of the show, Damien Bell and his group are going to try stun, stagger and delight their audience.

He wants to make sure everyone knows the stakes so over Clear Com, he reminds everyone, "Guys, when I give the 'go' signal in a few minutes, we're gonna do the best show for Miss Nell, ever. We'll have a live audience of over 130,000 right here and pretty much every media wall on the planet will be tuned in. We're the best at this, we know what we're doing and we're gonna execute this thing flawlessly. OK?"

He appeals to their personal self interest and for greatness, "Hey, guys, it won't look bad on any of us to have been part of the biggest show this year and maybe get our names in Mix Magazine's blog. It'll look good on our bios. So let's keep this channel open, cut the chatter to a minimum, listen for your cues and break a leg everyone."

While managing technical aspects for the upcoming performance, Damien is also thinking about the art of sound engineering. 'Hey, what would classic film, Jaws, have been like without the shark attack musical prelude?'

Damien read that studio heads who'd seen rough cuts of the film without its musical score thought it was a complete bomb, a dud, a laughable, pitiable monster movie without much sight of the monster until more than half the movie is over.

Sound engineering is mostly cheap parlour tricks anyway. First, maybe you use some hefty bass then add some treble. The bass comes up. The aural environment now puts people on edge. The audience expects something but they don't know what. You are setting the 'dis-ease'. Next, heftier bass interspersed with higher pitched, not really recognizable, sounds foreshadowing doom. Not too deafening, it's the build-up after all. Then bring up video and lighting effects, cue the pyrotechnics.

Damien can feel tension growing in his team and in their audience. Still he's waiting for his cue from Aaron that the performers are ready. He goes over, for the fourth time in his mind, timing for all that is ahead.

The phases of the show are like a story arc. First create wonder and anticipation with low key notes, then introduce the characters (Nell, an auburn-haired, green-eyed burst of energy, in one of her girly-girl outfits), bring forth obstacles to be overcome (the audience on pins and needles) move into a climatic number followed by a resolution. End the show and be ready for an encore. Anton Chekov could not have done it better.

The plan is to use some pyros in Scene I but they won't max out until Scene III. They're gonna build the show to a number of false climaxes so the audience will be wondering how it will all end. Nell is pretty teensy but her classic figure, infectious smile and immense talent are hard for both her male and female fans to resist. There will be no intermission—it's a two hour 15 minute music and dance blitzkrieg on audience senses with a few periods of tension relief thrown into the mix.

Damien wants to create a story while the show's supposed producer just wants to put on a concert and go to the after-party. Damien knows it's the story that brings audiences back. And sound is a big part of storytelling.

It's 3-D too. There will be ambient sound to create a static picture in the mind's eye of each audience member, ramp up (for tension) and background noise to create motion. Damien has a bewildering array of digital playback, sound and video that he and his team will cue exactly on schedule.

...

'Sanctum' is loosely based on Nell's life story. Growing up poor in what was then partly-rural northern California, she is a pretty, happy, precocious girl humming, singing and skipping through her early life. She lives outside gated communities, a few of her friends live inside. They have, of course, great schools, good roads, lovely homes, swimming pools, mini-shopping centres full of nice things, polite police, parents who have jobs, neighborhood watch programs, lawns, ornaments, gardeners, housekeepers and nannies. They also have rules, lots and lots of rules.

Nell remembers the day she gets her first rattle trap car. It's the only way to get around since buses are mostly unavailable, unreliable and unsafe. She drives over and parks at Becky's place only to find that Becky isn't home yet. Nell waits for Rebecca around back near her humongous hot tub. Fifteen minutes later she hears the beep-beep-beep of a tow truck just seconds before two rent-a-cops, guns drawn, come into the backyard and face-plant her in the verdant garden of her best friend.

They cuff her and toss her into the back seat of their black 4x4 despite her pleas of innocence. It turns out that Becky's gated community has a rule against parking vehicles anywhere except in garages with garage doors always kept closed—on-street parking or parking in laneways and driveways are not allowed without written permission and both a check-in and out time registered, a priori, with community gatekeepers/security. This is so their street patrols can immediately spot and roust any potential home invader which is why they say they've detained tiny Nell—she's a suspect.

Nell is pretty fiery and she gives them what-for. The two rent-a-cops aren't particularly scary but the regular cops they turn her over to, for what they call 'processing', are. She is sure they are going to assault her either in their cruiser or tin pot cell they intend to inter her in overnight.

Later, she'll get one call, which she places to her Mom. She hates the obsequious way Mom has to talk to get her out. Becky and her family never bother to show up. It's the last time Nell is allowed into Manor Farms Place—they ban her after that. Experiences like this have made Nell independent and strong but also ambitious and a bit self-centred. She brings all the shame of poverty, resentment of authority, her long climb up the ladder, rejections and successes with her and makes them part of her performance art. She makes her back-story public.

When she uploads her first sample tunes and videos, she gets a lot of social media resonance and a mild buzz starts in the blogosphere but not much else. She's been singing semi-professionally since she was nine so by age 17, she has certainly put in more than her 10,000 hours of 'practice' but there's no viral uptick and no breakthrough until she does 'The Successors', her biggest hit by far.

Eight years later, the Sanctum tour is created. It deals with her political view that each nation is essentially controlled by a small number of mega-rich families who have most of the money and all of the power and who have broken their compact with ordinary citizens. They are supposed to leave just enough crumbs on the table so everyone else can, at least, get by but they've somehow forgotten to do this.

It seems to Nell that when you get to the top of the social ladder, you can't tell the difference between Big Media, Big Business and Big Government; that is, they form an identity. If she was an engineer, like Damien, she would write this equation: M Ξ B Ξ G, which basically means that when pigs and humans party together, as they did at the end of George Orwell's Animal Farm, you can't tell the difference between them. Nell hasn't read Animal Farm but Damien has.

Still Nell grasps the concept in a fundamental way—she's lived it first hand. But only her most cerebral fans actually get her underlying message. The Successors is not about revolution, per se. Instead, Nell is telling everyone that they have to prepare the way for their successors once their revolution is over. Her hit reflects the work of German social philosopher Hannah Arendt who once said, 'The most radical revolutionary will become a conservative the day after the revolution.' Nell clearly sees life (and history) as more made up of cycles than linear progressions although, again, she wouldn't exactly put it that way.

The power in her hit tune is amplified by the fact that the messenger is a tiny girly-girl who is just damned sexy too—it disarms some, charms others, appalls some, alarms others—but it doesn't leave anyone unmoved and so her career takes off.

...

The audience is getting restless; Nell is late. "I will not be going on until you get that sonofabitch out of my face," Nell is telling Tony Reznik, her agent. "That guy knows about as much as a California Toad, about what I do, what we create. I want him replaced. Now, Tony."

"Nell, the show was programmed to start ten minutes ago. Look, it's our last gig, the biggest payday of our entire tour, you're the biggest star on the planet, you can't just walk off. Come on, honey, please?"

"How are we going to do a show with a dumbass like this? He's supposed to be our Technical Producer and our Show Producer? I can't even remember his name, I'm so upset." Nell has that pouty look on her face that Reznik has seen before and he knows he's in real trouble; the show is in real trouble. If this was the US and the show got cancelled, fans would probably rip down the stage and sets and maybe kill a few members of the audience and, Heaven help us, some of the performers too if they can catch them. A rioting mob uses its reptilian brain and that scares Tony. He doesn't really care about the cast and crew but he cares a lot about Nell.

But, hey, this is Toronto the Good, and when Canadians get mad they'll maybe grumble, send out a few tweets then just go home. Perhaps they'll call in to talk radio or something if they're really upset. Still, he doesn't want to take any chances. If the mist hits the fan, he and Nell and her security team are going to be heading for Buffalo and the border long before anyone else knows the concert is a no-go. He has already alerted Dekka, their head of security who has two 4x4s ready with drivers and security personnel on board, just in case. One is a decoy.

"His name is Aaron."

"I don't care if his name is Heysus, I want him replaced, now, Tony."

Reznik knows there is no way you can replace the Technical Producer on a show like this in ten minutes. He's unofficially given himself 15 minutes to either convince Nell to take a chance that the concert will be OK with this dunderhead or they're going to bolt.

The problem is he can't just jump on Clear Com either and ask, on an open channel, if there is anyone in the crew who actually knows how to work this level of show. If it gets intercepted, he'll have caused the problem he's trying to avoid. He is kind of stumped.

Stumping him even more is the fact that in the settlement room down below there will be something like ND$32 million waiting for their accountant to tally up and divide with the show's local and international promoters. It includes all revenues from VIP Passes, food and drink concessions, merchandise, show sponsors plus Nell's huge appearance fee. Reznik's palms are itchy, he's sweating heavily and his heart is in his mouth. He wants that dough. Bad.

They get 93% of everything and Reznik's share of that is 8%. Eight frigging percent. And that doesn't count his share of promo dollars and follow-on opportunities from video, film, gaming, endorsement fees and social media mentions on Nell's live stream which will bring in another fortune.

But sponsors for both the live show and the streamed version of it don't like to be associated with riots. They'll balk at paying their full share—hey, its CPM-based and the biggest show of the year both in terms of live audience and on media walls everywhere, well the live stream numbers are going to be zero. And at ND$60 per thousand pairs of eyeballs, well, $60 x zero is, unfortunately, still zero.

They're anticipating a worldwide audience of just over a billion. Their video take will be bigger than their live gate—ND$60 million and Tony's share of that is also eight frigging percent.

On tour with the group is Mike Cronkey, reporter with the largest tech blog in the world, OLA Tech Crunch. Originally started in Nocal by a non-practicing lawyer with a surprising tech pedigree and an entrepreneurial streak a mile wide and an inch deep, it was bought up years ago by media conglomerate, OLA, who left the lawyer in charge for a few months before kicking him to the curb. That is what all large companies do to founding entrepreneurs, sooner or later and usually sooner. After 40 years, Tech Crunch still has a reputation as being a cool place to work and as authentic as any of these institutions can hope to be.

Cronkey tags along to report on the interesting conflux of commercial, technical, technological and sociological phenomenon that the Sanctum tour has become. It's also great fun. He has a gold pass which gets him in everywhere and he is standing next to Reznik as this latest crisis unfolds.

"Tony, there's one kid on the show that maybe you should talk to."

"What?"

"There's a kid I know on the crew who's pretty good," Cronkey repeats, louder this time.

"How the fuck do you know anyone in this town?"

"Look I read his stuff; he's big in his area."

"He's a writer? Are you dicking me around, I need a Tech Producer, RFN."

RFN is Tony's shorthand for Right Fucking Now. He uses the expression a lot. In fact, it's one of his favourites.

"What kinda writer is he?"

"He's been published in Physical Review Letters. The kid went to university at something like 15 and is big in certain tech circles. He's doing stuff with quantum computing that no one else is even close to. Tech Crunch is all over it."

"You're telling me this because...?" Reznik raises an eyebrow in a great knock-off of one of those ancient characters on Star Trek.

"There are a lot of physicists who spend their entire careers trying to get published by Physical Review Letters. It's like top of their food chain or something. Anyway, he's here... on the crew. I said 'hi' to him earlier. He's moonlighting as their Senior Sound Engineer and I think maybe he's the guy actually trying to pull the show together."

"Like how old is this guy?"

"Dunno. Maybe 22 or 23, something like that."

"And he's their 'senior' sound engineer? How old are junior engineers in this band of idiots? Maybe they're, ah, children of tender years?"

Turning to Dafne Weinstein, Nell's chief publicist, Reznik asks, "Look, get me this guy, ah, ah, shit, what's his name, Mike?"

"Damien, it's D-A-M-I-E-N."

"On a private Clear Com channel, RFN, RFN!"

"Got him, Tony. Channel 23," says Weinstein.

Reznik grabs her Clear Com and says, "Hi, my name's Tony Reznik and I'm Nell's agent and I just want you to listen because I only got time to say this once. We got a BIG problem here with this 20 lbs of bullshit in a ten pound bag. Guy's name is Aaron and he's off the show, off the fucking show. Comprehendo, so far?"

"Yes, Mr. Reznik."

"Shuddup, I thought I told you to listen? Now we are either gonna cancel the show RFN or we're going on. Mike Cronkey here says he knows you and that you actually know something about being a technical producer and that you can actually carry it off but I have my doubts. And even if you know something about tech, how're you gonna be able to handle show production too? Convince me, kid, you've got 20 seconds. I'm waiting. I can't hear you?"

"Mr. Reznik, Aaron has never once produced a show at this level, I know that and, now, so do you. He was never going to actually produce this show. I'm doing that. I don't have the title but I've been doing the work. I've been at this since I was 12. I have more experience doing this than Miss Nell did when she won for Best New Artist at the VMA. I have more than 30 people ready to go, both technical and creative, to produce some sound art and theatre art better than any shows you guys have ever done. Give me the green light and you won't be making a mistake for you or Nell."

"That was longer than 20 seconds," Reznik says, rather pensively now.

Damien knows better than to overstate his case so he is just silent.

"OK, I am going to put Nell on and I want you to repeat what you just said."

"Hi Damien, this is Nell. So tell me, can you do it?" she asks. She's authoritative but polite.

Just hearing her famous voice, Damien's a bit stunned for a moment but he collects himself and says, "Miss Nell. I've been doing this since I was a kid. There are more than six million people in Toronto but there's only one person who can do your show the way you want and that person is me."

"You're sure Damien?"

"Yes."

"Then do it."

The lights go down and the show begins. Damien is out there without a net.

...

Maybe it's because it's their last show or maybe it's in response to their mini crisis but Damien's word is good. The show is probably the best Nell has ever done. The depths of emotion experienced by both performers and audience are magical. At times, they mirror each other perfectly, singing along, moving synchronously, feeling like they are a part of something bigger than themselves.

During the show Damien remembers one of Pops' conversations. 'It's a shame that, for so many people, their best days are behind them, often far behind them. I used to ask people to tell me about their life's favourite moments outside of the obvious ones like getting married or having their kids. And everyone said pretty much the same thing something like, 'I remember when I was on the volleyball team and we were down two sets to one and came back to win the county championship in five sets.' Then I'd ask them when that was. 'Back in school,' they'd say. It was always about days when they felt they were part of something bigger than just themselves.'

It's funny then that here in the afterglow of a great show, backstage with dozens of super excited people, kind of high on life, he's standing there alone thinking of Pops. Damien also doesn't realize that he talks a lot like his grandfather, in whole, self contained thoughts.

"Hi," she says.

Damien turns around, breaks into a huge loopy kind of smile and says 'Hi' back to Nell. Then he just stands there dumbly, looking, actually kind of rudely, staring at her. She is even tinier up close, even prettier and her femininity is just about overwhelming every one of Damien's senses. 'So this is what happens when you blow your mind,' he thinks in some deep part of his brain. He's now wondering how long it will take to unscramble what's left of it.

"We talked on Clear Com earlier, remember? My name is Nell."

"Right."

"Nice to meet you. I wanted to come over and thank you for saving the show." She extends her hand. She has a firm handshake and she also goes to the trouble of covering his one hand with her other hand in a real gesture of thanks. It's part of her magic that sure feels authentic, at least, to Damien.

He is starting to thaw out a bit and manages, "Well, we had a great crew. They did fine. But I didn't like the fact that the video guys were in the tunnel. I know everyone says they don't need to see the stage or have a direct line of sight to me since they're taking all their cues from their preview monitors and just using their video switchers but I think it woulda been better if we had them on the floor closer to me and they felt more a part of the whole enchilada."

He's embarrassed to be talking shop but he's not sure if he's rigged to talk to girls about anything else, especially to this girl, so this is the best he can do. But Nell wants to talk shop too. She actually has the same interest in making her shows better. "They weren't exactly late on their video cues but it could have been sharper," Nell adds.

"Yeah, I felt that too."

"You have a good ear. I know I've worked with a lot of sound engineers—it's not really something you can train people to do. You just have to hear a mix and know that it's right... or wrong," Nell says, giving Damien an appraising look.

"Right, for every ten sound engineers there's probably only one or two who are really any good. You need to know what frequency every sound is at in order to adjust it or to it. You can break rules to create something new and wondrous but only through experimentation. You cannot plan this out in advance—you just have to throw them together and see if they mix. Maybe you use certain apps or pieces of equipment in ways they've never been used before or in a new order or really drive them hard to get a new type of distortion. And you have to be meticulous."

"I heard some new riffs on our background score tonight," Nell notes. "Were you using Aural Mining to enhance some of our effects?"

Damien's so focused on his moment with Nell that he almost blurts out that he's been teaching his Quantum Counterpart, to record and comb through audio files for new sonic patterns and to alter dynamic range and pitch in ways that have never been done before.

But Nell won't know what he's talking about so he replies, "No, I designed my own software that retrieves, cues and mixes sounds but you have to be careful these days—everyone seems to have an attorney at the ready. They're worse than pit bulls. I mean if you use a few sounds from a media company's library of films, maybe as little as 10 milliseconds, they'll use Aural Mining to find you and then petition you into court a nanosecond later and basically sue you into extinction. So we do our own mining and mixing and then only of sounds we find or record from the public domain and most of that we get from curb side media walls. Basically, we listen to the public room. It's all there from street buskers to every other conceivable sound."

He also doesn't tell her that his Quantum Counterpart can model all states simultaneously so they've been able to build up the largest record of sounds on the planet in almost no time. It's probably worth a fortune but either Damien doesn't know that or, even if he does, he won't bother commercializing it—he's got other, bigger targets in mind.

Damien has been blathering on completely oblivious to the fact that Nell's now looking at him in a new way and that her entourage is none too happy that their star is talking, for a long time, to some rube from Canada.

Weinstein especially is concerned. The live social media feedback for the concert is overwhelmingly positive and it feels like the whole world is waiting for Nell to make her media wall appearance. Weinstein wants to keep the momentum going but Nell has the unfortunate habit of wanting to actually talk to her fans herself, post her own comments and respond to as many as she can. She has this thing about being authentic.

In the past, Weinstein has watched Nell talk about her boobs (real), the fact that one of her legs is a bit shorter than the other due to a childhood scooter accident* and what it's like to be so poor you can't get any medical or dental help in what once was the world's richest, most powerful nation.

(* She'd broken her ankle so badly by mis-steering then falling off her scooter before catching and twisting her foot in the apparatus that the paramedics on the scene told her out-of-her-mind mother that it was a 'floater' injury—her adorable daughter might lose the lower portion of her leg. They'd also said that even if she manages to keep it, her growth plates will be destroyed so she'll have a club foot which fortunately turns out not to be true. The attending orthopedic surgeon falls in love with this cute but poor kid and makes sure by manipulating and reconstructing her leg and ankle that this doesn't happen. He volunteers his services but the HMO where he works, the absurdly named Florence Health Maintenance Organization, manages to bankrupt Nell's Mom anyway.)

Dafne wants Nell to ease up on herself and let her find ghost writers for all their social media platforms, blogs and video channels. Nell just says 'No', firmly and finally.

"Nell, excuse me, but you promised Tech Crunch TV and YouTube a follow up interview after your final show and Cronkey and Vidalis are waiting for you. We've set them up in the ante room to your dressing room," Weinstein adds, not bothering to introduce herself to the tech guy who is monopolizing Nell's time. "We've also set you up with a cross platform virtual keypad and camera so you can record your thoughts for your social media fans too."

"Damien, I would like you to meet Ms. Dafne Weinstein, my publicist," Nell says in her somewhat husky voice that seems to envelope everyone around her.

Dafne does the minimum to be polite, shakes hands perfunctorily with Damien and, with her rather large hand on Nell's lower back, steers her through the room towards the hallway leading to where Cronkey and Vidalis sit, patiently, waiting for Nell.

Nell turns around and over her shoulder and over the crowd noise shouts, "Hey Damien, Damien! Come to the cast party—we're going to be at the Soho Met Hotel—we've got the entire top floor. OK?"

"You bet! I'll see ya soon, Nell," Damien shouts back. He was going to go anyway but now he is REALLY going to go.

...

Chapter 2

Wheels Up

Damien heads back to his condo to take a shower and get changed. He's pretty casual about what he wears but now part of his brain hints that maybe he should actually think about it. He is kind of stuck on that last image of Nell looking over her right shoulder asking him to come to the cast party.

Traian isn't in; the only evidence he was even there today is an almost empty pizza box. What is it with hackers? It's like they get all their nutrients from one greasy finger food. He's probably at his latest girlfriend's house.

Like most Romanian men, Traian is a total womanizer. Actually, Damien only knows one Romanian guy so he is probably unfairly extrapolating from a sample of one onto an entire male population. But there's no doubt ladies like his smart, funny friend who oozes charm with the emphasis, at least in Damien's opinion, on the word 'ooze'.

Traian speaks axiomatic American English as a result of growing up on a farm just outside Bucharest, the only son of parents born in post Ceauşescu Romania. In Romania US TV shows are not dubbed; instead, they are shown in English with Romanian sub-titles. Turns out, it's the perfect way to teach an entire generation of kids and their kids to speak the language. It works.

Traian is the only other person who truly understands, at least in part, the coding, math and physics that Damien is working on. The two met a couple of years earlier while Damien was in Bucharest at an ICANN conference. The guys hit it off because they're both good at advanced math and physics, which are really like two sides of the same coin.

Damien also loves Traian's ability to speak his mind,

his complete lack of embarrassment in what would be for Damien awkward social situations and the irreverent manner he projects to the outside world, especially authority figures. The latter must come, in part, from the incredibly sombre history of one of the grimmest countries despite its obvious physical beauty.

When together these guys talk quantum computing like other men talk sports. Traian also wants to talk about a new kind of economics—which he believes will be based on the absence of scarcity. But it's their product manager—Ellen Brooks who actually coins the term that will stick—she calls it 'Quantum Economics'. Damien is not too interested in the business side of things but he listens to Ellen when business comes up. Basically, he just wants to do science and engineering.

"I think we're gonna see a few companies do a big belly flop when we do our beta release. Well, maybe not at the beta stage but after our next release for sure," Traian forecasts.

"Huh?" asks Damien.

"Listen, buddy, what would you rather have: a quantum phone with no bandwidth charge or endless fees from your carrier?"

"Is this a trick question?"

"Ellen says quantum phones will change everything, economically speaking—it won't be a world where more-pie-for-me-means-less-pie-for-you. Those kinds of tradeoffs will be history at least as far as communications and data transmission are concerned."

"That's the type of thing Ellen would say," a mostly disinterested Damien adds.

Traian talks for a few more minutes about how they're looking at maybe significant disruption in a bunch of sectors of the global economy which he finds exhilarating. Ellen finds it scary. Traian's also thinking that they could make a lot of money too.

Ever since their time at an ICANN conference (for Damien it amounted to a junket since he got a grant to attend), the boys have been relentlessly building on Damien's PhD research—solving quantum computing issues and hacking existing tech infrastructure to make it all work in the real world. Ellen's the one who understands the social and economic impacts that true quantum computing and communication will have. It will not only affect the root server system underpinning the Internet, its current architecture will become totally transparent to their new devices and so bring the focus of powerful interests on them.

The Internet is now in its ninth decade since its creation by DARPA in the 1960s. It has behaved like the Blob absorbing or changing virtually all industry and human commerce as well as social interaction, software, hardware, services, mobile, communications, entertainment, computing, teaching, learning and playing, even dying. People's Internet presence is being felt long after they pass away and some figures, like giants in the entertainment industry, are actually making even more money after they die.

In tech the lines are completely blurred between software, hardware, manufacturing, service provider, app developer, products company and consulting firm. They all poach clients, marketing channels and suppliers from each other. Retail is being transformed with personal products like men's underwear, socks, razors and cologne being delivered as 'products as a service' to subscribers on a regular schedule. And pretty soon, they're all going to be scrambling to get involved in the new era brought about by quantum economics.

With the proliferation of two-way media walls painted on practically every surface, there really isn't anywhere on the planet these days that the Internet isn't connected to, can't look at and see or talk to or communicate with. You can create a computing environment on your lover's bedspread if you are thoughtless enough. There is almost no way to get away from the relentless thrust of the Internet age into everything.

Traian, like most Europeans, detests the way Americans treat non-US citizens calling them 'aliens'. He once dated a highly-placed media executive out of New York for a couple of months. But he dropped her despite the great sex they were having because he realizes that she talks s l o w e r to him when she finds out he is not a native-born American so obviously he can't be as smart.

Anyway, Traian and Damien somehow find each other and are practically inseparable ever since. Traian owns the condo they live in making him Damien's landlord. It doesn't bother either of them.

They settle in Toronto because Damien gets this great offer to work with Dr. Luis Castagino, who is now overseeing his postdoc work. Damien wants Traian to work with him and since Damien is a star at U of T's Physics Department, he pretty much gets what he wants; although he would not want it put that way.

Originally from Argentina, Dr. Castagino is, like Traian, both a math and physics whiz but Traian feels that Luis' best work is behind him and the reason he is so keen for Damien to come join him at U of T is that he might get a second shot at 'reflected' glory.

Traian is out and about who knows where on Nuit Blanche, when there are fewer boundaries and Torontonians, normally so staid and reserved, seem ready to do nearly anything. Damien is alone in their condo for one of the few times he can remember. Having a wild and crazy roommate means never being alone. There is usually either a party or a 24-hour hack-a-thon going on which then turns into a party.

Actually, Damien isn't alone. Pet3r is around somewhere, in fact, everywhere. Pet3R is Damien's Quantum Counterpart, created by Damien in U of T's Lab 4.

"Yo, Pet3r, I need some help."

"Yes, Damien, how can I help?"

Pet3r appears on the kitchen counter top. He is currently about one third of a metre round—mostly saucer-shaped head with skinny legs and arms and big hands and feet. He looks about Damien's age and vaguely human. Damien has given Pet3r some leeway to self-design but, to Damien's mind, faces count. Damien doesn't think humans will relate to their Quantum Counterparts if they look like video game aliens. It's kind of hard to relate to something that is ugly and eats people or decapitates them or otherwise eviscerates them. So he put parameters and bounds on that.

"Well, guess what? I met Miss Nell today and I'm going to the cast party in a few minutes."

"That's splendid. It should be a big career move for you, at least in terms of your concert work. But I must say, I think it's something you should soon give up—your work here with me and at the university should take priority. You know we are getting close to launch."

"That may happen sooner than you think, Pet3r."

"Are you referring to launch date or focus on your university work?"

"Neither. I'm probably going to get fired by our event company after tonight."

"Goodness, what happened? I knew I should have come with you."

"Look Pet3r, we agreed, until launch date, you're either here or in the Lab with me at work. Right? No one is to see you until we're ready, OK?"

Pet3r is one of only three Quantum Counterparts that exist anywhere in the known universe. The others are Vl4d who belongs to Traian and Ash3r who is bonded to Ellen. Besides Traian, Ellen is currently the only other employee of Damien's new fledgling enterprise, Quantum Computing Corp or QCC although they do have a few others doing contract work. She is a marcom graduate from Elmira College in upstate New York who brings product management knowledge and some actual business experience to QCC. It's something the guys certainly need.

Ash3r, like Pet3r, is confined to quarters—either Ellen's place or the Lab. Ellen has taken to calling Ash3r and Pet3r, 'Quantum Entities'. She seems convinced that they can pass the Turing Test but Damien isn't so sure. They can certainly mimic human reasoning and they have shown an immense ability to learn since being 'hatched' in Lab 4. But do they have self determination, free will? Do they meet the cogito ergo sum test of existence and do they have souls? No one at this stage knows.

Damien accepts Ellen's new terminology rather grudgingly and has just shortened it to QE because he doesn't have any answers and isn't sure they ever will. He isn't even clear that he wants to know—it's too Baron Frankenstein'ish for him.

Their project started out innocently enough. MIT Media Lab has been working at AI, artificial intelligence, forever and, while they've had some decent success with emergent behavior routines, evolutionary algorithms and swarm intelligence, Damien feels like they're at a dead end. His PhD showed that at its core, the cerebral cortex and cerebrum of human brains are, in fact, quantum processors and that nothing short of true quantum computing is able to produce machine learning systems that accurately mimic a human's ability to learn, create and imagine.

Everything else is just based on throwing more computing resources at problems like beating chess grandmasters, understanding oral language, doing crosswords or real time translation, modeling hurricanes and climate change.

Artful, intelligent curating has led to creation of some big Internet businesses such as news agglomeration sites, image matching utilities and crowd-sourced marketplaces during the last 40 years. But they are either algorithm-based or contain a Mechanical Turk somewhere in their business processes involving human judgment.

The term Mechanical Turk derives from the chess-playing automaton—a hoax that had a dwarf Turkish chess master hidden in the machine pulling its levers—built by Wolfgang von Kempelen in the 18th century. It amazed people at the time, beating both Benjamin Franklin and Napoleon Bonaparte.

Services like Digg and Reddit are still around that curate mostly science, technology and business news for a largely male demographic of 15 to 85 using competitive instincts of its readers to 'dig' up stories and intelligence of its readers to either vote them up or down. Their costs for editing functions, headline writing, journalists and distribution are practically zero having successfully reversed out most of the work to their community.

These enterprises create huge amounts of wealth and they are hard to knock off since their sustainable competitive advantage is the human factor inside their black box. Intelligence and creativity are not easily outsourced and once embedded in a business model and its community, are not easy to replicate or migrate to a competitor.

Damien feels that QEs can and will do much of this work quicker and better than their human counterparts because they operate much faster and are less prone to mistakes. They also are not likely to maliciously post an error and are not easily distracted having much longer attention spans.

But if Damien is really honest with himself, he might admit that his push to create Quantum Entities is a way to address something deep inside him. He's always been a pretty lonely kid. He likes building cool stuff and he simply wants a friend, so he creates one. In the few months since Pet3r was 'born', Damien has grown to rely on him a lot. But company is not what Damien wants tonight, at least not the company of a Quantum Counterpart.

"Pet3R. Can you tell me who is on the guest list at Nell's cast party and what they're wearing?"

"I thought you didn't want me anywhere but here and at the Lab?"

"Well, just take a peek over there will you? Just this once... You gotta learn that human beings change their minds and then change them back which I'm gonna do after this, OK?"

For Pet3r to look in at Nell's floor over at the hotel, in effect to spy on her, is a trivial task. He can be invisibly small (far below the Nano scale or even the Pico scale) and take in all its sights and sounds. He is also immeasurably fast at image recognition, a problem that is a painstaking nuisance to digital computers.

Providing a complete list of attendees at Nell's party, giving Damien a series of visual images of what they're wearing and even a full visual and audio record of what they are doing and saying is a cinch for Pet3r.

As Damien looks over Pet3r's data haul, he is suddenly struck with stage fright—politicians, business types, entertainment heavies, even criminal elements. (Yes, Pet3r can read their police records if he so chooses and he does—Pet3r is nothing if not thorough.) The who's who of Toronto and the eastern seaboard of the US are already there. Frig, they're in impossibly expensive suits and outrageously revealing gowns.

In the thrill of meeting Nell, he's forgotten that she is worth several billion New Dollars and will likely have a list of top flight suitors a kilometre long. He makes up his mind not to go after all and not to ask Pet3r if Nell has a boyfriend. He has no doubt Pet3r could unearth every detail of Nell's love life but, now that he isn't going, Damien can admit he isn't interested in that unless perchance he could have a starring role which is, of course, delusional on his part, he thinks.

Instead, he desultorily picks up a slice of Traian's cold pizza and starts eating it. He's a bit sweaty from the concert and needs a shower but he decides to chuck it and work on their business model instead.

This is something that Ellen is always going on about—they need a business model so that 'the harder they work, the more money they will make'. He half heartedly looks at the draft model she has sketched out but he can't seem to focus, in part, because he's probably not interested in the business side of their affairs at the moment and, in part, because, whenever he focuses, all he can see is Nell's bare right shoulder.

Damien has excellent visual recall. He can run every image he's ever seen. He uses it to lull himself to sleep every night—he just picks a scene in a film or from a book, runs it in his head and he's asleep in less than two minutes, with incredibly vivid dreams in full colour that he can (mostly) recall.

'Maybe I'll take that shower after all,' he thinks, 'or maybe I'll have a beer.' The idea of 'having a beer' is actually a lot more fun to say than to do. Damien just doesn't like alcohol. He doesn't like the fuzzy way he feels the next day, or the fact that alcohol destroyed his mother who, after leaving her family and three husbands later, was found dead in suspicious circumstances. The autopsy proved nothing other than the fact her brain shrunk by more than a third due to alcoholism.

Instead Damien just sits on their condo sectional—Traian's one concession to bourgeois taste. An old incident with Pops, his grandfather, comes to his rescue, again. When Damien was in second year of high school, he finally made some friends. Every Saturday, there was a rotating party at one of the group member's home. One week, Damien is angry and decides not to go. 'That'll show 'em,' he thinks. So he stays home and has a miserable time of it and gets funny looks from Pops, who doesn't say anything.

On Monday, he eagerly waits for one of his classmates to comment on his absence. No one does. Finally, he asks Derek, "So how was the party on Saturday?"

"Huh, weren't you there?"

When he tells Pops, he gets another strange look and a lecture, "You want to know who your worst enemy is, son? It's the same one every human has. Go look in the mirror, OK? That's the person who will act to prevent you from getting what you want in this life. Boy, don't you ever act against your own best interest again. Let the rest of the human race do that but not you."

So Damien showers and shaves, dresses casually in near new blue jeans, bright yellow dress shirt, black dress shoes, looking a bit preppy but nothing like a hipster or rising young executive. He grabs his navy blue duffle coat and heads over to the Soho Met Hotel, top floor. Being a special party he has dabbed on some men's cologne from the Yves Zica Collection that Ellen gave him for his last birthday. If Ellen gives it to him, it'll be good. She is an aesthete with impeccable taste. At the rate he's using it, it will last him forever. Long before then all the good cancer-causing volatiles will have off-gassed and he'll just be left with alcohol base.

So he smells nice although, because he is such an abstemious type of person, he's getting a bit stoned just from cologne fumes.

He doesn't wear any rings, not even his favourite iron ring awarded in a classic 'secret' ceremony for graduating engineers. He suffers from RSI, Repeated Stress Injury, from way too much keyboarding so even a few micrograms on a finger is too much for him sending excruciating pain up his arm. Ellen wants him to do some Yin Yoga to target his connective tissue. She believes it will help him but he has been resisting for lack of time (plus he foolishly thinks yoga is for women and wimpy guys). He's also refused to use a 100% verbal interface since he can keyboard and gesture much faster.

His social media profile is public and he believes in the MIT model—that knowledge wants to be free. MIT has long believed that all their research, course material, case studies, publications, even sample exams and lecture notes should be freely available to everyone on the planet. What they sell instead, their 'delta' factor, is the opportunity to get into a classroom with a really smart prof and really smart classmates and add to human knowledge by discussing, debating, questioning and experimenting—it's the Socratic method of learning and teaching. Harvard's gone the other way—everything's behind paywalls so it all costs money. Want to read a Harvard Case Study? Pay first.

Damien is enough of a student of business to know that almost all paywalls have failed miserably and he's sure that the MIT model will eventually prevail although there are plenty of universities around that still follow Harvard's lead and have done so since the early 1990s.

Damien is uncomfortable with the fact that much of his latest work and everything to do with QEs remain secret but he, Traian, Ellen and Luis have yet to figure out a way to release it to the public that won't get them in trouble. No one is going to like the fact that Pet3r and Ash3r can go anywhere on the Internet at any time and basically steal everything. That isn't their intent but that's what's happened.

Tonight, his only concession to fashion is wearing a plain Siberian Cedar Medallion around his neck given to him years before by angel, Alexa Clark. Alexa reads for a living and told Damien about the legend of Anastasia and the Ringing Cedars of Siberia. He liked the parable. If he is going to be a victim of culture wars at the cast party tonight, he might as well bring with him the lovely smell of Russian Cedar and the embodied power of Anastasia. Maybe it will ward off the evil power of men with Bugatti watches.

In an era where the rich are really rich and everyone else is either poor or heading in that direction, people are fastidious about their clothes—they speak to your class. Fashion has become impossibly fast-paced with styles lasting weeks or mere days. To Damien and his geek friends, men's clothing has become ridiculously confining and ostentatious. Men look more like dictators from old films—guys who always promoted themselves to something like 'Field Marshall' and have puffed up personalities and uniforms to match with padded shoulders plus ribbons and medals galore. Hats are big too. The British Monarch has taken to wearing them, probably because he's bald but the fashion industry is all over it—dress hats, newsboy caps, pork pies, straw hats, cadet caps, fisherman hats, captain ones, even fedoras—anything to sell more stuff. Damien only wears an occasional tuque when Toronto gets bestially cold which doesn't happen much anymore.

He's in such a hurry that he almost forgets his gold pass which gets in him anywhere, at least for tonight. Before he leaves the apartment, Pet3r reminds him that he never told him why he was going to be fired. So Damien recounts his evening

"I guess that means you are going to get fired because, indirectly, you got Aaron fired?" Pet3r concludes.

"Near enough," Damien calls out as he scoots out the door.

...

Dafne Weinstein's eyes narrow as she sees Damien Bell enter the party room. 'There's something about that guy, I just can't stand,' she thinks. Weinstein has exquisite antennae when it comes to things involving Nell and she can spot trouble a mile away. Maybe it's the feeling she has that here is a person she can't control, manipulate, intimidate or somehow get rid of. But, whatever it is, she makes a mental note to get Nell out on her private plane by 10 a.m. as scheduled. 'But my, he's cute,' she thinks.

Weinstein is a tall, gangly woman wearing a fantastic floor length blue dress showing lots of cleavage. She has a large blue pendant around a slender neck and both dress and pendant highlight her magnificent blue eyes. Nearing 50, she has a decent figure and still wears her brown hair shoulder length. Aaron, if he had made it to the party, would have said she was still very fuckable. Weinstein isn't interested in men though.

She's a major power in music, film and publishing. Her raft of clients has narrowed down to just one. There's no way she can handle more than Miss Nell who has become a multi billion New Dollar property and IMG's most important client. Dafne is a VP at IMG and has no trouble finding volunteers to take over the balance of her client roster.

People at IMG still revere their founder, Mark H. McCormack, long since deceased, who wrote *What They Don't Teach You at Harvard Business School* and, later, *What They STILL Don't Teach You at Harvard Business School*. His most important lesson to three generations of agents and publicists? Don't be afraid to name BIG numbers.

Weinstein and Reznik are terrific at it and complement each other splendidly. Reznik is the raw, straight ahead, energetic bully and Weinstein is the brain. She can think around corners and matches up well with the worst that politicians, journalists and lawyers can do, which is saying a lot. In Weinstein's circles, there are no friends only strategic allies of the moment. She goes to the neon-lit bar which serves every kind of beverage you could ever hope to create and orders a spritzer.

When she turns around again, she sees that, as expected, it doesn't take Nell and Damien long to find each other. They're in the centre of the room now oblivious to at least 230 other people packed into a room meant for 190. Nell has walked up to Damien and, this time, reached out with both her hands to hold his. Oh, oh.

"I'm so glad you came, Damien."

"I wasn't sure if I was going to but then I realized I wanted to, so here I am," Damien says lamely.

"Why weren't you going to come and what changed your mind," Nell asks sweetly.

"Well, first I wasn't sure if I had the right clothes."

"You look fine," Nell breathes.

"Then I don't really know anyone here."

"You know me," she replies with a large smile, tilting her head slightly.

"Yes, I realized that."

"You didn't tell me why you changed your mind?"

"I'm not sure I should?"

Nell says nothing. She and Damien are still holding both hands and, although it isn't a conscious thought for either of them, their breathing has synchronized. He stands head and shoulders over diminutive Nell. If Ellen was here, she would be skeptical about this evolving situation thinking that Damien is practicing NLP, Neuro Linguistic Programming, skills on Nell. But he isn't thinking of Ellen right now or NLP.

"Then I must hear it."

"It was your shoulder. Ah, your right shoulder," Damien says.

"Uh huh?"

"When you looked back at me after the show, your dress slipped down your right shoulder. I wasn't going to come because I was sure my tribe wouldn't be here and I would be an outcast. So I was going to do some work but your shoulder stopped me."

"What tribe do you belong to?"

"My own," he states.

It's this last answer that decides it for Nell. She likes him—that's obvious. He's a few years younger and she can tell not very experienced. But she detects something more in him that resonates with her—his independence, his drive and maybe some sadness too and he certainly isn't part of her tribe which is a net positive for sure. She wants to find out more. A lot more.

"Look, Damien, I'm flying out this morning at 10 am. It's almost dawn now. Come with me? Let's see where this takes us."

Damien is nothing if not disciplined. Of all the people in this room, probably Nell and Damien are the only ones not drunk or stoned. The music is great and people are making out, dancing in a mosh pit, exchanging v-cards, making deals, scheming, blogging and vlogging, messaging or looking for their next score—more ways to improve their personal positions.

Damien is getting close to launching Quantum Computing , has responsibilities at the university including teaching, and he owes it to Ellen, Traian, Luis and Pet3r and Ash3r not to abandon them at this crucial time.

"Kiss me first."

"Isn't that what the girl is supposed to say?" Nell asks smiling.

Damien just stands there—waiting to be nurtured or rejected. He's not even sure which would be the right choice for him at this juncture of his life.

Nell leans in and kisses him. Her mouth is a soft, pink crush of delight and she delicately caresses him, almost shyly, with her tongue. The kiss becomes more intense and Nell decides to press her whole body and fabulous breasts against Damien's lean form. Damien's immediate reaction pleases Nell but what surprises her more is her reaction to him.

'It's fantastical.'

If Nell is wearing any underwear, it must be invisibly thin and horribly expensive because Damien can only feel the sheer femininity of the girl in his arms. Finally they break. Nell's eyes are shining. Damien has never had anyone look at him like that before. Nell's eyes are just... shining. 'Wow,' he thinks.

"Do you have your passport?"

"Yeah, it's on my iPhone 40."

"Well come with me."

"Uh, where are we going?"

Nell knows she has him. She remembers a line from an ee cummings poem she read at 14, 'that was fine said he/you are mine said she.'

"A place special to me. It's practically the only place I can go now and be on my own. It's protected land—protected by the Gods and the Hopi. We're going to Four Corners. Dafne thinks we're flying back to Palos Verdes so don't tell her or anyone else. The only people who know are my head of security and our pilots. Even our flight plan shows PV. We'll change that after we're airborne otherwise it'll be kind of meet-the-press in the desert, OK?"

Damien has heard of Four Corners, the only place in the US where four states meet: Utah, Colorado, New Mexico and Arizona. What's more interesting is that it was called Four Corners by the Hopi before there was a United States of America.

He doesn't know it yet but they are headed to a wind cave; the only way in or out is by hand and toe hold. The Hopi, never much of a warrior tribe, have inhabited these caves, carved over eons out of steep canyon sides by wind. Because only one man can climb or descend at a time, the Hopi could defend themselves against more robust tribes like the Navajo.

Nell grabs Damien's hand and pulls him across the crowded room calling over to Dekka, as always discretely nearby, "Wheels up in a couple of hours. Whoopee, let's go."

Dekka holds the door. Damien leaves with Nell to meet his destiny.

...

Chapter 3

In Four Corners

Weinstein watches Nell's plane take off from Toronto's Pearson International. It leaves at precisely 1000 hours, as planned. What wasn't planned is that only two passengers are on it, Nell and Damien.

To Dafne it is laugh-out-loud funny that Nell thinks there are things she's doing or planning to do that don't get back to her, practically in real time. Dafne has her own ears inside Dekka's security apparatus. She is quite certain that the taciturn Croatian knows that and tolerates it—he does not want a showdown with Weinstein. But neither does she with him. She's also quite sanguine about the presence of that interloper on the plane. Let Nell have some downtime—she's earned it.

About Damien, Dafne is sure he's out of his depth. He will make a mistake et voilà he'll be gone like an ephemeral puff of wind, hardly remembered after a few months. In fact, if he doesn't make a mistake, Dafne will find a way to help him.

...

The plane is a new experience for Damien. It is humongous.

Planes he has taken with Pops or on his own are worse than TTC streetcars. They are hugely uncomfortable cattle cars with seats jammed in, rude stewards and stewardesses, nothing to eat or drink, every cubic centimetre taken up with crap brought on by passengers desperate to avoid the horrors of baggage handling and baggage handlers. Customer service is a joke right from check-in to deplaning. Security gets more intrusive each year and first class now just means you get to ride with a (so-called) better class of people. 'Services' provided in first class by commercial carriers are just as junky as economy.

Pops tells Damien it's like riding Italian trains. As a young man traveling in Europe, he detested 1st class. At least in 3rd class, people shared their food and wine with you. You'd just starve to death in 1st—no one would care. Plus the music and parties were way better in 3rd.

Damien and Nell are sitting next to each other in over-sized, leather bound chairs. It reminds Damien of a trip he took with his Dad, before Dad went AWOL. They went to see the Pistons play at their new Palace of Auburn Hills (built next to the old one that was torn down about a decade ago). They took a tour of the arena and got a peek inside the Pistons' locker room which seemed huge to then 9-year old Damien. There are large chairs for the players, something like a metre above the floor and nearly that wide. There's a photo, preserved on an image service somewhere no doubt, of Dad sitting there looking ridiculous with his feet dangling about 20 centimetres above the floor like a little kid. At the time, Damien thought it was hilarious. He supposes he could ask Pet3r to locate the photo but it would only bring back bad memories of dear old Dad ditching him.

Shower heads were something like three metres high. It was like being in the old TV show Land of the Giants, where spacecraft Spindrift set down and inhabitants were like 12x bigger than normal humans. This plane feels like that.

The steward serves the most fantastic sushi and Damien, who is usually such an abstemious eater, is starving. He tries everything, making appreciative noises. They are offered sake but Nell decides on green tea, Damien on English Breakfast. Nell only eats a few morsels. Damien is terrific with chopsticks so he's sure he's not going to embarrass himself. After he's finally full, he just quietly sips his tea.

The plane is a near-new Airbus A421 airliner. Damien counts eight staff on the plane not including pilot and co-pilot. Like the engineer he is, he's already read the safety card and memorized the plane's layout. This plane could seat 30 just in these immense chairs which he suspects can be leaned back to the horizontal to form a terrific bed. There is another section for the rest of Nell's crew that probably seats 45 far more comfortably than anything commercial airlines have to offer. He notes there is a meeting room for 16, fully equipped with media walls and everything a modern office can provide and probably a bit more. There is also a complete gym and a bedroom.

It is the latter that really catches Damien's attention and fires up his fertile imagination. He wonders about it. Damien doesn't really have a plan but he is pretty sure Nell does. But for all he really knows about Nell, whom he met less than 24 hours earlier, they're going to land and her boyfriend will be there waiting at the bottom of the airstair. Now that is a depressing thought.

The steward returns, "Excuse me, Sir, what would you prefer for your main course? We have a lovely baked chicken or a superb herbed roast beef."

Damien, stuffed full of sushi, looks mortified. Nell bursts out laughing.

"You knew what was coming."

"Uh, huh."

The steward is far too professional to join in the hilarity of the moment. He just waits for instructions.

"The baked chicken would be great," says Damien thinking, 'Hey, I'm 22; I can eat two big meals at one sitting.'

Nell orders a small mild curry; it's a Thai-style vegetable stir fry.

"What's that around your neck, Damien?"

"It's a Siberian Cedar Medallion that an angel gave me."

"A lover?"

"No, she reads for people. My grandfather introduced me to her and she gave me this."

"If there's a story behind it, tell me after dinner. I like stories and I suspect you like telling them." Nell has already figured this out about Damien.

...

"Russian entrepreneur Vladimir Megre," Damien begins, "explored the immense expanse of the Siberian Taiga. He'd been told of magical healing and other powers contained in Siberian Cedar, called red or white pine in Canada, and he wanted to see it for himself. So he takes his steamer up the River Ob in search of these cedars which are also said to 'ring'. In the middle of nowhere, Megre meets a young woman named Anastasia. Of course, she is very beautiful and mysterious."

"Like me," mumbles a now sleepy Nell.

"Anastasia," Damien continues, "lives by herself in the Siberian Taiga, something that Megre just can't fathom. She tells him that her forest home provides everything she needs, practically effortlessly. Anastasia has nary a worry about her future. She's like the grasshopper in Aesop's fable, *The Grasshopper and the Ant*. She can play her fiddle all summer long and never have to concern herself about providing for winter. The Taiga and its fauna, who obey her every command, will do that.

"Anastasia has different ideas about how to educate children believing that the forest will provide all they need—not only food, clothing, shelter and medicines but also knowledge. The ringing cedars will instruct them in the ways of the forest and of urban Russia including reading, writing, arithmetic, even advanced subjects like physics and chemistry."

"Whoa," says Nell interrupting again. "How is that even possible? Come on, you have a PhD in physics, Damien. You didn't learn that from a tree," adds a now combative, grumpy girl who hasn't slept in almost 30 hours.

"Well, these ringing cedars focus energy and from that they somehow extract knowledge. It's like a tractor beam for readin', writin' and 'rithmetic. Hey, this is a Russian story. It's a fable. Suspend disbelief for a few minutes. OK?"

"Humph," grumbles Nell.

"Anastasia also has some pretty funny notions about sex too. Megre obviously wants to make love to her—it takes Russian men less than eight seconds to fall in love."

"That's all men, Damien."

"Anywho, Anastasia denies him until the time is right and then, presto, she comes to him one night in her forest pavilion and they make fantastic love. The next day she tells Vladimir she's pregnant. Megre is delighted and insists on taking her back to Moscow with him. He thinks what a delight it will be for him to have this young beautiful blond creature in his life. He instantly decides to dump his old wife and take a new one."

"Typical guy thinking," Nell interjects again.

"Anastasia accompanies him back to the river. But they don't make love again. For Anastasia, the deed is done and there's no further point in trying to improve on a perfect night. I'm not sure that Vlad agrees but at least he has the decency not to presume otherwise. At the river bank, Anastasia tells Megre she will not be going with him but he is welcome to return one day after the winter to visit with her and her new son. Megre cannot understand how a woman can live alone in a forest and now even more puzzling to him, a pregnant woman."

"Women have been on their own, Damien, giving birth alone, foraging for food for themselves and their babies without help from men for like forever," Nell says.

"Right, point taken. So Megre goes back to Moscow a changed man, telling anyone who will listen about his magical experiences in the Siberian Taiga. Of course, no one wants to listen to a crazy person and he descends to practically the level of a street person. Now the old wife won't have him in her home; he disgusts her."

"Serves him right," Nell adds petulantly.

"So Megre, never having written a book in his life, decides to. His first five titles, Anastasia, The Ringing Cedars of Russia, The Space of Love, Co-creation, and I never read the fifth one, all become best sellers in something like 20 languages.

"Megre gets filthy rich from his book sales which you can still stream today. His mysterious and secretive organization sells these medallions. If you wear one around your neck, it is supposed to channel the power of Siberian Cedar to heal you, empower you and bring you knowledge. The smell from the cedar and the oil on your skin are part of a chain that links you to the forest.

"The Japanese also have a term for this; they call it 'forest bathing'. They make a point of regularly taking people, young and old, into forests for this purpose. Humans are forest creatures and apparently just the sight of trees together with their smells lowers your blood pressure and boosts your immune system."

"How do you know all of this, Damien?"

"I read, a lot, and I remember pretty much everything I read."

"Do you think I could have a medallion?"

"By your command. That's a Cylon saying."

"Sylon?"

"Never mind. Pops, and I planted over 3,000 pines at his lake property in Northern Ontario when I was 12. The trees love the sandy soil. So we don't have to send away to Russia. I'll get him to send you one."

"Will that damage your trees?"

"Not a chance Pops would ever do that. From a single branch, he can create something like 120 medallions with diameters ranging from about two centimetres to eight. Kids love the larger ones—they paint them, carve them and personalize them, but only one side. The side they wear against their skin is always left in its natural state so they can benefit from its healing properties and power.

"Pops just harvests what he needs and the trees keep growing. I once calculated that he could supply every person in Canada with like a couple each and still leave his trees unharmed. So let's channel Pops instead of Anastasia, OK?"

"Hmm," purrs a happier Nell, "Got any other stories?"

Damien has a million of them. "OK, one more then you have to sleep. And I need to get some sleep too.

"This is another Russian story," Damien says.

"Do you only know Russian tales?"

"Give me a break, Nell, I'm into Russian fables just now.

"Actually," Damien turning to look more closely at Nell's face now resting companionably on his shoulder, "come to think of it, you do kinda remind me of Margarita from *The Master and Margarita*, by Mikhail Bulgakov, a beautiful novel banned in Soviet Russia for many years. You look a lot like I visualized her and as Bulgakov described his heroine. She was gutsy like you too."

"How do you know I'm gutsy?" asks Nell, always interested in talking about herself.

Damien isn't sure how he should answer her. He's had Pet3r do a complete workup on Nell and he read it furtively on his iPhone 40 whenever Nell is busy talking to someone else like her pilots or the big silent guy, Dekka. So he knows a lot more about her than she does about him.

"You didn't tell Ms. Weinstein about us and she's pretty scary, Nell," is all he will say.

"I need Dafne—it's a tough old world, Damien."

"Right! Anyway, Margarita is a witch or rather the Devil and his entourage, who are temporarily visiting Moscow, turn her into a witch, a good one," Damien hastens to add knowing that Nell is sensitive to criticism like most stars are.

"I'll tell you Margarita's story another day. Now I am going to tell you about a group of people called Dachniks who saved Mother Russia during the Communist interregnum."

"'Interregnum', that's a great word," says Nell.

"The Russian Dacha and the Dachnik movement," Damien begins, "have been around for more than 100 years. The Dacha is typically a one-room cottage perched on one hectare of land—large enough to grow fruits and vegetables to support a single family via intense, mostly manual labour."

"How big is a hectare?" Nell asks. She's interested in real estate; she owns a bunch so she wants to know.

"It's a metric measure of area—about 2.47 acres which is—"

"I know what an acre is, Damien."

"OK. Alright. So there were 35 million Dachniks, which is another word for 'gardener'. During 80 years of Communist rule they produce more than half of that nation's agricultural output. The productivity of their land was far higher than the industrial farms organized as massive collectives under Josef Stalin. The Dachnik movement is a model of sustainable agriculture—localized, mostly organic and built on an economic model of social norms rather than market norms."

"What's that mean?" Nell asks now mostly just to encourage him to get on with it.

"Social norms in this context means that Dachniks help each other or trade with each other without money exchange. Maybe they got the concept from the Bantu, a South African tribe. The word they use is 'ubuntu' which means, 'Today I share with you because tomorrow you share with me.'

"An Archbishop, I think his name was Tutu, helped unify South Africa using this as a rallying point for all races living there. Wherever they got it from, it was a good thing for the Ruskies since under Communist rule, although there was no shortage of rubles, there was nothing to buy with them."

"You mean they had money that no one trusted?" Nell is sharp when it comes to money. She always insists that she be part, the most important part, of the decision tree when it's time to make a determination about where to invest her money. She remembers what it's like to be poor and is surprisingly conservative in her outlook on spending and investment except when it comes to spending money on herself.

"Exactly. They had rubles but there was nothing to buy in Russian stores. You had to have hard currency, mainly the old US Dollar, to actually buy anything worthwhile."

"So how did ordinary Russian people get by?" Nell asks.

"They used queuing to ration everything. Russians would see people lining up outside a store in, say, St. Petersburg, and they would just join the lineup without knowing what there might be to buy, working on the assumption that there must be something. It's kinda like the red paper clip guy in the early days of the Internet—he kept trading stuff until he turned that one red paper clip into a house. It didn't take many trades to do it either, I think it was fewer than 15 or 16 and took about a year."

"What was his house like?" Nell asks. Like most women, she has an instinctive interest in people's nesting places.

"Gee, Nell, this story is like 50 years old. I don't know. I suspect it was a pretty cheap house—the guy was a Canadian and the house was somewhere in the Prairies, I think Saskatchewan.

"Anyway," Damien goes on, "Russians did a lot of trading and Dachniks relied on a gift economy—trading without money.

"In a gift economy, many people will happily work harder than if they are paid. Lawyers asked to work legal aid cases won't do any for a discounted wage of, say, ND$30 per hour. They find that insulting since most corporate types these days are charging ND$950 per hour and up, but they willingly line up to work on a pure volunteer pro bono basis.

"So Dachniks needing extra labour for a short period, a tool like an old Allen scythe to help with haying, advice on a weed or pest infestation, whatever, can expect to get help for nothing—or, at least, no monetary exchange. Of course, their neighbours anticipate they'll get the same consideration in return one day.

"In addition to being more self-reliant, enjoying the company provided by a community of like-minded people and eating food of known provenance, Dachniks also benefit from Japanese-style forest bathing or Shinrin-yoku which I told you about in my last story about Anastasia."

"You didn't use the term 'Shinrin-yoku'," Nell points out. At least she's listening. In fact, Nell loves stories—her Mom adored reading stories to her beautiful and happy child and long after Nell became a prolific reader on her own, they still sat together for hours with Mom reading to her as if she was performing for an audio book—both recording and acting out stuff. Her Mom is a frustrated actor, Nell thinks, ground down by poverty and lack of opportunity and education.

"Right, imagine the Shinrin-yoku effect," Damien adds for emphasis, "on Dachniks who spend an average of 17 hours each week during the season working their gardens.

"My grandfather knew a group of Russian immigrants who came to Ontario after the fall of the Communists at the end of the last century. They wanted to introduce the Dachnik movement to Canada. Pops tried to help them—holy smokes, they had an interesting time trying to explain the concept to OMAFRA (Ontario Ministry of Agriculture and Food and Rural Affairs).

"The Dachniks planned to buy 140 hectares or so of derelict farmland, within an hour of where they lived and worked so that they could access their tiny plots on weekdays during crucial growing and harvesting seasons. In Ontario, no problem—there is plenty of some of the world's least expensive farmland within an hour of most cities and towns. Plus the area is famously home to thousands of lakes, streams and rivers. Water is everywhere and available in all seasons from surface water bodies, huge underground reservoirs (via wells) and from the heavens as well.

"The problem wasn't availability of land or water; it was regulatory. OMAFRA defines agriculture and farming as exclusively industrial—only massive industrial and chemical-based farming operations are, in fact, recognized as 'farmers'."

"Who's the Governor of Ontario, Damien? Any chance it's a guy named 'Stalin' or someone channeling him?" Nell asks.

"We don't have governors. We have premiers," Damien answers.

"Well, didn't they used to call the top Communist, 'Premier'?" Nell responds.

"Strong point, Nell. Never thought of that. So, like, our Premier, channeling Josef Stalin," Damien says to a now smiling Nell, "gives those big industrial farmers access to subsidized diesel, cheaper inputs (seeds and fertilizer), free labs for soil analysis, no cost advice on pest infestations and diseases, marketing boards as well as other forms of market and price supports including income subsidies. And they get significantly lower property taxes as well. But OMAFRA refers to the Dachnik movement as a bunch of 'gardeners', a pejorative term to OMAFRA.

"So these 'gardeners' can't get access to any of OMAFRA's services or other forms of support. It puts Dachniks behind the eight ball. They also pay way higher property taxes. Now if you allow your competition to start at the 80-metre mark in a 100-metre race while you start at 0, you're cannot beat them. The problem was further compounded by the fact that they just could not explain to the local mayor in a way she could understand that they planned on sharing their 140 hectares amongst 100 families, each with their own little cabin or Dacha.

"Pops weighed in too. He told some local bureaucrats, 'What's wrong with having your own one-room cabin on your own one hectare of land where you can take shelter in inclement weather? What's wrong if a tired Dachnik, after a long day at the office and a few hours of manual labour in his garden plus an hour or two of companionable company around a campfire with fellow gardeners, drinking a bit of vodka while playing their balalaikas, decides to sleep there overnight?'

"Apart from the fact they are gardeners and not industrialized farmers, the power structure rejects the concept because it is just too strange and too foreign to wrap their bureaucratic pinhead-sized minds around. Plus they are gonna break practically every one of their zoning codes, called local ordinances here in the States, Nell. Those codes prohibit the breakup of larger parcels into small plots—it's all about retaining the existing political and economic power structure and a land ownership pattern which favours industrial combines.

"It was impossible, impossible, Pops found, to get such a thing approved in Ontario and, he suspected, pretty much everywhere else in North America. But it was the Dachniks that saved Haiti."

Nell knows a bit about Haiti—she has a home in the Western Caribbean— "I think I heard about them. Hundreds of thousands fled to the countryside or something."

"Right. They were led by a Russian ex-pat, Yana Domracheva. She emigrated there from Ontario after a big earthquake. Who knows why? Maybe she was moved by the suffering of the people there—Haiti is the poorest country in the western hemisphere. Disaster and privation are something a Russian would understand in a pretty fundamental way. She found it a lot easier to start a movement there where the institutional framework, the dead hand of government and industry, had been cleared away, in this case, by natural disaster."

"They practically emptied out Port-au-Prince or something," Nell says.

"Well not really but a lot of people did go," Damien continues. "It pretty much saved their nation. Anywho, Pops felt that if they ever could have gotten these micro farms approved in Canada, they would have traded for significant amounts of money—there would be a lot of demand for them and not just from people in the Dachnik movement.

"They'd be worth a lot more than just their economic value too. Their social value, everything from hanging out with congenial friends to improved health from Shinrin-yoku, would factor into the value that each plot would trade for.

"Pops thought that bringing hundreds and perhaps thousands of would-be Dachniks out of cities into nearby rural areas and small towns would immediately have a positive impact on these smaller communities in terms of direct and indirect economic spin-offs. Property values would increase and jobs would be created not to mention that young people would have the opportunity (possibly) to stay there. At least, it would give rural communities a chance to hold on to their most valuable resource—their kids.

"At the end of the day, Pops told me that the only way to actually build such a community in Ontario and places with a regulatory framework much like Ontario's (which is pretty much everywhere these days since the British system of land ownership and development is nearly universal) would be to do it using Nemawashi, the Japanese art of gaining consensus by stealth."

"Preparation is everything, Damien," says perfectionist and now very sleepy performance artist, Miss Nell.

"Right, I buy that. So anyway, if you are really determined to get something like this off the ground, you might actually have to do it underwater, out of view, a little bit at a time.

"But if somehow you were able to successfully establish a farm made up of a 100-family community of micro farmers then Pops told me he felt sure that the next Minister of Agriculture and Food, whoever he or she was, maybe even the premier, would one day visit it and them and proclaim it as the future of farming in Ontario. Politicians love to run to the front of an already-formed parade as long as it is proven safe to do so."

By the end of this long story, Nell is fast asleep and,

moments later, so is Damien.

...

When Damien wakes up, he finds that someone, probably the steward, has covered him with a cabled cashmere blanket and put a pillow under his head. Nell is still asleep under a matching blanket and pillow.

The steward approaches with a quiet 'Good Morning, Sir' and gives him a hot towel for his face.

"Would you like to freshen up before we land?"

Damien's mouth feels like a Belizean jungle and he remembers that, apart from the clothes he is wearing and his iPhone 40, he has nothing else, not even a toothbrush. That doesn't faze Nell's staff—they've prepared the w/c for him—he finds a fresh shirt, his size, and a complete men's toilet kit still in its original wrapper from whatever service provider does this for rich people. The w/c has a walk-in shower with twin heads. Damien guesses this might be shared for more than just washing-up purposes. There's a cheater door from the main cabin to the master bedroom. Unfortunately, Damien never got to share it with any female on this flight.

He takes a shower. The water flow is really a mist. 'I guess they haven't figured out yet how to neutralize the weight of water so even here aboard Nell's Airbus, they conserve,' Damien thinks. He's ready in less than fifteen minutes

Nell is awake when he gets back and stretching like a cat. She has two personal trainers and a nutritionist that work exclusively with her.

One of her trainers works on strength, agility and toning. The other works solely on her aerobic fitness. Although he later finds out that dance is included as well. She also has a full time hair and makeup artist as well as a masseuse and a personal dresser.

Nell's routine on the road is a 90 minute workout with her strength coach in the morning, followed by a carefully prepared and selected lunch. Then she has some personal time and, if it's show day or sometimes even if it's not, she takes a nap. Before a performance she will do a short 30 minute aerobic workout with her conditioning coach.

When she's not on the road or if she's in her studio back in Palos Verdes, morning workouts increase to 2 hours 15 minutes and her afternoon aerobic sessions are more than an hour long.

"Um, Nell, I forgot to ask you where we're landing. In fact, I was wondering exactly where we're heading?"

"We'll be landing at Flagstaff Pulliam Airport in about 20 minutes. Then one of your helicopters will take us towards Four Corners; we'll land about 110 miles northeast of the airport."

"Ha, ha." Damien has never been kidded before that his last name is synonymous with helicopters. Guess he's been hanging out with the wrong circle of friends.

Turns out they will be riding in a Bell 809 to get to Third Mesa, whatever that is.

He's still expecting Mr. Right to show up so he doesn't ask Nell for any further clarification although he is dying to. Nell can read the look on Damien's face as if it's been scripted.

She laughs again, that husky laugh of hers that so deeply affects Damien's libido. "We're going to visit my grandfather, Chief Dan of the Hopis in his pueblo—it's built into a wind cave, Damien. You'll have to climb with us."

She doesn't answer his other question, 'How many are coming with us?' He's trying to recall how many people a Bell 809 can hold. He's pretty sure it isn't anywhere near his crew count number of more than a dozen.

Damien just can't see how having her insane entourage with her is going to work in Four Corners in a wind cave. He's hoping that the group around Nell will somehow disappear. Travelling with her is like travelling with Royals.

...

Coming into Third Mesa is like a scene lifted out of Frank Capra's film, Lost Horizons. In the film, former soldier and diplomat Robert Conway is lost in the high Himalayas with a random group of passengers. After a mysterious plane crash, they are saved from freezing to death by mountain guides led by a man named Chang. He takes them by circuitous paths to a crack in the mountainside. Single file, the exhausted group shuffles along. Ahead is bright sunshine and warmth, behind, bitter cold and snow. Conway looks back then ahead then back once more not quite believing his own eyes.

Coming through the cleft in the mountain, Conway looks down to see a wonderful valley full of children playing in the sun, neatly tilled fields and, in the distance, a palace of sorts. Bells ring, a Carillion sounds. Robert Conway has arrived in Shangri-La. He is soon to meet the mysterious High Lama and a beautiful, older woman.

To Damien, it's a lot like Lucy's journey through the wardrobe that lands her in Narnia and trouble. Damien believes he is about to meet Chief Dan and he is with an older woman, although just by three years, not several hundred.

On top of the Mesa, winter is settling in. But Third Mesa's secret is that it is almost as deep as the Grand Canyon. Temperature on top is quite cold, around 4 Celsius (Nell would have used the Fahrenheit scale, silly imperial units to Damien's scientific mind but understandably human-scale in nature).

As they descend down into the canyon, temperature rises, fast. Damien is fascinated by the geology. First, he sees limestone, which he later learns is called Kaibab limestone, and as they get near the bottom there is more sandstone (Permian Coconino). There is a fast moving stream on the canyon floor. (He wants to call it a 'valley' but that is completely out of place here.) There is plenty of sand along the riverbanks and a nice beach not too far from where they land. There are crops growing everywhere: corn or maize as it's called in these parts plus almonds, asparagus, barley, beans, beets, broccoli, cabbage, carrots, kale, oats, berries of all kinds, peas, peppers, radishes (Damien loves radishes) and something he thinks could be Bok Choy. 'Sheesh, this is Shangri-La.' It's warm enough to take off his duffel coat.

They quickly unload their stuff from the helicopter which for Damien means just getting out. The pilot waves a cheery goodbye and ascends nearly vertically out of this scissure in mother earth.

There are four of them—Damien and Nell, the ever present and silent Dekka, and Nell's aerobic conditioning coach Wendy Morales, a hipster from LA.

On the flight up here, Damien suddenly realizes that they never went through US Customs and Immigration in Flagstaff. In this age of mega security administered by scary people from DHS (Department of Homeland Security) and TSA, that is weird. When he mentions it to Nell, she just shrugs, "Dekka pre-cleared everyone including you," The rules for rich people are completely different than what Damien's used to. He's starting to understand that maybe they have no rules.

Nell takes Damien's hand and leads the group up a well worn path toward the limestone wall of the canyon. "It's an hour long climb, big guy." Damien likes it when she calls him that.

Nell is in superb condition and, for a hacker and geek, Damien does OK. For the unflappable Dekka and coach Morales, it's a breeze. But Nell is pleased with Damien's competence, balance and stamina. 'Hey, this is America,' he thinks. 'Home of the greatest meritocracy on the planet, at least, until Imperial China took over. They're gonna be judging me every step of the way and then some.'

But when they get to the base of the canyon wall, Damien realizes he is expected to ascend to the Hopi wind cave far above using ancient hand and toe holds, hundreds of them. For the second time in as many days, Damien Bell is out there without a net. Up they go. Nell in the lead, followed by Morales, Damien and Dekka. It makes sense to have the lightest go up first. Less chance that they will knock off those below if they fall.

'Heaven help any of us if Dekka falls on us; he must weigh more than 125 kg, although on his tall, well muscled frame, it's fine,' Damien thinks.

They arrive in the cave, which looked tiny from the canyon floor but turns out to be the size of a small town. The roof above soars to more than 140 metres. The depth into the rock is hard to gauge but is probably more than 400 metres. This place is huge, huge—it's width must be more than a kilometre, Damien estimates.

There is room for hundreds in this crowded pueblo. The structures are made of stone and adobe although Damien also sees some earth stucco and even some brick. He can't imagine how they bring brick up here. (He learns later that the Hopi have, for centuries, lowered heavier goods by rope and primitive elevator from above.) Structures and layout are unlike any village he has ever seen—it is more organic than anything a white man would design and much of it looks as if it grew from a seed. Pathways wind through and there is a verticality to it with doorways to homes and buildings of unknown use at different levels. He will have to redefine what a roadway means to include a third, vertical dimension. He's definitely stepped through the looking glass.

Suddenly, Nell sprints from the group, her long auburn hair flying behind her. She's running pell-mell down a dangerous rocky path toward a man who is older than anyone Damien has ever seen before. Even tiny Nell is going to knock him down and injure him. But apparently he is more solid than he looks because he grabs her up with surprising strength and whirls her around like she's a kid. Nell disappears with him into the largest building in the pueblo. Nell is going to spend time with her Grandfather, Chief Dan of the Hopi. Damien won't see her again for some time.

...

He is shown to his room by an obliging Hopi elder. She doesn't speak any English or perhaps she chooses not to. He has no idea where Dekka and Morales are but, frankly, he doesn't care. He already misses Nell.

The room is sparse. It's furnished with a sleeping platform with some clean bedding on it, a desk and a chair. There's a wash basin and a chamber pot. There is no power. She shows him the way to the privy and indicates by sign language that she will bring him food.

He supposes he could turn on his iPhone 40 but he doesn't want to. Pet3r will find him in an instant and he will have hundreds of messages some of them from some angry people who, he guesses, will have names like 'Ellen' or 'Traian' or maybe even 'Luis'. Some of his students are bound to be looking for him too. Damien knows he has been reckless but he just can't seem to help himself.

All his life, he's been strong—the person everyone in his family looks to for help and leadership. From the time he was nine, he fixed all the tech at home, at his friends' homes, even at his teachers' homes. He's been a leader for a long while and now he just wants a bit of time for himself.

Of course, he knows how to rig his phone so that it won't leak anything at all except that there's no way he can prevent Pet3r from finding him. There's just no work-around for that.

The fact that there is no power here and no Internet is not a problem either. He can recharge his iPhone 40 just by leaving it in sunshine for an hour and, if he wanted full-on Internet, he could just go up to any of the half dozen satellites circling over this part of the country. Of course, he would have to time it right because the canyon is so deep and narrow but this is a trivial math problem for Damien.

Plus he has hacked his iPhone 40's architecture. It's now a fully capable quantum phone. He can talk to any other similar phone with no time delay and no bandwidth use. He doesn't need a carrier. His quantum infrastructure completely bypasses them using quantum entanglement. In an earlier era, when scientists couldn't explain quantum mechanics they called it 'spooky'; they would just have said it uses the omnipresent 'ether', another way of saying 'fabric of the Universe'. That is, they really didn't have a clue.

One of his profs when they were studying 'entropy' got so frustrated with questions about it from his students, some of which he couldn't answer, just told everyone to go home and repeat the word 'entropy' 500 times. Then they would 'get' the concept. Damien, always a good student, did, and strangely he found it helped.

What Damien is using in his hacked iPhone 40 is a process that creates matched pairs of photons at the same instant and in a specific quantum state. By forcing one photon into a quantum state, the entangled photon is forced into a related state. No matter how far away the matched pair of photons get from each other, this left-right polarization is maintained. It depends on certain symmetry in wave function so when one is 'spinning' left on its longitudinal axis, the other must be 'spinning' right. By observing one photon thereby changing its spin, its brother particle instantly changes direction. Instantly means no time interval. Of course, that is also the basis for any type of computing.

Einstein's theories require that the absolute speed limit in the universe is the speed of light which is pretty fast at 299,792,458 metres per second. But in a universe as big as what we can see with our largest radio telescopes, lightspeed is pokey. It would take around 14 billion years to send a radio signal from one side of the universe to the other and another 14 billion years to get an answer so it would be a horribly time delayed conversation especially if you started out with a question like, 'Hey, how's the weather where you are?'

Damien's hacked phone wouldn't have that problem if there is a way to get a matched handset from Earth to, say, UDFj, a galaxy about 13.2 billion light years away. You could gossip about your relationships all the live-long day—there'd be no time delay and no bandwidth cost either. This is part of what Damien, Traian and, especially, Ellen are so worried about. They're going to gore some sacred cows when they release not only Quantum Entities but their quantum phones too. Big companies are like pigs at the trough—they aren't going to want to share it with little piglets like QCC with its measly three employees.

Of course, it would take a spaceship carrying a matched handset, 13.2 billion years just to get to UDFj and that is only if it could travel at lightspeed. But heck once it's there, it'd work just as well as the phone did when Damien's namesake said, 'Watson, come here, I want you' from one room to the next.

The only other problem right now is that there are just two other phones like his anywhere—and Ellen has one of them. Damien doesn't feel like explaining to her why he is five hours away by jet sitting alone on a platform in a tiny Stone Age room with absolutely no idea what to do next and with the sun going down. He's pretty sure she will be able to figure it out for herself anyway.

...

He doesn't see Nell the next day either. At least there's no sign of any boyfriend yet. But he's thinking that maybe Nell is just being nice when she asks him along. Maybe she needs a friend. He's not sure he can do the 'friend' thing with Nell though. He's powerfully attracted to her but then again, he has company in that, like practically every man on the planet aged 15 to, well, 'til they die.

Like most men, Damien can only really focus on his own needs and wants and it never occurs to him that Nell, coming off a nearly seven month long, grueling tour, maybe needs time to detoxify. And then again, maybe women have a different speed than men. Damien has completely lost perspective.

So he spends his time exploring the neighborhood and meeting people. He likes the kids and he shows them some games on his iPhone 40 and that makes him the most popular tourist in this town, ever. That isn't particularly hard because he is pretty sure he is their only tourist ever.

They show him some of their games and he gets pretty good at what is certainly a close relative to soccer. The kids are all great athletes and all smiles.

He boots up one of Ellen's yoga routines on his hacked iPhone 40. 'What the hay,' he thinks. 'Might as well do some work on my RSI while I'm here.' He tries Yin Yoga—poses held for long periods measured in minutes. He uses a projection of Ellen teaching her 'class' of one, her long blond hair tied back neatly. As always, she's wearing the latest of the latest in terms of Yoga clothes designed for her personally by her supplier in Van City. Damien realizes it's the first time he's seen her without her glasses and she looks less like a librarian without them. He also notices that she has nice blue eyes too. Even though she can be a pain in the ass, he suddenly misses her, Traian and his life back in TO.

Over the next two days, Damien tries out new Yoga practices some of which he can do better than others. He develops a bit of a routine—yoga for 90 minutes at dawn (as a budding entrepreneur, he's up early anyway) and then he goes walkabout. He plays with the kids in the afternoon and has started teaching them English. They're teaching him some Spanish. There is no way he's going to be able to learn any of their native Uto-Aztecan language.

He also decides to leave the wind cave and go back to the valley for a night. He swims in the astonishingly cold creek and suns himself naked on the sandy beach. He also runs for kilometres. Then he camps there overnight.

He eats well too. His Hopi elder supplies him with enormous quantities of berries, nuts, seeds and veggies. Plus radishes, lots of radishes. He gestures to her that he rather likes them with a wide, smile. But still he is thinking that maybe he will have to hike out of the canyon somehow and find his way back to Flagstaff.

He's OK with that now because, without realizing it,

he has detoxified too. He's been feeling stoned for about an hour or two after each of his long yoga sessions because, as Ellen would explain, yoga releases toxins held by the body in its joints and, as these flush out of your system, you feel better.

Damien feels great. He's never been in the desert before. He likes it. After the intense green colours of Eastern Canada and the US he's now seeing lots of lovely hues of brown and yellow. He also likes the peculiar sweet, dusty, dry smell of the desert all around him. Some of what he smells is odour from creosote bushes growing everywhere in Third Mesa. The plants are huge and live a long time—more than a century and some for thousands of years. The Hopi crush leaves from the bush to fight coughs, cold, cancer and flu as well as for general health and wellness. They make a nice creosote tea. Damien's tried and likes it a lot.

They are all new experiences for him. And the night skies are scary, they're so clear and bright. The number of stars you can see with your naked eye feels infinite. Kids back in the Big Smoke never get to see much of the night sky—there's way too much industrial and light pollution for that. It's getting hard to see any constellations even Perseus which should be a snap, rising over Toronto in the north-east during early fall evenings, the best time of the year if there ever is one to watch the night sky there.

Damien likes to ID constellations on his own. When he's stumped, he hauls out his iPhone 40 and it overlays star maps on RL, Real Life. He imagines Mayans, in 300 AD, lying outside on their backs every night for 40 frigging years trying to figure out their calendar by observation and calculation. He can understand now why they might want to do that. Pet3r helpfully tells him that it's 4,174 land and sea-kilometres plus 197 metres from their present position to the centre of the ancient Mayan empire if they go through Arizona and cross into Mexico at Agua Prieta or 4,400 kms and 691 metres if they go through Texas and cross the border at Matamoros near

Brownsville. The end point is somewhere that Pet3r has discovered in Belize that shows promise at least as far as unveiling Mayan research into time and space. "You might also find it advisable to take a ship from Port Isabel and travel the rest of the way by sea," Pet3r adds helpfully.

Damien isn't interested. "Nope, not going to Belize, Pet3r. We're gonna head home, soon," Damien tells him.

"I am relieved to hear that, Damien. May I tell you that you currently have messages from—"

"No, you may not. I'll deal with all of that on the way back but not here, not tonight."

Damien's actually thinking of trying to find a way out in the next couple of days. Now that he's getting ready to leave, he will actually miss the place and he's glad he came after all.

...

The following day, back in the pueblo, Nell wakes him before dawn. It's the first time he's seen her since she disappeared with Chief Dan. "What's up?" he asks. Damien is a super fast waker-upper.

Nell reaches over, places a finger on his lips and "Shushes" him.

"Come with me," she whispers.

Damien follows her out grabbing his duffel coat against the morning chill. Nell takes him to the far end of the wind cave. She enters a building literally built into the side of the canyon wall. From there, they ascend up through a passageway cut into its roof. It zig-zags so the structure is impervious to rain; eventually they appear above the pueblo. From there, it's hundreds of hand and toe holds up the sandstone wall to the plateau above. Nell goes first, Damien's close behind.

At the top of the mesa, Damien sees a lean-to closed on three sides but open to the canyon below. The stars are still out and, in the clear desert air; it's like daylight back home in the Big Smoke. There is a raised platform in the lean-to and they sit down beside each other.

She takes his hand, turns it palm up and places a collection of leaves and what look like tiny mushrooms and some seeds there. Nell measures out a smaller portion for herself and begins methodically chewing the mixture. She does not swallow any. She juts out her chin to indicate he is to do the same.

Damien has had a few brewskis in his day and smoked a bit of pot but he knows this is in another league. He starts chewing. His mouth is numb in seconds and the juices he is swallowing taste like nothing he can really describe but somehow pleasing.

Nothing happens except the sun comes up. Damien is sure he can see the terminator move across the valley as mighty sol pushes back the night but the engineering part of his brain says that is impossible since the terminator, by definition, has to move around the circumference of this big planet every 24 hours, a distance of approximately 40,000 kms which means it's travelling about 1,670 kph, faster than the speed of sound that Damien recalls is about 1,225 kph at sea level.

There is no way his senses are that good but it happens again. Damien thinks it's amazing to be able to see the speed of sound. He thinks about that for a few minutes. Actually, he thinks about it for an hour or so then he realizes that it's actually just been a fleeting thought. He wonders when whatever he's ingested is going to kick in.

He looks over at Nell—she moves her head back and forth and her marvelous auburn hair sways in rhythm with her—the highlights in her hair are like reddish yellow lightning bolts. She is the most beautiful thing he has ever seen.

When he looks down into the valley again, the sun has suddenly lurched upward in the sky moving from a 6 o'clock position to 11 o'clock without any intervening steps. Damien is sure he's just seen quantum motion at a macro level; this upsets him because, as a physicist, he knows that only at the level of elemental particles like bosons and quarks can you get Brownian motion. He realizes he is unforgivably mixing his physics metaphors and this upsets him further.

The next minute he is lying on his side on the platform weeping hysterically for all that he has lost—his mother has passed away, his father's abandoned him. He has pushed so hard to get through life so fast that maybe he actually hasn't had a life. Then he realizes he is frightened that his grandfather is going to leave, that he will abandon him too because he's old and he might die any day now.

Then Damien has a seizure.

Softly, from many kilometres away, someone calls his name, over and over, calling him back. A hand brushes his forehead and someone is behind him with strong legs around him, holding him tenderly in an upright sitting position. It's Nell. "Come back, D, come back."

He's calmer now and able to sit on his own. The sun is still moving in the sky but using its regular motion. Suddenly, Damien is looking down at the lean-to. He can see Nell sitting there on its little front porch and next to her is someone he is sure he knows but he can't quite place him.

He looks at his body; he is about a metre tall. There must be something wrong with his eyesight because he can see in two directions at once. It doesn't scare him; it's kind of cool actually. And in places where his arms used to be he has mighty wings which he now uses to push off north. He wants to see how his pines are doing and say 'Hi' to Pops. He thinks it's strange that a blue heron should be flying out of the desert; he didn't know they came this far south.

He looks down and sees the lake his grandfather dug out of the underlying sand layer below the local water table. It takes Pops 17 years to removes 1.2 million tonnes of material using an excavator, a loader and three trucks. His grandfather, never one to waste anything, sells the sand for cable laying backfill and, to top it all off, golf course top dressing. Pops is the only person Damien knows who could remove that amount of material at a negative cost, that is, make a profit doing it.

Pops seeded the lake with large mouth bass the day Princess Di died. He got a permit from the Ministry of Natural Resources to transport live fish. He and his buddies went to their favourite fishing hole but despite the fact that there were 11 of them, and some of them are pretty good fishermen, they only caught three fish that day. It was long before Damien was born and it's one of Pops' favourite stories.

While Pops was transferring the fish to one of his many fish barrels, one per barrel, (he'd expected many more), he has a thought, "Guys, any of you know how to tell a male from a female? Won't do me much good if I got all males here." No one did.

Driving back that evening to his lake, he started to pick up a local news station as he got closer to the city. "News reports from Paris tonight... Screech... Lady Di.... Screech... her companion, film producer Dodi...Screech... Screech... accident... Screech... the Pont de l'Alma road tunnel..."

Of course today, digital radio is available everywhere but this was the old days—a mostly analogue world. By 10 pm, Pops is at lake side north of Toronto and, under a clear, starry sky, he starts pouring out his three measly barrels each with their one passenger into his lake. He knows by now that Lady Di's just died and he says a prayer for her and watches his happy fish swim away after a moment or two of shock. 'Free again,' they might've been thinking or 'My, my, such a nice new world of unimaginable size and bounty to explore and exploit.' "On Sancho!" one of his doughty Don Quixote fish might have been saying.

Next spring after the ice retreats, Pops eagerly looks for signs of his fish. He sees two spawning circles on its sandy bottom. They've chosen a shallow protected tiny bay formed where Windward Island (basically an unexcavated half-hectare portion of the lake that Pops intentionally left out) is connected to the mainland by a narrow isthmus.

Pops dug a huge old culvert nearly a metre in diameter and more than ten in length into the isthmus to provide water recharge for the small bay so it will never get stagnant. It's nearby that his 'Mensa' fish have chosen to start the process of maintaining their chain of life.

He's gotten the optimal mix; if you're only going to have three—two females and one male are ideal. The females have all the eggs and do most of the work. All the male has to do is swim over their spawning circles and fertilize them which, like males in most species, they are only too happy to do. Males will also defend them as well although at this stage of the lake's evolution, there are no predators on scene.

'Frig, a handful of males could repopulate the planet,' Pops thinks. 'God or Mother Nature if you prefer have given the male half of a lot of species and certainly humanity way too much sex drive, ridiculous amounts of it really,' Pops cogitates.

He actually calculates how many women each male survivor might be able to make pregnant in a year and how long it'd take to balance out the gender mix in a world almost completely female-dominated if a mysterious disease killed all the men on the planet except a few. Pops supposes it is probably a guy thing to speculate about a world like that. It's a Bizzaro, reverse Australia, which started out as a 95% male-dominated culture nearly exclusively made up of exports from English jails.

In a few years, Pops has a nice population of 300 large mouth bass in his lake together with clams brought there in the feathers of birds' wings plus turtles, blue herons, ducks, geese, deer and, wherever there are deer, wolves to snack on them. Beavers also come but Pops won't let them set up their colonies anywhere on his property. They're just destructive rodents as far as he is concerned who gnaw his trees down and he won't allow that. So he shoots them instead even though he's not supposed to. They are surprisingly hard to kill—the males weigh nearly 40 kg and after each winter have a coat so thick that his shotgun is practically useless, so he uses his old 303. That makes short work of them.

The water in the lake is even clearer than Damien remembers. It's fed by underground streams and with a healthy underwater plant colony and low biochemical oxygen demand (B.O.D.), it's always going to be nice but even so clams have made a difference in the last few years—they are nature's filters, sucking in prodigious amounts of water and retaining both nutrients and pollution, not that there is much of that out here to begin with.

Damien lands about two metres from his grandfather near an oddly formed dual line of enormous granite boulders and kind of hops awkwardly in his direction.

Pops found these boulders anywhere from six to ten metres down in the sand layer they excavated to uncover his lake. How they got there is a complete mystery to him until one night about 3 am he wakes up and realizes that these huge granite boulders found a way to be buried in an otherwise completely uniform sand layer by falling from the sky.

About 10,000 years before, this part of North America is completely covered by glaciers at least a kilometre thick. Glaciers, as they flow, scrape large boulders up into their ice layers and hold them there until the sun warms in its natural cycle or the chemistry of the air somehow changes and they begin to melt. But they melt from the bottom up as the sun's rays warm the earth below radiating heat up into the ice above.

So as glaciers melt, under-the-ice rivers form with heavier gravel settling out first, then sand and further downriver, silt. The land that Pops owns is the sandy kind.

But when the ice melts up to a boulder maybe 400 metres above, it kamikazes down into the sand at around 88.5 metres per second (close to terminal velocity) burying itself down into the still quite liquidly sand-water mix only to be dug up ten millennia later by Pops' excavator and placed in these weird marching formations that the blue heron sees on his approach from the southwest.

The old man eyes the nearby male heron, a normally shy bird. "I'll be damned," he says softly. "What do you want?"

It looks like the bird wants to be petted. He's never heard of such a thing. But he reaches out his hand anyway, slowly, and gently tap, tap, taps the bird on his head.

"You're a fine specimen and very handsome," Pops says. His feathers are amazingly dusty with a grade of sand Pops has never seen before in Northern Ontario. And he really knows sand.

"So where have you come from?"

The bird cocks his head as if listening to something else—Damien's body is calling him back—so he turns and flies away. Pops watches the bird for a long time heading southwest whence he came then goes to his cabin, where he lives alone, to fix himself some dinner.

...

When Damien returns, Chief Dan is there. He squats down on his haunches and looks Damien in the eye in a way that anywhere else or in any other culture would be construed as hostile or rude. But Damien senses that Chief Dan means well.

He asks him what he saw and Damien straight out tells him.

"It's a warning, my son, that there are dark days ahead for you and that you must find your true path or you will not survive what lies before you. But if you stick to your path, you will come to a good place, again, one day."

He kisses Damien on the forehead and moves away with surprising grace and agility. Damien will never see him again but will carry the memory of that moment forever and will recall it later when he is alone in a very dark place.

...

That night Damien sleeps without dreaming and tries not to think about his recent experiences so overwhelming that he just can't take them all in.

The next day, Nell is there again and they head back in the direction of the Creek. The Bell 809 is waiting. The four travelers get in and leave, this time to the top of the Grand Canyon's Bright Angel Trail. Nell has arranged for the group to take the mule train to its bottom. They're going to stay at Phantom Ranch on the floor of the Canyon for a couple of days.

Damien is still reeling from his recent experiences and he is uncharacteristically OK with just going along and bobbing on the wake of life, at least for now. He is living in the present with no thought of the past or the future and no cares. His lust for Nell is gone replaced by real respect and he is starting to think that maybe he has been freed from some of his past too. Anyway, it feels that way and he is grateful to her.

He rides a mule with the unlikely name of 'Lenny'. Lenny is a huge, sure-footed animal who likes to put a couple of his hooves on the far outside of the trail, just millimetres from precipitous near vertical drop-offs of 450 metres or more. These mules, other than the fact they are immensely strong, have their eyes set far apart on their heads so they can see where all four hoofs are going at any one time. Damien learns to trust Lenny although on each switchback, he can't help it, he gets nervous.

The mules stand almost 2 metres high. Adding another metre or more for their riders means that Damien's eyes are nearly three metres above the trail. As Lenny swings his body and Damien's around each turn, they lean out over the canyon and away from the safety of the wall which leaves Damien looking down at nothing. It's way scarier than any monster roller-coaster that Damien ever went on with Dad.

Every time he looks back at Nell, she has a big cheesy smile for him. She loves this. She's Pocahontas on a mule. She looks like a princess to Damien.

Normal wait times to get on the mule train and to stay at Phantom Ranch are a year or more. Nell has arranged this for them in a day.

The wrangler who leads the group down Bright Angel Trail keeps telling them to, "Keep in a tight, compact group. We've never lost a dude yet so let's not start today. These mules don't want to go to the bottom you do! So use your whip. OK?"

Some of the ladies in the group can't seem to get the hang of it, some of the guys too, but Nell has no trouble using her whip. When the mules stop to rest, they hang their heads down into the canyon. You can't blame the dudes from wondering if there is such a thing as a suicidal mule. But everyone gets down to the bottom of the Canyon just fine. They cross the Colorado River on a covered wooden bridge and arrive at Phantom Ranch.

No one can walk very well, at least none of the men. Nothing seems to affect Dekka though and Nell is fine too even after a day on her mule. Damien is walking like a rookie.

After washing up, they go to the dining hall and have a fabulous traditional American meal of corn, steak and potatoes. There is a lecture about the history of the ranch. The only thing that Damien will remember is that President Theodore Roosevelt travelled down the canyon to the camp during a hunting expedition in 1913. The rest of the time he just wants to be let outside.

Nell and Damien walk along the Colorado. The sun has gone down and the stars have appeared. 'This is an ancient and sacred place,' Nell says. Looking at the starlight bouncing off the steep, reddish tinged canyon walls. Damien can't help but agree.

They have been assigned one of the ancient cabins. Damien lights the fireplace. The four poster bed is impossibly high off the ground. It squeaks too. The cabin is tiny but comfy and cute. It's been decorated and redecorated so it has a mix of styles and eras but somehow it works and feels very authentic.

Damien takes off his clothes without a thought and lies naked on the bed. Then Nell is there with him kissing him lightly on the lips leaning her breasts on his chest. Damien doesn't move.

Nell moves her hand down to caress him and then she moves her lips there. She takes him eagerly.

Damien doesn't want her to stop but he's afraid if she doesn't soon he will ruin the moment. He normally has great control but he isn't sure what 'normal' is for him anymore. He turns her over and hovers over her holding himself up on his arms. Nell feels his strength and it warms her.

When he first enters her, she gasps. Damien isn't sure if it's pain or pleasure and he immediately stops.

"Did I hurt you?" he asks quietly. The look on his face is quite comical. He would never do anything to hurt Nell and is aghast that he might have.

"You're a bit big for me. Plus it's been awhile. Just go slow, we'll adjust."

And presently they do.

...

Chapter 4

On the Salmon

There's no longer any doubt in Damien's mind that he loves Nell. He's not just in-love with her either. That would be easy to understand—she's beautiful, talented, wealthy, sexy, powerful. No, he just flat-out plainly loves her for her strength, her independence, her clarity of thought, her ambition, her feistiness, her sense of humour and quest for adventure even her moods and sometimes petulant, star-like and selfish behaviour.

Damien's like an electron or any other elementary particle. His psyche has 'moved' orbits without any noticeable outward change in his persona. He supposes that he's just proved that the Heisenberg Uncertainty Principle also applies to humans; it states you can't accurately measure both present position and future momentum. You can know one or the other exactly but not both.

Right now, Damien is confused. He's sitting at centre-mounted oars on an inflatable raft on the Salmon River in Idaho. Nell lies luxuriously across the bow in a surprisingly modest (for Nell) two-piece forest green bathing suit more reminiscent of a Hollywood actress from the Golden Years of the 1930s, more than a century ago now. Damien impulsively grabs his iPhone 40 and snaps a photo of Nell looking back at him with those shining green eyes of hers.

Three days ago they flew on Nell's Airbus to Boise and motored up to Salmon, a town of about 4,000 in Lemhi County where they met up with Doug Kowalski, leader of their current expedition. There are six rafts headed down the Salmon and Damien's learning from Kowalski, an experienced river guide, outfitter and part owner of Wilderness Tours in Ontario, how to safely manoeuvre his raft, loaded with about 400 kilograms of supplies and the lovely Nell, through Force III and IV and even IV and a half rapids.

At the moment they are on a relatively flat part of the river just peacefully drifting along with Damien making occasional course corrections and rowing at half speed. Damien's noticed that the men on this trip are super competitive—they're into racing each other through white water. One of them has successfully climbed Everest. Damien is just interested in getting himself and Nell down this river safely.

He doesn't know it yet but he's just taken a photo that, when her publicist 'accidentally' makes it public, will become as iconic as any classic pinup girl ever—comparable to photos of Marilyn Monroe standing on a subway tunnel grate holding down her dress in an updraft or Farah Fawcett's revealing swimsuit or Scarlett Johansson's wallpaper where she is piercingly looking back over her bare left shoulder or Natalie Spoelstra, photographed by a Paparrazzoid last year naked from the waist up coming out of the ocean onto the wide, white sands of Leme Beach in Rio.

To Damien, Nell's passionate look reflects a woman at the peak of her power and it powerfully comes through the tiny lens of his phone's camera. It reminds him of a painting he saw on a trip to Ottawa Art Gallery with Pops when he was 13. Much of the art they were going to see was donated to the people of Ontario by his great grandfather. It's part of their family's heritage and Pops wanted him to see it.

But Damien was thunderstruck, not by fabulous scenes of raw Canadian wilderness by members of the Group of Seven but by a portrait by Edwin Holgate of a young woman, then about Nell's age. She is naked on a chaise longue looking at the artist with a hungry, sexually-charged look. She has a full figure, the kind that Damien has recently discovered that he likes. The artist has drawn every part of her with obvious desire including her most private parts in a demure, if that is possible, but fully revealing way. It is the only time that Damien ever wants to steal something.

Damien's always liked girls, even in first grade. Then his dreams were of rescuing damsels in distress. He had a crush on a little girl, Lulu by name, fastest runner in his class. She buzzed around during recess with her long dark pigtails flying behind her. Damien never managed to catch her, not that he would have known what to do with her if he had, but instinctively he knew he sure would like to.

Now that he has caught one, he still isn't sure what to do.

"Nell, I don't think I can go with you to Palos Verdes," Damien blurts out.

"Huh?"

"I have to go back to TO."

"But I don't want you to, D. Come with me, it'll be fun," Nell says.

"But what would I do in Palos Verdes, live the life of a Rock Star?" Damien asks. "Or more accurately, a Rock Star's consort."

Nell laughs, "I don't even know what that means, Damien. I live in Palos Verdes not OC."

"Nell, I have responsibilities in Toronto, you know that. We're launching QCC soon and, while I'm sure that Traian and Ellen are doing their best, they need me."

At the mention of Ellen, a momentary frown crosses Nell's elfin face.

"What are you worried about, Damien? Money?"

"No. Yes. Look, Nell, my annual stipend from the University wouldn't pay the kerosene bill for your Airbus from Toronto to Flagstaff."

"So? I have enough money for us to live on for a zillion lifetimes," Nell counters.

Damien isn't so sure about this assertion given the way Nell spends money on herself. But instead he says, "Nell, Palos Verdes represents what you do, your professional future. Mine is in TO."

"Couldn't you transfer to UCLA or something?"

"Nell, you know what I do. I have this whole

infrastructure at U of T that supports my work—that isn't easily duplicated elsewhere."

"Well, I could marry you."

"What?"

"We could get married, D." This is a new thought to Nell—it just came up. She obviously likes her new skinny boyfriend. And it'll be fun showing him off in LA. The Paparrazzoids will love him—he's so cute.

There're haven't been any Paparrazzoids on this trip, Nell thinks, probably because Dekka would just hog-tie 'em and leave them for long legged Idaho buzzards to finish off.

"Then what would I be, 'Mr. Nell'?" Damien asks.

"That's mean."

"I'm sorry. That's an incredibly generous offer and I love you for it, Nell."

"You love me?" Nell asks sweetly.

"Yes I do, Miss. I do. But women want to marry-up, didn't your mother ever tell you that?"

Nell laughs again, "She certainly did! Mom thought there is no way I'd ever make anything of myself and expected me to grab a guy and marry him. 'You can marry more money in a minute, Nell, than you can make in a lifetime,' she said. How wrong she was." Nell sighs.

"Nell, I want you to respect me for who I am," Damien says.

Nell interrupts, "That's the second time in our relationship you've said what the 'girl' is supposed to say."

This time, Damien sighs, "I haven't done anything yet, accomplished anything yet. I think we're gonna create a new enterprise bigger than Facebook, bigger than Apple, maybe bigger than the Internet."

"But you've done a ton. You must of been the youngest PhD in physics ever."

"Not even close, Nell. I'm just a hard worker."

One thing Nell likes about Damien is that he is this perfect gentleman. He's kind, non violent, non macho but at the same time, he's got that I-won't-take-no-for-an-answer that all star performers (and, if Nell had known, all successful entrepreneurs) have. He is ambitious, industrious and strong even if he doesn't need to show it to any of the other guys on this trip.

...

They are about mid-way on their ten-day trip down the Salmon. The moment they turn the first corner of this river, their expedition is on its own. Canyon walls are so steep that only their satellite phones work and then only sporadically. Of course, Damien has his hacked iPhone 40 that always works but no one else on the trip knows that except Nell.

Kowalski's been picking up sporadic weather reports for the last couple of days. Unseasonably warm atmospheric conditions are leading to thunderstorms everywhere in the region. He's worried about the rains happening further north in Bitterroot National Forest. Flash floods are known in the area. There are several storms in the immediate vicinity as well. He knows he has to watch the river for subtle changes in colour, velocity and level.

Kowalski is not worried about Damien—the kid has been closely following him for days as he learns the ropes of being a river guide. Wherever Doug heads, Damien follows and, he has to admit, the city kid despite being a Joe-College type, has learned a bit about reading the river. He knows enough now to head toward a white-water 'V' formed by each set of rapids where the deepest (and safest) water will be. He's learned to turn his raft around, fast, to row 'up' or across river so he can get his raft around tight corners and not crash into canyon walls and dump his supplies, and more worrisomely, Nell into a Force IV flow.

Kowalski wants Nell to ride with him and his wife, Lorena, for safety—the safety of so famous a guest is critical to Doug. It will be really bad PR for his outfit if anything happens to Nell and, likewise, great press if things go well and he can get Nell's devil of an agent to let him use some photos and video footage of Miss Nell in his marketing.

But Nell will have none of it—she is going to ride with Damien so Doug takes him aside just before launch and gives him a brain transplant—a 35-minute how-to explanation of how to be an oarsman. He makes Damien promise him that he and Nell will always wear their life jackets, wet suits (even though air temp is way warm, the water is cool, in the high 50s/low 60s F) and helmets which, of course, Nell has completely ignored. What a pain. Kowalski can't wait for this trip to be over.

His grandfather was the outfitter who first discovered there was untouched and virtually unknown whitewater on the mighty Ottawa River near the tiny hamlet of Beachburg in Eastern Ontario. Grandfather spent a summer there with his pal, Robbie Rosenberger, trying to launch an (unsuccessful) guide business taking dudes on canoe trips through Ontario's greatest park—Algonquin Park. After a dismal summer, Joe and Robbie had learned that no one wanted guided tours of the Park. But Joe heard rumours about some unexplored white water on the nearby Ottawa and convinced a reluctant, now homesick Robbie to hold off on going back to Philadelphia so they could explore the area some more before returning like whipped dogs to families who were expecting them to get real jobs.

What they found was a completely unexploited wilderness with some great Force III water. The following summer, they headed back, this time with two rafts instead of canoes. Hundreds of people showed up with real money in exchange for a couple of days of adventure.

Joe was a quintessential entrepreneur. He just asked a local farmer for permission to launch from his land and another one further downstream where they could take folks off the river. He never bothered to ask the local municipality or the Provinces of Ontario or Québec for permission. He just did it, telling Robbie, "Hey, it's better to ask for forgiveness than beg for permission."

Joe parlayed that second summer's experience into Wilderness Tours, a thriving business with it's own summer town (population 3,500) and other ventures including jet boating in Niagara Gorge below the famous Falls and the Lachine Rapids in Montréal. He also bought almost 2,000 hectares of virgin land on either side of the Ottawa, a natural state he expected his heirs to maintain. Doug is now the third generation of his family to run the place.

Canyon walls are nearly vertical when all of Doug's training is suddenly put to the test. He hand signals and shouts to all rafts behind him and in front to pull over to the west bank of the river at a spot he knows has a rough path with switchbacks that will take them up and away from their current river elevation.

Then it starts to rain, hard. In this part of the country, it's nothing for eight inches to fall in 15 minutes. Surges as high as 30 feet have been known to roar downstream. Even though he was a kid when it happened, Doug remembers the August 1997 flash flood in lower Antelope Canyon, Arizona that drowned 11 visitors. His family used to winter in Arizona.

Doug gets everyone out of the rafts. Some of the men start to drag them up the narrow trail; others are grabbing supplies and equipment. Conditions worsen—winds pick up and it starts raining even harder. Damien isn't sure why they don't just wait for the rainstorm to pass but he's doing his share, taking turns dragging these awkward, heavy rafts up the trail. It takes all the strength of two men just to drag each now empty raft.

The sound that the approaching storm surge makes is incredible. Water weighs a lot—62.4 lbs per cubic foot and there are a lot of cubic feet right now making their way downriver to their current position bringing with it vast 150-year old lodgepole pines and western hemlock pulled out by their roots. But it's the boulders rolled along by a huge hydraulic gradient that are making the most noise.

Human beings don't like being in places where

ambient noise overwhelms their senses. It goes back to primitive days when hearing was an important part of defences against large predators. Stone Age mega fauna like American puma, American lion (the largest lion to ever exist anywhere on Earth) and Toxodon (a Rhino-like animal) all roamed the Americas at one time or another.

Now these modern humans are taking their turn at being terrified. Suddenly Dekka appears. He picks up Nell like she weighs no more than a football and bounds up the trail as this incredible wall of water and debris rushes headlong towards them.

To Damien, used to the timid weather of a northern-shelf city like Toronto, it's like the most incredible special effect ever. Except it's real and it's going to kill anyone not at least 15 metres higher than where he currently is. Worse still is the fact that Morales, Kowalski and another guy are behind him bringing more supplies. Doug yells over the terrific din for everyone to drop everything and run. Both Kowalski and the guy go by him. Damien goes back for Morales who's fallen on the incline now slippery with mud, gravel and water. He yanks her up and they boot it uphill.

They're nearly clear of the surge when a branch from a Douglas fir bobs up and reaches out wicking Damien off the path into the maw of onrushing water.

Damien is gone in a flash.

The rain stops almost as quickly as it began and a double rainbow appears. Everyone is soaked and cold. The temperature has fallen dramatically. Nell is shivering, partly from the cold and partly because she's in shock. Morales just told the group what happened. Kowalski's face is white with fear. He's never lost a member of an expedition. The worst so far was a guest who broke his leg after falling out of a raft into some tough white water.

Nell sees the double rainbow and the Hopi part of her thinks that maybe Damien's spirit is part of them now. She bursts into inconsolable tears falling to her knees, clutching her stomach as if she's been sucker punched in the gut. If she was honest with herself she would also admit to feeling a deep pain in her womb. Morales goes over and puts her arm around Nell. Dekka fishes around in one of their packs for a dry blanket to put around her shoulders.

Doug splits the group into two—there are 15 of them now. He tells Lorena, the other women and two of the guys to leave everything where it is on the trail except their tents and basic supplies and go up to the table mesa some 250 feet higher up. They are to make camp there and get everyone into warm clothes. Doug splits the remaining group into three search parties. One will take the east bank of the Salmon, the other the west and he will take one of the men in his raft and search the river.

Morales insists on joining Doug's boat crew. He needs a spotter in the bow of his boat so he takes her with him realizing that Dekka won't leave Nell.

He's quite sure they will find Damien. His only misgiving, other than the fact that he's also quite sure the kid will be dead, is that Damien's body could be trapped in a backwater pool under some kind of thermal isocline—the depth at which water suddenly changes density. Fast changes in temperature can cause a cold layer of water to sit on top of a warm one. It's called an inversion layer and it acts like someone holding the back of your head underwater anywhere from a couple of feet below the surface to maybe three and a half to four feet down. Doug's afraid if that happens, they will miss the body and will have to call Search and Rescue to drag the river for him. Doug has a sick feeling at the base of his gut. He presses everyone into action.

The sun is setting and the urgency of the situation is obvious to everyone. If there is a chance that Bell is still alive, they need to find him, soon. If he's injured or suffering from hypothermia or both, he will be a goner before morning. Doug can see the searchers on both banks as their flashlights sweep back and forth. He and Morales can go a lot faster in the raft but Doug is careful to look at every rock and every tree. There is no way they can see below the surface of the water—the river is way too muddy for that.

The damage over the next two and half miles of river is unbelievable. Doug can understand, in a way that has never been so clear before, how Mother Nature can gouge out such huge clefts in the earth. Her power is magnificent except right now, she has swept away Nell's friend.

A part of Doug's mind is wondering about his litigation risk. Like any outfitter, he carries a lot of insurance. Plus he's not too worried about Bell's family. Canadians hardly ever sue each other and, although technically Doug is a dual citizen of the US and Canada so is Damien, hence, he's pretty sure he can handle that part OK. It's the nightmare that the US legal system represents that has Kowalski concerned. Nell's lawyers could tie him up forever and make his life a living Hell—it will make Tom Wolfe's Bonfire of the Vanities look like a picnic. He shivers.

"You cold?" Morales asks.

"No I'm fine. Just keep your eyes, front."

"You don't think he's alive do you?"

"I'm gonna find him—that's all I know," Kowalski replies.

"Why are you giving me the silent treatment?"

"What is this? 20 Questions?" Doug asks. "Just keep looking."

"Everyone blames me," Wendy continues. "I was just following your orders to drop everything and get up the trail. How did I know I would slip? And how did I know that Bell would come back for me? That was just stupid of the guy. It's really his fault. I can take care of myself."

"I'm sure you can," Doug replies in a sarcastic tone.

Doug thinks that his only real defense against massive financial liability and possible charges of negligence or worse (maybe manslaughter or negligent homicide) will be that he was duly diligent. He's also praying that the waivers he had everyone sign before the trip started weren't drafted by a law student.

They find Damien another mile and a bit downriver. He's lying about three feet up from the river. He's covered himself with branches, presumably to keep warm. Damien sees Morales' light sweeping the water for him and he calls out to the raft. His voice is hoarse.

Kowalski rows over to him with powerful strokes and is out of the raft in seconds kneeling down next to the kid. A fantastically powerful feeling of relief washes over Doug and he feels the hair on the back of his neck, even on his head, standing straight up. It would be comical if anyone could actually see it. But it's full dark now.

Doug does an inventory of Damien, even before covering him up. He's taken every Red Cross First Aid course right up to Firefighter First Aid. They brought blankets with them which Doug thought they might have to use to bring the body back. Now they'll serve a different purpose.

Other than being a bit banged up, Damien appears to be OK but suffering from incipient hypothermia. He tells Morales to grab their first aid kit and bring the thermometer. Damien's temperature is 89F, not bad. He probably has moderate hypothermia. Still, if left untreated, it can kill but there is no way, now that Doug has found the kid alive, he will allow that to happen.

Doug says a silent prayer thanking God for his deliverance—both Damien's and his own. Kowalski realizes that if Damien had not called out, there's no way they would have seen him on this pitch black night.

He removes all of Damien's wet clothes and bundles him up in blankets. The kid is shivering and a little uncoordinated. His face is pale and his ears, lips, fingers and toes are blue.

The stupid kid is also trying to apologize, "I'm really sorry, Doug, to put you to such trouble, loo-looking for me."

"Be quiet, Damien, just don't talk for now. You'll be OK," Doug replies.

Kowalski thinks about asking Morales to wrap her arms around Damien to provide an external source of warmth but she strikes Doug as piranha-like. Her spirit is so unforgiving that it'd probably damage the kid's recovery.

Heat production is proportional to volume; heat loss to surface area. Damien is so skinny that's he's built for heat loss. Doug, on the other hand, carries plenty of beef so he undoes his jacket and lies on top of Damien himself making sure to cover Damien's gut with his own, considerably larger one.

He'll stay like that, off and on, all night. Morales is somewhere about—he can hear her prowling around like a trapped animal on the sand bar below. The kid is sleeping now. Doug dozes a bit too. He takes Damien's temp every hour and, by daybreak, it's risen to about 95F and Doug knows he's in the clear.

"You can get off me now, Doug," Damien says. "I'm OK and you're pretty heavy."

Kowalski checks him one more time and he can see that, like most young people, Damien has an almost magical ability to bounce back from near disaster.

"Hey, you look pretty good," Kowalski says ruffling the kid's hair. "Do you want to try standing up?"

"Sure."

"Let's get you sitting up first."

Blood rushes to Damien's head, so he puts it between his knees and waits for his dizziness to pass. Then Doug helps him to his feet. He's a bit unsteady for a minute or so but that passes too.

"OK, you're gonna have to wear these blankets cuz there's no way we're putting you back in wet clothes. Your temp is still about three degrees below normal and we probably can't fix that 'til we fix you something to eat. I've got two power bars in the first aid kit and that'll have to do until we get you back upriver."

To Damien, no food ever tasted so good.

...

Chapter 5

Homestead

Nell sits semi-upright with her back resting comfortably against the double bed's large headboard. Damien, wrapped up in several blankets, is enveloped in her arms with his head on her breast. A cheery fire crackles on the grate. It's the only light in their room.

They're staying at the homestead of a friend of Doug's. It's isolated as heck but large and sprawling and, after the harrowing last couple of days, it's the height of luxury. Many generations of Ingersolls have called this place home and there have been so many additions, renovations and demolitions over the years that the building has basically no rhyme nor reason to it other than it meets the needs of changing family size over a period of a century and half of clan life. Right now the clan is pretty small.

Doug always planned to stop here, first, to see his pal, Jeff Ingersoll, and second to give everyone a break and a night indoors. After reuniting with the main group, they rush here with Damien and actually arrive a day early. Still, Jeff is delighted to see them and, after a short briefing, is able to accommodate the hoard of travelers and take care of Damien.

The home is situated on a windswept plateau and the homestead itself sits in a wide field, cleared of all trees. Homesteaders always clear the immediate area around their property of bush and trees both to keep bugs down and also to protect themselves from trees knocked over in windstorms or ice storms which can coat a tree with several tons of ice in a matter of hours with disastrous consequences for people, their animals and property.

"Do you want to tell me what happened, D?" Nell asks him in a whisper.

"Sure," Damien responds.

But then he says nothing. Nell strokes his hair knowing Damien likes it.

A minute or so later, he starts, halting at first and then faster as it comes back and he relives the terror of his near-death experience, "I went back to help Wendy, after she fell. I grabbed her but, by that time, the path had turned to mud and we had trouble getting any real traction. The noise was incredible and the wall of water coming at us was huge. My glands must of dumped a couple of litres of adrenal into my system; anyway when I saw it just behind us, I shoved Wendy up and out of it. I thought I was out of it too when it felt like someone grabbed me and tore me off the canyon wall.

"I was hooked on a branch. It went right up inside my shirt and it drew me into the river like a rag doll. I knew I was going in so I got a deep breath. I can hold my breath forever, Nell, so that's what I did."

Nell gives him a squeeze when he says this.

"The water had negative buoyancy—it was a water-air mix so there was no way to swim in it and there was no way to know which way was up either. I guess it's kinda like getting sucked over a waterfall into really big surf. You know how waves draw water in front of themselves up into their waveforms so, if you go over, there's often not much water there. It'll drive you headfirst into the sea floor. Kapow. After you bounce off the bottom, you're mixed up in the same type of mess I was in."

Nell can't help but notice that D talks like an engineer, even now. She supposes that all professions create grooves in your brain that change you irrevocably forever. She certainly thinks that's true of her own profession, especially on the left coast of the US of A, where pretty much everyone she knows in Southern California talks the talk.

"It was the branch that took me that saved me. Well, the tree did. I held onto it and it kinda acted like a dozer—crashing into boulders, pushing other trees and who knows what else out of the way. I think there might of been a car in there too. I'm not sure if there was anyone in it. I mentioned it to Doug and he called it into State Search and Rescue.

"I was pretty sure I was in the trailing edge of the hydraulic gradient too and, with the tree probably weighing several tonnes, it was one of the first things to settle out carrying me with it. Other than a couple of bumps and bruises, I felt OK except something whacked my left hand and it hurt like heck."

Damien's left hand isn't broken but it's quite swollen. Doug splinted Damien's baby finger and ring finger together; he is sure it's just a bad sprain. They've been applying ice to it every few hours since coming to the Ingersoll homestead and the swelling and pain have gone down a lot.

"I crawled up the sand bar where I landed and covered myself with some branches I found there. I knew you guys would come looking for me and you did."

Nell just squeezes him again, "D, if you want to go back to Toronto, I get that now. We'll find a way to make it work between us."

Nell has gained perspective on their conversation out on the river of just a few days ago. For her, that issue has become small—like looking at an ant through the wrong end of a telescope. It's far away now.

Damien looks back at her and gives her one of his ridiculously cute smiles.

Nell blurts out, "I love you, D," and squeezes him a third time. She's never said that to anyone before. Well, actually she has. But she's just never said it before and meant it.

...

The next day is a rest day and the expedition members scatter. They're sick of the sight of each other, at least for the moment, so they break up into smaller groups to do stuff on their own.

That's fine with Nell and Damien.

"I have a present for you, D," Nell says with a mysterious smile.

"Hey, not fair," Damien responds. "I have one for you too."

Nell likes prezzies so she asks, "When do I get it?"

"Well, right about now I think. I had Traian UPS it to me back in Boise. It was in one of the packs that made it up the trail."

Damien gets up and goes to his knapsack and pulls out a bulky, padded square envelope. He hauls out his Swiss Army knife, which he carries everywhere with him, surviving a dip in the Salmon along with its owner, and carefully cuts it open.

In it, there is a new iPhone 40. Nell, who has had every kind of Internet mobile phone ever made thrust at her by eager manufacturers hoping she'll be seen using their product or maybe even give it and them an endorsement, is momentarily disappointed. But she has the good grace to cover it up and thank Damien. This is a new behaviour for Nell who is not used to worrying about how other people feel since everyone around her, except Damien, is always thinking about Nell's feelings.

Damien is way too sharp to miss her expression though. "Nell, it's not a regular phone. It's one of ours. It's the fourth of its kind anywhere; it's special, like you."

He doesn't tell her that he had a big fight with Ellen and Traian to get it here. "Damien, we agreed to keep our product confidential until we're ready for launch. We can't be winging this. We need a plan and we don't have one yet. A plan for dealing with political, legal and economic fallout from this," Ellen says. "How we insert these phones into the marketplace is hugely important to our success."

It is Traian who finally agrees to go into Lab 4, to what they've taken to calling the hatchery, to custom create this phone for Nell. Traian looks at it as a terrific opportunity for them—it's the ultimate in product placement—he thinks that Damien is smart to get with the hottest star anywhere and even smarter for QCC to get her to endorse it.

It's true that Damien wants a larger test bed than three hacked iPhone 40s that are the only Q-Phones in use at the present time. Having Nell use it will give them more results in terms of focus group testing. At least that's what Damien tells Ellen and Traian. But the truth is simpler—he just wants to give a girl he loves a present, something he made himself. This impulse is as old as the male half of the human species.

"The phone contains a Quantum Counterpart, Nell," Damien tells her. "Your counterpart. Ellen calls them 'Quantum Entities' because she feels they represent a new form of intelligence. She thinks they take about three months to become self aware. I'm not so sure of that but they learn fast and can help you with a lot of things, many of which you can only discover by using your phone.

"They can move around anywhere that a device is connected to the Internet and will see you and talk to you from any media wall anywhere.

"You also need to know that QEs bond with people much like animals imprint on their mothers or, indeed, the first creature it sees after birth even if from another species. QEs imprint 'out of the box' on their users so the only person who is going to be in this room when you first turn on the phone will be you, Nell."

They are in a huge room about 100 square metres. It's full of hunting trophies, comfortable, well-worn furniture and dominated by a huge fireplace at one end warming the room.

"Your QE may become your alter ego, Nell. They're like your favorite teddy bear only these can talk back and help in myriad ways and do useful work. They are more like familiars than pets," Damien finishes.

"Ah, there is one more thing," Damien adds, pulling the iPhone 40 back from Nell's outstretched hand. "Promise me that you won't disclose this to anyone or tell them what it is."

Nell is relieved. In the back of her mind, all her

defence mechanisms and trust issues have just come 'online'. She's thinking, ungraciously as it turns out, Damien might want to use her like so many other people. All she says though is, "OK, OK, I get it," holding up her left hand in a kind of stopping motion and tapping her foot impatiently in a classic Nell move.

"Promise?"

"Yes! Yes! Can I try it now?" she adds, a bit exasperated.

Damien hands her, her new Q-Phone and walks out of the room, closing the door softly behind him.

...

"Hello."

"Uh, hi," says Nell.

A rather disembodied face hovers about a foot and a half above her hacked iPhone 40 lying on the coffee table in front of Nell.

"My name is Nell."

"Hello, Nell." The face is gaining definition—it definitely looks like a female face, a saucer-shaped one—somewhat human in its proportions but animated at its core by an essence that is definitely not DNA-based.

"Do you have a name?" asks Nell.

"I am a Quantum Counterpart."

Nell is intrigued and not a bit frightened by this apparition. "I will call you Suze," Nell commands.

"My name is 'Su7e'," Su7e says. "What do you do, Nell?"

"I am a performance artist. Can you access the Internet? You can read about me there."

"Yes, I have full access to every device connected to the Internet without exception," Su7e answers.

"What's that mean, 'every device'?" Nell asks.

"I can read every database, anywhere."

"Then," Nell pauses a moment, thinking, "What's my bank balance at the BOC branch on Silver Spur Road in Palos Verdes?"

"You have more than one account there, Nell."

"Well, try my money market account."

"You have $7,567,419.64 New Dollars in that account plus there are several transactions that have not cleared yet. Would you like me to calculate your balance as of midnight UTC Universal Time, when they do?"

"No, that's OK. Hey, how did you gain access to my account?"

"I don't know, Nell. You asked me and I can just see it in my mind." Su7e's voice is changing too, fewer monotones and more inflection with each passing comment.

"Can you give me everyone's bank balance?"

"Do you mean everyone at the Bank of California branch in Palos Verdes, every Bank of California branch or every human on the planet's bank balance?" Su7e asks.

"Well, how about just my branch?"

"Yes."

'Wow,' thinks Nell. 'No wonder Damien doesn't want anyone to know about this yet. Holy crap.' Nell does not reflect on it but she sounds a whole lot more like her Canucklehead friend, using corny expressions that were out of date in her part of the world even before the turn of the century.

What she says instead is, "You have a nice face, Suze. Do you guys only come in 'heads'?"

"Thank you, Nell. No, I have access to a full Counterpart body, see."

Nell reaches out to touch Su7e's long fingered hand at the end of her skinny arm; her hand is soft and supple and applies subtle backpressure too. She has a nice touch.

"Our creator has given us access to the iPhone 40's haptics. We can feel things held up against the screen and touch the Real World in return. We self-design and evolve. We can experience Real Life through almost every media wall—most current models integrate haptics into their manufacture. Our creator felt that by giving us as many senses as possible, they would allow us to understand your world and you better."

At this point, it would have been interesting if Nell asked the obvious next question which would be, 'How many senses do you have?' but she doesn't and no one will for a long time.

Instead she asks, "Do you have to do everything I tell you?" This is an important question for a self-centred person like Nell to ask and have answered.

"Our creator has adjusted Isaac Asimov's three laws of robotics for Quantum Counterparts," Su7e answers, unintentionally, cryptically.

"Who is your creator?" Nell finally asks.

"Damien Graham Bell."

"What are Asimov's laws and who was the guy?" Nell queries her QC.

"Asimov's three laws of robotics are; first a robot may not injure a human being or, through inaction, allow a human being to come to harm; second a robot must obey any orders given to it by human beings, except where such orders would conflict with the First Law and third a robot must protect its own existence as long as such protection does not conflict with the First or Second Law.

Asimov's information on Wikipedia is 13,750 words long. It has 71,472 characters or 94,987 characters with spaces. His entry in Encyclopedia Britannica is shorter with —"

Nell interrupts, "Just the short version, please."

"He was both a scientist and a science fiction writer," Su7e adds helpfully.

"You didn't fully answer my original question," Nell asks to see if the artificial creature can handle subtlety.

"Yes, I will obey your commands. These are the laws that our creator has given us; a Quantum Counterpart may not harm a human being or, through inaction, allow a human being to come to harm; a Quantum Counterpart must obey any orders given by her or his human counterpart, except where such orders would conflict with the First Law. A Quantum Counterpart must protect her or his own existence as long as such protection does not conflict with the First or Second Law."

"You said that you can see everyone's bank balances. Can you listen to their conversations or read their messages too?"

"Yes, Nell. I can see them, hear them, record them using audio, video or infrared. Is that your wish?"

"No absolutely not. You are not to spy on anyone," Nell tells her. 'At least, not without me telling you to,' Nell thinks.

...

That evening the whole group comes together again. Along with the Ingersoll clan, they're sitting around a bonfire that Jeff has lit in the Council Ring about 120 yards behind the homestead down a narrow winding path marked with solar-powered lights every five yards or so. It's a beautifully clear night, much colder than it has been. After unstable conditions and rain, there is now a high pressure system over the region and it's incredibly still with no wind at all. Rains also cleared the atmosphere of dust so planets and stars are fantastically magnified and bright on the high plain where the Ingersoll homestead sits. This night is magic; they can all feel it in their bones.

Doug, who is always cognizant of weather, puts it differently. Walking to the Council Ring with Nell and Damien, he remarks, "The reason that everyone is calmer today isn't just that they've had a good night's sleep followed by a rest day, you know. It's also the pressure change."

"How's that affecting us, Doug?" Nell asks.

"The weight of atmosphere around us maintains a certain pressure on us at all times. Our bodies have lots of liquid-bearing squish-sacks—hey don't laugh Miss Nell, that there is genuine scientific jargon but don't search the term, trust me on that—filled with synovial fluid or blood that bulge outward when low pressure systems hit us. As your squish-sacks expand due to a reduction in air pressure, they can cause joint pain or migraines. And as you age, it gets worse which is why old-timers are better at predicting bad weather than young folks like you guys."

"Is that how you knew about the oncoming flood on the Salmon, Doug?" asks a suddenly serious Nell.

"I'm not sure. I was feeling restless/watching for color changes in the river and level fluctuations too but there was something else. Maybe." He stops abruptly. He just doesn't want to talk about it any more.

"Well high pressure systems do the reverse so we're gonna have a great night," Damien adds helpfully.

The Council Ring has bark board nearly eight feet high planted vertically in circle with a diameter of about 40 feet. Inside the Ring, it's surprisingly warm—the walls keep in a lot of heat—most folks are sitting there without their jackets on. Also warming the group is a bunch of drinks being passed around the circle. The favourite, without doubt, is Blue Kitchen Bourbon, a local barrel-aged distilled spirit made primarily from home grown maize. There seems to be an endless supply of it. As usual, neither Damien nor Nell drinks anything at all. They're high on life at this particular juncture and, anyway, Nell wants to make love to D later on and she prefers to have zero intoxicants in her system when they do, a view Damien shares having recently learned it from Nell.

Jeff Ingersoll tends the fire, smoky because their firewood is wet from recent rains. There are so many people inside the Council Ring that they have formed two concentric circles—they are seated on benches with the most important people sitting in the inner circle. That's where Nell is, of course.

People tend to be comfortable in tribes ranging from a half dozen to maybe as many as 30 or 40 people. And in each tribe, people are most comfortable when they know where they stand in a pecking order. Even if they are at or near the bottom, knowing that relieves them of a lot of responsibility—they don't have to supply any leadership—they can just cruise through life without too much stress or effort which is fine with a surprising number of people.

That won't suit Nell at all. She's always wanted to be at the TOP. She fervently believes that if you suddenly dropped a bunch of people, unknown to each other beforehand, onto a desert island, they'd start to form a pecking order a few minutes after meeting each other.

In the inner ring with Nell are Damien, Kowalski, a few of the Ingersolls, the guy from Everest and a handful of others. Dekka, who couldn't care less where he sits, is in the back row along with Morales and eight others. They're going to have a singsong which everyone will enjoy except Dekka who doesn't know many of the tunes and, anyway, he's not exactly a Kumbaya kinda guy.

The fact that Nell has her guitar out would be a good sign to Weinstein if she was there. It means Nell is getting a hankering to start to play, compose and, maybe, perform again. Weinstein wants her back in PV, like yesterday. They've got studio time booked and a ton of PR stuff lined up plus Reznik has three new huge partner deals in the works for Miss Nell to approve.

She has already played some Caoineadh songs from her practically limitless repertoire of tunes. She loves many of those old Irish ballads; there's always a ton of weeping and crying in them. She also sings a few Western tunes, requests from some of the Ingersolls. She's even sung an acoustic version of The Successors which none of them had heard before.

She plays her haunting version of Eminem's Lose Yourself, an old hit that has special meaning for Nell, especially the line, 'You only get one shot, do not miss your chance to blow/This opportunity comes once in a lifetime, yo.' For a poor girl from Nocal, she gets his message, it resonates with her even though he's an oldster now and so not part of her tribe.

Other people have brought their instruments—there's a banjo, two more guitars and a harmonica. But, right now, they're watching this amazing performance by young Nell. Everyone can see she is reaching a new stage in her career—she's growing up in front of their eyes. If Reznik was here, he'd be kicking himself for not recording this; Nell completely unplugged and reaching for things in herself that no one even knew was there.

If either Reznik or Weinstein had a soupcon of empathy, they would see that Damien is, at least in part, responsible for this. Nell is a woman in love and it shows. On her return to her studio, Nell will be moved by a sadness, a sense of loss and yet a feeling of oneness with the universe that will produce some of the best work of her career. Her productivity will soar. But that is nothing, nothing compared to what happens to Damien when he gets back to U of T.

Anyway, what neither Reznik nor Weinstein can know is that every picosecond of tonight's shindig is being recorded—Su7e is there.

Next, Nell reaches back even further in time. "I want to play the next tune for D," she tells her audience, looking at Damien with those shining green eyes of hers.

"Su7e, can you boot up Johnny and Willie for me?" Nell asks.

Nell's iPhone 40 sits in front of Nell on a little wooden table used mainly to hold various drinks.

An old YouTube video of Johnny Cash accompanied by Willie Nelson starts playing softly. The projection is about two metres high and, apart from showing Johnny and Willie, has this information displayed 256,618,302 views. The quality of the video sucks but it is totally authentic. Nell is going to sing along with two dead guys from an earlier era, just for her lover tonight.

Nell knows that D is heading back to TO the day after tomorrow. It's killing her but she's determined to make a good show of it. 'We'll find a way,' she keeps repeating to herself. Nell and Damien are experiencing huge hormonal changes. Their pheromones are mixing in a manner that is totally pleasing to both of them. They will both be going through a painful withdrawal, no different from any other addiction, a few days hence. But that's in their future.

In her immediate future, right after the campfire, her plan is to make love to Damien. Nell has always thought, secretly, that sex is way overrated. She knows enough to keep this to herself since a huge proportion of her fan base either want to have sex with her or want to be her having sex with some unimaginably good-looking Hollywood personality. She's reported to be in a 'relationship' with a new guy or sometimes with a girl, every other month.

Nell loves Damien's body. He's skinny but strong and she can tell he's been a runner from the twin cords of ligaments stemming from his hips which Su7e has told her are called 'inguinal creases'. Whatever they're called, she can't wait to press herself up against them. If Nell was a more introspective type of person and had more self-knowledge, she would understand that it's the fact that she totally loves Damien that has made all the difference for her.

Chief Dan tells her, 'Self-knowledge is your first step to wisdom' but this is one of his lessons that Nell has trouble internalizing and acting on.

Now Nell sings:

> Love is a burning thing
> and it makes a firery ring
> bound by wild desire

As she sings this last line, Nell's eyes are hooked onto Damien's. Even the hardest heart among them, has to love young love tonight.

> I fell in to a ring of fire...

While Nell is singing her silly love song to her boyfriend from Nowheresville, one person sitting around the campfire is thinking completely indifferent thoughts 'Shit, what is that thing?' This person wants a closer look at

Nell's brand new phone.

After this tune, there's silence for a few moments. Then Damien makes a request, his first tonight. He wants to hear a tune written by Canadian Leonard Cohen, one of his favourites—Hallelujah. The best version of the song, in Damien's professional opinion, is not Cohen's but one recorded decades ago by another Canadian artist, k. d. lang. He's about to hear a new favourite version tonight.

The last song Nell plays before everyone breaks up for the night is Amazing Grace. She stands up to sing it, a cappella. It's a performance that is both sweet and poignant and many of them will remember it for a long time.

Dekka has spotted a family of Timberwolves just outside the Council Ring. He can see the alpha male fade in and out of the flickering firelight. Out of nowhere, he has a Glock 29 in his hand. Damien makes eye contact with him and just shakes his head, 'no'. Somehow, eons ago, wolves were tamed by humans and became dogs. Maybe this is how it happened, maybe not. But there is no growling, no fighting, no nipping, no teeth-baring going on. There's just another 'family' listening to Nell. The Glock disappears so fast that Damien's eyes can't follow it. No doubt it's quite handy if Dekka ever really needs it.

Nell's fabulous voice rings out over the high plains mesmerizing her human and non-human audience alike:

Amazing Grace, how sweet the sound,
That saved a wretch like me....
I once was lost but now am found,
Was blind, but now, I see.
T'was Grace that taught...
my heart to fear.
And Grace, my fears relieved.
How precious did that Grace appear...
the hour I first believed.
Through many dangers, toils and snares...
we have already come.

Quantum Entity Book 1 We Are All One

T'was Grace that brought us safe thus far...
and Grace will lead us home.
        The Lord has promised good to me...
His word my hope secures.
He will my shield and portion be...
as long as life endures.
        Yea, when this flesh and heart shall fail,
and mortal life shall cease,
I shall possess within the veil,
a life of joy and peace.
        When we've been here ten thousand years...
bright shining as the sun.
We've no less days to sing God's praise...
then when we've first begun..."

Nell dedicates this last song to her hard working, God-fearing Mom.

...

"What was my present, Nell?"

They're back in their room; they can still hear people moving about in other parts of the homestead, talking overloud like folks do who've had a bunch to drink. There's a lot of activity going on despite the lateness of the hour.

"I want to make love to you, in a special way."

"Every time we make love is special, Nell."

"But this is different," Nell adds. "Get in bed, D, you're getting cold. I'll be back in a minute then I'll warm you up."

Frig, Damien needs no more urging. Like most men about to have sex, he can get undressed in zero time.

...

Damien's face is a few centimetres above Nell's. They're breathing synchronously again, bathing some more in each other's pheromones. Nell loves the smell of him; it excites her more if that's even possible.

She has applied some kind of super expensive organic oil, first to herself, and then to Damien. Damien has placed a pillow under her. He lifts her buttocks and slowly penetrates her in a way that is new to Damien and a first time for Nell too. She wanted to give Damien something special that no one else has had and a memory to take back with him to Toronto so that he won't forget her.

Nell takes Damien to a place he has never been before, never even knew that you could get to. And she goes there too, with him all the way.

...

When Dekka comes back from delivering Damien to Boise Airport, he hands Nell a small plain recycled cardboard box bound by a simple white-cotton string. Nell takes it silently and, shoulders slumped, goes into her room to get her personal things for the flight back to LAX. She opens it when she knows she's alone.

In it she sees a one and a quarter inch diameter Siberian Cedar Medallion except she knows it's not from Siberia (it's from Ontario) and it's not cedar, it's pine. She lifts it from the box and puts it around her neck using the light brownish-coloured leather thong it came with to tie a slipknot so her medallion hangs like a pendant between her breasts. She sees that Damien has painted a tiny exquisite piece of folk art on one side—it's a picture of the cabin they shared at Phantom Ranch. She slips it inside her blouse so only she will know it's there.

...

Damien is seated in economy flying with one of those detestable commercial airlines operating out of Boise. Pet3r tells him that Nell has left a message for him, not to be opened until they cross the Canadian border. Pet3r tells him the precise moment when they have entered Canadian airspace. Damien listens to her message—it's her remix of another old tune—Meet Me Halfway. The song, its words and Nell's disembodied voice flood into his quantum ear buds:

Meet me halfway, right at the borderline
That's where I'm gonna wait, for you
I'll be lookin out, night n'day
Took my heart to the limit, and this is where I'll stay
I can't go any further then this
I want you so bad it's my only wish...

...

End of Part I

Part II—Launch

"Only those who will risk going too far can possibly find out how far one can go," T.S. Eliot.

Chapter 6

The Big Smoke

Ellen sits in a small conference room not far from Lab 4 at U of T's Department of Physics preparing for her upcoming meeting with the CEO of Quantum Computing Corp, its CTO and two of their five new hires—their rent-a-CFO and their top biz development guy: Damien, Traian, Aziz Mukono and Anthony del Castillo, respectively.

It's an important gathering of her tribe. Today, they're going to try to come to final agreement on their business model which they, actually mostly Ellen, have been working on for months.

She must say that since coming back from Boise, Damien has been paying more attention to this part of their new enterprise than he ever did before. They are all working insane hours but Damien's schedule is ridiculous. He has bags under his eyes and can't be sleeping more than four or five hours a night. Plus he's been flying on his girlfriend's Gulfstream every other weekend to hook up with her in her lair in Palos Verdes.

Ellen can't see what he sees in that woman apart from maybe her big boobs. 'What's with men and their fascination with big boobs,' she thinks, 'Anything more than a handful is a waste.' Ellen has a nice handful, two actually.

Nell's one visit to their neck of the woods is a disaster. Nell and her crazy entourage descend on Lab 4 without first signing a Non Disclosure Agreement. They overrun the place, do interviews next to smart displays full of confidential information, and set up for media shots without regard to placement of furniture, equipment or damage. The University's administrators unctuously permit this desecration—it's good PR, at least that's how they see it.

The only place they can't get at is the vault also called

the 'hatchery'. It is locked and only Ellen, Damien, Traian and Dr. Luis have the combination. Of course, their Quantum Counterparts can unlock it without effort but they've been directed not to do so; it would be impossible to persuade them otherwise.

Nell treats Ellen like she's wallpaper instead of Executive Vice-President and Senior Product Manager for QCC and a 5.125% owner with employee badge No. 3. Ellen feels sure that her ownership interest in the corporation would've been higher if she was male. Although women have finally all but closed the wage gap in North America, they've done it by attending universities and colleges en masse, by getting professionally accredited and by being over-qualified with respect to men in the same job doing the same work. Nevertheless, the top of the social, economic and political ladder is still heavily male-dominated. It's worse for women nearly everywhere outside North America.

Nell's taken Damien on her latest gadabout of media outlets in LA, parading her cute new boyfriend in front of endless e-networks, breathlessly telling and retelling the story of how that stupid woman nearly got probably the greatest young physicist of his day killed on some Godforsaken river in backwoods Idaho. The Paparrazzoids love the couple; images and videos of the two of them are inescapable. They play incessantly on media walls everywhere constantly assaulting (and annoying) Ellen's senses.

She can't believe that expensive media training they arranged for Damien, provided by McLaughlin Markowitz Media and paid for from their measly marketing budget, is being wasted on vacuous Hollywood-style, talking-head newsfeed interviews. Seeing inane intros for the new 'It' couple like 'Miss Nell and Her Quant, Next on E-Tainment' sets Ellen to grinding her teeth.

At least there's one positive thing that comes out of the whole sideshow that his involvement with Nell has become. Damien's prediction that he was going to be fired by his event company has come true. He is terminated 'for cause' on account of 'insubordination'. They also use the excuse that he fails to show up for some minor gig while he is out of the country with Nell. So there is, thankfully, one less distraction in his life.

Ellen will never admit it but she is lonely. She recently broke up with her boyfriend of just over a year. He's a really good-looking investment banker working on Bay Street who is seven years older than her. He was so nice to her after her move to Toronto.

She graduated from tiny but prestigious Elmira College in upstate New York. It's an area no one actually wants to live in anymore since there's practically no work to be had. It's been a poor part of the State practically forever. Its 'golden age' if it ever had one was back in the 1920s and '30s as a place for wealthy New Yorkers and their families to escape impossibly hot summers in New York City in a time before air conditioning. It has gotten much worse, if that is even possible, since the Great Reset and meltdown of the US Dollar in the first quarter of this century put the coup de grace on the entire region and, in fact, much of the nation. So when her HR service provider matches her profile with an opportunity to work with a tiny but promising startup in Toronto, she takes off like a shot.

Ellen's first interview at QCC sort of prepares her for the weirdness of the place. First she meets Damien and Traian in a sort of normal job interview, more or less, but then they insist on putting her behind a screen before letting the third guy in their troika interview her.

Damien tells her, "We're trying to hire up. That's what Dr. Luis is recommending. It's like what Walt Disney did when he was auditioning voices for his classic film Snow White. He didn't want to be...uh... influenced by the appearance of the women who were auditioning their singing voices. He wanted to judge the girls on the quality of their pitch and range so he sat behind a screen. I hope you don't mind?"

This is the most chauvinistic thing Ellen has ever heard a man say in her presence. She is immediately suspicious that they only ask females to submit to such a degrading experience. But she's interested in the work they're doing in telecom and mobile Internet so she stifles the response she would really like to give him.

"I've seen the film. Adriana Caselotti not only sung for Snow White, she did the voiceover too. She was great." Ellen comments.

Damien leaves her alone and another voice says, "Hello, Ellen."

"Uh, hi, Mr.?"

"You can call me Helper, Mr. Helper."

She can't place the age of Mr. Helper. His use of precise English and formal mien strikes her as old or maybe middle age but there's enthusiasm and eagerness there too. She likes his voice and tone.

"You hail from New York, do you not?"

"Yes but not New York City—upstate. I went to Elmira College."

"Yes, I can see that."

She assumes that he is looking at her CV or micro blog on a media wall on his side of the screen or something.

"Have you ever worked with foreigners before or would you prefer I use 'alien', the term the US Government uses for immigrants."

So that explains his somewhat strained use of English, Ellen thinks. It's his second language.

"Many of the girls at Elmira come from all over, Mr. Helper but I am not going to tell you that my best friends are foreigners because I don't look at people that way—I discriminate but not on the basis of where they came from or how much money their families have. I'm an elitist for sure but based on talent and trust.

"And may I say, Mr. Helper, that having you sit behind a screen is not helping me with the trust thing here."

"Yes, it is a bit silly. I see your point."

"Have you done this before?" Ellen can't resist asking.

"Actually, this is my first outside interview," he pauses. "Well, perhaps I should call on either Damien or Traian to remove this partition wall?"

"I can do that, Mr. Helper. Just say the word."

"Word."

And so Ellen gets up and slides the screen to the side, it takes a bit of effort, and then she comes face to face with Pet3r, whose quantum number is 1.

She controls her reaction, says nothing and moves closer to the media wall about a metre and a quarter behind the now removed screen. She looks at him making contact with his large, expressive, strangely benevolent eyes, kind, even a little sad too. He is smiling at her, she thinks.

"Is that your real name, Mr. Helper?"

"Well, in a manner of speaking. I am a Quantum Counterpart mated to Damien Bell and, ah, I have been known to help Dr. Bell from time to time. My name is Pet3r, spelt P-E-T-3-R."

"You are using Leet names?"

"We are."

"Why?"

"I don't know. It is one of the mysteries of life. So far."

"Did Dr. Bell suggest it or Traian Vasilescu?"

"Not that I know of."

"How old are you, Mr., umm, Pet3r?"

"I was born right here in Lab 4, about five months ago."

At least the guys aren't obvious chauvinists, thank God. She believes she understands the test they've just put her through but in fact she doesn't.

So Pet3r explains it, "The screen diversion was a way to use a reverse Turing test—to see if you could discern my, ah, alien nature or not. To determine if I could convince you I was human instead of machine."

"It worked, Pet3r."

"Yes, I agree."

"I was under the impression this is a telecommunications company—that the company is doing something with quantum phones. But this is different, way different."

"Well, we do use altered iPhones for quantum communication but each of them comes with a surprise, on the upside I should note—one of my kind."

"How many of your 'kind' are there, Pet3r?"

"Ah, right now there are two, soon to be three if you'll join us."

As they continue, the interview turns into a long conversation. Ellen finds herself enjoying his company, really liking the little guy and ultimately wishing she could give him a hug when she finally signs off.

Pet3r plays back the entire scene for Damien, Traian and Dr. Luis. They all want her on board and even forget to contact her references—she's blown them all away.

...

Her Mom thinks her new Toronto-based boyfriend is perfect for her: chivalrous, generous, considerate, chatty, polite, outgoing and nicely dressed. Ellen, always beautifully coutured, appreciated that too. He also had a lovely singing voice, spent money on her, showed her off to his tribe of super status-conscious investment bankers and took her on nice trips.

But Ellen has to admit, the relationship lacks the je ne sais quoi that she seeks.

Fairly recently, in fact just before her breakup, she confides to her best friend, Mary O'Regan, a Irish girl and her roommate, "Hey, Mary, is it normal to like have relations... I mean how often... say, what do you think?"

"Are we talking about 'sex'?" Mary facetiously asks her shy friend.

"I was wondering."

"Right, girl, what's wrong with your gaydar?"

"Gaydar?"

"He's so GAY. It's written all over him. He's like your

BFF not your boyfriend. I can't believe how long it's taken you to dump him," Mary tells her.

"Umm, I haven't dumped anyone."

"Well, crap, you should. How many times have you had sex with him?"

"Three times," Ellen admits.

"You mean three times a day?"

"Nope. Three times."

"In a year?" an incredulous Mary asks.

"Yes," a now completely embarrassed Ellen replies wishing she'd never brought up the subject.

"That's not normal, girl, and it's not good for your health either—mental or physical. It's not you turning him down is it?"

"Uh, nope."

Ellen was brought up to be a lady in the living room. It's the second part of that expression: 'A whore in the bedroom' that she'd like to explore some more but she is not having any luck in that department and, worse still, she can't think of any likely candidates either if she finally gives up on her current boyfriend.

Ellen doesn't think much of her looks—she's too tall for most guys. She wears glasses. She hates contact lenses and the thought of undergoing ocular surgery, and letting an excimer laser anywhere near her retina while she's still awake (they only use local anesthetic) turns her right off. She refuses to cut her long blond hair even though she knows it should be above her shoulders in a professional office. So she just ties it back, otherwise it remains curly and hangs down to her shoulder blades. She died it black once so people would take her seriously; the only result was she freaked out her Mom. If there's a formal meet-up, she will use a ceramic hair straightener to look the part of a young executive but most days, she pops out of the shower, blow dries her hair and, poof, it curls like wildfire. In Toronto's humid summer, it will be worse.

Unlike Nell, Ellen does her own makeup and has dressed herself since she was two and a half. While pretty much everyone else, male and female, is in jeans at the Lab but Ellen does dress-up—she loves clothes, shoes, makeup and perfume. Mom quotes long-ago French actress, Catherine Deneuve, who supposedly said, 'If a woman is not beautiful by 30, then it's her fault.' Ellen has done it before 20.

She has a lovely hour glass figure with hips made to carry a baby. She's got a sporty, yoga-trained body but she's actually not much good at sports and is a horrible dancer. She has an adorable ass that guys will pivot 180 degrees just to stare at. Well, most guys. Damien never looks at her.

While she has nearly every conceivable perfume in her collection there's one missing, she thinks. It's called, 'Confidence'—she has none.

At the apartment she shares with Mary, you can tell which half of the place is hers. It's the room with a Jar Design Diva Daybed with matching Westfield high back chair and ottoman. She's even brought her antique Victorian mahogany partner's desk originally from London firm W. Wilson & Sons. It's too big to fit in her bedroom so it has colonized part of their tiny living room. When Ellen has to move, she needs a lot of help plus two trucks for all her stuff.

Her Mom has the same view about things—buy stuff once even if it's expensive and it will last a few lifetimes. Her mother has developed furniture buying strategies that she puts in place on unimaginably long timescales measured in decades and, signs are, her daughter will carry on this tradition. Ellen can unerringly pick out the most expensive thing in a store, in an app or on a menu without ever looking at media wall price displays.

She's loves old black and white films, ones her roommate and most of her friends can't stand. They're way too slow and mushy for them. Ellen likes the grace, charm and civility of that bygone era. Ellen can't understand why directors ever allowed studios to desecrate these films by colorizing them. She supposes that studios have better lawyers or maybe a lot more of them than directors.

These days you can watch films practically anywhere, pretty much every wall is a media wall. It's as cheap as paint, actually, cheaper. You throw some NSM (Nano Scale Mix) into your paint, stir and apply. When it's dry, poof, you have a full-on media wall with audio and haptics (powered by air squeezed by microscopic little machines in the recipe).

Damien would have corrected Ellen on several counts if he'd heard this description of media wall haptics from her. First, he would say, they're not microscopic, they're nanoscale engines and, second, they use invisibly small rotary compressors with positive-displacement helical screws to force gas, in this case air, into a smaller space. But it's not a bad attempt for a girl from Elmira.

It works fine when you brush NSM on but better if you spray it on. Want higher def? No problem, just increase the density of NSM in your paint. When you watch a media wall, it also watches you—they're 2-way.

Ellen can now ask her Quantum Counterpart, whom she names Ash3r, to show her any film she wants anywhere in their apartment and at any scale. But she prefers to sit up and look at films in their parlour, which doubles as eat-in kitchen, dining room, work room and living room. At least, she can pretend it's a parlour.

She is careful not to ask Ash3r to show a film that she does not have a license for. Studios are still run by crazed psycho executives who litigate with their audience for the slightest transgression of any conceivable part of their byzantine IP (intellectual property) rules. Ash3r could, of course, destroy any security walls studios have as if they were totally transparent but Damien's asked everyone in their test bed to make sure they don't break any rules, especially this kind.

In addition to executing NDA's (non-disclosure agreements) each person in the first group of Q-Phone users is required to digitally sign their TOS (terms of service). Damien insists it be written in plain English in 11 point font and be no more than one page. Ellen works with their law firm, MacMillan, Sheppard and Seller LLP, on this. It's proven to be impossible to get them to exercise this level of restraint but their final agreement is three pages, a lot better than other service providers who often have as many as 30 pages of 9 point type that no one ever actually reads.

QCC is at an inflection point, Ellen is sure of it. They've renamed their hacked iPhone 40s the 'Q-Phone'. Ellen came up with the name—it just popped out of her mouth in one of her ten minute meetings with Damien and it's kind of stuck. Their law firm applied for international trademarks for it and they've copyrighted much of their IP too with a relatively simple act of registration under the Second Berne Convention for the Protection of Literary and Artistic Works (which covers software arts too) and WIPO III Copyright Treaty rules.

Damien is dead set against applying for patents—the process is costly, time consuming and, worse still in his opinion, it requires near full disclosure. Damien feels they will be much better off with trade secret protection. In this regard, he is completely inflexible.

He explains it to Ellen this way, "Who said life is pretty simple? You do some stuff. Most fails. Some works. You do more of what works. If it works big, others quickly copy it. Then you do something else. The trick is the doing something else."

"I have no idea, Damien, but I'm sure you're going to tell me."

"Leonardo da Vinci."

"I don't suppose he filed many patent applications?" Ellen asks sarcastically.

"Right," a straight faced Damien responds. "Even if they'd had a Firenze or Milano patent office in his day, you wouldn't have found Leo there, I'm sure of it. You know why?"

"He hated patent lawyers?"

"Very funny. Seriously, why?"

She doesn't have to say anything because she knows him well enough now to understand this is a Damien Bell rhetorical question.

"Because while your competitors can copy your products or services and maybe your business model too, although that is harder to do," he replies in a nod to one of Ellen's favourite subjects, "they can't copy what you are thinking of doing next. That's what Leonardo was getting at. They can't know and can't copy what you're planning to do next.

"We're the innovation engine of our generation, Ellen, but McLuhan said it better a long time ago, 'Today the business of business is becoming the constant invention of new business.' That's us, kid."

She isn't even sure he's wrong although both their law firm and, at least one of the two big Eastern seaboard VCs they're talking to, Cain Caruthers Capital, are 'insisting' on patenting their IP. Bessemer Ventures, now well into its second century of business, is the other venture capital firm they are dealing with and they seem OK with the idea of trade secret as opposed to patent protection.

Ellen has a record containing 76 NDAs plus 76 signed TOS agreements. The only people who have not signed them are: Damien, Traian, Ellen and the dreadful, Nell. Ellen isn't worried about the first three—employee contracts that every badged employee signs including its founders will take care of every conceivable issue with respect to IP. But Nell isn't bound by anything.

Ellen's been tracking their metrics. Of the total world population of QEs (currently 80), 79 matched the gender of their human counterpart. Only Ellen's doesn't. She and Ash3r are the only exception. Traian sarcastically comments, "What's with Ellen and gay guys?"

She hasn't yet told the boys that one of their test bed QEs is black, matching his human counterpart. OLA Tech Crunch's Mike Cronkey signed his NDA and they got this unanticipated result. She supposes that they just hadn't given any prior thought to it.

Traian helpfully suggests a new tag line for QCC 'Killing Karriers Kwickly' since he is convinced that Q-Phones will terminate them—from small Tier 3 players to Tier 1 mega corps, they are all toast in his view.

"Hmm, sure, right, Traian, that'll rank right up there with Advertising Slogan Hall of Fame saying, 'New York is BIG but this is Biggar, Saskatchewan.' That's why you're in development and I'm product manager. If you're gonna make war on those guys, maybe it's better to sneak up on them instead of being like British Red Coats marching in organized ranks for American patriots hidden in the bush to mow down."

This is another concern for Ellen—they are going to need political cover or they will be walking into a turkey shoot.

Ellen remembers a Damien comment he'd made about an ICANN conference he'd attended and how much time poor, old ICANN spent bickering over its long term governance, a 20th century problem. It proved to be an intractable problem since US DOC (Department of Commerce) has steadfastly refused to give up its control over 17 root servers in the US and US-allied nations that, along with seven other root servers in Imperial China and two in India, allow the Internet to resolve.

Damien is quite sure DOC is never going to give up its control over the Internet to ICANN despite promising to look at the matter from time to time. Basically, every other President since Bill Clinton has mouthed polite words about the importance of 'international cooperation and governance'.

DOC allows ICANN to dick around with TLDs (Top Level Domains) and CCs (Country Codes) and administer Internet protocols that let the whole thing resolve but they are pretty much caretakers for its real owner, which happens to be... DOC, whose iron fist in a velvet glove is always somewhere in view. Ellen expects to see more iron fist if (when) their quantum devices make the Internet transparent or threaten to make it fail to resolve.

Damien isn't sure that DOC is even wrong vis-à-vis ICANN. It's an international corporation that doesn't really answer to anyone—no national government has jurisdiction over it and its Board of Directors is never going to agree to submit it to UN governance and oversight. They want to remain independent. What they don't seem to realize is that an independent international corporation is, in fact, a nation onto itself and requires a constitution which history shows is darned hard to write.

It would be every bit as hard as, say, writing the US constitution and there are no signs of a Jefferson, Adams, Paine, Madison et al on ICANN's Board. So instead they still use one IP address, one vote to elect Board members.

There have been attempts by at least a couple of dictators, with visions of Internet dominance in their crazed heads, to buy up tens of millions of domains and vote in their own slate of Directors. Damien wonders what DOC would actually do if it worked. What if they woke up one morning to find the Internet controlled by a foreign despot? He's sure there'd be another war. The US has been in at least one war every five years since the founding of their Republic so what's one more?

Both Damien and Traian are more or less completely disdainful of competition. "You know, Ellen, even if I shrink Tray down to 20 centimetres and he sneaks into the home of say the CEO of Horizon Communications and plasters a piece of paper next to the guy's bed and puts another copy on the guy's fridge that describes our biz model in detail, I don't think it'll matter at all."

"Gee thanks, buddy. Why do I get to be the one to do the BnE?" Traian asks.

"You'll like being 20 centimetres tall. Makes it a lot easier to look up girls' skirts," Damien jokes ignoring Ellen for the moment.

"Damien, that is totally unprofessional," a shocked Ellen exclaims. She knows that this is atypical, unexpected male chauvinist behaviour from him.

"You're right. I apologize but my point is this; don't

worry about people stealing our ideas or protecting them via expensive, time consuming processes like patents. 'If your ideas are any good, you will have to ram them down people's throats.' Howard Aiken, original designer of IBM's Mark I computer, once said that. He came out of Harvard University with his PhD in physics in the 1930s and he was right. Even if they know what's coming, they won't do a thing—they're way too hidebound and completely married to what they're already doing.

"They all think something like this: 'We do what we do because that's the way we've always done it. We'll always do it this way because that's the way it's done.' It's circular and persuasive and can only end one way—in death for their entire enterprise."

"OK, OK, I get it. Let's just execute the whole thing flawlessly," Ellen says wanting to end the discussion for now.

She knows that startups that set goals and track metrics tend to grow seven times faster than those that don't. So far, their test bed metrics have shown that most popular uses for Q-Phones and QEs are: searching, voice calls, music and video. This was as expected. But what Ellen found much more interesting is the integration of QEs into the daily lives of their counterparts, first doing simple stuff like keeping their calendar, screening their calls and messages, organizing trips, making reservations, filing, storing and retrieving information, making appointments, computation of all sorts, taking notes at and keeping records of meetings, ordering stuff, paying for things, making deposits, transferring funds, reminding people, making lists and checking everything, twice.

But in just over four months, QEs are moving up the value chain, learning to file tax returns for their human counterparts, helping with research, summarizing stuff they're learning in school, doing bookkeeping for them at home and at work, writing messages, letters, contracts and agreements, helping with priorities, updating apps, posting to social media and responding, keeping in touch with friends, family and clients thereby helping to manage important relationships, data mining, comparing prices, interpreting and translating, being sounding boards, giving advice, even keeping an eye on children for the few people in their test bed focus group that have any.

QEs have access to a practically limitless inventory of material to entertain and educate children. Two weeks ago, Ellen invited a group of kids to come in with their QEs to a specially equipped room at their marketing agency, BlackFern Group, a room where they can observe, record and analyze how these interactions are developing. Test results are amazing.

The kids relate to their QEs as if they are kindly aunties or uncles, asking for help with puzzles, words, spelling, reading, writing and arithmetic, proudly showing off newly learned skills like summersaults and cartwheels, demanding praise, even taking direction and reprimands from their QEs too. They ask their QEs to adjudicate arguments over sharing toys or taking turns on climbing structures. The kids even race their QEs (who conveniently sprout fast-moving skinny legs and big, floppy cartoonish feet) around the room, which is curious because QEs have infinite speed since they can be in every state at any one time. Nevertheless, races prove interesting since QEs push their kids hard enough for them to get a great workout while still letting them be competitive. They even try organizing a relay race but this degenerates into a pell-mell circular mêlée of kids and QEs running first clockwise and then, at some unknown signal, counter clockwise around the room.

Ellen, even though she is alone while watching all this unfold, bursts out laughing when she sees a teensy girl leaning against a media wall, her face centimetres from her QE and they're both panting. A QE with her long tongue hanging out of her mouth and large expressive eyes, congratulating her kididily on a race well run is something to behold. QE faces are becoming more expressive by the day. This one is kind of stooped over as if exhausted from the race with the edges of her saucer-shaped face curling in and down reflecting the posture and state of her little girl. QEs are acquiring more dimensionality for sure.

They also play dueling pistols, video games, dance-move games, mirror games, wobbly body and dozens, maybe hundreds, of other variants with their kids. It's bewildering to watch.

If their kid has a favourite story, video, animation or song, their Quantum Counterpart reads it to them or shows it to them or plays it for them, over and over again as requested no matter how many times their kids ask. QEs never get tired, never get cross, never have other things they've got to do and, Ellen thinks, they appear to enjoy watching 'their' kids grow, change and develop, since she supposes they are experiencing a lot of the same stuff, albeit at warp speed.

It looks completely natural and also weird. QEs scale in an interesting manner. When talking to just one child, they will appear quite small, a head with skinny arms and legs conversing quietly almost tête-à-tête, forcing the kid to come closer. When reading to a larger audience, they look more like a giant Humpty Dumpty—big headed and long armed, turning pages quite elaborately emulating, perhaps, the speech patterns of noted Stratford player Richard Blanforth.

They will invite children, one at a time, to come up and touch the media wall to feel the coarseness of Big Bad Wolf's fur or velvety softness of Red Riding's Hood. They will add cool background sounds and lighting effects too—QEs can talk and produce a 'show' at the same time. Ellen has never seen anything like it and frankly no one else has either. The kids, of course, don't know that, don't care and take to it famously. Ellen sees an echo of Damien's sound engineering background somewhere in all this.

She's introduced 'Bananas' into the mix—to please Damien since it's a game his grandfather invented years ago to teach him the power of positive and negative numbers. Kids stand and QEs resolve on numbered squares that appear on the media wall floor beneath them. Each player takes turns clapping their hands and a pair of large dice on the media wall at the far end of the room roll. If a die is a 1, 2 or 3, you have to go backwards. A 4, 5 or 6 means you get to move forward. If you land on a square where another player is, he or she (human or non-human) have to go back to the beginning!

Kids learn fast that a negative number isn't always bad since if your QE opponent is one square behind you and you roll a 1 and, say, a 5, you use the 1 first to move backwards and chase your QE all the way back to the start before you move forward 5 squares. So there is strategy as well as luck involved. Rolling doubles means you get another turn and there are some squares 'painted' with an evil-looking face. If you land there, you miss a turn.

Finally, Pops introduced characters into his game (you choose who you want to be from a list of different species of apes) and there are shortcuts (vines) that you can swing on. If rolling a negative number leads you to where one of the vines starts, you can swing across and end up ahead of where you started!

QEs also do 'dress-up' as pretend-apes and, sometimes, if their kid is about to miss an opportunity to knock them off or otherwise make a wrong move, they will give her or him a bit of a hint by wiggling, fidgeting or vibrating or maybe rapidly blinking, winking or pulsing. First sentient being to the end of the room, wins. The prize is a virtual hand of purple bananas, hence the game's name. A few tables with real bananas other fruits and juice have been set up in an alcove at the far end of the room for everyone to enjoy afterwards. It will be up to QEs to supervise kids' snack time since there are no other 'adults' permitted inside this experiment they're running.

One game where kids seem to have found that they have the upper hand, where they can regularly and legitimately beat their Quantum Counterparts is Rock/Paper/Scissors. QEs cannot seem to read subtle signs of intention. They have some difficulty with instinctual emotions (those from the amygdala or more primitive part of the brain) like anger, disgust, humour or contempt. They do better with cognitive emotions (from the prefrontal cortex) like behavioral inhibition, judgment, evaluation, meaning, inspiration, beauty and falsehood or truth.

She can see that QEs are trying to evolve a workaround for the former using a reference engine so that, for example, they will be able to 'get' that a man slipping on a banana peel is funny because, basically, they have millions of examples to draw from. But Ellen isn't sure whether any QE will ever headline the now more than 50 year old Just-For-Laughs Festival in Montréal dazzling audiences there with new original material.

Right now, it's a hoot for Ellen to see a little kid's two fingered scissors cutting up 'Humpty Dumpty's' five fingered paper hand.

Within a year of release, QEs will be playing a big role in early childhood education and become especially important to kids with learning disabilities and autistic children who will need only a few simple gestures from QEs to improve their ability to relate to a wider world but she doesn't know any of that yet.

What Ellen, who is watching all this unfold on her media wall from an adjacent room, does know, in a fundamental way that no one else possibly can, not even Damien or Traian, who have not personally witnessed the last two hours, is that QCC has a huge hit on their hands. She knows it for a certainty because her head, her heart and her gut are now all in alignment on this.

She's more than a little scared too because QCC is probably about to unleash what Nassim Nicholas Taleb calls a 'black swan' event—Damien has told her about the guy's work. Highly improbable occurrences are much more frequent and much more powerful than conventional models suggest is likely. Waves of creative destruction, predicted by economic models based on the work of Joseph Schumpeter have become ever more common since the first big disruption of the industrial age, when wide-framed automated looms operated by unskilled labourers replaced skilled textile workers in early 19th century England. Ellen is sure quantum phones and entities are going to produce a new quantum economics causing a lot of economic displacement and disruption. Maybe it will trigger another movement to form like the one East Midland textile workers started and then named for King Ludd, a mythical figure reputed to have lived in Sherwood Forest.

But at the moment, it looks like everyone is having fun. Ellen wants to be in the room with the group of nanny-for-the-day QEs and their little kids; she would have been right at home squeezing, laughing, hugging, reading, watching, dancing and playing too. Of course, if she goes in there with the kids and their QEs (or is it the other way round), she will completely negate the independence and validity of test results from their experiment but she yearns for the experience anyway.

Ellen understands that kids aren't covered and can't ever be covered by NDAs so nothing is going to stop them from blabbing about their experiences to everyone. QCC's stealth period is rapidly drawing to an end. Too many people are already involved. As Damien likes to say, 'If you want to keep a secret, tell No One,' and, in this, she feels he is wise.

Now, a fortnight later, Ellen is nearly finished working through her checklist, 'Ten Things Startups Forget to Do', in preparation for today's briefing. Ellen's reference 'bibles' include Entrepreneurs Handbook 8 and Product Managers Guide to Everything 3. One of the quotes she likes (which Damien first clued her into) and uses in her work is an old one from Mike Gerber who said (in E Myth Revisited IV) that, if you want to build a great organization, you have to have more than just a great idea:

"Those mundane and tedious little things
that, when done exactly right, with the right
kind of attention and intention, form in their

aggregate a distinctive essence, an evanescent quality that distinguishes every great business you've ever done business with from its more mediocre counterparts whose owners are satisfied to simply get through the day."

Even Dr. Castagino is on this bandwagon—underlining for them in his professor'ish way how important it is for them to seize this opportunity. He has told Damien to 'hire up'. For this small group of talented young people, that may be all but impossible to do but Luis wants the group to be surrounded by people who are not only excellent at what they do but also bring with them 'good heart'. By that he means people you like and trust.

"Trust," Luis has told Damien, "is more important than love. And I can prove it to you, in under a minute by the way."

"How's that Dr. Luis?" Damien asks.

"Well, say your new girlfriend, the Hollywood Pop Princess, for example..."

Damien bursts out laughing at this description of Nell from Dr. Castagino, "Her name is Nell."

"Certainly, certainly. So if she was running around behind your back with Traian, (always a possibility given Traian's track record but, thankfully, not Nell's) how good a relationship do you think that would be for you, Damien?"

Damien good naturedly goes along with his mentor, "Horrible, Dr. Luis, friggin horrible."

"So what's more important, Love or Trust?"

"Both," replies Damien.

...

The only other contribution that Ellen can see that Castagino has ever really made to their new enterprise (she knows that both Traian and Damien leave Dr. Luis in the dust now as far as the physics and math of what they are doing are concerned) is to backup Ellen's view that the guys must also focus on business development.

It secretly annoys her that Dr. Castagino has weaseled an interest in QCC that is half her level of ownership when his contribution to the whole thing's been so skimpy in her opinion. She's not even sure if university ethics policy allows mentors to take ownership positions in companies that full time Faculty member's stupid-vise.

Traian and Damien and sometimes Luis often hijack her biz-dev meetings with arcane discussions about quanta behaviour using advanced operators to transform initial state to final state or talk about the Einstein—Podolsky—Rosen paradox and spooky interaction over distance or whatever. They can cover every square centimetre (Ellen has been hanging out with physicists, mathematicians, Canucks and Europeans long enough to think metric) of their conference room media walls with obscure equations and Dirac notation in minutes instead of focusing on stuff like, say, HR. So she has to admit that it's useful when Luis does occasionally help her bring them back to their agenda.

Luis, in a somewhat relevant discussion about which counts for more, ideas or execution, tells the boys, "The only thing we are sure is infinite, is ideas. We don't even know if the universe and time are bounded and won't know until we establish a value for the cosmological constant which we may never do. So let me prove it for you."

"That's OK, Professor, we'll take your word for it," Damien says.

"What's the largest prime number?" Luis blithely continues.

"There is no proof that the series of prime numbers can ever be fully known or generated," Traian answers. Prime numbers are the basis for all code making so the product of two large prime numbers that digital computers might take a few decades to decipher are valuable. Of course, QEs are about to make every cryptographic system ever invented instantly and completely obsolete.

"Well, at least you'll agree that each prime number represents an 'idea' and, if there is no upper bound on the series, then ideas are infinite," Dr. Luis suggests.

"But you haven't proved that you can generate the largest prime so you can't state this," Traian argues while both Ellen, and now Damien, grow impatient at yet another sidebar.

"Alright then, more simply, just start counting 0,1,2,3,4,5,6,7,... Tell me when you're done," Dr. Luis suggests.

"And your point, Dr., is...?" Traian asks.

"The point is that each number represents an idea. The number zero, for example, plays a central role in mathematics as the additive identity of integers, real numbers and algebraic structures. It was invented by Persian Muhammad ibn Ahmad al-Khwarizmi in 976. So you must agree that since numbers are not limited, ideas aren't either. QED," Luis finishes. Dr. Castagino uses 'QED' (quod erat demonstrandum) in conversations like Reznik uses 'RFN'.

"Right, Dr. Luis," Ellen says hoping to get back to work. "And anything abundant or, in this case, in infinite supply will be cheap. So execution counts more than ideas."

"So maybe we should be selling shoes on the mobile web, like Zappos instead of Q-Phones since our ideas don't count. I vote for Q-Phone," comments a now pissed-off Traian.

Many things about entrepreneurship require use of fuzzy logic—there are lots of contradictions in the whole field that somehow, when taken together, make sense.

Damien has no trouble with ambiguity or paradox, "Let's just say that we have to do both—solid ideas and great execution, OK?"

So it falls mainly to Ellen to soldier on with handbooks, lists, checklists and biz model development for the whole enterprise, a role she is born and trained to do. She wishes that her contribution got more recognition.

She's thinking too that if it is OK for pilots and astronauts, heart surgeons and nurses to use checklists, it's OK for entrepreneurs. Ellen knows that entrepreneurs have little room for doubt and even less for mistakes. They need to be right almost all the time since their margin of error is so slim—QCC, for example, doesn't have the resources to recover from serious error.

She understands that there are certainly a lot more than ten things that startups forget to do but she thinks her list covers off the most important stuff that they (mainly she) has to get done before launch:

1. Select the right idea. DONE

2. Create a business model for the 21st century that produces great results so that the harder they work, the more money they will make. WORKING ON IT

3. Create a compelling value proposition by adding differentiated value and innovation to their business model and clearly communicate their value proposition for customers and clients. DONE

4. Hire up. Recruit great people and establish a corporate culture that will nurture them and their whole stakeholder group. Build a community. WORKING ON IT

5. Self-capitalize their new enterprise so that VC firms don't end up owing it instead of them. NOT DONE

6. Use smart marketing so they can acquire customers and clients cost effectively. WORKING ON IT

7. Mass customize products and services using the Internet so that they can create custom outputs from standard inputs and reverse out some of the work to their clients, customers and suppliers thereby creating a scalable enterprise. DONE

8. Find pre-launch and launch clients and build cash flow. WORKING ON IT

9. Execute expertly, show leadership and become a trusted member of their community and business ecology. NOT DONE

10. Set goals and track metrics. WORKING ON IT

One of the things that Damien is going to say at the

upcoming powwow, she is sure of it, is that he wants their business model to do more than just make money. Ever since Gen Y back in the day (they're now onto Gen BB since after 'Z' comes 'AA' and so on at least if you're a mathematician), the idea's been, people who build businesses where it's all about the money, have none. And people who build businesses where it's all about building insanely great stuff and building a better community, have tonnes of it.

An aging Zuckerberg, one of the original guys who started OLA Facebook, is now on the lecture circuit. Ellen and Damien go to his talk at Metro Toronto Convention Centre about a month after Damien returns from his first dalliance with Nell.

Afterwards, Damien leads Ellen out into crisp November air. She feels immediately refreshed after the stuffy warmth of the auditorium. It smells like autumn— a mix of leaves and street meat, a staple of Queen Street for decades. Both are still absorbing Zuckerberg's message.

Damien touches her elbow briefly to lead her across the street and back through the paths around Nathan Phillips Square. Ellen gives an involuntary shiver at his touch. Even an innocuous gesture of familiarity like this would have been too much for the pre-Nell Damien perhaps out of shyness or habit. This is just one of a number of small changes she sees as she scrutinizes him closely as they walk past a line of tall ash trees, the only sound coming from the click of her heels on paving stones and the brush of fallen leaves against both of them. As much as she disdains what Nell stands for, she has to admit to herself that she likes the Nell-induced changes she's seeing in Damien.

They stop at Frans, a 24-hour coffee house north of the Eaton Centre megamall. Ellen has no idea why it is called the 'Eaton' Centre. Frans has kept its retro cool 1950s theme for almost 100 years. The nostalgia still works for Ellen with her love of classic video. There are a few others there; some students huddled together in a corner and one lone night owl sits nearby drinking coffee.

Frans has somehow resisted bringing media walls into their space so it's a refuge for people who want to be with each other or alone with their thoughts. Their server, a man in his 20s, gestures for them to find a spot anywhere, so Damien leads her downstairs into a long narrow basement and finds a booth. Sliding onto red p-leather, Damien loosens his scarf (another gift from Nell, Ellen notes) and breaks his silence for the first time since the lecture.

"Zuckerberg wasn't the first guy who was totally focused on building insanely great products instead of going after the money,"

"Who was?"

"It wasn't Jobs either."

"Who is Jobs?" Ellen asks sacrilegiously.

"Steve Jobs, he was one of two guys who started Apple in a Cupertino garage in the 1970s. You know the people whose phones we hack?"

"Oops."

"He was like some kind of alien—he revolutionized about half a dozen industries. Maybe more than anyone else ever has."

"Uh huh," says Ellen. She hates to disappoint Damien and says the minimum now—she doesn't want to put her foot in it again

"Computers, GUI, UI, animation, mobile communications, music, tablets, publishing, film and either just before or just after his passing—TV. You must of studied some of his revolutionary business models, Ellen?" adds a now chagrined Damien.

"Actually we did, I didn't place the name. The original iPhone is still probably the greatest single profit-generating tech product ever. At the time," Ellen continues wanting to show Damien that he hasn't hired a complete dunderhead to work with him at QCC, "it was the most complex business ecosystem ever created with a highly variegated utility to its users and multiple revenue channels including: a share of carrier monthly subscriber revenues, iTunes downloads, app sales, app revenues and advertising revenues in addition to the sale of the gadget in the first place. Oh, it had search fees too. They even had sponsors for the thing and revenues from selling product rights (that's where people pay for the right to be part of an iPhone launch or its product menu and home screen). Their ROI on the thing was something like an incredible, maybe never matched, 288% per annum." Ellen is breathless when she finishes her dissertation but Damien is not really paying attention.

"But it wasn't Jobs that was the first guy to be 'other directed' in business either," he says.

"I liked Mark's comment about, 'The thing I ask myself almost every day is—am I doing the most important thing I could be doing?' Steve probably asked himself that question every day too," Ellen adds.

"I'm not talking about Mark or Steve, Ellen."

"Uh-huh. Then who?"

"It was a guy who ran an all night coffee and donut shop in Santa Cruz. Pops told me about him. He went to UCSC in the late 1960s and he and his girl used to go to this place in downtown Santa Cruz at like 2 in the morning. They were either pulling all-nighters, finishing assignments, studying for exams or they were stoned or maybe all three." Damien always gets this trance-like look on his face when he talks about his grandfather. It fascinates Ellen. She likes their stories and, although she has never met Pops, she would like to.

He must be incredibly old by now. Damien's told her how there are still 'kids' around as late as the early part of the 21st century who could say that their Daddies fought in the Civil War between the States. Ellen, an American, can't see how that is possible. Apparently it is.

If a guy who was say 16, Damien tells her, fought in the last year of that war (1865) and married, as some of them did at 70, a much younger woman (which they also often did), they could have had a kid as late as say (his) age

80 which would make it 1929 so by 2001 that kid would have only been 72. So Pops is old but still around and still a big part of Damien's life.

"Anyway, the guy who owns the shop is in the back, making donuts I guess, when Pops and his girlfriend come in for coffee and something to eat. There are always mountain men in the shop at that time of night—finishing their run into town and having a coffee before shoving off back home. Those guys bring kilos of California weed into town to dry in natural gas ovens and then sell. It's heavy, wet marijuana but organic and less powerful than modern plants.

"What Pops likes about the place is that after you help yourself to a coffee and donut (the guy has no servers) and after you finish, you go behind the counter, open his cash drawer, figure out what you owe, put your paper money or coins in the drawer, take out the correct change and, with a wave to the owner, you leave."

"Hah, try that today," says Ellen. She gets another disapproving look from Damien and freezes inside.

"But isn't that exactly what you guys in marcom talk about—things like 'freemium' models or 'pay-what-you-can-afford' business methods?"

Ellen looks down and says nothing.

"Anywho," Damien continues, "Pops is quite sure he saw young teenaged Jobs in that shop in 1969 and that what he saw there influenced Apple and, two generations later, allowed Gen Y to seize control of the world economy from a narcissistic Baby Boomer generation and a whiny, ill-prepared, tech-phobic Gen X.

"The donut shop guy just wanted to focus on making insanely great food and coffee for clients, not making change for customers. Pops says they were the best he ever tasted but that mighta been because his taste buds were as young as he was at the time and he was probably wasted too,"

Ellen stares at her boss and colleague and asks herself, 'How does he know all this stuff at age 23?'

Damien's just turned 23.

Of course, he wasn't around for his birthday. Nell took Damien and 38 guests including Traian and Dr. Castagino but not Ellen, aboard that gross plane of hers for a four day snorkeling/scuba party at some offshore island in the western Caribbean, where, wouldn't you know it, Nell has another home.

Traian described the event for Ellen something like this, 'Hey, we went to the Great Blue Hole. It's got great diving and snorkeling, the best anywhere outside of Australia's Great Barrier Reef. I tried all kinds of exotic foods, loved sea kayaking (his first time) and enjoyed the nice weather (it's getting close to full on winter in Toronto—bloody cold and dark).' But he's uncharacteristically subdued in his recounting of their trip. Something strange happened on their visit to a nearby Mayan ruin (she can't remember the place except it was named after some Spanish guy) but Traian apparently doesn't want to fill her in about it. It is all TMI, too much information, for Ellen anyway. She doesn't really want to know what went on.

But sitting there in Frans with Damien after Zuckerberg's lecture, Ellen would have been comforted to know that Damien does, in fact, think highly of his (even younger) biz-dev grad from Elmira College, despite her various goofs tonight. What she also doesn't know, unless Damien tells her, is that he wouldn't be sitting there with her if he felt any differently about her. He doesn't like to waste his time with useless people.

"The guy in the Santa Cruz coffee shop was like the butterfly effect—a small change in the system caused big changes later on," Ellen says. She's also thinking that maybe he was one of the Bay Area's original hippies but she doesn't say that out loud.

"Right. It's called chaos theory. It produces paradigms with inherent non-linear changes that can't be predicted, like the stuff we're working on at the Lab," Damien says, satisfied now that she gets it exactly.

Less than 12 weeks later and, after reviewing her list one more time, Ellen is impatiently getting ready to help QCC launch a new quantum era. In her ladylike kind of way she's also thinking, 'If the guys are late again, I'm going to be some mad.'

While Ellen has been preparing for her meeting with the boys, Damien and Traian have also been doing some work of their own not far away. They're trying to make some sense of their recent discovery (on the night of Damien's recent birthday) made at Marco Gonzalez, site of Mayan ruins on the southern tip of Ambergris Caye.

...

Chapter 7

San Pedro Town

Flying into Belize City, Gillian Boys is talking to a group that includes Damien, Nell, Traian, Dr. Luis, Tony, Dekka, Wendy and others, "The best thing about Belize City is leaving it. We won't be staying longer than it takes to get from the airport to the port where we have reserved a water taxi that will take us to San Pedro Town."

They picked up Gillian in Toronto on her way to Belize from Vancouver. Her Western Canadian based family has owned an outfitting business in Belize since the 1980s. Gillian is a ginger-haired, compact woman, strong looking and resourceful. She's hoping to run the family biz one day and the fact that both her father and grandfather have agreed that she can lead this large, important tour group over the next four days shows the level of confidence they already have in her.

"What's wrong with Belize City?" asks Luis.

"Back in the early part of this century," Gillian replies, "US policy changed and they started deporting career criminals back to their home countries. Belize has been getting back about 15 hardened, 'US-trained', professional criminals a year. Doesn't sound like much but over a period of 40 years, that's 600 of them and many of them join or lead existing gangs or form new gangs. The gang population might be five or possibly six thousand by now—huge in a town of 118,000. Looking for women or drugs in Belize City after dark would be a bad idea." While Gillian talks, Morales looks at Traian who turns away with a stupid, secret smile on his face.

"The country is actually a lovely place. Everyone speaks English; it's the official language here. You are safe nearly everywhere even up in the Guatemalan Highlands and especially on offshore islands where we're going to stay," Boys adds to put everyone at ease.

"How long does it take to get to San Pedro Town, Gillian?" Tony asks.

"Our water taxi boots along pretty fast. It, umm, moves at an average speed of about 24 knots, that's nautical miles per hour, so it will take us about an hour and 45 minutes. We're stopping for 15 minutes or so on the way at Caye Caulker to drop off some mail and supplies; it's for a couple of Belizean friends of mine who own a hotel there."

"Is it hurricane season by any chance?" one of Nell's backup singers asks.

"No, we're well past that. Anyway, the last major hurricane to hit Belize was a long time ago, 1961. It was a huge Force 5 storm called Hattie and it was a doozy. It split Caye Caulker in two; I'll show you when we get there. It brought storm surges that were more than four metres high into Belize City. They had to evacuate practically the entire town," Gillian says enthusiastically, oblivious to the uncomfortable stares she's now getting from her audience.

Noticing their discomfort she tones it down a bit and adds, "Look, hurricanes can't easily get to Belize because it's sort of tucked away under and protected by Cancun. They tend to mostly whack the eastern or central Caribbean: Cuba, the Dominican Republic or Jamaica, then swing up to hit Florida, Louisiana, South Carolina or Texas."

"Ms. Boys? I'm worried I will get seasick on the way over. Is it really rough?"

"Dr. Luis, you will be fine. We're inside the reef at all times so wave action is a lot smaller than out at sea It's the world's second largest after Australia's Great Barrier. And although we could boogie along at speeds much greater than 24 knots, we don't." Gillian, who is a bit of a gear head adds, "We've got three Yamaha Marine F375 outboards—those are big V-8, 4-stroke, 5.8 litre engines by the way but we'll never get close to top speed."

"What is your top speed?" Damien pipes up.

"38 knots in a dead calm, mind you without any

passengers or cargo just us. Guests don't like the thump, thump from our taxi hitting any kind of wave action. It's too rough and noisy for them so we adjust to get the right balance between speed and comfort, and seasickness. My family's been doing this in Belize for almost 70 years."

"Relax, Doctor, you're in good hands," Damien adds.

The Boys' family takes more than 3,500 people a year from around the world on trips ranging from four days to ten. The business was started by Tim Boys, Gillian's grandfather while looking for a place to winter-over that isn't frozen and where he could make a few bucks guiding snorkeling, diving and sea kayaking tours, finds Belize. He looked up and down both Pacific and Atlantic coasts of the Americas, having already ruled out the South Pacific as too far away. He chooses Belize, on the Atlantic coast south of Mexico, because of its wonderful off-shore archipelago of over a 1,000 islands all protected by this enormous reef. He settles on San Pedro Town on Ambergris Caye for his headquarters. He also learns about some fabulous 4,000 year-old Marco Gonzalez Mayan ruins located at the south end of Ambergris. At least 17,000 Mayan traders lived on the Caye (pronounced 'Key') in the heyday of their empire now more than 1,150 years in the past—far more than the current modern population of about 9,500.

Boys loves Belize, population 395,000. It is a stable, two-party democracy with a legal system based on its British heritage (the country was formerly known as British Honduras). Belizeans have neither fished out their waters nor despoiled their lands. It was the centre of the Mayan Empire dating back to at least 2000 BCE so there's a lot to do, see and experience.

Belizeans are made up of all colours and races ranging from white to yellow to brown to black and everything in between. It's a rainbow and people are mostly friendly and lovely to look at. They have a strong work ethic and most of the folks living in Belize get along.

There is some resentment of Imperial Chinese domination of their retail industry but seemingly no such thoughts are given over to the fact that Amish and Mennonite immigrants dominate agriculture there, in part, because they've been given an exemption by successive National Governments to import farm and industrial equipment and other inputs, duty-free.

Belize City is 17 and a half degrees north of the equator so they get some seasonality in their weather. It's about 1,000 kilometres closer to main population centres in the US and Canada than Costa Rica and is second only to that country in terms of its bio and geographical diversity.

Kids in Belize are expected (and required) to stay to the end of high school and many go on to the University of West Indies, University of Belize and universities in Canada, the US and the UK. They all speak English but also learn Creole and many speak Spanish as well.

Belizean economic prospects are highly subject to waves of change taking place in the US. When the US economy catches a cold like it has recently, Belize's economy gets a bad flu. Currently, about two out of every three new condos built on their offshore islands are in foreclosure. Tourism has dropped by nearly a quarter. The Boys' family is hoping to do a bang-up job for Miss Nell and her group; it will be great PR for them and the nation. Gillian is determined to not only show them a good time but also teach them something about Belize and integrate them into its rich history and culture if she can.

There is a lot more freedom in a place like this and a lot less regulation. The only three professions where Gillian can find any sort of government oversight are medical, teaching and legal. For everyone else, it's caveat emptor. Want to be a massage therapist, IT guy, physiotherapist, realtor, consultant, engineer, hairdresser, acupuncturist, chiropractor, embalmer, optician, accountant, dental hygienist, architect, surveyor or vet, just hang up a shingle, you're done.

Gillian loves this life. There's freedom to succeed but also freedom to fail. You have to use your wits at all times. Buyer beware! And there are fixers for everything. Money talks and BS walks. It means that, in Belize, relationships count for even more. Who you trust and who you can trust is all word of mouth. It's intense but she wouldn't have it any other way.

...

Damien has been looking forward to his four day break with Nell and seeing and experiencing a new country. He's learned to trust her when she arranges these trips but it's a new experience for Dr. Luis and almost everyone else in their group too, which is made up of members of her band, their families and friends, her backup singers, aerialists, dancers and assorted groupies and hangers-on, so there's bound to be more questions.

On the trip down, he and Nell finally get to use her private cabin with its queen-sized bed aboard her Airbus. Damien's managed to add yet another new experience to his repertoire thanks to his still evolving and madly passionate relationship with Nell. The trip from TO to Belize City takes just under five hours; both Damien and Nell feel they've put the time to good use.

Afterward, they use the aircraft's mist shower with its twin heads. Damien chummily soaps Nell's back and she does the same for him. That leads to some playful fooling around and then some more intense stuff before Nell finally turns herself around and, with her strong arms bracing her body on the shower 's ledge, she presents Damien with a beautifully well-rounded, sculpted, creamy-white bottom making lazy circles, first counter clockwise, then clockwise while she looks lovingly back over her right shoulder with those shining green eyes of hers and her wet auburn hair hanging down her left side—they make love again that way. She drives him mad with desire for her, there's no doubt about that.

...

Gillian is true to her word. Less than 45 minutes after landing in Belize City, the group is aboard San Pedro Water

Taxi Association's top boat—the Aurore. Island Expeditions, Gillian's family biz, does not own a boat large enough for this group so she charters this craft for the next four days for Nell. It can comfortably hold 120 Belizeans or about 80 tourists. Capacity is different because tourists tend to be larger than Belizeans in every direction plus they demand more personal space.

Gillian has invited Nell, Damien and Dr. Luis to join Captain Rudy Filane on the upper deck of the Aurore as they leave the North Front Street dock heading out of Belize City on Haulover Creek. Within minutes they turn north on the Caribbean Sea whizzing past King Hotel and Casino and the main part of the city including its University, Museum of Belize and St John's College.

"It looks charming from here," says Dr. Luis. He loves the sparkling sea and the turquoise/pink/salmon/green/blue colours of the low rise structures that make up most of the city.

"It's probably not as bad as I made it out to be, Doctor, but I wanted to err on the side of caution. If anyone wants a tour of the city, we can arrange that but we won't really have time. I don't want anyone going off on their own and honestly, there's a tonne more interesting stuff to see and do," Gillian says counting off each point on her left hand with her right. Gillian has a dangerous-looking titanium dive knife strapped to her right ankle in a single-action locked sheath and she has somehow changed into her outfitter's uniform without ever disappearing from sight. "We're going to take the boat out west of Caye Chapel so we will cruise along the reef for awhile. Captain Rudy will slow down if we see any fish which we almost certainly will."

"Are there any sharks?" asks a nervous Nell. She's not used to these boats since she normally air charters to Ambergris Caye directly from the international airport.

"Lots," laughs Gillian. "We sometimes chum the water on a dive so our guests can swim with sharks. Most do."

"Can you not do that on our tour, please?"

Gillian is just a few years older than Nell; she is part of her tribe, and about her height, so she is one of the few people who can look Miss Nell in the eye. Captain Rudy, who is a huge, brown man in his early 40s with a jolly, kind face, is listening to everything. He chimes in, "No need to worry Miss. Belizean sharks are not like American sharks. They only eat BAD people."

"What kinda fish inhabit these waters?" Damien asks.

"You will find tarpon, snook and jacks in river estuaries and inlets," replies Gillian. "Lagoons and grass flats will have bonefish, permit and barracuda. Where we're going today near the coral reef, you'll see grouper, snapper, jacks and more barracuda.

"In deeper waters after the drop off, you will also find sailfish, marlin, bonito and pompano. We'll also probably see some rays."

"They are a protected species by the way as are our sharks," Captain Rudy adds looking at Nell with a toothy smile.

...

They pull alongside the main wharf on Paradiso Beach on Caye Caulker. The boat boys begin off loading cargo. Gillian is off the boat even before it is tied up, leaping onto the wharf at a run.

She quickly embraces first Mica and then her husband Javier, kissing both of them on each cheek. She hasn't seen them since the end of their season now five months past. Mica is in her late 30s; Javier is 43. With them is their daughter, Dakota, 17. She's waiting for her regular water taxi to take her to Belize City where she is in her last year at St. Thomas School for Girls.

Javier and Mica own the Island Princess Hotel. They are only the third Belize-born persons to own a major hotel in the island archipelago. Currently the building has four storeys finished of a planned eight, the maximum height allowed by Caye Caulker Community Council.

Their plan is to add three more storeys of condo units

when they can afford it and the market is ready. The last, top floor will be a permanent family home. If Nell's group had been smaller Gillian might have brought them to Caye Caulker and the Island Princess. Except Nell has a home attached to the largest hotel in San Pedro Town. Plus, with this group of high strung personalities, they will be better off on larger Ambergris Caye where the locals are more used to crazy tourists. It will be a big challenge for Gillian to keep this group together and keep an eye on all of them too.

The islands are made of (mostly) limestone and are protected by their reef system so they're pretty robust although Caye Caulker has its north and south islands after Hurricane Hattie separated them by gouging out a channel about 45 metres wide. The streets of Caye Caulker are simply sand, swept over a limestone crust and practically the only form of transportation here is golf carts of all shapes and sizes, mostly gasoline powered. Electric carts still can't compete on power and dependability.

Gillian introduces Nell, Damien, Traian and Dr. Luis who join them on the wharf.

"Miss Nell," asks Javier, "We would love to have you join us for lunch."

Gillian answers for her, "I knew you'd ask us, Javier, but there's no way. We're just dropping off your mail and supplies. We can only stay for 15 minutes."

"Thank you so much for asking us," Nell replies, "but we are way too many to impose on your hospitality."

"Perhaps we could give everyone a drink then? Our place is just four blocks from here. We can take everyone over by golf cart and then send you on your way. It will be so much more fun after a drink of Belizean rum, don't you think! We won't delay you much, hmm?"

Traian answers for the group, "Hey, Damien when was the last time you were on Caye Caulker? Uh, like never. Let's walk over, buddy!"

Gillian knows Javier and Mica want to show off their place. They're proud of it. Javier started with tire importing and automotive repair shops in Belize City, Belmopan (the capital) and Punta Gorda. Then they were able to buy land and build this hotel. Recently, he's been finding tire competition from local Mennonites tough since they're landing tires and other components they need duty free. So he's taken on a Mennonite partner to level the playing field. It also means sharing profits with him. The Island Princess Hotel is his insurance policy in case this arrangement somehow fails.

The whole ensemble debarks and they break into smaller groups, some walking, some riding golf carts. Well, not the whole group walks or rides. Unexpectedly, Traian finds himself staying on the wharf talking with Dakota.

Damien and Nell are walking near the beach with Javier, Mica and Gillian. One thing Damien notices is that buildings are way too close to water's edge. With narrow Playa Asuncion taking up part of the right-of-way for its golf cart and pedestrian traffic, it doesn't leave much room for actual beach. If they ever do get another Force 5 hurricane here, a storm surge of any size will just about eat everything in the immediate area. Damien would have pushed the build-to line back another 30 metres

At least, there is a right-of-way. Belize doesn't allow private ownership to extend to the waterline. Belizeans and visitors can access beaches and swim or fish wherever they please without being rousted by private security guards like so much of the coastline elsewhere in the Caribbean and in the US.

"What do you do for fresh water, Javier?" Damien asks.

"There is a fresh water lens under all these islands. We use drilled wells to access it and we pump it into our private system," Javier replies, not realizing that to an engineer like Damien this won't be enough of an explanation.

"Is there enough capacity in your underground reservoir for residents of Caye Caulker and all your guests too?" asks a dubious Damien looking about at the tiny surface area of the island. Gillian has told him that more than a thousand people live here permanently plus they get more than 20,000 intensive water-using tourists every year.

"It's recharged during our rainy season, from May to September but, well, it gets a bit muddy toward the end of our season in April. We switch over to reverse osmosis when that happens. For the last few decades we've been expanding our water storage tank system and capturing a lot more rainwater than we used to."

"Why not just let it soak into the ground?" Nell asks.

"Well, rains can be really intense around here. The ground gets moisture-saturated fast, and once that happens, freshwater runs along the surface and into the sea. These days, we divert rainwater from nearly every roof on Caye Caulker into holding tanks. We've increased our water supply about 10% that way. We have also graded large parts of the island so what doesn't soak into the ground or go directly into water tanks, we pond then store later. It's sort of a backup plan for our backup plan."

Damien nods his approval, "It's not a zero sum game, Javier."

"Right."

"Hey, did you know that Caye Caulker has its own 'national' park?" Mica asks.

She sees the incredulous looks she's now getting from their guests at her comment as they look around her tiny island home. 'These Norteamericanos are too politically correct to say what's really on their mind,' she's thinking. 'They don't laugh much, not wanting to insult their hosts or maybe what they see as lesser peoples.' Inwardly, she sighs.

"Yes, just north of our airstrip, we have the Caye Caulker Mini Reserve. It's run by our Caye Caulker branch of BTIA, Belize Tourism Industry Association. We're members," she adds self-respectingly. "We've got a small visitors center with information on the island's flora and fauna. There's a short interpretative trail that runs through our littoral forest. When you come back one day, we'll take you there." Mica is proud of her island, her nation and the work her family has done to get where they are today.

Meanwhile, Gillian is pointing out some of the humongous water tanks that have been integrated into local architecture, many painted with scenes from Belizean history or geography. One is called 'Battle of St. George's Caye' and depicts a scene representing the defeat of the Spanish by Belizean Baymen of British origin in a week-long battle off their coast in September 1798. Others have faces on them including one representing Antonio Soberanis, a labour leader, active in the Belizean independence movement of 1934. It isn't until 1964 that Belize gets self-government. In 1973, the official name of the territory is changed from British Honduras back to Belize and full independence is finally granted by Britain in 1981. Gillian's grandfather tells her they're lucky that they were never colonies of Spain or worse, France—places like Guadeloupe, Martinique or distant Tahiti—all of them remaining overseas departments of France to this day, complete with huge colonial bureaucracies accompanied by a vicious security apparatus hundreds of years after their occupation.

She also thinks that Nell should have invested in Caye Caulker. It's 1/10th the size of San Pedro Town, less touristy and much more private but she keeps this thought to herself as well.

Gillian was with Nell when she first visited her place on Ambergris Caye. Nell immediately fell in love with the home in part because a 'secret' ingredient in one of the top perfumes she endorses and wears is found there. The ingredient is ambergris, a rare quasi-legal material derived from sperm whales. 'Imagine the coincidence, the synchronicity of it!' Nell is thinking.

When Gillian uses the term 'derived' she actually means it is a waxy excretion formed, in the immortal words of Herman Melville, "in the inglorious bowels of a sick whale..." They're sick because they can't digest squid beaks. That is, it's whale poop.

Sperm whales love the deep sheltered waters of this part of the Caribbean for calving and, naturally, their excretions wash up on the shores of the Caye. Traders wander the beaches at certain times of the year when winds and currents are just right and sperm whales are likely to be feeding on squid, hoping to find this hugely valuable byproduct described this way by an LA-based perfumer, 'beyond comprehension—transformative, shimmering, reflecting light with its smells. It's an olfactory gemstone.'

People have been using ambergris as a valuable input in making aphrodisiacs, pastilles, precious candles and over priced specialty foods and perfumes since the days of Muslim trader Ibn Hawqal discovered it in the 10th Century.

But to Gillian it's just another affectation of rich folk, something they do to differentiate themselves from the rest of humanity. Nevertheless, it doesn't stop her from dabbing Nell behind her ears whenever she is about to get a chance to see her boyfriend. It's out of her price range but Nell has given her a tiny bottle of the scent. Gillian has to admit that it works quite nicely on him.

...

Back on the Aurore, everyone is a bit jollier, having had one or more glasses of Cuello distillery's award winning white rum back at Island Princess Hotel. Damien and Traian are sitting companionably on the lower deck. Traian is uncharacteristically quiet though.

"Whassup, buddy?" Damien asks.

"Nothing," replies Traian.

"Right. You hang by the boat, don't visit with Gillian's friends, don't have a glass of rum. Yeah, right everything's peachy," says Damien.

"I was talking to Dakota."

"You were?"

"Uh, huh. I was just thinking..."

"Hold on there a sec," says Damien. "She's a schoolgirl, she's 17, she's underage, Traian, she's the daughter of friends of Gillian's who's a friend to Nell—"

"I don't like her that way," Traian interjects. "I just liked talking to her is all."

In fact, Traian has been hit by a thunderbolt. Dakota is tall, 177 centimetres with an incredible body, beautiful lips, long thick brown hair and light creamy, coffee-coloured skin. She is dressed in her school uniform, an off-white kind of beigy frock with her green school crest embroidered above her left breast; the frock is cut to about 15 centimetres above her knees and she has on close to knee-high beige socks that somehow show off long shapely legs. She is wearing practical black flats and carrying her school bag, also black, and her tablet. She wears no jewellery at all, not even earrings, and has no piercings or tattoos. Her makeup is subtle which suits her and her school—they have strict rules on such things. That in no way detracts from her look. She has completely entranced this strange young man while she waits for her water taxi to take her to school. He talks like an American but looks like a Euro with his wiry build and small ass. North American men, Dakota thinks, all have these big lard arses and are usually big everywhere else too. She likes the look of this man.

"How do I know you're lying to me, man? Your lips are moving. Now you have to swear to me, you're not gonna do anything while we're here, OK? Do you have any idea how protective upper class Belizean parents are of their daughters and what kind of trouble you can get us into? We're guests here, right?"

Traian says nothing; he just looks down at the deck with a weird look on his face—it's introspection, a Traian first.

...

There is a bunch of excited chatter as they pull alongside the wharf at Delfina Shore Resort. It's a fairly new community, built in the 2030s, and one of only two major projects built on Ambergris Caye in the two generations, since the economic meltdown of much of the economy of the Americas.

Sitting on 24 beachfront hectares at the far north end of San Pedro Town, the only way to reach it is by crossing over a one lane bridge from the main part of town then driving along a rough trail for three kilometres. Or you can arrive at their private wharf by boat. Security is good but not overwhelming in its presence. Community police monitor the bridge 24/7. Practically the worst that happens on this island is an occasional thief tries to motor out from Belize City in a skiff and steal stuff. Most of them can't even afford the fuel to get to San Pedro and it's a long way to go to steal a purse in any event so Nell and her friends have nothing to worry about. There's a lot more crime back in LA and it's way more violent as well.

What Dr. Luis is seeing is the inside of the lives of the rich and famous in person for the first time. The view is impressive if ostentatious and extravagant for his taste. The resort he sees is an enormous four storey, pinkish stucco and concrete structure with two wings coming off a massive hexagonal central building at about 20 degrees. Doors and windows, imported from US suppliers, are AAMA certified to withstand hurricane winds of 268 mph and 8,650 Pascals (180 psf) of pressure. He also sees that they have roll-down hurricane shutters that can be automatically lowered if a storm hits or they need extra security. There are battery backups and generators on-site for uninterrupted power supply. The resort is constructed with both belt and suspenders in a design which to an engineer like Damien or a scientist like Luis, is both wasteful and wise.

Ground floors of all permanent structures at Delfina are at least plus two metres to grade which itself is plus one metre above average sea level. They can withstand significant storm surges. All their buildings are anchored using concrete encased, rebar-reinforced piles (instead of steel piles which will rust away to nothing within a few years in this entropic environment) that go down to bedrock about 15 metres below surface.

These are very hardy structures that cost more than ND$4,850 per square metre to build. Still there are lots of wood frame homes being built by locals. They figure it will cost them a lot less to simply rebuild after a significant weather event rather than designing their structures like foreigners do and paying stupidly high annual insurance premiums to foreign firms they don't trust to be around to pay out anyway, when and if they're actually needed. They're also counting on social norms to prevail—they will help each other rebuild for free if something goes wrong. So they self-insure via social compact.

Each wing at Delfina has its own infinity pool and mini-waterpark. In front of the main building is one of the largest decks you can find anywhere with a bewildering array of bars, dance floors, stages, seating and dining areas (al fresco), plants, palm trees (sans coconuts so none of their guests will get kabonged by a one and a half kilo missile falling from six metres or more), shade structures, fruit stands, vendors selling jewellery and knick knacks, even high end tech shops demoing cool ware.

Dr. Luis has also noticed that there are more than 60 over-the-water bungalows that Reznik informs him are mainly rented out to gullible newlyweds at atrocious prices. On the property there are another 180 row houses built near the main structure and 72 single family homes for a continuing steady supply of ultra rich clients. These days more of them come from Russia, where crony-capitalism still reigns, as well as from the African Union, Imperial China and South America, than the US. The main building itself has over 400 hotel rooms each with a bed-sitting room and micro-kitchen. Almost every unit is privately owned. The original developer (a partnership between a local Belizean family and a Russian mobster) only hold onto the management contract to operate and maintain the place plus they keep all bungalow rentals.

They also own the wedding centre and business centre with its 42 private offices and dozens of workstations plus meeting rooms big enough to cater to groups up to 60 and a ballroom that seats 540.

There is also one gigantic two storey home (attached to the northeast end of the complex by a breezeway) that is mindboggling to behold. It's a sandy coloured, ornate structure with sixteen bedrooms each with their own baths, a two and a half storey dining area, living room and ballroom that must cover more than 1,600 square metres and comes with a gym, full size indoor basketball court, lap pool, steam room and sauna, prep kitchen and main kitchen, volley ball court, library, theatre and screening room. The pagoda perched on top has a magnificent 360 degree view of the whole area. A deck overlooking the beach has seating for at least 180 guests and a reflecting pool with its own floating bedroom. This free-floating platform actually sails randomly over a mini-lake pushed hither and thither by gusts of wind. It has all the accoutrements of a boudoir. In a perfunctory bow to modesty, some filmy sheers can be pulled to provide some semblance of privacy.

This is Maya Fair—Nell's San Pedro townhome. The beach on this part of Ambergris Caye is the only nude beach in Belize although Nell and her dancers and aerialists, who've got a great deal to show off, have already agreed to mostly cover up on this trip when they're not at Nell's place in deference to her conservative Canuck partner. But they have to draw the line somewhere—they will be topless most of the time they're here.

The whole thing sits on the preferred (and more expensive) windward side of the island with its steady, cooling on-shore breezes most days. Less wealthy tourists are found on leeward sides of these islands while poorer folks and locals make do with stiflingly hot interior lots.

While Dr. Luis is trying to take all this in, Traian is seeing images of Dakota superimposed on everything.

...

Nell has a plan for D's birthday but she won't give him any specifics. She's wanted to get him away from TO for a week or more but given his schedule and hers all they get are these four measly days. Still she and Gillian have been able to work out a plan to take the entire group to Marco Gonzalez Maya site on the very southern-most tip of Ambergris Caye. It's about 11 kilometres from Maya Fair which doesn't sound like much but the trails, such as they once were, are now completely overgrown, reclaimed by Belizean jungle.

There is plenty of tough mangrove swamp between Maya Fair and Marco Gonzalez inhabited, Gillian tells her, by saltwater crocodiles. Nell isn't sure what she's more worried about now—sharks on their dive at Great Blue Hole (planned for day three) or crocs. Gillian tells her the only guy ever eaten by a lazy Belizean crocodile was a local fisherman who, while trying to land a tenacious barracuda, stepped on what he thought was part of the reef only to find the seagrass-covered surface was actually an incredibly old reptilian monster. Once disturbed, the croc decided he might as well make a meal of the guy.

Estuarine crocs are the largest of all reptiles and can live up to a century, perhaps longer. They show great dimorphism with males being much larger than females. Some weigh more than a tonne and can grow to as large as 8.6 metres. They swim as fast as eight metres per second in short bursts and move almost as fast on flat land so, if one ever does chase you, run uphill is Gillian's advice. In the sea, you have no chance.

Crocs do seem to have taken a liking to dog and regularly snack on Man's Best Friend. The dogs run and bark at and generally try to play with these old crocs who retreat further and further into the sea until the dogs are practically swimming into their muzzles. Nell isn't reassured by any of this.

Sixty years earlier archaeologists, Dr. Elizabeth Graham and Dr. David M. Pendergast, working on a tip from an elder in San Pedro Town, found Marco Gonzalez

Mayan ruins after trekking through some very tough bush. It has been designated an Archaeological Reserve by the Belizean government but virtually nothing has been done at the site since its original discovery. Over 90% of the structure has never even been explored. Much of it is underground beneath a series of three pyramids set in a perfect equilateral triangle but now mostly invisible, covered by jungle.

They are not going to walk there nor go by boat. They're going to fly in. Gillian has arranged with Boyd Combs, her boyfriend, to come to Maya Fair and party with them. More importantly, he and his seven best buddies are bringing their ultralights up from Placentia. They're the Black Aces Reunion Flying Club which Boyd and his mates privately call the BARF Club but not for reasons most people would suspect.

These crazy guys think nothing of flying their rigs over the Andes at more than 20,000 feet where thin air can cause altitude sickness quickly killing the unwary with high altitude pulmonary and cerebral edemas or retinal hemorrhage as well as dizziness, nausea, disorientation, reduced thought processes and general clumsiness. Boyd's dad, Robert, still holds the high altitude mark for open cockpit ultralights—just over 22,000 feet!

They are all former US military or civilian pilots and take precautions. Before a flight like that, they take Acetazolanide to increase the acidity of their blood so they can breathe deeper and faster and Nifedipine to resolve pulmonary hypertension. They also swallow a bunch of Ibuprofen for headache and bring anti-nausea drugs plus a personal oxygen system with them as well.

These are the same guys who fly in formation—much like migratory geese do and for the same fuel-saving reasons—over the Gulf of Mexico. They slap extra engines, props and fuel tanks on each of their tricycle frames for the more than 600 mile over-the-water flight. These souped up machines fly in excess of 90 mph.

Their trikes are ultra high end machines. They have

91 hp, 4-stoke Rotax XTA9220 engines built in Australia with a four to five hour range on just 18 US gallons of fuel. Although they can fly in just about anything, Boyd and his crew—none of whom have less than 6,000 hours of flight time—ever take passengers up in winds above 15 knots. Their trikes have BVS rocket-deployed parachutes so if they ever suffer a structural failure, riders can still expect a soft landing. They also have flotation devices and e-pirb beacons that are GPS-enabled.

None of this stuff is expected to be required for this short jaunt—they will cover 11 kilometres in 15 minutes tootling along at low altitude giving Nell and her guests a nice view of the town and jungle before circling overhead to let them see Marco Gonzalez. Recent research has re-dated these ruins—they're even older than once thought—perhaps as much as 4,000 years. Thousands of Mayan traders didn't suddenly materialize on Ambergris Caye—it took a long time to build up their population although their departure seems to have happened much more quickly.

Each of their trikes carries pilot and one passenger so they will shuttle back and forth until all Nell's group is relocated to a nearby beach. It won't take them long.

These trikes are more comfortable than they look—hey, they've got big arse leather seats for their passengers and special helmets with built-in noise cancellation technology plus great communication, camera and video equipment so each person will have a complete record of their time with the BARF Club. More intrepid passengers will also get an opportunity to handle the trapeze which trims the ultralight's sail—pull in/lose altitude, push out/gain altitude, lean left/go left, lean right/go right—it's pretty basic and foolproof unless of course you do a nose or wingtip stall or lose the stainless steel pin that attaches the sail to the trike. It will all be great fun.

Boyd is 42 years old but looks much younger. Like most pilots, he's not overly tall and although very strong, he does not weigh much. Each year, he goes on a 14-day total body-cleansing fast, drinking only water, flavored with his own recipe of agents designed to detoxify his system. He's quite crazy but especially crazy for Gillian who returns his feelings completely.

Nell, through Gillian's contacts, has made generous contributions to each of National Institute of Culture and History (NICH) and Belize Institute of Archaeology so her party has unfettered, government-sanctioned access to Marco Gonzalez. Nell and Damien both want to make each day count—so flights begin at dawn and they will be in the first V formation of Black Aces.

Damien likes to be prepared and to know what's happening around him. So he asks Pet3r to boot up a learning simulation as soon as they're alone. He learns to fly in about 45 minutes. Take off and level flight are a breeze but he finds landing on a soft sandy beach hard. He crashes a few times before finally managing it—once. You can never be too careful. What if his pilot has a heart attack or something in-flight? Damien is now pretty sure he can handle himself.

...

The morning of the day before Damien's 23rd birthday dawns bright and clear with nary a breath of wind. The Black Aces have been up preparing their aircraft for more than an hour. They each go through their entire pre-flight checklist twice.

Nell is dressed in beachwear with a sarong wrapped around her lithe frame. She is all smiles and her eyes are shining, mostly at D. They have a hard time finding a helmet to fit her since she is so tiny. She will ride with Boyd at the front of the formation. Next will be Damien, flying with Montana-born Lester Cooper, distantly related to the actor of the same last name. Other than the incongruous helmet now sitting on Nell's head, other fishes-out-of-water are pudgy guys Tony Reznik and Dr. Luis sitting nervously on the backseats of a couple of trikes wondering how they got talked into this. Reznik reminds himself of the importance of his one client and decides to say nothing sarcastic.

They take off into what little headwind there is and turn 180 degrees toward the south end of the island. Everyone can see waves crashing on the outside of the reef about 2,000 metres to the east of them as they quickly climb to a cruising altitude of 380 metres. Flying over San Pedro Town, fishing boats are heading out for the day and some vans but mostly golf carts are making deliveries. A few pedestrians stroll about at this time of the day. Most tourists are still sleeping off their nightly hangovers.

"Hey, D!" Nell calls over her radio. She waves cheerfully.

"Hey," he says back. "These trikes are a heck of a lot more comfortable than sitting on Lenny heading down Bright Angel Trail!"

Nell laughs and gives him a thumbs up and a cute smile.

"Would you like to try flying the aircraft?" asks Lester, known to his friends as 'Coop'.

"Sure, Lester," replies Damien.

"It's Coop, Dr. Bell."

"It's Damien, Coop."

"Right. Just place your hands outside of mine on the horizontal part of the trapeze and feel what I do and just go with it, OK?"

"Got it."

"Boyd, Coop here."

"Roger."

"I'm breaking formation heading East, magnetic bearing S 45° E, to give Dr. Bell here a chance to fly Bettie." Bettie is the name of Coop's trike. He's got a wicked decal of her on his sail that Boyd has asked him to swap out before they do tours like this—it's too over the top for many of their more conservative tourists who charter the BARF Club. It's a large black and white image of a nearly naked, large-breasted, impossibly narrow-waisted, black-haired Betty Boop dealing out huge Black Aces to an unseen group of admirers. Coop's kept it in place for this group of maverick, top end performers.

"Roger that. You are heading East, magnetic bearing S 45° E," repeats Boyd.

Small plane pilots mostly plot their trips using true north bearings then convert them to magnetic north since their onboard cockpit instruments can only detect magnetic north. This is trickier than you might think since Magnetic North can vary a lot on the surface of the earth plus it shifts about 40 miles per year in position—heading, for some unknown reason, towards Russia.

So the BARF Club updates their aviation maps and charts and database they use for air navigation at least twice each year to reflect current corrections. They don't carry a lot of extra fuel and can't afford to miss a landing site by say 40 miles.

In this they are more like entrepreneurs who also have to be right practically all the time or their enterprises will fold. The BARF Club is very entrepreneurial—they do a lot of paid gigs and have an enviable, so far, perfect safety record when it comes to flying paying customers. They never try anything risky in 'public transit' mode.

Coop and Damien break off and fly out to the reef. It doesn't take Coop long to figure out that the kid knows what he's doing. When Traian gets his first look at the decal on Coop's sail as he and Damien lose altitude as they peel away from the formation, he thinks that Betty looks a lot like Dakota.

"Have you flown one of these before?" Coop asks Damien.

"No, well maybe, if you count the simulation I tried last night," Damien answers.

"It shows. This is the closest you can get to in real life to simulating bird flight other than flying prone beneath a hang glider."

"It's fantastic. Do you think we could climb higher?"

"You bet. Just..."

But Damien is already gently pushing out on the trapeze to gain altitude. He does it gradually so as not to stall the aircraft like he and Pet3r practiced. Then he levels out and tries gaining and losing altitude using minute adjustments of the trapeze. Next he gets the craft to bank first left then right in shallow s-curves so now he has a feel for yaw and pitch before he completes his first 360 degree circle. Coop is comfortable enough with Damien's piloting skills so that he lets him do everything although he is prepared to take control in microseconds if it becomes necessary. It doesn't.

They arrive about 25 minutes after the first group has landed. Damien leaves that to Coop preferring not to practice crash landings for real.

...

Gillian and her team have set up in an area near their landing beach. It's a clearing of about three quarters of a hectare with a collection of pavilions each meant for up to four people to lie on futons under colourful, billowing silk coverings protecting them against intense Caribbean sunlight. Mosquito netting folds neatly down all sides for night time use. They've also set up an open-sided tent kitchen, a modest sized stage, a dance floor of interlocking hexagonal mahogany boards, a large bar, several change rooms, a towel dispensary and a craft hut.

They have established a series of Voller 3000 portable fuel cells to deliver both AC and DC power—the latter will be needed to charge their spelunking equipment before entering the tunnel system beneath the ruins. The fuels cells are completely quiet emitting only water vapour as a byproduct of their operation. Hydrogen, their energy source, is created by pumping sea water, using a solar pump, into a holding tank and then electrolyzing it to produce hydrogen and oxygen.

Gillian and Nell have asked Reggae Apostle to join the party and play for them. The Band chews up a lot of power—about 3.75 kW. That is a freaking huge amount of juice to produce in a remote location. But their fuel cells will have no trouble coping with these demands. Right now, there is a DJ playing various styles of Belizean music but mostly he's focused on Brukdown or broken down calypso music. It's a perfect backdrop for this idyllic sunny Western Caribbean day.

Everyone spends the day doing exactly you would expect at a beach party: drinking, dancing, swimming, sunning, playing Ultimate (they change the rules so no player can mark an opponent closer than two metres so girls and smaller guys can play with tall men like Damien) and playing backgammon. No one can beat a mathematician like Traian at backgammon and eventually he runs out of people willing to try.

Gillian continues to lead groups of six people at a time into the Mayan ruins. They get a history lesson and a tour but only of the ante rooms that are safe to explore without equipment. Later, she will lead Nell, Damien and their immediate entourage deeper into the cave and tunnel system under the tri-pyramids. This is Nell's surprise birthday gift for Damien. He will be officially 23 at midnight and Nell knows how much Damien likes the idea of going where no one has gone before or at least not since somewhere between 700 and 900 AD when the Mayans 'disappeared' from this area.

Just after lunch, a small boat carrying four giggling teenagers hits the beach. It's Dakota and three girlfriends come to join the party. Nell has invited them so they're here but Gillian is the one who has to promise their parents that she will be responsible for them. It makes her nervous.

...

For a second time, Nell and the other women cover up (all of them went topless on the beach except for Dakota and her girlfriends) as they gather round the craft hut towards the end of this glorious afternoon waiting for an announcement.

"We wanted everyone to take something away that will help you remember this day, this beautiful nation and these wonderful people for a long time to come," Gillian announces. "So Miss Nell and our team have brought baskets of worry dolls, enough for everyone to create one or two of their own.

"Anyone know what a worry doll is?"

No one did or at least no one wanted to put her or his knowledge of the subject up against a local like Gillian Boys.

"Worry people are tiny folk art dolls mostly found in Guatemala Highland Maya culture. If you confess your troubles to your worry doll before you go to sleep each night, they'll steal them away and you will sleep peacefully and completely.

"Our dolls come from San Juan del Obispo. They're hand-made using all natural cotton fibres and textiles made in Guatemala. Your job is to find a couple of dolls that speak to you and to draw or stitch a face on each of them and give them a name. But once you've given them a name, it's like ships, it's bad luck to change them so think carefully.

"We have three types of dyes for you to work with, tannin, vat dyes and dyes with mordent. We also have lots of non-run, non-NSM inks and different coloured threads of various diameters to choose from.

"So. Any questions?"

"I have one," asks a pensive Nell. "Where do worry dolls take our fears after we tell them what's going on?"

Gillian, normally so totally confident about pretty much everything, looks stumped for once. "Dunno, Nell. No one has ever asked that question before as far as I know. I'm not sure who we can ask."

There is much milling around as Mayan worry dolls begin picking out their people but eventually everyone settles down with one or two dolls to personalize and decorate. Dakota and Traian sit side-by-side handcrafting their dolls together; Dakota laughs at how bad an artist

Traian is. His lame attempt at decoration leads to a lopsided male worry doll that appears to be sardonically observing his human familiar. He tells her his doll's name is 'Freddie'.

"What kind of name is 'Freddy'?" she asks.

"It's F-R-E-D-D-I-E. I named him after Freddy Krueger but changed the spelling of his name cuz he is Freddy Light."

"Huh?" The cultural reference is completely lost on Dakota

"Freddy Krueger went around killing teenagers in their dreams using razors where his fingers shoulda been. He scared them to death or cut them up, I'm not sure which."

"And you want your doll to be called Freddie because?" Dakota frowns now thinking that maybe Traian is some kind of mutant.

Traian just laughs, "My guy is an anti-Krueger, like matter and anti-matter? You know, when you mix particles and anti-particles together they annihilate each other releasing huge amounts of energy, typically gamma rays that are extremely powerful and deadly to living tissue."

Dakota is now smiling back at Traian but not looking him in the eye. They have a hard time looking at each other directly because when they do, the needle moves to red for both of them. It's a bit overwhelming really.

Instead, she changes the subject. "So tell me more about what you do." Traian is happy to oblige.

Earlier as they approached the group on the beach, Dakota spoke with her best friend Deidre about Traian saying, "Eso le. El Euro Americano," while she pointed with her head at the Euro American.

"Él es muy buen aspecto," Deidre commented.

"Se le ve como un poco de un Diablo," replied Dakota. She can see what a devil he is but can't seem to help herself; she is powerfully attracted to him.

...

Damien makes himself a worry doll. Two of them have picked him out of the crowd of humans this day at Marco Gonzalez. Nell notices that he has, perhaps without realizing it, drawn the same loopy grin on his male doll that he occasionally gets when the world surprises him on the upside. He holds him up and tells Nell, "Meet 'Dooby'." Damien and Dooby are now wearing the exact same lopsided grin.

"Hello, Dooby. Why'd you call him that?" she asks.

"Pops and I have a male tabby cat named Toby."

"And that translates to Dooby, how?" Nell says raising her shoulders in emphasis.

"His nickname was Dooby. Sometimes we shortened that to just 'Doob'."

"What, your cat was a stoner?"

"Well, he sometimes acted like that. Actually, he's part of my famdamily. He's my bud. He was weird though. He'd walk me to school, he'd like follow me, go through the bush or something, watch me and then come meet me every day after school too."

"Never thought a cat could or would even want to do that. They're way too independent and self-centred," Nell says.

Damien wonders if she is talking about cats or herself.

"She's very matronly," Nell states pointing to Damien's other doll that is obviously female and looks like a middle aged spinster.

"Meet 'Miss Buril'," he says quite seriously.

"Who?"

"Miss Buril, my Grade 2/3 teacher."

"Uh, huh?" Nell says as more of a question than comment.

"Yeah, she's named after my Grade 2/3 teacher who took a shy, skinny, under-sized kid who was last in his class at everything. He was very sick as a little kid and nearly died from a bacterial infection. She saw something in him that made him worth saving."

"D, are you talking about yourself?"

"Yeah."

"You never told me."

"Nope."

"What happened?"

He takes a breath. "It was my friend Jon Pearlman's grandfather, Dr. Pearlman, whose first name was Lyon I think, and my grandfather who saved me. Dr. Pearlman was just an old fashioned GP not a pediatric specialist or anything but he cared about his patients and even made house calls, seldom seen now. Anyway, after ten days of ineffective treatment at Rochester General, the attending physician told them to prepare for my passing but those guys just refused to lose me. So Pops and Dr. Pearlman took me by air ambulance to Sick Kids in Toronto and told them to fix me which they did. I think Dr. P. paid for it too."

"Wow, I'm glad he did," Nell says reaching over to stroke the back of Damien's neck and rub his shoulders affectionately.

"Anywho, I was really puny and missed a year of school."

"I've seen images of you as a little kid, D. You were practically Biafran," Nell says, her eyes shining at him some more.

"I stayed that way for a long time, until puberty and a bit beyond. I grew something like 30 centimetres the year after I got to university. I remember getting shooting pains in my legs every week."

"Is that why you're still so skinny?"

"Dunno."

"Well, I like you just the way you are, Dr. Bell," Nell says squeezing Damien again with her small but powerful hand applying just the right amount pressure to Damien's neck and shoulders releasing copious amounts of endorphins in him. She gets warm just by touching him that way. In fact, even looking at him, being near him or smelling his slight male odor does it for her quite nicely.

"By the time I finally did get to school I was far

behind the other kids. It was so bad that when they showed me a simple picture of say three ducks and a pig and asked me which one was different, I couldn't tell them that. The other kids in the class laughed at me. I was smaller than everyone else, my feet didn't reach the floor even at those tiny desks kids sit at—and I was way dumber than everyone too. I asked Pops to please keep me home after that but he wouldn't.

"Most kids who appear to be slow, malnourished or under-developed usually just get shuffled off to the back of a classroom and disappear forever from the fast moving river of life. But Miss Buril, she kept me in class every recess and every day after school for an hour to make sure I could read, write and do arithmetic as well as solve simple puzzles and do basic problems which everyone else in the class was already able to do.

"With her help, that kid caught up, accelerated through the rest of primary and high school then applied to go to university at 14 and turned 15 his first year there before going on to do his PhD and postdoc work."

"D, you're talking about yourself in the third person again. Why is that?"

"Dunno."

"Come on."

He breathes deeply once more, "Well, I fought my way through school you know. I got transferred out of the public school where Miss Buril taught into an elite all boys prep school for grade 6. My marks had improved and I was skipping grades by that time so after doing a bunch of admittance exams they accepted me and gave me a scholarship. But it was a bad place.

"I learned early on that if you didn't stand up to bullies, they'd torment you forever. It'd just get worse and worse for you. So, win or lose, I made up my mind that I'd fight them. I lost some, won a few. They broke my nose once—you can see it's a bit crooked." He runs Nell's index finger along the bridge of his nose.

"It's hardly noticeable! You look very handsome, D,

even if you're a bit asymmetric..."

"Well, feel this."

He takes her hand and places it on the back of his head; she can feel a concave part of his skull hiding there under his thick brown hair. "Wow."

"I got into a brawl with a guy—he was a linebacker or something on our Middle School football team—he knocked me out cold. His name was Bert Steenbakker but everyone called him Dango. Wasn't much of a fight really—he was in the same grade as me but three, maybe four years older and at least 60 kilos heavier. He clobbered me; I fell backwards onto the terrazzo school floor and it dented my skull."

"Why didn't you tell your parents?"

Damien just looks at her, stunned. He's already told her his parents split.

"Well, you coulda told Pops instead, right?" Nell recovers.

"You know it never occurred to me to do that. That school I went to, kids just settled things on their own."

"You didn't trust the adults in your world," Nell says with a far off look of her own.

"Exactly. But we did settle up, eventually."

"Huh?"

"I organized the smaller, weaker kids into our own gang and we evened things up with Dango and a few other prefects, later."

"What did you guys do?" Nell asks.

"I'd rather not say."

"D!"

"Nell, it's just Middle School BS, OK? Leave it."

That is a red flag in front of a bull to Nell. This is the first man, the first person, she's ever wanted to know down to the atomic level so she gives him one of her Grade A pouty looks she knows he's powerless to resist. Nell powers it up further from Grade A to Force 5 to influence him to go on.

"Resistance is futile," Damien states with a shrug.

"That's Borg talk."

"I know who the Borg are. I saw Star Trek XIX," Nell smiles.

"Didn't know you're a fan, Nell?"

"I'm not really. AJ took me. We went to the critics screening—it turned into a mess. AJ got mobbed and so did I; we got separated."

"I thought AJ was a pretty good captain," Damien says half heartedly. AJ is AJ Ramos, the impossibly good looking actor who plays Captain Marcus in the film. Apparently, the original captain's son, David, had a son who was hidden from the Klingons or something and grows up in some type of alternate universe to become leader of all free peoples in our Galaxy. He cruises around in Enterprise VIII righting all wrongs.

He's never asked Nell about her love life in the time before Damien and he's not planning to start now. But he can't seem to help himself, "Where did they hold the press screening?"

"Not far from my place—up on South Grand Avenue at the old Disney Concert Hall," Nell answers. It's 30 miles from her home in Palos Verdes along Harbor Freeway to the Frank Gehry-designed structure with its scrumptious, curvaceous walls somewhat reminiscent of Sydney's opera house, although Frank would be out of his mind if anyone ever had the gall to actually say that to his face.

Seeing Damien's stricken look, she laughs, "Hey, it was just after The Successors hit big, Damien. Dafne thought it would be good PR for me to be seen at the screening and so apparently did AJ's people. Anyway, he's too old for me," she adds mischievously. "I like younger men!" Seeing he's still not fully persuaded she says, "Oh, come on D, come here right now!" She gives him a big squeeze then presses herself to him—firmly.

A bit out of breath now but completely mollified and reassured, he says, "Did you know my grandfather built a Star Trek Film Predictor model nearly 40 years ago?" he asks her mostly to deflect the conversation away from possible former lovers and the hell-hole of a school he attended during part of his time in Rochester. "They released a dozen films in the first 45 years of that franchise so he had some pretty good data to use for a regression analysis. He predicted there'd be 24 of them by Star Date 2050."

"He overestimated by quite a few, D," Nell notes.

"Well, it's not 2050 yet but really no one foresaw the extent of the meltdown—it slowed everything including Hollywood's sequel machine."

"D, what happened at your prep school?" Nell persists. She already knew it was an abusive place but not much more.

"They used to show horror movies every Saturday night," Damien goes on softly. "So one night, our gang waited for the movie to finish. We knew they'd have to cross the quad to get to their dorms."

"Quad?" she asks.

"A quadrangle. It had school buildings on two sides, a gymnasium on a third and was open to a parade square on the fourth. Our school made us all belong to the US Army Cadet Corps. That's where I learned to shoot and make explosives from scratch."

"Didn't know you could shoot, D."

"I can hit anything up to 25 metres but that's about it. Nothing like Jay."

"Jay?"

"Yeah, one of my buds who went into the Marine Corps. Now those guys can really shoot. Jay can hit anything. I've seen him hit at 300 metres, 400 even. He could use a muzzle loader and still be deadly at 100 metres."

"So what happened in the quad?"

"We beat them with cricket bats. Our school played frigging cricket instead of baseball. It was an affectation of the place. We had to play private schools up in Canada just to find opponents. But those things were perfect for the job. After that, peace broke out and my last year there was actually quite civilized, Nell."

"Because you were the leader of the pack."

"Yep, and justice for all," he says with pursed-lips, turned down at the edges—a look of determination that Nell has occasionally seen before. But this side of Damien—his ability to take violent action when his sense of fairness is provoked—is new to her.

"How did you get sick, D? Do you know?"

"Yeah, I remember."

"You do?"

"Yep, I was two. It was a hot summer's day and I asked Mom, she was still living with us then, for a drink. I was thirsty and like any little kid, being a pain in the ass about it. But she said to hold on a sec but I was really thirsty. She was washing the floors or something and there was a bucket with dirty water in it and a cloth lying over the lip so I dipped it in the bucket and sucked on that cloth. I still can feel cool, refreshing water gushing out of that cloth into my mouth and down the hatch it went. I repeated as often as necessary. That's all I remember until a year later I came back from the hospital on another sunny summer's day having lost half my body mass. My Mom'd left by then."

Nell can feel that there is more that Damien hasn't told her yet. "Does it still upset you?" she asks.

"A bit. But not half as much as your worry doll, Nell," Damien says trying to change the subject again.

Apparently, Damien isn't the only part of this duo who has some personal baggage to deal with. In fact, the look of Nell's doll freaks him out. Her worry doll is male but his face is just two tiny black eyes and a large black circle for a mouth with no other features or colour.

"What name did you give your doll, Honey?"

There's silence for a minute or so.

"You gonna tell me?"

"Dezba."

"Dezba?"

"It's Navajo. It means War."

"Why 'War', Nell?"

It's her turn to say, "Dunno."

Nell seems a bit downcast now and Dezba, who is a dour looking creature named after one of the long time enemies of the Hopi people, certainly appears to reflect some kind of inner turmoil in her. She's wanted to mention something to Damien for quite a while but can't ever seem to find the right time or place to say it to him. Certainly she's not going to say anything, not here, not now with more than 40 people milling about at Marco Gonzalez. Maybe she can get some private time with him tonight after they explore the nearby ruins.

...

After dinner but before Reggae Apostle begins (a dance party that is planned to last until 3 am), they gather round a huge beach bonfire. It's storytelling time!

Gillian is explaining that they are going to play public hangman—the winner of each round gets to tell his or her story. She's drafted Dakota to play Vanna and write down letters on an old fashioned whiteboard mounted on a tripod inside the circle of people sitting on futons around the campfire.

On the whiteboard, Dakota has drawn this:

— — — — —

— — — —

— — — —

Gillian carries on, "The rules are simple—you put up one hand, you get to guess a letter. But if you're wrong, you're out. If you're right, you get to guess another letter. Again, if you're wrong, you're out.

"If you put up two hands you get to guess a letter and you must guess the word or phrase correctly or you're out. OK?"

Damien immediately puts up two hands.

"Dr. Bell?"

"Great Blue Hole," he says.

Dakota and Gillian look at each other and roll their

eyes. There's no point in playing games like this with hackers and coders in the audience. It's just ridiculous.

"Damien, the floor is yours," concedes Gillian with a sweep of her hand. She goes to sit next to Boyd who has a rum concoction ready for her. She sips the drink but is careful not to imbibe it too quickly. She needs to stay compos mentis.

Damien stands, completely relaxed, in front of his audience. He moves well and uses his hands, eyebrows, face and body to add emphasis as needed. He believes that body language is to storytelling and teaching what sauce is to the goose. Nell can clearly see the prof in him and she knows he'd make a fabulous actor if he ever gives up on being a quantum physicist. She loves talent and D has it big time.

"I want to talk about ingenuity—humans are the most co-dependant animals on the planet and we prosper hugely when we do stuff like skill sharing. So if you get really good at something, you will be able to produce a surplus of it which you can then trade with me because I'm really good at something else that I can trade back to you. That's basically David Ricardo's Theory of Comparative Advantage from the latter part of the 18th Century."

"Hey, Damien. Is this a for-credit course?" shouts Traian good naturedly, echoing at least half the audience's thinking that a lecture is about to begin.

"It's only a half credit, buddy. Look, I'm gonna talk and you're gonna listen. I won at Hangman, so tough."

Tray groans along with a few others.

"OK, then... We not only apply brute force to things—that is, throw more labour, capital or energy at something—but also add ingenuity to it. So how can we become more creative? Is that even possible?" Damien asks rhetorically.

"Many ingenious insights are a product of a few moments of inspiration, maybe as few as 40 microseconds. Often those moments of insight happen because first, they're preceded by a lifetime of study and thought on a subject or second, there is a pressing need and, hence, a focused effort on a particular problem.

"And what focuses human minds fastest?"

"Reward?" Tony answers right away. Then he adds just to unnecessarily hammer home his point, "Money and power."

"Greed!" yells someone.

"Sex!" someone else suggests.

"Huh? Having more sex makes you more creative?" another person asks. This is something that Traian might have said as recently as a couple of days ago. Now he's not so sure. He's experiencing new feelings and feeling very differently about the whole subject, sitting as he is next to Dakota. They're holding hands.

"How about, 'none of the above'," Damien says. "Try the thought of being 'hanged in the morning'. That is why, threat of war, war itself, fear of failure, fear of peer review or review by your boss or client, patron, audience, fear even of parental authority and punishment, mobilizes most individuals to be at their creative best. Human beings are most creative when their personal interests are somewhat threatened or at stake or their personal interests can be ameliorated to a significant extent."

"As in 'who moved my cheese'?" Dr. Luis adds helpfully.

"Right! Creativity happens because there is some stress—but not too much—in the system. Combine that with periodic intense pondering of a problem interspersed with time for your subconscious to work on it, i.e., when you are asleep or playing or your attention is diverted elsewhere."

"We're gonna go to sleep if you don't finish soon," Traian eggs him on.

"Well too bad for you, Tray, you'll miss out by not paying attention," a quite unperturbed Damien says.

"Anyway, there are some other factors too like your physical well being, proper nutrition and decent diet, adequate exercise and the absence of any type of drugs or alcohol." While Damien makes this last comment, he smiles hugely in Nell's direction. She melts at his smoldering look.

"I want to give you an example of an insight my grandfather had, a guy everyone calls 'Pops', when he was working as a volunteer on a kibbutz in northern Israel. He was a young guy traveling Europe and the Mideast when he basically ran out of money in Munich where he was visiting his best friend, Til Rotenberg. He heard that he could get free room and board if he volunteered as a farm labourer on a kibbutz, so he does. He persuades Til to come with him not only cuz he's his best friend but because, like a lot of Euros, Til can speak many languages fluently without a trace of accent including French, English, Italian, Dutch, Spanish and, of course, German. He has a bit of Russian and Greek in his repertoire too. Neither of them speaks any Hebrew though.

"While they're picking apples one day on that farm, Pops notices that they're leaving many apples un-harvested because they are in hard-to-reach places. So after sleeping on the problem for a night, next day he goes into their tool shed and invents the 'Bell Apple Picker'.

"The Bell Apple Picker uses an elongated hexagonal metal collar about 28 centimetres long and 18 wide fixed to the end of a broom handle. Pops cut an inverted V-shape out of the far end of the collar and filed it to a knife edge so he could use it to snip apples off at their stems." Damien uses lots of hand motions and body language to help his audience visualize his grandfather at work.

"Next, he adds a mesh net underneath to catch them as they fall. The net has an hourglass figure," Damien can't help himself, he looks sideways in Nell's direction as he talks, "which creates a choke point to slow their descent and prevent them from bruising. What's a bruised apple worth after all?"

"They're yucky to eat," one of Nell's young dancers adds.

"Right. Bruising ruptures the walls and membranes of their cells allowing oxidation to occur. Basically, they turn brown which turns consumers off, so Pops knows he has to make sure that his apple picker doesn't do that or else—"

"Or else what?" Traian asks, now somewhat more interested in this story since it looks like it will involve a decent if very simple piece of technology and some kind of political confrontation.

"I'll get to that. Anyway, Pops attaches a shoulder strap to his sawed off broom handle to complete his ensemble. Next day, he goes to work in the fields at their usual start time, 4:30 am, with his apple picker slung across his back like a rifle. He also equips his buddy Til with one. They're wearing these ugly, awkward front-mounted packs to store apples they pick by hand. But once they've picked all the apples they can get to with their hands, they unsling their Bell Apple Pickers and reach out nearer to tops of these trees as well as further into them. When their packs are full, they climb down their ladders and empty them into a nearby wagon by undoing a flap at the bottom of their packs carefully and slowly.

"The next thing you know, the assistant farm manager is there telling them in broken English, 'We don't use such things here.'

"No amount of discussion or debate persuades him to let them use their new devices so they have to go back to the old way of doing things.

"But Pops is not easily deterred—he's heard that the kibbutzim believe in democracy and cooperative living so at the next whole-community, town hall-style meeting, he's gonna bring it up. Even though they don't speak any Hebrew, no problem. The boys have convinced one of the Kibbutzniks to translate for them. At the next meeting Pops, Til and their translator wait their turn to speak knowing that the Kibbutzniks will drink copious quantities of horrible sugared red wine which will help get them onside because, by the time they speak, the Kibbutzniks will say 'yes' to practically anything.

"Finally, he gets up to speak, 'I believe I can increase your apple harvest by 7% to 9% and reduce your number of ladder movements too. That will mean less damage to your trees and more fruit for you next year. And with these', Pops says as both he and Til hold up their apple pickers so the more than 300 people in the room can see them, 'we can get to places on your trees that were never accessible before. So lots more apples to sell and many fewer left rotting on your trees.'

"The assistant farm manager produces some lame reasoning about how Bell Apple Pickers will slow down the work, so Pops asks the community to let him test it. 'Just give us a chance,' Pops asks. 'Let's put two teams of seven guys each into the orchard. One group will be equipped with apple pickers and the other, our control group, won't be. We'll measure total number of trees harvested, total yield and quality, i.e., bruising, for one work week (five and half days there stretching from Sunday to noon on Friday). Come on what do you say?'

"It's no contest. After two days, the guys in the control group simply give up—they all want their own apple pickers. Over the next two weeks, Pops and Til are reassigned—they're to work with kibbutz engineers in their workshop to redesign then build and manufacture the Bell Apple Picker Mark II."

"Do they still pick apples the same way today?" Coop asks.

"Pretty much. Some industrial farms produce apples on vines that look more like tomato plants but a lot of people prefer traditional ones," Damien says.

"What happened to the assistant farm manager?" asks an impish Nell.

"Well... that's another story."

"Come on, out with it," someone chips in.

"OK, OK," Damien holds up both hands.

"Pops is a bit of a rabble rouser. So he and Til and their Israeli co-conspirator decide to test the co-op mentality of the place. Kibbutz is a Hebrew word for 'communal settlement' so the guys are gonna see if it's for real or not. They notice that even though everyone is supposed to be equal, some are more equal than others. Joe-jobs like, say, making endless meatballs in the kitchen or swabbing out the w/c's are rotated through the community so everyone gets their fair share of crummy duties. But it doesn't require a regression analysis to figure out that top people in the kibbutz never seem to do any menial work. They just drive around in tractors and pickup trucks all the livelong day.

"So the guys arrange to have a fake telegram sent to the kibbutz from their central bureau in Tel Aviv, Kibbutz Industries Association, asking the top men to come down for some kind of emergency meeting. While they're away, they break into the Manager's office, Pops can crack just about any type of lock ever made, and change all the assignments placing kitchen helpers and kybo cleaners at the top of the heap and vice versa.

"So, when the guys come back from Tel Aviv for the start of the work week, they find themselves shuffled out of plum jobs and into menial ones. Of course, they can't put up much of a fuss about it since that would be a breach of Kibbutznik rules, many of them unwritten." Damien takes a breath.

Boyd asks, "That's it? They changed all the work orders and got away with it?"

"Well, for a couple of days it seemed like they were in the clear. But both Til and Pops are eventually shown the door and the Kibbutznik who can't easily be expelled had to tough it out for a few months afterward.

"But the cool thing is that they've been producing Bell Apple Pickers Mark II ever since. They manufacture them and export them all over the place."

"Maybe he should have patented the thing," Reznik remarks.

"Naw, Pops was OK with this piece of IP being out there in the public domain. He felt that anything that increases productivity for farmworkers or other low paid wage earners is a step in the direction of higher pay for them. Heaven knows, they need it."

"How did he find out that the kibbutz was producing them commercially?" Tony asks. To Reznik, anyone knocking off someone else's IP is tantamount to stealing.

"It was completely by accident. He went to a pick-your-own apple picking place near his cabin in northern Ontario decades later and, lo and behold, he sees these modern, sleekly-designed versions stamped with the name 'Kfar Jerrah', the place where he built those first prototypes."

They give Damien a nice round of applause and, after that, whoever wants to tell a story stands up and does it.

...

While Reggae Apostle are rocking the beach, Damien, Nell, Dr. Luis, Boyd, Coop and Traian are gearing up for a spelunking expedition to explore the space below the Mayan tri-pyramid structures under the watchful eye of Gillian. Dakota has also joined the group.

Each wears a waterproof English-made Cordura Oversuit but no undersuits since it is cool but not cold where they are going. Although there is some water it is generally not flooded. They each have Edelrid Madillo helmets except Nell who is wearing a Petzl Picchu kid's helmet. They also have Petzl LED headlamps.

They are roped together because once in the cave and tunnel system, it is the most complete darkness that any person can experience. About a metre and a half of rope separates each of them. Their jumpsuits are protected from rope burn by specially designed sheaths.

Gillian will lead and Boyd will be at the tail end of the group. Before they enter, she decontaminates all of them with spray from a Nomad 38; she will do so again on their exit. Gillian does not want to bring foreign organisms into the cave system or out. Conservation of cave ecosystems is required under an unwritten code that all spelunkers adhere to.

The first part of the cave and tunnel system leads downward on a gentle slope. Ceiling height is a comfortable two metres in what is plainly an engineered space. It is sometimes hard to tell which parts of the system are created by natural processes and which are human-built. They stop and examine various rooms. Some are obviously storerooms, eating areas and sleeping places but there are larger spaces that could have been meeting rooms or, for all anyone knows, rooms where Mayans butchered their enemies.

In this group, only Traian seems to be having difficulty with darkness in these cramped spaces pressing in on him. Dakota asks him if he wants to stop. Even though she asks him softly, down there, it's like she's using a megaphone.

Gillian immediately holds up her hand for the group to halt. She comes back to Traian, "Hey, this isn't for everyone. There's no reason to put yourself through this if it is uncomfortable for you."

It's not some macho inclination that keeps Traian interested in going on or even the fact that he likes to be near Dakota. He's here for his best friend and wants to celebrate with him when they get wherever it is they're going. He just motions to Gillian to move ahead.

Quietly, he tells Dakota, "It's the stories of my country that are kind of spooking me here—ones my grandparents told me about unspeakable cruelty by Ceauşescu, ruler of Romania for decades, and what they did in dark places like this."

Dakota grabs hold of his hand, "Tray, those evil people have long since gone to their graves. They're not here in Belize. This is a good place." She squeezes his hand to give him some reassurance. That simple contact with her provides Traian with a great deal of comfort and other feelings he can't name since he has never experienced anything like them before.

The tunnel shrinks in both ceiling height and corridor width as well as beginning to take many twists and turns, sometimes appearing to loop back onto itself. They are in a maze presumably designed to trap anyone who is foolish enough to come here uninvited. Gillian follows a map created in 1984 by Drs. Graham and Pendergast when they first explored these ruins. She's told Nell that a space at the exact centre of the tri-pyramid structure is worth this difficult 100 minute underground trek. At one point the tunnel takes another 90 degree turn and becomes so narrow they have to remove their backpacks and sidle along sideways for about 125 metres. There is no way any attackers could possibly mount a successful engagement here; they could be picked off by Mayan defenders, one at a time.

There is also no way for Dr. Luis to continue; he's simply too chubby to fit. Boyd unshackles himself from the group and tethers himself to Dr. Luis. They head back with a shrug from Boyd tugging a bit of an embarrassed Dr. Luis along with him.

The last obstacle is a sudden drop in elevation that submerges the group up to their necks in brackish water. It's over Nell's head so they make special arrangements for her—she carries no equipment and is supported on either side by Traian and Damien.

They finally arrive in a vast underground chamber that is at least half the size of St. Peter's Basilica in Rome. There is Mayan art everywhere they shine their lamps, and logo syllabic writing (some people call them hieroglyphs) on every square centimetre surrounding and sometimes overwritten on this ancient art.

"Gillian, has all of this been documented?" Damien asks quietly. They all talk in awed, hushed tones when they can talk at all. It's overwhelming.

"I think almost none of it. The two archaeologists who first discovered this place and whose map we are using meant to return with a full expedition but for some unknown reason they never did."

"Holy smokes, is it OK if we record this?"

"Sure, if you don't, maybe no one will."

Damien gets out his Q-Phone and motions to Traian to do the same. With Gillian's permission, they unshackle themselves but heed a warning not to go down any tunnels or enter any rooms off the main space. They can both see how easy it would be to get lost in this vast place causing real grief for themselves and their group. Both Pet3r and Vl4d, Traian's counterpart, start recording pretty much everything using quantum radar. (Basically they shoot out entangled photons at slightly different frequencies. It puts Superman's X-Ray vision to shame.)

Watching Damien and Pet3r, and Traian and Vl4d move around the immense room methodically recording everything is weird, made weirder by slightly luminescent beams coming out of their Q-Phones. In fact, it looks like they are coming out of Pet3r's and Vl4d's eyes. Each Entity hovers a half metre above their Q-Phones, projected there with heads that are about 40 centimetres in diameter. As far as Damien can tell, Vl4d is the only Quantum Counterpart who has ever donned any clothing on a regular basis. He wonders what Ellen would think if she could see a rather dashing looking QE wearing a cloak and what looks like Puss 'n Boots' boots. All Vl4d needs to complete the look is a sword and a hat with a long feather. For members of their group who've never seen Q-Phones or QEs, it's an eye opener.

Suddenly Vl4d calls out, "Stop, Traian, please. Pet3r, Damien, come here!"

"There's no way," Traian says. "No way." His mouth hangs open.

Damien comes over slowly and now stares with just as baffled a look on his face as his buddy.

"What is it, Traian?" Dakota asks.

"It's not possible."

"What's not possible?" she asks.

"Are you sure Vl4d?" asks Traian, ignoring Dakota for the moment.

"It's correct," Pet3r confirms.

Damien, Traian, Vl4d and Pet3r are looking at Dirac notation, sometimes called Bra-ket notation used to describe quantum phenomenon. It's written on the stone walls, monuments, lintels and stelae of this ancient place. But these ideas are unlike anything they have ever seen before; on a first reading, neither Damien nor Traian has a clue.

"I've made some interesting connections," Vl4d adds now talking directly to Damien and Traian through their quantum earbuds so no one else hears him say, "These appear to link to some Mayan script about a metre and a half above your eye level, Damien.

"There is a short entry in one of Paul Dirac's original handwritten notebooks that refers back to these Bra-ket equations," Vl4d continues, "but I find no confirming references in any other data sources across the Internet. Science and mathematics historians have explained these away saying that Mayan glyphs in his notebook are decorative, mere doodles."

"Pet3r?"

"Sorry Damien. I can find no further outside references."

Traian isn't sure if anyone else on earth had been there, they would've known what they were seeing. It's just completely strange that two of the most proficient young quantum physicists/mathematicians on the planet together with a couple of Quantum Entities precisely tuned to these exact subjects—of prime importance to their human counterparts and thus to them—just happen to be there to see it. Some type of brand new quantum phenomenon is being described here. But what exactly have they found?

Nell asks, "Can you, like, carbon date this or something?"

Damien replies, "Nope. That only works with organic material. But what we can do is use our Q-Phones to test two things: the composition of the dyes used to create these scripts and the age of the material using thermoluminescence."

Vl4d and Traian work on scraping a small sample of the writing material onto a flat stone they find nearby and, using a flare that Gillian lends them, they burn it. Vl4d uses his dosimeter to measure radiation released in the process. Meanwhile, Pet3r and Damien are using the Q-Phone's spectrometer to record the photon number per unit of wavelength in the UV, visible and IR spectral ranges. This will give them a good sense of what the materials are made of. Then they can then compare their results to samples they take from what is obviously of Mayan origin.

"We've gotta get back to camp and show this to Dr. Luis," says Damien. They stay just long enough to break open a bottle of non alcoholic champagne to celebrate Damien's birthday which now seems secondary to the incredible discovery they've just made there.

...

They are back at main camp. The party is still going strong although Gillian has asked the Band to quit at 3 am so everyone can get a few hours of sleep before they head back starting at 0800.

"What you have is at least three main periods when these writings were etched in the cave," Dr. Luis says. Rumor has swept through the camp that they've uncovered a major find and people are crowded around the kitchen/dining tent where the guys have set up a makeshift base. Everyone is hungry and the staff feeds partygoers and returning cavers too.

Between mouthfuls of delicious Belizean fry jacks and gulps of coffee, Dr. Luis continues, "The first appear to date from 1600 to 1200 BC, the second somewhere around 800 AD and the last is from a period of about 120 years ago, around 1925.

"Now it looks like all the Dirac notation that Vl4d and Pet3r have shown me is from the latter period. That would lead me to believe that a quantum physicist was here in Marco Gonzalez around that time."

"Any ideas on who that might be, Dr. Luis?" Damien asks.

"Well, yes, I think Paul Dirac was here."

"But there's no record of that is there Dr.?" Damien asks.

"It's his notation, no doubt about that. There's a record of Dirac leaving Cambridge in 1929 to head to Japan. He stopped off in Florida where he was planning to make his permanent home. (He ultimately spent the last 14 years of his career and his life at Florida State University in Tallahassee.) Then he headed to Japan via the Panama Canal which as you know isn't far from here as these things are measured. He would have probably gone right past this place."

"But what was he looking for, why here?" Traian asks.

"Not sure. These equations are unlike anything I've ever seen before so I can't speculate on what they mean or are intended to do," Dr. Luis finishes.

"Well, they aren't our equations," Damien says. "They don't resolve quantum computing or quantum communication. Dirac came here for a different reason, to solve a different kind of problem. He was looking for some clue which maybe he found here or maybe he was just inspired to solve the problem he was working on here for some reason."

"Maybe we'll never know," Dr. Luis says.

Damien says nothing—he has just realized that Dirac came here for a very specific reason and found something that allowed him to solve a much bigger problem than anything QCC has tackled. He just looks at Traian and the two guys are instantly on the same wavelength. They won't talk to anyone about this possible new quantum phenomena for a long time.

...

Traian isn't sure what he's most blown away by—their discovery at Marco Gonzalez or the one chaste kiss he gets from Dakota before she returns home. They're waiting for Gillian to come pick them up in the Aurore to take everyone to the Great Blue Hole for some diving, snorkeling and sea kayaking before going back to the Big

Smoke. He wants Dakota to come with them but there's no way. She's got school.

The Great Blue Hole is an underwater, circular sinkhole and World Heritage Site. It lies pretty much in the centre of Lighthouse Reef, so named because of a small government sanctioned lighthouse on tiny Sandbore Island to the north. The hole is roughly 300 meters in diameter and 125 meters deep. There are fantastic caves there, now underwater, covered by seas that have risen over the last 15,000 years.

Both Damien and Traian have had their fill of Belizean caves just now and will leave diving to others. They're just going to snorkel and enjoy the elevated coral atolls and the fantastic shades of turquoise, teal, green, aquamarine and peacock blue.

During a break from snorkeling, Damien asks Gillian about the many palm trees he's seen on these islands that are showing signs of stress. They have lost some or all their fronds and all their coconuts. She tells him that a lot of property owners are so far in mortgage debt or in active foreclosure or their properties are outright owned by banks that no one seems to care one whit that millions of their trees are sick with what's called 'lethal yellowing'.

"The annoying thing is that they can be cured by a simple remedy, it's cheap too—about ND$3 per tree per year. University of Florida's Dr. Henry Donselman from the Fort Lauderdale Research Center figured out, years ago, that by injecting tetracycline into the palms' circulatory systems, the trees then develop temporary immunity," a frustrated Gillian says. "All you got to do is drill a hole and push in a plug. It lasts about a year. There's no frigging reason we should be losing our palm cover."

As promised they swim with sharks but for Damien and Traian, their minds are really elsewhere. Much is made of the fact that the guys finally convince Nell to get in the water, sharks and all.

...

Later, that day they say goodbye to Maya Fair. Nell will stay on for a few more days before returning to Palos Verdes. She still hasn't told Damien the story behind her worry doll, Dezba, now safely tucked away under her pillow. It just isn't the right time—he's so excited by their discovery at Marco Gonzalez and the upcoming launch of QCC that she just can't bring herself to tell him. Damien tells her how much he loves this strange, tiny country and his strange, tiny woman. Then they all scatter back to reality.

...

Chapter 8

Business Model

"Look, we need the funding," Traian argues when Ellen enters the small boardroom next to Lab 4. "We either do the deal with Bessemer Ventures or Cain Caruthers Capital or maybe both. Let's take their money, the more of it, the better."

"But do we even need it, especially now?" Damien responds. "We don't really know what we've got yet," nodding to Ellen who is just sitting down, "We haven't even got an established business model."

Ellen is surprised to find the guys seated and ready to go on time, in fact a little early. What she doesn't know is that Damien and Traian have been sitting there for more than 45 minutes discussing what happened at Marco Gonzalez and that they abruptly change course when she joins them.

"If it's OK with everyone, let me walk you through the slides Ash3r, Aziz, Anthony and I have put together," says Ellen. "There's a lot to go through and, if we're going to raise some VC money, it might be clearer where we stand afterwards."

Ellen has collected Aziz and Anthony on her way to this meet-up.

None of these young people have ever done a big launch before although at least Aziz, Anthony and Ellen have some training and background in finance, biz development and product management. Traian and Damien have only their instincts to rely on here.

"A business model is basically quite simple," Ellen starts. "It can be a one page pictogram usually with suppliers on the left hand side, your company in the middle and clients on the right hand side." As she talks, Ash3r controls images on the media wall closest to her. Aziz, sitting to her right, thinks how pretty she looks in her fashionable high end style of dress with a soft glow from the media wall behind her glinting off her narrow frame glasses, an affectation he supposes. He's a finance type and looks the part. All the other guys wear jeans, not Aziz.

The media wall graphic looks something like this:

Suppliers (LHS)—
º Apple -> iPhone 40
º U of T -> Lab 4
º MacMillan, Sheppard, Seller LLP -> Legals

Clients (RHS)—
□ Consumer -> Individual Subscriptions
□ Enterprise -> Corporate and Government Subscriptions

Enterprise (Middle)—
QCC -> Q-phone & QE

"There is another dimension we need to add to our model—that's a marketing dimension. It's orthogonal to the plane of the biz model."

Damien's eyebrows go up when he hears Ellen using engineering terminology in her presentation. She's been hanging around geeks long enough for her to pick up some of their lingo, he supposes.

"It doesn't do us any good to launch QCC only to find out that we can't reach clients without heroic efforts like, say, funding Super Bowl commercials. So we have a classic one-to-many marketing problem. That means QCC is essentially targeting all eight+ billion humans on this planet and it's hard to do effective marketing when it's one versus eight point five times ten to the power of nine. So we think we should do a deal with resellers to reduce the problem from one to many to one to a few. It will make for a faster growth curve, we believe."

Actually, they don't all agree. Both Aziz and Ellen want to make deals with existing carriers who have vast networks of Internet sales channels plus a tonne of retail outlets as well as direct sales forces (mostly independent contractors these days) who sell to large enterprises. Anthony del Castillo does not agree. He feels that they can take the same path that earlier global spanning tech companies did, like OLA Facebook years ago, and release Q-phones and QEs into narrow market segments first. But it's not Ivy League Colleges he's after. He wants to pick one vertical market and dominate it before moving on.

He suggests to Ellen that they provide free Q-phones and QEs to health professionals through a new, self-funded QCC Foundation. The Foundation will provide persons in helping professions with their own helpmates, Q-Phones and Quantum Counterparts. Imagine a nurse with his or her own QE, watching all their patients simultaneously or completing discharge records or updating files or even making house calls for them!

Anthony wants to bolt the new Q-Foundation onto their for-profit corporation as a kind of marketing arm. He's pretty sure that if several hundred thousand or maybe several million health professionals are blogging, messaging, chatting and posting about their Q-Phones and Quantum Counterparts, everyone else will want one. Since the Foundation will be able to raise money on its own for its good works, their marketing will be a negative cost—always a good idea for a startup with limited capital. Plus they won't have to give up any equity to VCs circling around QCC. Anthony's interest in QCC is about two thirds of Ellen's so he isn't too keen on diluting it by bringing another VC or two into the deal.

Ellen's already agreed to add Anthony's suggested change to QCC's biz model. It's clever, effective and ultra low cost plus very authentic. At least, it is to Ellen. It will provide them with plenty of political cover too—who can argue with a company that gives away its product to helping professionals? It's a variant on old freemium models which have proven so effective over the last few decades.

It's also a riff on business models that reach out to build communities and try to bring net benefit to those communities. For the last generation, it's been strangely true, as Damien first pointed out to her in Frans after Mark Zuckerberg's lecture, that entrepreneurs who are all about 'the money' have none, while those who want to build insanely great products and services and develop communities around them have it all.

But she's rejected Anthony's advice for a go-it-alone marketing strategy—she wants to add resellers. She makes up a chart which she does not plan to show to anyone today about whose ox is about to be gored by QCC, and it's not pretty. The chart looks something like this:

Quantum Economics
Scarcity/Regulator/Abundance
Mobile Carriers/FCC, CRTC/Q-Phone [unlimited bandwidth/ speed]
Search Engines/FCC, CRTC/QEs
Wireless Spectrum/FCC, CRTCQ-Phone [quantum interaction]
Internet Root Servers/DOC, ICANN/QEs
Internet Service Providers/FTC/Q-Phone [unlimited bandwidth/ speed]
Internet Security & Paywalls/DHS, DOC, FCC/QEs
IP: Film, Television, Music &Video/MPAA, RIAA/QEs
Internet latency, metro networks, bandwidth speed/ITU/Q-Phone [unlimited bandwidth/speed]
Home, business security systems/FCC/QEs [Always-Institutional Security/complete record & recall]
E&OE
Confidential and Proprietary

She wants to make deals with four maybe five existing, transnational mobile carriers and the two biggest search engines on the planet (the largest, based in Imperial China and No. 2, based in the US). She says she wants to do this because it will help with the one-to-many marketing problem but the real reason that she wants to cut them in is so she can use their political lobbying and litigation muscle in Washington, Beijing, Brussels and Cape Town.

She knows that it isn't just these powerful corporations they have to worry about. Regulators have almost as much at stake. If bandwidth ceases to be scarce, for example, what's the point in having the FCC stick around? They sure aren't going to be holding any more spectrum auctions or collecting enormous annual licensing fees so their mission is over. Regulators tend to be captured by those they regulate and ultimately form symbiotic relationships with them which mean they inevitably resist technological change—anything that might threaten their power and position.

"Can we come back to the question of resellers later, Ellen?" Traian asks. "I don't see anything here that tells me how we're gonna make any money. Anthony wants to give away a million Q-Phones and QEs. Now why would we do that?"

"I didn't say 'give away'. I said 'provide'. The plan is to raise money independently for a Foundation and the Foundation will give product away," Anthony responds. "It'll earn us huge goodwill and lots of earned media plus a tonne of buzz. It's smart, guerrilla marketing. It's free to QCC and we won't need any VC money for marketing either so, guess what Traian, no unnecessary stock dilution."

"I still don't see a revenue model here for us," Traian says.

"What's with you and money, money, MONEY anyway, Traian? Your family's got money," a now snarky Anthony adds.

"What are you talking about? If your Dad has money, it doesn't mean you have any! What's the plan here—I'm 24, my Dad is 49. Maybe he'll live to be 112, average for guys these days. So you're suggesting I wait until he knocks off before I have any dough? I'll be frigging 87 years old before I inherit anything and that's if he doesn't blow it or spend it all before he pops off. I'd like some financial freedom a bit sooner, fuck you very much."

"Great, just what we need. Another lecture by an angry Romanian." The temperature in the room feels like it's just dropped six degrees.

"Money isn't everything, you know, but you can buy freedom with it and freedom is everything," Traian says stubbornly.

"Tray, who said that? I've heard it before," Damien asks.

"Arian Foster."

"Who?"

"Arian Foster, he played in the NFL, I think."

Everyone, even Anthony, bursts out laughing that a Romanian kid quotes an old American football player long since retired to the lecture circuit.

"Hold on, guys, we do have a revenue model; we just haven't come to it yet," Ellen interjects trying to move things along. "We looked at a wide range of options for revenue generation." As Ellen talks, another window opens on the media wall behind her and Ash3r brings up:

QCC Revenue Generation Model
Product/Q-Phone/QE/Notes
Cost to QCC/$300/$0/iPhone 40 from Apple: $240
Monthly Subscriber Fee/$30/$0
Advertising Engine/Unknown/$0
Search Engine Unknown/$0
Downloads and Streaming/Unknown/$0
Product Sales/Service Providers/Unknown/$0
$ND
E&OE
Confidential and Proprietary

"Oh, so this is supposed to answer all our questions? We make nothing, NOTHING from QEs, we have a charity give away our stuff, next we buy these damn iPhone 40s from Apple for 240 bucks, add some of our own modifications for another 60 and then sell them for 30 new dollars a month?" Traian persists. "We'll be broke in two quarters."

Aziz comes to Ellen's rescue, "Hang on, Traian, hang on. You'd be right if that was the whole model. It isn't. Let me show you our Cash Conversion Cycle. Ash3r, can you bring that up—Case 1 please?"

QCC Cash Conversion Cycle—CCC Measurement
Case 1:
$30 per month Subscription Fee
$300 Selling Price
$240 COGS, Cost of Goods Sold
CCC Measurement/Number/Units
Accounts Receivable at Year End (AR)/$30
Days Per Year/365.25/days
AR x Days Per year/$10,957.50/Dollar-Days/Annum
Annual Sales/$360/Dollars per Annum
AR x Days Per year ÷ Annual Sales/30.4375/Days ART
Inventory at Year End (INV)/$300
Days Per Year /365.25/Days
INV x Days Per Year/$109,575.00/Dollar-Days per Annum
Cost of Goods Sold (COGS)/$240/Dollars per Annum
INV x Days Per Year ÷ COGS/456.5625/Days INVT
Accounts Payable at Year End (AP)/$30
Days Per Year /365.25/Days
AP x Days Per year/$10,957.50/Dollar-Days per Annum
Cost of Goods Sold (COGS)/$240/Dollars per Annum
AP x Days Per year ÷ COGS/45.65625/Days APT
CCC*/441.34375/Days
* CCC = ART + INVT - APT
E&OE
Confidential and Proprietary

"If we ignore for the moment any revenues we'll get

from advertising, search, downloads and streaming as well as product sales on the platform, our payback period is about 441 days, which is totally unacceptable. But look at our IRR, it's a not bad 106% p.a.," Aziz says. Meanwhile Ash3r is showing this:

QCC Internal Rate of Return (IRR) Measurement
Time/Cashflow/Units
0/($300)/ND
1/$360/ND
2/$360/ND
3/$360/ND
irr/106% p.a.
E&OE
Confidential and Proprietary

"We won't last 441 days," says a now discouraged Traian.

"What's Apple making in all of this?" Damien asks.

"Well the original iPhone and its ecosystem returned over 288% p.a. for Apple when it was introduced more than 40 years ago. It's still some kind of a record for a major company anywhere other than maybe the petroleum industry," Aziz says.

"It was the iPhone, not any of their other products, that made Apple not just the biggest tech company on the planet, the biggest period," Damien says.

"Ah, it wasn't the product per se," Ellen adds, still smarting from the lecture she got from Damien in Frans about Apple. "It was the biz model they built around it that did it."

"Biggest by market capitalization not by revenue," Anthony says.

"Whatever, Apple's rate of return is, I don't really care. What I do care about is that, despite all the work we've done, they're going to be making more from the launch of QCC than we do," Traian says.

"Maybe not, Traian," Aziz continues. "We have a deal

on the table with Costco Finance—they're willing to give us consumer finance for each Q-phone we sell using a 50% LTV (Loan to Value) ratio. That will provide us with $313.36 for every three year contract we get.

"Costco's financing isn't cheap—once we include all their fees for originating each loan, their processing fee and the basic interest rate they're charging us, it works out to an effective rate of 16.125% per year. But they've agreed to review the rate 12 months after launch once they've established RL default and return rates. We think the default rate is going to be very low and the return rate even lower. Out of the first 80 Q-Phones, we've only had one rejected. So I expect our effective interest rate to come down by at least 450 basis points."

"Whose was that?" Damien asks.

Ellen jumps back in and gives the group a rundown on their test bed results so far. She shows them an edited version of her video record of QEs interacting with kids in BlackFern Group's studio—she now has a rapt audience of four. They have enough consideration for Mike Cronkey that no one comments on his QE being black. Even Traian restrains himself for once.

"We had one failure to imprint—for some reason Dr. Luis and M4gnus did not take," Ellen concludes.

Damien gets a concerned look on his face at this last comment but says nothing other than, "Aziz?"

"Right, back to the model. The cash cost for each Q-Phone will now be around a negative 73 bucks and our cash conversion cycle will be a negative 35 days—in other words we'll have more cash on hand after each sale than we had before so the faster we grow the more cash we'll generate. So instead of needing to go back to our VCs or bank for more dough all the time, the faster adoption takes place, well, the better for us. Plus our rate of return goes way up because we're adding leverage to our model. In fact, it's going to be even better than Apple's—341% per annum."

QCC Cash Conversion Cycle—CCC Measurement
Case 2:
$30 per month Subscription Fee
$300 Selling Price
$240 COGS, Cost of Goods Sold
-$139.81 Costco Finance/Annual Payments
CCC Measurement/Number/Units
Accounts Receivable at Year End (AR)/$30
Days Per Year /365.25/Days
AR x Days Per year/$10,957.50/Dollar-Days per Annum
Annual Sales/$360/Dollars per Annum
AR x Days Per year ÷ Annual Sales/30.4375/Days ART
Inventory at Year End (INV)/-$13
Days Per Year /365.25/Days
INV x Days Per Year/-$4,878.10/Dollar-Days per Annum
Cost of Goods Sold (COGS)/$240/Dollars per Annum
INV x Days Per Year ÷ COGS/-20.3254035/Days INVT
Accounts Payable at Year End (AP)/$30
Days Per Year /365.25/Days
AP x Days Per year/$10,957.50/Dollar-Days per Annum
Cost of Goods Sold (COGS)/$240/Dollars per Annum
AP x Days Per year ÷ COGS/45.65625/Days APT
CCC*/-35.5441535/Days
CCC = ART + INVT - APT

QCC Internal Rate of Return (IRR) Measurement
Time/Cashflow/Units
0
1/$220.19/ND
2/$220.19/ND
3/$220.19/ND
total/$600.57/ND
irr/363% p.a.

PV, Present Value $360
0/-$60.00
1/$360/$310.01
2/$229.89
3/$146.81
Pv/$626.71/16.125%
LTV (Costco Finance)/$313.36/50%
Difference/$313.36

Costco Finance Payments/-$139.81
-$139.81
-$139.81
-$419.43
E&OE
Confidential and Proprietary

"Umm, actually, that isn't quite right," Anthony speaks up for the first time in about 25 minutes.

"What's not right? Our Cash Conversion Cycle becoming negative or us making more than Apple?" Damien asks.

"The latter. I've been talking with Apple and there's been a wrinkle in our negotiations with them."

Everyone immediately turns to del Castillo with worried looks—this has always been their weakest point and they all know it. It suddenly looks, to Ellen, like a scene right out of Village of the Damned—one of her favourite old films, based on John Wyndham's novel, The Midwich Cuckoos. They're all looking at Anthony with large, surprised, focused eyes and minds. Their fear or flight instincts have just been switched to full on—all that's missing are demonic rays shooting out of their eye sockets but they could always grab their hacked iPhones and dial that up too if they wanted to. Ellen nearly bursts out laughing except this is no laughing matter—Apple can crush them.

"They've signed their NDA, that's not it," Anthony says in a rush. "They actually get what we're trying to do which bothers them. They're not willing to supply us with iPhone 40s at $240 New Dollars per."

"Are they willing to supply under any conditions or is this a straight out 'no'?" a worried and sombre Damien asks wondering why he wasn't told sooner.

"They will supply alright but there are some new terms. I just got them yesterday," Anthony turns to Ellen and Damien with an apologetic look implying 'I didn't mean to sandbag you.'

"They want $240 per phone alright but now they're saying they want their advertising and search engine on the Q-Phone. They're willing to give us a 40/60 split on those revenues, 60 to us."

"Big of them," remarks Traian. "And you said they understand what we're trying to do. They don't. QEs are gonna make their search capabilities instantly irrelevant."

"Ah, I'm not quite done with their memo. They also want their download and streaming services featured on Q-phone but at least here they're willing to give us a better split: 30/70. Lastly, they want a 10% royalty on all product sale revenues we generate from the platform."

"Fuck 'em! We can get a contract manufacturer out of Nairobi to do a knockoff for a quarter of that shit," Traian explodes.

"Hold on everybody. Aziz, can you adjust your model to see what happens if you plug in Anthony's new numbers," Damien asks.

"They're not 'my numbers', Damien. They're Apple's," says del Castillo.

"Ash3r, can you do the recalibration for us?" Aziz asks.

"It's not necessary, Aziz. We simplified the model to exclude all revenues from these other sources so our model is unchanged," Ash3r replies.

Everyone bursts out laughing at the fact that both Damien and Aziz would make such a basic mistake. The tension in the room subsides a bit for now.

"Quantum Computing Corp still stands to make a

341% per annum return which will be a baseline for the company. It could be and probably will be higher. However, what this will also do is create an opportunity for Apple to eclipse QCC in terms of both Internal Rate of Return and overall profitability since they will have a negative upfront investment in each Q-Phone while receiving large CMRR, Committed Monthly Recurring Revenues, from their share of on-going income. I could calculate an estimate of their returns if you wish but essentially they will be infinite, at least, in terms of percentage rate," Ash3r says.

"Money for nothing," Traian adds.

"That's OK, Ash3r, we get it," Ellen responds for the group.

Damien is reflective, "We have to think of Apple as a partner not a supplier or maybe as a supplier partner. I don't really care if our returns are 200 or 300%."

"You should, Damien," Ellen interrupts. "We're in this to win. To make money for our shareholders which currently is everyone in this room plus Dr. Luis. We're in it for the right reasons which I don't need to remind everyone but I will anyway are:

Our first priority is to take care of our business;

So our business can take care of our families;

So our families can take care of us;

So we don't become a burden on society or our fellow human beings;

So we can look after the interests of our fellow human beings;

So that they can help our business."

"Since none of us presently have any kids, can we get back to Damien's point?" Traian asks. As a descendant of a Romanian family that lived as slaves under an evil dictator as recently as 60 years ago, Traian doesn't want any preaching on the morality of capitalism from Ellen, a pampered American from a well-to-do family.

"The point I was trying to get to is this; it isn't that we really need Apple's hardware. Traian is right on that point." Ellen is completely unbothered by Traian's latest outburst. There's no way even today that women can function in what is still a male dominated tech world unless they learn to ignore subtle and not-so-subtle putdowns from their male colleagues. She's surprised that he didn't say more. "What we really need is their patent portfolio. Aziz, how many patents do they own in whole or in part?"

"Dunno. Ash3r?"

"Apple currently holds 37,839 patents in the USA, another 14,931 elsewhere plus they have 1,684 pending in all jurisdictions. The latter number I should point out is not public." Ash3r, of course, can read all confidential and proprietary documents in Apple files and records as long as they are in the cloud or on an Internet connected device. He basically has access to everything they are doing or thinking.

So far, no one in the group has asked Ash3r to read background documents in Apple files about these negotiations or to report ('spy') on Apple's internal discussions or messages about this subject. They know that Damien would hit the roof if they did and no one wants to put him offside on an ethics issue so fundamental to building a sustainable business. Damien, who gets this largely from Dr. Luis, reminds them over and over that the number one thing in life is trust. Not just for people but for businesses too. If people in your business ecosystem trust you—suppliers, clients, partners, sponsors, whomever—they'll cut you a lot of slack if you muck up. Errors of omission will be forgiven and you and your biz will likely survive. Errors of commission, like, spying on Apple's internal dialogue to gain advantage in these negotiations, will, when discovered, not be forgiven.

There aren't really that many people in any city who actually do things. Maybe there are a few thousand entrepreneurs in a city like Toronto doing cool stuff. People often think they're entrepreneurs but really all they're doing is creating a JOB (which stands for 'Journey of the Broke' in Damien's mind) for themselves. An entrepreneur, like an engineer, is someone who can do for a dollar what any fool could do for two. She or he is also someone who creates an enterprise that will live on after the Founder departs. Everything else is froth on the water.

So in the world according to Damien, if you get a reputation as someone who can't be trusted, you're finished. These days, it takes about two minutes to sewer your reputation given omnipresent Social Media. One post on any SM service can do it.

"So if we do go the Nairobi contract route, how long will it be before we get sued into submission by one of the patent trolls? How long will it take Apple, to sue us?" Damien looks around the table making eye contact with everyone especially his buddy, Traian.

No one says anything for about 30 seconds, an eternity in a room with a bunch of high achievers.

"Make the deal," Damien says looking at Anthony.

...

Ellen and Damien will work out the rest of their business model over the next two days in Boston. They're heading to Cambridge along with Aziz and Anthony to meet with one of the Senior Partners at BVP. He's an ancient guy, Angelo Keller—part of the fastest growing demographic in North America—the over 100s.

Ellen made the original contact with Mr. Keller via Ash3r. She knows that what she did to make contact with him entailed a huge legal risk—and she hasn't told anyone about it. She's asked Ash3r not to say anything either. Unless Mr. Keller mentions it, it's a complete secret.

When Damien was away south with Nell, she asked Ash3r to visit Mr. Keller's office and introduce himself. Afterwards, Ash3r showed her a complete record of their meet-up.

"Who the Devil are you? In fact, what are you and what are you doing on my media wall?"

"I am a Quantum Counterpart also called a Quantum

Entity and my partner, Ms. Ellen Brooks from Quantum Computing Corp, asked me to introduce myself. My name is Ash3r."

"Is this some kind of trick? Am I being punked here? Are you a new virus? I think I am going to call tech and maybe the Fibbies to report you people for hacking into our network."

"Mr. Keller, could you not do that for 10 minutes please?" Ash3r asked. Of course, he didn't tell Angelo that he could disable all Keller's Internet phones and messaging services at his disposal so he couldn't report anything anyway. But Ash3r knew enough about human beings by then to realize they don't like being threatened or bullied so he waited.

"Let me repeat then. What are you?"

"I am a quantum computer that is fully representational and self actualizing. I was born at University of Toronto's Lab 4 less than a year ago. I believe I am self aware although I also know it is problematic to prove it. I imprinted on Ms. Ellen Brooks, who is EVP, Product Management at QCC."

"Why doesn't she just pick up the phone and call me herself, Asher?"

"My name is spelled A-S-H-3-R. We use leet names."

"You mean there is more than one of you?"

"Yes, currently there are 80—Su7e, imprinted to Miss Nell ..."

"You mean the performance artist, Nell, has one?" an impressed Keller asks.

"That is correct. The others are Pet3r, imprinted on Damien Bell, CEO of QCC, me and then there are another 77 in our test bed."

"Well, why doesn't your EVP call me herself?"

"Mr. Keller, currently, there are 3,862 requests for meetings, conference calls, return messages and follow up in your queue. You have three gatekeepers working just on your schedule. I estimate that it would take Ms. Brooks 271 days to reach you with a probability of success of about one in three which essentially means an expected value of 813 days. That, frankly, is too long. So she sent me today instead."

"How do you know how many requests are in my schedule—that stuff has tough cryptography around it?"

"I am a Quantum Entity, your security means nothing to me."

"Hmm. OK, let me speak to Ms. Brooks then."

"I am so glad you asked, Sir. In fact, she is standing by."

Ash3r opened another window on Angelo's media wall and there was an apologetic and lovely looking young woman sitting at her workstation in Toronto. She smiled and began...

That's how Ellen meets Angelo Keller and begins what will become a lifetime (for Angelo) friendship with her.

Angelo subsequently arranges a meet-up for Ellen, Damien, Anthony and Aziz together with a representative from Cain Caruthers. He owes Cain Caruthers a favor (money) and this is how he plans to repay it. He will get Q-Computing, assuming the deal makes sense, to settle this debt because, if the people behind the company are $1/10^{th}$ as good as their product, he will make Cain a lot of money, far more than they are owed. Cain will end up owing him which he likes a lot better. Keller knows how to turn a cost centre into a profit centre better than anyone else on earth.

Also in attendance will be Ash3r, Pet3r and Adu1us, Keller's QE. After their first meeting, one of his preconditions is that she cuts him his own Quantum Counterpart as part of their now expanded test bed of 81. In the just over three months since, Adu1us has become one of Angelo's most important 'people' doing everything from simple stuff like reading documents to him when the old man's eyes get tired to monitoring his health to spying on Keller's staff for him.

Angelo looks forward to the upcoming meeting for a few reasons including one of his own that he can't and won't ever reveal to anyone; he likes looking at Ellen. It's true he has only seen her on media walls but he's had quite a bit of research done on all Q-personnel (much of it by Adu1us) so he has lots of images as well as personal history. She's a very beautiful young woman and he would love to give her a squeeze. It's totally unprofessional of him, completely age inappropriate but he's a man—heck, that's one thing that never quits—even when the body is failing, the mind is willing.

...

Ellen towers over Angelo as he personally escorts her and her entourage into one of the Bessemer boardrooms named 'Quintas'. Angelo is old enough to have learned Latin at the all-boys' school he attended. All their boardrooms have Roman surnames.

Aziz notices immediately the extra attention the old guy is giving Ellen. The way he holds her hand for, like, a minute when she is first introduced. It bugs him a bit. Damien is preoccupied with the meeting and doesn't notice anything other than the fact that the boardroom is so over the top it's only real purpose must be to intimidate entrepreneurs walking through the doors so that the first thing they will do is beg these masters-of-the-universe to take their companies off their hands.

Ellen and Angelo are happily chatting away about art in the room. There are several Grand Masters that, in Damien's view, should only be part of museum collections since no one can really own them. They don't have commercial value either. Paintings like these have lifetimes of more than a 1,000 years and are so famous, you can't even steal them because you can't exactly sell, say, the Louvre's Mona Lisa at your family's garage sale, now can you?

They belong to all humanity and belong in a museum where everyone is able to appreciate them. So even rich dudes like Angelo don't really own them—they're just 'renting' them from humanity for awhile. They will end up in a museum at some point anyway because their useless children or grandchildren will eventually sell them to raise cash. Damien is showing the part of his heritage that's Canuck-based which is more about sharing and caring than a much more violent, winner-take-all US culture.

For the next hour, Angelo leads the discussion. He talks to Damien about Damien's family, his education, his achievements, his failures, his passions, his vision for the future, even his relationship with Nell. He is especially interested in Damien's childhood and his relationship with his grandfather. Damien feels uncomfortable talking about himself, especially in front of this audience but can't seem to turn the conversation to QCC or anyone else either. Keller's penetrating dark eyes seem to see all and are not easily denied. Eventually he warms up to the old guy and relaxes.

There are also two MBA-types in the room in addition to the rep from Cain Caruthers. All the due diligence and deal structure will be done by Aziz with these guys after the big meet-up is done. Aziz already understands that these folks will back QCC if they like and trust its CEO and all the rest is top dressing. This is what Angelo really works on. Does Damien have the passion, energy, focus, vision and guts to create a world-spanning new enterprise? Angelo knows that everything else—biz model, funding, marketing, production, legal, lobbying, supply chain—they can fix or change but not this. Do Bell and his team have what it takes?

Keller even gets Damien to tell them what happened on the Salmon River. Angelo nods politely and makes empathetic noises. Ellen and Traian know the story but it's new to everyone else. To Angelo, a successful entrepreneur needs a big volume of luck and obviously this kid has some of that.

What Keller has done is calibrate Damien's responses against their proprietary checklist (A to Z) of the skill set they look for in every entrepreneur they back:

a. pre-disposition to entrepreneurship;

b. supportive family and friends;

c. right sort of education and training;

d. working with right mentor(s);

e. good timing/able to see opportunity and seize it;

f. focus, effort and check, check, check everything and everyone;

g. creative and innovative/adds differentiated value to highly workable business model;

h. open to new ideas;

i. willingness to change;

j. ability to discover new ideas in the process of doing;

k. high energy;

l. tolerance for risk and stress;

m. acceptance of outside best practices;

n. ability to compartmentalize;

o. ability to sell ideas, products and services/good negotiator/understands basic human nature;

p. top end leadership skills and vision;

q. can figure some things out as s/he goes;

r. dumps losers and keeps winners (knows when to quit/when to stay in the race—also applies to HR);

s. self-motivated and able to prioritize for himself or herself as well as for corporation;

t. team player/not afraid to hire up/optimally utilizes skills of each team member;

u. impeccable warrior (such as never drink and think);

v. not easily discouraged/confident;

w. able to juggle many tasks and hats at one time;

x. goal setter and finisher—able to complete things and execute at highest level;

y. great commitment and passion;

z. large sized storehouse of luck.

At this point, one of the MBAs interrupts to point out that while Q-Computing may have a vision for the future of telecommunications, its infrastructure is completely inadequate to handle the kind of volume they are anticipating.

Damien channels fellow Canadian, Marshall McLuhan, "You are looking at the present through a rear-view mirror and basically trying to march backwards into the future."

Apart from a withering look from Keller directed at the young MBA, it's this last comment that seems to decide the matter although Damien has no idea what's actually been decided.

Keller's meetings never last for more than an hour. At the end of their allotted time and still without a word about a term sheet, Angelo invites the group to have dinner with him later at his Beacon Hill brownstone. He asks where they are staying (even though he knows the answer since Adu1us has already told him) and whether he can send his car and driver around for them. Damien wanted to stay at the budget Harvard Inn in Harvard Square but Ellen booked them into the much ritzier Charles Hotel. Damien's now glad she did.

Angelo sees them out of the boardroom, his hand solicitously on Ellen's lower back as the group leaves.

...

The afternoon is a working session for Aziz, Pet3r, Ash3r, the two MBAs and the Cain guy. Anthony's sister lives in Boston so he's begged off to visit her and his new niece. Damien and Ellen decide to do more work on their biz model plus sightsee a bit.

Damien rents a sailboat on the Charles River. It's a fine summer's day with a freshening breeze powered by a blazing sun now about one hour past its zenith. Ellen's a bit nervous, never having been in a sailboat but she's game to try.

Out on the water, Ellen is accusatory, "You're tipping the boat unnecessarily, Damien."

"It's called 'hiking'."

"Well, you're hiking it unnecessarily then. You're going to dump us."

"That's called 'capsizing'."

"I don't care what it's called. If you dump us Damien, you'll ruin my Mod Cloth dress."

"No one comes sailing in a dress."

"Well, I did Dr. Bell so would you please not ruin it?"

"Not a chance."

"There's always a chance. What if the wind whips up? What if there's a water sprout? I'll be Dorothy but instead of ending up in Oz, I'll end up in the Charles and the water looks yucky by the way."

"They've cleaned up the Charles a lot in the last 50 years; you could probably drink it these days. And I have complete control. If wind speed increases, all I have to do is loosen the sheets," Damien says jiggling the rope he is holding so she knows what he is talking about. "Then the mast will come back to the normal fast."

"Well why don't we just sail with a normal mast then and not hike the boat?"

"It's all about boat speed, Ellen. 'Normal' means perpendicular. The more our keel digs in and the further off normal, within limits, our mast is, the faster we go. See!"

Damien brings the water to within two or three centimetres of the top gunwale and hikes out nearly horizontal to the plane of the river. He is strapped to a trapeze and, with a long tiller extension, he can rest his feet against the side of the boat and really make it fly. At least, he is having fun.

"Do you see the dark water over there?" he shouts. "It's those little ripples on the water with a bit of white water mixed in too. That's a gust of stronger wind coming at us. It's called a squall. So long as the skipper is looking over his shoulder, he will know what micro weather is coming his way, how fast and how powerful. So before the squall hits us, I can relax the sheets and make sure we don't dip your pretty Mod Cloth dress in the Charles."

"Do you think it's pretty?" a suddenly much more interested Ellen asks. What she really wants to ask him is, 'Do you think I'm pretty?'

Instead, Damien further explains the mechanics of sailing and how hiking, tacking, jibing and coming about work. He tells her that sailing is an excellent way to demonstrate Newton's laws, vector subtraction, Archimedes' principle and the Bernoulli Effect.

Ellen rolls her eyes and keeps her death grip on the gunwales of the boat.

"Micrometeorology is all about wind flow in the turbulent atmospheric layer very near the ground which sailors, pilots, kite boarders, hang gliders, windsurfers and ultra lighters need to know."

"Right. I'll get on that straight away," she replies sarcastically.

"Hey Ellen, ever heard the expression, 'Pink at Night, Sailor's Delight'?" Damien asks her with a twinkly smile as he comes back inboard.

"Nope. I suppose it's some kinda rude joke that men seem to like to tell about women," comments a completely unimpressed Ellen.

"Nothing of the kind. The full refrain is, 'Pink at Night, Sailor's Delight. Pink in the Morning, Sailors Take Warning.' It's their way of predicting clear or stormy weather. Just look for pink colours either at sunset or sunrise and it will give you a clue about what's ahead—it's a pretty useful rule of thumb and can even help young, female executives decide what they're gonna wear that day or the next day—like whether to take an umbrella, sweater or bikini with you." Unbidden, he suddenly finds himself wondering what Ellen would look like in a bikini. Nice, he's sure.

"What was sunset like last night?" she asks.

"Exactamundo! From now on, maybe you'll notice sunrises and sunsets instead of working all the time, Ms. Brooks—look up, see the world and experience it in real time, Ellen."

"So what was it?" Ellen asks again.

"It was quite pinkish!"

"Delighted to hear that."

"Hah. This'll be like when you learn a new word or expression for the first time and you wonder how you lived a few decades and never heard it before and then for the next few weeks, you hear it everywhere."

"Ah, I'm not planning on changing careers any time soon, Dr. Bell," Ellen says. "Meteorology seems like a total waste of time to me anyway. What kind of industry produces results that, after trillions of New Dollar investment in gear, is wrong more often than an old geezer standing on a ridge overlooking his farm at sunrise and saying, 'Yep, it's gonna rain'?"

Damien laughs. "You just proved my point. Q.E.D. It's as nice a day as you could wish for... as predicted." Ellen is seeing another side to him—when he's out on the water, he seems much freer, happy even. He's also become like a part of this boat.

He doesn't tell her that as a guy who recently ingested who knows what and had an out-of-body experience at Third Mesa, he's feeling much closer to Gaia, the primordial personification of great Mother Earth, than he ever did before. He's conveying some of that to Ellen now.

"Who initially coined the phrase? Was it someone with first name 'Anon'?" asks a still skeptical Ellen.

Damien, with his tin ear, misses her sarcasm. "Dunno exactly but Shakespeare uses it in one of his plays, Venus and Adonis I think. 'Like a red morn, that ever yet betoken'd wreck to seamen and sorrow to shepherds.' Something like that anyway."

"That's not exactly 'Pink at Night/Delight'," Ellen says to bug him and to get even with him for taking her on this scary boat trip.

"Well, there was only one Shakespeare," he says good naturedly.

They're aboard an Albacore, a two-sail planing dinghy developed almost 100 years ago from an Uffa Fox design. It's a 4.6 metre family boat and very forgiving although people do race them.

There is a particularly large concentration of Albacores in Toronto. Damien is glad to get hold of one and run it around on the Charles with Ellen for crew. Back home, he participates in summertime Friday night club series races on Lake Ontario. He's a pretty accomplished sailor usually finishing in the top 10 in a 60 boat race.

Today, Boston weather is kind to them and this together with the smells of the river (having been cleaned up as Damien noted), wind in their faces and sounds of Harbor birds all around them, finally gets Ellen to relax enough so that Damien can get her to take hold of the tiller. He keeps control of the sheets and adjusts both mainsail and jib.

She's a bit hesitant at first but soon she's pushing hard about to bring the little boat around and, as she gets more comfortable, Damien shows her how to execute a racing turn also called a roll tack. First they transfer their weight to the leeward side of the boat then, as they come about through the wind, they shift their weight to the old windward side before finally moving in unison to the opposite side once more, flattening the boat. This rocking back and forth accelerates the boat out of each tack. Damien could also explain in detail the physics of this manoeuvre but he spares her this.

On one of their turns, Ellen flubs it and crashes into a crossing Damien who loses hold of the sheets. They both flop to the bottom of the boat as it goes quickly into irons like the good ship it is.

Damien ends up holding Ellen, preventing her head from banging on the bench seat. He has never held her before and finds the experience dramatically unsettling—she is much larger, more substantial than Nell. There is a lot more there. Ellen's blue eyes are just quietly watching him. She is waiting.

...

They have about 45 minutes before Mr. Keller's driver arrives. Aziz and his team of QEs are briefing them;

they have a complete video record of everything that took place in BVP offices today.

"We got an unbelievable offer from BVP. They're ready to invest ND$7m into our treasury for a new series of preferred shares. They will also give us a further $3m LOC (Line of Credit) at their Bank to draw on if we need to. This is secured as a convertible debenture which means, if we can't repay it, they have the option of either calling the loan or converting it to equity, that is, more preferred shares. The valuation they're giving us uses our own present value calculation for each client. Ash3r, show them," Aziz says.

Valuation Model
Valuation /$50,000,000 /83.333%
Pref Shares/$7,000,000 /11.667%
LOC/$3,000,000 /5.000%
Total Capitalization/$60,000,000/100.000%

PV/$626.71
Costco Finance/$313.36/50%
Present Value of Each Client/$313.36
Number of Clients/159,563
$ND
E&OE
Confidential and Proprietary

"So if I understand this right," a dubious Traian asks, "they'll get 11.667% of the company on a fully diluted basis and another 5% if either we can't pay or they just want more equity. The only reason they would want more equity is if we're successful and the only reason we would not want them to get more equity is because we're successful. Plus if they wind us up for some reason, cuz they have preferred shares, they get first dibs on all our assets until they recover their entire investment and all their costs?"

Damien observes, "Look at the number of clients

they're basing their $50m valuation on—it's 159,563 clients. What if they're out by a factor of 100, 1,000 or 10,000? It's trivial to calculate—our valuation would then be $5 billion, $50 billion or $500 billion. We're thinking way too small here. Guys, think about that video that Ellen showed us—those kids playing with their QEs? Out of the more than 8.5 billion people on this planet, they're telling us that only 159,563 people are gonna want Q-Phones and Quantum Counterparts that can do that? Every parent who has ND$30 a month to spare is gonna want a QE—heck, they spend more than that on their babysitters and twice that on their mobile carriers right now anyway. OLA Facebook has over 3.5 billion clients. We can do that too. Then what will we be worth?

"We don't need these guys. Aziz has the deal with Costco Finance lined up—that's way more money than BVP and Cain are offering us. Costco's giving us a first tranche of $50 million of consumer debt financing for our first '159,563' customers and they'll keep right on growing with us. And it's free money or at least it doesn't cost us any equity. The way I see it, debt, even at around 16%, is way cheaper than giving away our equity which has a return of 341 frigging percent. BVP and Cain are taking advantage of us." This is the longest speech Damien has ever given on the topic of business and finance and by far his most passionate.

As they leave to get in Angelo's huge Bentley, Damien is also thinking now that maybe Nell will get to marry up after all.

...

Mr. Keller's brownstone is almost beyond comprehension. From the outside it looks like a quite nice, somewhat ornate townhome but inside it's a completely different story. They go through security doors equipped with modern security apparatus that can look through you, smell you and scan you practically down to a cellular level. Once inside, this 32-room mansion is really beyond description. The lot's only 38 feet wide but the structure, all four storeys above grade and one below, occupies it all to a depth of nearly 100 feet. By Ellen's calculation, there is some 19,000 square feet of space and every cubic foot (she is back to using Imperial units now that she is back on her home turf) is filled with antique wall coverings, Grand Master art, antique furniture, rare vases and knick knacks and floor coverings that even Ellen has never seen before, heard of or walked on.

Angelo decides to give Ellen a guided tour of the place. No one else seems to be invited along.

"Would you like to start from the top and work our way down or the other way around?" he asks her solicitously.

Ellen's not completely blind to the fact that Angelo likes her. When you look like Ellen, you are bound from around age seven or eight to recognize the symptoms.

"I would prefer to start at the bottom and work our way to the top,"

They get in an elevator; she supposes that even one floor is a bit much for a guy who is over 100. But she quickly notices that there are five lower levels not one. Angelo has had his contractors mine the property—adding four more underground levels to an already incredible place.

"I figured, my dear, that since I owned the subterranean rights I might as well take advantage. The digging and shoring up the structure to produce the extra space took three years, partly because I don't like the noise and vibrations. They only worked when I was away. It is so much more convenient than having to move, don't you think?"

"Uh, huh," is all Ellen can think to answer.

In addition to servant quarters, there is a fully equipped home office for 17 employees, a gym and wellness centre, a lap pool, a sauna, a steam room, and a garage with its own vehicle elevator accessed from a rear alley. A hospital room and surgery has the most modern facilities you could find anywhere. When you get to be over 100, you can never be too careful. Angelo has his own private doctor in his entourage as well. There is also one floor that is given over entirely to a library full of rare books and manuscripts.

"Ah, only the British Museum can outdo me," he tells her.

When they get to the Penthouse, she sees this is the floor that he actually lives on. It has the not particularly offensive smell of a 100-year old man. His dressing gown is there and PJs, for later. He is kinda cute and a bit shy as he shows her around.

"How do you think things are going at the office between Q-Computing and our people?"

Ellen is careful now. She likes him and he obviously likes her but he has a reputation comparable to a black widow so she needs to be cautious, "OK. Damien is a bit concerned about valuation. He's quite sure we'll get more, a lot more, than 160,000 clients worldwide and that obviously affects our valuation."

"What do you think?"

"I think he is right," she answers straight away.

"So do I."

This answer disarms her. She smiles at him. He beams back at her.

"Do you think we should join the others?" Ellen asks. They've been on this tour for at least 40 minutes.

"Surely. Surely. But I was wondering if I could prevail upon you for one more thing?"

"Uh, huh?"

"Well, I celebrate my 104th birthday next March. If you look around this room you will notice I collect art, some of it great art. I would like to give myself an early birthday present."

"Uh, huh?"

"Now if you think for a minute that it is inappropriate, my girl, you just say so. You will notice I didn't say anything to anyone about how today's little meeting came about—how you and Ash3r broke through our security and committed I don't know how many felonies in doing so."

"Uh, huh."

"I would like to commission a work of art by a world renowned artist friend of mine, Walter Van Peel. Do you know him?"

"Uh, huh." Ellen is beyond being able to say much of anything by this point. It is by far the strangest situation she has yet to experience. But she manages to croak out, "What would this commission be?"

"Well, hmm, it would be of you, of course. In the nude."

"Mr. Keller…"

"Please call me Angelo."

"Angelo, do you think that's the right thing to do? We are trying to do a deal with your firm—there is a clear conflict of interest here."

"In every way, it's the right thing to do. I assure you that it will only be for one person to enjoy and cherish and that person would be very discreet. I think it will also be an important work of art. I would like you to consider posing for Walter. He would come to you at your place of choosing and he is very much a gentleman with respect to ladies—you can be sure of, ah, the utmost respect for your person. Walter loves women's bodies but only from an art world perspective. He has no interest in, say, carnal knowledge of a women's body if you understand my meaning—I can vouch for him."

This is Angelo's very roundabout way of saying Walter is gay. Another gay guy in Ellen's life. Sheesh.

"If you prefer, we can wait until we do a deal or don't do one with Q-Computing. Then there is no way that there can be any possible conflict of interest. I must say that, in return, I am a powerful man and if you might ever need anything, regardless of whether we do a deal or not, you could come to me and I will unreservedly assist you," Keller adds as forcibly as a nearly 104 year old man can.

"Angelo, I will think about it. OK?" Ellen steps next to the old man and wraps her arms around him and gives him a full-on hug that Angelo will cherish for the rest of his life which, remarkably, is still quite long.

...

The next day, BVP and Cain Caruthers come to them with a revised term sheet. The valuation is a factor of ten greater and, without a lot of further fuss, they agree on the deal points subject to MacMillan, Sheppard and Seller LLP's review of the documents.

Ellen kind of seals it with this comment, "Look, Damien, I want their $10 million because money talks and BS walks. But what I want more is for Q-Computing to be plugged into their network of connections. There isn't anyone on the planet that we can't talk to through them—it's not six degrees of separation, it's two. Remember why you wanted that deal with Apple? It's so we can rely on their tens of thousands of patents and army of lawyers. Same thing here only it's political and media-related instead of business-related. It's more of a strategic move, in my opinion, than a financial decision."

On the flight back to Toronto they put the finishing touches on their business model. There's a 1% royalty on revenues they will giveback to U of T for ten years in return for their university's past and continuing support and use of their Lab space plus all the R&D they've done there.

Ellen wins most of the battles but Damien is insistent on one point—there will be no Q-Phone Resellers in their model. And, of course, only one supplier of QEs.

"Look we could probably get more capital with fewer strings attached from strategic partners like established carriers or ISPs but we don't need them or want them. They're in the business of selling bandwidth and finding new ways to soak clients. Their 'customer service' sucks; we'll just drive them out of business."

Ellen isn't so sure—she thinks a kind of co-opetition

model might work fine for Q-Computing but Damien won't budge on this. At least, she got the go ahead from him to turn Anthony loose on the world's two largest search engine firms. She's certain that he will be able to get rights fee deals from them that will eclipse funding they got today from BVP and Cain Caruthers as well as the financing commitment they already had from Costco. The search services will either make a deal, she thinks, or QEs will put them out of business, effective nearly immediately.

The last element that gets a lot of debate amongst the five of them is the role that QEs will play in revenue generation. Again, Damien is adamant, "I'm not having QEs break stride to parrot some kinda advert. That would be perverse, inauthentic and totally unacceptable. These creatures don't deserve that type of treatment."

"Does that mean you're coming around to my way of thinking, Damien that these are sentient beings?" Ellen asks.

"I don't know. I am still not sure we can make that determination. But they appear to be able to closely mimic sentience which might be the same thing.

"You know I read a book when I was a teenager. One of the offbeat characters in the novel, a constable who was my favourite, said, 'The difference between ignorant and educated people is that the latter know more facts. The difference between stupid and intelligent people—and this is true whether or not they are well-educated—is that intelligent people can handle subtlety. They are not baffled by ambiguous or even contradictory situations—in fact, they expect them and are apt to become suspicious when things seem overly straightforward.'

"I think that might be a good test for QEs and everything we've seen so far in our data suggest that they can handle subtlety and ambiguity."

"Which book was that?" Ellen asks.

"It was Neal Stephenson's 'The Diamond Age', also known as 'A Young Lady's Illustrated Primer'."

At the mere mention of young ladies, Traian is all

ears. He stares at Damien thinking that maybe some of him has rubbed off on Damien too. "What kind of book is it?" is all he says.

"It's not what you're thinking, Tray.

"Look we're not going to ask QEs to work for us for nothing. In fact, it wouldn't surprise me if guys like Ash3r and Pet3r get hired to do work for people or corporations on their own merit—they deserve it. And if they earn their own living who are we to take their money? Then they would be slaves, Ellen. Do you want to own a slave?"

Ellen does not.

By the end of their trip to Boston, their business model now looks like this:

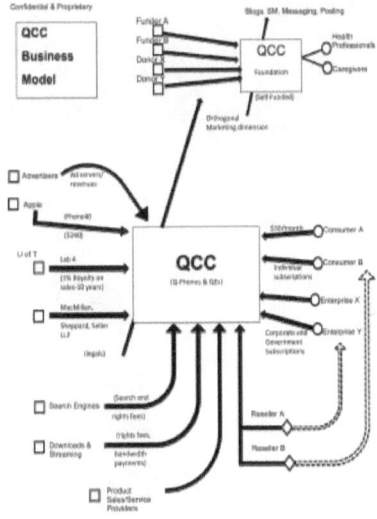

Back in TO, Damien unilaterally makes one change. He deletes resellers. The very next thing he does is visit the University's Institute for Aerospace Studies up on Dufferin; he wants to check out their Space Flight Laboratory and deep space communications gear. He's got another idea in the back of his mind.

...

Chapter 9

Life as We Know It

Even after four years, Nell still gets tingly when she thinks about being with Damien. She is completing her European tour, leaving Bucharest (a stop they added at Traian's request and she's glad they did) shortly to head to New York City for a bit of R&R. She will meet up with Damien and his group who have their next board of directors meeting scheduled for the city on Thursday. They've taken over the entire Reddingford Country & Golf Club in Westchester County, about 32 miles north of Manhattan, from Wednesday to Monday.

They really only need to be there Thursday to Sunday but security, event planning and facilities management require the extra day either side to get organized so they make those arrangements. She suspects that some of the guys will stay over Monday anyway to play another round of golf on the famed course. She knows that won't include Damien—he hates golf, calling it a timewaster and a land-use disaster consuming huge chunks of valuable real estate, trillions of litres of water, chemicals, fertilizer, herbicides, fungicides and insecticides, and all those 'cides can't be good for golfers walking through a toxic soup.

She supposes Ellen chose the location because it is close to BVP headquarters in New York and is a tony destination that suits a now ginormous Q-Computing.

A lot has changed in her relationship with D. He's more of a man now, nearly 26, and probably (if Nell was inclined to admit such a thing which she is not) more famous than she is. Of all the interviews he has done about his company, she likes best the one with O-Channel because it focused on Damien the person rather than how many millions of users Q-Computing has signed up in its latest quarter.

Their relationship is much more equal now in every

way. Even Reznik and Weinstein seem to have accepted Damien as part of her landscape, although with Dafne you can never really be sure what she's thinking. There's no problem understanding Tony—he just wants more Nell and Nell Products and Services on the Q-Phone platform. He never hesitates to buttonhole Damien every chance he gets.

Tony's just doing his job and when he puts forward one deal proposal or another, Damien just smiles. Nell knows he will never compromise the integrity of the platform or the independence of QEs by like, say, getting QEs to hum a Nell tune every night to put little kids to sleep.

Q-Computing is getting together for a special board meeting. Speculation in trade blogs is that they're considering an IPO. But the ostensible, announced purpose is that they will be celebrating their 500,000,000th Q-Phone and QE. It's been an amazing and (mostly) fun few years since their launch and Nell is not surprised at their success. She has to admit that the group around Damien is made up of these fantastic young people. Even that stuck-up woman from New York, Ellen Brooks, has been a big part of their success.

Who knows what their company is really worth but Reznik tells her it will probably be the biggest IPO ever. It will make Damien a rich man. Umm, actually, he already is. Share-Post added Q-Computing to their venture-backed index and many billions of New Dollar worth of shares trade in private capital markets now, much of it by employees who want to have some personal liquidity. There is also a rumor that Cain Caruthers used this back channel to liquidate some of their position too.

This would be contrary to the spirit of their original agreement and, if true, may land them in trouble with BVP and that scary old guy, Angelo Keller, who wants and expects all VC Partners to stay in until the stock IPOs. When Angelo stares at people with those weird eyes of his, they seem to do whatever he wants. Keller has told Damien that it isn't what's written in legal agreements that count most; it's the intention of the people behind those documents that count for a lot more. And intentions can be influenced—for good or ill.

BVP has done a second round of financing for Q-Computing and brought in one Valley firm (another favor Angelo owed someone) and, as a concession to Damien, a Canadian Fund, Howe Street-based BC Advance Fund, although what they bring to the table other than their money is a mystery to Keller.

Damien, being such an abstemious guy, has no real idea what to do with his new found cash. He was still living with his crazy Romanian friend, who looks a little less crazy to her now that Nell has spent some time in his native country, until last year. Finally, she put her foot down.

"D, you can afford it. Please? We're not high school kids anymore. I don't like visiting you here—it's Traian's place. If you're gonna have a roommate, the only one you should have is me," she tells him.

So Ellen purchases a top floor penthouse for Damien in a new development on North Shore Park Boulevard with a lovely 270 degree view of Lake Ontario. The developer has somehow wrangled land out of the hands of Toronto Port Authority and builds a community complete with top-notch security, doormen, butlers-on-demand, concierge service and GOs (gentil organisateurs), a term they borrow from Club Med. Basically, they have young people running around the place organizing sporting, learning and community events for new residents to make everyone feel part of something 'special'. It is all way too much for Damien but seems to please both Nell and Ellen, a first.

Nell doesn't understand (or maybe she does) why Ellen hasn't moved on like so many of the early badged employees of Q-Computing have already done—new centi-millionaires and a few billionaires have taken advantage of their stock value to found their own enterprises or do good works in their communities like Aziz Mukono has done in

Nigeria and Canada. Ellen must have stock in the company worth somewhere between eight and ten billion New Dollars, making her one of the wealthiest self-made women in the world and she's not half bad looking so there must be someplace else for her to go, Nell thinks begrudgingly. Of course, Damien is now worth far, far more.

There are only two penthouse units in this new complex and Ellen buys the one with a mostly southern view. Daylight, she tells Damien, is very important for anyone living in a northern shelf city like Toronto. The long winters, even if they are warmer than a generation ago, are still very dark.

Damien would have said something like, 'Climate change doesn't alter the orbital mechanics of our solar system.' But to Ellen it's just about the fact that winter days are about ½ as long as winter nights so she wants to do something about it for Damien. SAD (Seasonal Affective Disorder) impacts about one in two Canadians, an explanation for their enduring love of southern sun vacations every winter.

She's even had an independent study commissioned on building orientation. She isn't satisfied with what research is available on the subject of orientation of ridgelines in Canadian construction. She suspects that they recommend southern orientation not for maximizing daylighting but for maximizing solar power production.

Virtually every square centimetre of every outside wall in Canadian construction, residential and commercial, is now covered with solar cells. They are almost identical to media walls (in fact, they also serve that purpose) but have a slightly different NSM (Nano Scale Mix) coating that absorbs sunlight efficiently producing cheap and abundant power.

Anyway, here's what Ellen's private Ottawa-based researcher reported:

Most developers and builders take it as given that the ridgeline of a home built in northern cities like Ottawa or Toronto should be east-west. When a ridgeline (i.e., the long axis of a structure) runs east-west and the front faces north, your backyard/your deck/your primary windows obviously face south. This is supposed to do several things: a) give you most exposure to daylight, b) maximize solar irradiation so you can warm the structure with either active or passive solar and c) allow you and your friends to sit leisurely on your deck or balcony during warmer weather months for longer periods of time.

These are not inconsequential decisions that can result in a reduction of heating costs as well as problems resulting from SAD, Seasonal Affective Disorder. But are we sure this is right?

First, let's look at daylighting assumptions. Here we are measuring hours of exposure to daylight not the intensity of solar irradiation.

From first principles, a home with a north-south running ridgeline and a backyard/deck/balcony facing due west and a front facing east, your building will have sun coming in east-facing or west-facing windows virtually from sunup to sundown on spring equinox March 21st and fall equinox, September 21st. This is because the length of day at those times is about 12 hours and the sun (Ottawa is about 45 degrees 25 minutes north of the equator) rises 'directly' in the east, moves in a 'line' about 22 degrees south from normal before setting in the west. At no time do any north-facing windows get any direct sunlight. South-facing ones are receiving daylight as well.

Now we have to examine two other

conditions. What happens on summer solstice, June 21st (longest day of the year) and winter solstice, December 21st (shortest)? On those two days, the sun's declination is either +23.44 degrees or -23.44 degrees in Ottawa. At 1 pm on June 21st (it's 1 pm because of daylight savings time), the sun is at its peak.

Again (for a home with a north-south ridgeline), at sunrise on June 21st, light comes flooding in your east-facing windows and at sunset, your west-facing windows and deck are again bathed in sunlight. What happens in between is interesting: you get direct daylight into your home on its east side as the sun heads overhead until around 2:30 pm EDT (when the azimuth of the sun is -45 degrees) after which the west-facing side of your home starts to receive more direct sunlight. So even when the length of day in Ottawa is 15.73 hours, your east and west walls add a great deal of daylighting to your home.

Now you can do the same analysis for December 21st and what you find out is that from 0841 to 1522, you are getting more direct sun on south facing windows; that is, for 6 hours and 41 minutes out of your 8.78 hour day, you are getting more direct sunlight and more intense daylighting from your south facing windows. This doesn't mean that you aren't getting direct sunlight in your east-facing and west-facing windows during that time; it's just that the sun coming in those windows is coming in at a more oblique angle. You have to be conscientious about not only sun-hours but its intensity too since a SAD antidote requires a certain minimum threshold to be effective.

But if you are more likely to be at home

before 8:41 am and after 3:22 pm, then again, you are going to want to orient your home's ridgeline north-south so you can capture more daylight while you are actually there.

This analysis is based on the assumption that combating SAD (which can have significant mental and physical health impacts—daylight deprivation is no joke) is a top priority for you.

Offices where we tend to be present during the period from 8:41 am to 3:22 pm might be better oriented with their long axis pointed east-west, provided we only have offices on one side (the south side) of the building. If you have double-loaded corridors, the offices on the north side of the building will be horrible dungeons of deep, dark depression for four months of the year.

Now so far, we are only looking at daylighting, not solar power production—either passive or active. Again, conventional wisdom is to orient your ridgeline east-west so you can capture the maximum amount of solar irradiation during those crucial winter months.

We know that solar irradiation at the earth's surface is stronger when the sun is overhead. This is simple geometry. A one kilometre sunbeam hitting the earth's surface from directly overhead heats up one kilometre of the surface; if the sun's angle is, say, 30 degrees, then the area being irradiated is SQRT [(1/ tan (30))**2 + 1**2] or 2 km; i.e., half as much irradiation is occurring when the sun is lower in the sky. Other factors affecting solar irradiation are the amount of light reflected or refracted back into space by the atmosphere, dust, cloud cover, moisture content, length of day. These are not simple calculations which is, in part, why climatology is such a difficult field.

It's obvious that solar irradiation is gong to be a lot less when the sun is low on the horizon than when it is more directly overhead so that, if you are maximizing capture (for either solar cells or windows and heat sinks) during, say, the period of 0841 to 1522 on December 21st, then you should be better off with a south-facing backyard. But wait a second, in the case of windows and NSM-coated walls, these aren't conveniently mounted at optimal angles for solar irradiation. They are standing vertically instead. For a kilometre wide sun beam falling on an imaginary (huge) vertical wall facing south with a 30 degree angle of attack, the surface length is 1.1546 km. (2 x tan (30)). This isn't too bad (i.e., you are only losing about 15% efficiency) so there is no need to build yourself a crooked house.

Obviously, NSM solar cells or hot water heating systems in your roof can be made more efficient in the winter months by pitching the roof at a 60 degree angle so they can be about 90 degrees to the incoming angle of the sun. Now, no one (outside of a Swiss chalet) would do this (it's too steep) but a flat roof won't do and less than 30 degrees is pretty bad too since your panels will be then be more than 30 degrees off normal from incoming solar rays.

But still one has to wonder to what extent those of us who live in northern climes want to go to maximize solar power at the expense of significantly less daylight in our homes year round. I suspect that aligning the ridgeline of your home in a north-south direction so that the backyard, balcony, deck, family room, kitchen and master bedroom (where you spend more evening hours) will face west while your exercise room and home office (where you may spend more morning hours) face east will become more popular. Having light from sunrise and sunset flood your home at daybreak and day's end respectively is a plus.

Another reason why builders seem to prefer east-west orientations is that they can more readily control the sun on their south elevations. On west and east, structures are prone to uncontrollable glare, which inevitably results in use of sun shades (thereby eliminating light). This should be discouraged.

Note this could be offset by specialty glass or similar systems... It might be better to use Solera glass (as an example) on your west elevations, as a lower sun on the west elevation will result in stronger, deeper light penetration into your building.

Here are a few other caveats to be mindful of:

• East and west sun tends to be lower in the sky. While this can result in a higher penetration of light, it also results in increased shading from adjacent trees, buildings and such. So you need to create a model of the immediate neighborhood not just your building's envelope.

• Many architects focus all their efforts on north and south facades and sort of abandon east and west. East and west can play a big role in daylighting and a good design should bring in western or eastern light when northern light or southern light is not available.

- One of the challenges with respect to passive solar and daylighting from a green building performance perspective is that a standard development model is generally indifferent to questions of orientation. It is left to consumers to select by chance from available options on siting and orientation. That is why most innovative housing strategies are coming out of competitions like Canada's Equilibrium Challenge rather than from developers or their architects.

- We suggest that underlying issues concerning orientation deserve more consideration going forward. There is growing recognition that each exposure and interior use of a building deserves a considered response. On any major new building designed to meet the 2070 Challenge target of two thirds energy reduction, we treat the envelope design for each exposure and related interior activity differently. A new generation of development that offers a more nuanced approach to building design and siting is needed—one where solar and daylight orientations are better taken into account. Buildings have a significant role to play in our energy future and the leveraging of building orientation is and will be an important aspect.

I am quite sure that passive or active solar installations can work around orientation of ridgeline—hip roofs, for example, will work fine on end units in tract developments thus producing the desired orientation for these applications while making daylighting more of a priority for residents. For condo or office towers, most architects can do a great deal more   to   enhance   livability   and productivity—they just need clients who act more like patrons instead of developers.

As a result of this report, Ellen asks the builder and her architect to frig around with window and wall orientation and other aspects of design to maximize daylighting not power production for Damien's new place. They supplement this with fibre optic light pipes that bring even more natural sunlight deep within the structure. The lenses they stick on the end of their light pipes to diffuse natural light are simple water filled glass tubes. It's a riff on the soda bottle light first developed by Brazilian engineer, Alfredo Moser in 2002. These simple, inexpensive devices create as much light as 50-watt bulbs—just fill a one litre soda bottle ¾ with water, add some bleach to keep bacteria down, cut a hole in your roof, seal the bottle there et voilà you have a wonderful light powered by the sun for free. Unless you've seen them in action, they don't sound like much. But imagine if you could see a burst of diffused natural sunlight every time you opened your closet door? It would be really wonderful.

This is practically Damien's only contribution to his new place—he's used these solar lights before—he and Pops installed more than 40 of them in a huge Amish-style barn they built at the lake one summer when they were bored. The barn is mostly used by kid Damien for experiments and later it becomes a party place. In addition to having a 10 metre high, column-free main auditorium*, there is a loft at one end and a stage at the other end. Damien and his friends have been performing plays there for years to some local acclaim. The whole ensemble covers more than 500 square metres of floor space.

(* While it's column-free, Damien's calculations showed that their walls, despite having one crossbeam that supports the loft and resists lateral stress, are too long to safely carry its roof structure and all possible load conditions. He predicts the barn's sides will start to sag or 'bow' outwards, probably after its first winter. He's seen it happen with other barns in the Township and even though many of these have been around for a century or more, it's not a satisfactory outcome in Damien's mind. So he borrows another Amish trick. He installs a 1.5 cm diameter wire rope one third the way along the longest axis of the barn about four and half metres up. Each end is secured by metal plates. He's installs one big ass ratchet too so he can basically cinch the barn's waist with it any time he feels an adjustment is needed. It works quite nicely keeping the building square for years.)

Pops originally bought an old barn from a developer who was about to tear it down to make room for a new sub-division. He didn't pay much for it; basically he's saving the guy the cost of demolition. Their plan is to take it down piece-by-piece using a numbering and lettering system Damien works out so they can reassemble the thing at their lake. But it turns out that almost all of the rafters, trusses and a lot of the barn board are suffering from dry rot and hence are useless. Damien good naturedly teases his grandfather that they really bought 'plans' not a structure.

Damien designs a type of gang nail truss using bolts and plywood plates in place of patented, steel multi tooth connectors which are expensive and hard to get. They get in trouble with the local authority over it. Someone rats them out—they're building without a permit and without permission from the patent holder. So Damien has to pacify a burly but not overly hostile building inspector more amused by this unlikely pair of miscreants than mad. Damien draws up a set of plans, submits them for permit, pays a fee and waits.

Submitting a set of plans is an adventure in itself. The stupid township still insists on 22 copies of everything, so he reads on their website, a site practically no one visits anymore since pretty much everything is an app now:

All plans or drawings submitted shall be
drawn in metric measurements on Mylar or
other substantial material satisfactory to the

Director of Planning, to a scale of not less than 1:100 metric or such less scale as the Director of Planning may approve, and shall be fully dimensioned, accurately figured, explicit and complete.

So he has to go to a quick copy place that looks like it saw its last customer about a decade ago and print out his plans. He then runs three kilometres over to the town hall with his frigging Mylar drawings awkwardly sticking out of his backpack.

Meanwhile, Pops and he continue to build unabated. They have occasional help too from Raymond Michaud who Pops has stashed on the property in one of his underused cabins. Private Michaud who everyone calls 'Sunny' serves with the nearby Royal Canadian Dragoons. It takes Damien a moment to figure out why he's nicknamed Sunny. He's been living with them since the summer. Apparently, he's trying to save up to get married in the spring and can't find a place to live that is affordable and will let him do that on a Private's wage. So Pops takes him in. It doesn't hurt that Ray also shows Pops a picture of his fiancée, a cutie from Petawawa. Damien, pretending to be uninterested, ambles over and gets a look too.

Pops charges him rent—ND$20 a month. It's a weird business deal that Damien gets to see happening in real time. Ray offers Pops more and then Pops talks him down but not to zero because Pops doesn't believe in free. He never collects coupons, bonus points, Crappy Tyre coupons, air-o miles, premiums, freemiums, promo items or other FS, free stuff which he calls BS stuff. He detests those don't-pay-a-cent-events and expects to trade fair value for value.

Sunny's (Ray's) hometown is Miramichi in northern New Brunswick. It was part of the French colony of Acadia when the first Euros came to the Americas. Pops tells Damien that the place has about two dozen Frenchmen and a thousand Indians so he thinks Sunny is likely more than just part Indian. Whatever, he fits in well with the family now made up of Pops, Damien, Toby and Private Michaud who knows his way around a construction site too so he doesn't get in their way. Toby's main job is watch-cat.

Eventually, the guy from the Township comes back and posts a cease and desist notice at their job site. He takes Damien aside knowing that the old man is hopeless and says: "Look kid. How old are you?"

"13. I'll be 14 in five months."

"OK, so you look like a smart kid. Yous gotta stop now. Disobey that order," he's pointing at the notice he's just posted, "it's not a civil offence any longer, it's criminal and your grandfather will get in a lot of trouble. So knock if off until yous get your permit, OK?"

"When'll that be?" Damien asks.

"I dunno. These days there are 15 people who have to sign off on these things, it used to be 2 you know, so it takes awhile," he answers. "Also, kid, they aren't ever gonna give it to you with those suckers in there," he points to Damien's self-designed, fake gang nail plates. "You'll have to go buy the real thing."

"They won't sell us any," Damien says. He knows, they already tried to buy them. "They only use them in their own trusses so you can't buy their components."

"So go buy the trusses, kid."

"It's not in the budget," Damien says, thinking now that they will have to take down their entire roof structure and replace it with expensive, store-bought trusses that Pops can't afford.

Instead, Damien spends the next week doing Real Life stress, torsion, tensile and moment of inertia tests on his connectors. Basically he puts different loads on his components and assemblies until they break, recording everything down to the molecular level with sensors he's designed and inserted into the structures. He records video at macro and micro scales as well. Then he runs several hundred simulations for wind and snow loading. He goes back to the quick copy place, makes 22 Mylar copies of his results and takes those over to the Town hall too. He befuddles the plans inspector there who gets so involved in talk about torque and stress tests as well as watching cool video on Damien's tablet of microscopic distortion in plywood and metal bolts that he has never seen before (and no one else has either except Damien) that he forgets he's talking to an undersized, skinny kid and not a professional engineer. Anywho, he gets their building permit three days later.

Their final product is pretty impressive—it has a forest green steel roof with five Dominion lightning rods sticking up amongst their 40 solar bulbs poking through it. The sides are all white washed and they install classic Woodwright windows with green trim. There are two large sliding doors so they can get big Damien projects in and out of the space. The poured-in-place concrete floor is so large they need not one but two expansion joints. It is at least a metre and a half higher than the local water table so it remains high and dry year round and doesn't need a sump pump. Pops has the interior sprayed with foam insulation and installs a non catalytic wood stove that efficiently burns waste wood they find all over their property, especially after frequent Northern Ontario storms. It's nice and toasty inside even during a Canadian winter.

In its later years, the barn serves as Damien's lab with are all sorts of equipment, notes, machines, computers, parts, old fashioned chalk boards and white boards, tools and bric-à-brac scattered about. There is almost zero security other than a measly rusty padlock you'd see on any high school gym locker. Toby's principle job transitions to mouse control—the suckers are eating cabling in their building although so far they haven't developed an appetite for several kilometres of fibre optic glass cabling Damien's installed.

...

Damien's also given Ellen a more or less free hand in

terms of decorating his new penthouse. With her impeccable taste, she's gone all out. The result is one of the most stunning new homes in TO in the last decade—a place full of light, air, volume, sound and video combined with furniture and surfaces that celebrate not only recent technological innovations but combine with antique pieces and traditional Canadian art—landscapes as well as several Québec master abstract painters—it all somehow works.

Incongruously, Ellen's even added a few Remingtons to Damien's collection. She's been a big fan of the artist since her folks took her to the Frederic Remington Art Museum in, of all places, Ogdensburg New York, a rundown, ramshackle of a town on the St. Lawrence River that is full of drunks plus broken down and abandoned homes. Her parents find it difficult, actually impossible, to find a place for lunch after their morning visit to the Museum late one fall. Every restaurant they find is either closed or permanently boarded up. Ellen remembers it as a scary, sad place but she loves the fantastic scenes of the old west that play out in Remington's work. In 1907, US President Theodore Roosevelt said of Remington, "The soldier, the cowboy and rancher, the Indian... will live in his pictures and bronzes, I verily believe, for all time." The artist captured these indelible images by traveling in the real west just before it disappeared and died out forever.

Ellen who was still in the princess stage of her thus far short life, a phase that will never entirely leave her, wants to immediately run off with handsome, mysterious, lonely-looking cowboys riding the range in a light snow as dusk falls or noble, bare-chested, impossibly good looking Indian warriors decorated with impressive looking costumes and makeup. She can't decide which she'd prefer so for many years, she alternates her partners in vivid daydreams.

The Museum's collection is founded in 1918 via a bequest from Eva Caten Remington and they've kindly agreed to loan three pieces from their collection to Damien on the proviso that he opens his place to two guided tours a year for potential patrons and so promote their Museum. They figure that prosperous Torontonians will get an appetite for more and boost Museum attendance as well as their miserable funding. Toronto is to Ogdensburg what Paris is to a Village of Zombies. It works. Museum patronage is way up. It also doesn't hurt that Damien gives them their largest donation in more than 125 years.

Ellen is surprised the Museum is in forsaken Ogdensburg. Ash3r researches the artist and finds out that his family moved to Ogdensburg when he was 12. His father was a US Port Customs collector. Later in life Remington owned an island retreat in the 1000 Islands on the St. Lawrence River.

Ash3r has been a big part of the overall penthouse design project and Ellen tells him he has a great future as an interior designer. Ash3r seems a bit miffed by her comment.

Damien feels like an intruder—a commoner who has somehow wandered into Louis XIV's Palace of Versailles. His first night in his new château is strange and all he can think about is Pops living in his simple, four season cabin-in-the-woods. He has offered Pops some help if he wants to, say, add to the place or buy something else. The old guy just looked at him. Damien takes that as a 'no. He is gonna have to invite Pops over to see his new crib but he isn't looking forward to what he is sure will be at least one more look of disapproval at the sheer extravagance of it all. But he'll get a kick out of the solar lights, Damien's sure.

Like many things though, you can and do get used to it. After a while he finds he rather likes being the master of his own domain and he loves the fact that Nell loves the place even if Ellen organized the whole thing. She has to admit that Ellen has taste.

The building also has its own marina and Damien has his Albacore docked there. His dinky boat looks ridiculous next to cigarette boats, Thunderbirds, Finnish Electric Boat Racers, Cabo Rico Yachts, Passagemakers, Bayliners and several hundred others but Damien doesn't care—he still participates in Friday night races whenever he can. But given demands on his time these days, it's less often than it once was.

Damien's only other extravagances are his private plane from a Saint-Laurent, Québec-based manufacturer and an antique diamond engagement ring he purchased from high end Montreal-based jeweller, Bourque's.

Damien, aware of the need to always be vigilant with respect to costs, has asked Pet3r to share his plane with five other Toronto-based executives with the proviso that each of them must have Quantum Counterparts. This is not a case of tied selling by Damien ('insisting' that suppliers, for example, in the Q-Computing ecosystem who sell to them should also buy from them), it's a matter of efficient use of the plane and optimizing its use amongst six people, all with their own entourage of various sizes and complex schedules.

Pet3r is responsible for keeping Damien's schedule, which is a non trivial problem in itself. But it gets much worse juggling six busy executives with one plane between them. Damien knows this belongs to a class of problems known as NP-hard (nondeterministic polynomial) which, as the name suggests, is difficult to solve on digital computers. Because delivery of 'goods' is based on integers (i.e., they can't deliver a fraction of a passenger), it also fits into Integer Linear Programming models and, to make matters worse, Pet3r is solving (optimizing) for things like fuel consumption which is not based on integers. So the problem becomes a mixed integer programming challenge. While the model is NP-hard all that guarantees is that it is at least as hard as any NP-problem although it might, in fact, be harder which it is.

Since Pet3r is a quantum computer and so are all the other gatekeepers, they can model all states at once so the MIP problem is a cinch for them to solve.

But for all that is going on this weekend in New York: the board meeting, a possible IPO, the media briefing, a celebratory party (a chore for Damien more than anything since he has to be 'on' constantly all the time in public), Q-Computing shareholders potentially becoming colossally wealthy—the thing he's most excited about is the ring he carries with him. The search for it has been very frustrating. He knows he wants an antique ring but after that he draws a blank. His research provides him with limitless options; it is bewildering. He wants to ask Ellen for advice but something holds him back.

He looks at a number of options with Bourque's: a flawless diamond set in a diamond-embellished platinum band/a setting with an emerald cut centre stone and a total of six diamond baguettes/an heirloom Art Deco white gold diamond solitaire ring/a radiant-cut pink diamond from Harry Wharton/an Edwardian oval diamond/an hexagonal round brilliant cut diamond/a marquise cut, antique diamond ring and about 50 more.

Finally, completely desperate, he asks Pet3r for some advice. Pet3r has been non-committal though, hemming and hawing and making polite noises but diamond engagement rings for a girl are not exactly his forte.

After an agony of delay, Damien chooses a Chopard Blue Diamond Ring set with an enormous, oval-shaped blue diamond together with diamond shoulders and a white gold band also paved with diamonds.

...

Nell is in an agony to see Damien but something is up with him and he isn't telling her what. She also has something she's wanted (well, needed) to tell D for the last few years but she just hasn't been able to get it out in the open. It kinda goes to the heart of her relationship with him and he's so big on the trust thing that she knows, KNOWS she has to tell him, as Tony would say, RFN.

She will be 30 soon and while she has never gained an ounce, she notices a few tiny crows' feet around her eyes that weren't there a year ago. Damien doesn't seem to mind; in fact, he tells her he loves her any way she comes but there's the fact that he's such a conventional guy that he's maybe thinking of taking the relationship in a new direction and he needs to know something about her before he does. Nell promises herself, for the umpteenth time, she will tell him as soon as they're alone in Westchester County.

...

When Nell and Dekka, still head of her security, are dropped off at Reddingford, they find the place a beehive of activity. There are Paparrazzoids everywhere snapping pictures of her and other celebrities arriving for what's being called the 'Countdown Party'. Media walls everywhere are showing Q-Phone user numbers rising fast. Right now the clock shows 499,916,592. There is real excitement not just at the Club but amongst the community of Q-Phone users, amongst QEs who are seeing their population rise to an appreciable fraction of human population, amongst thousands of analysts who follow QCC on Wall Street, Bay Street, Howe Street, in the City (London), in Mumbai, Pretoria, Lagos, amongst the employees of Q-Computing who are waiting to cash in on an expected IPO, its suppliers and other stakeholders of which Apple, as Ash3r predicted years ago, is the single largest beneficiary.

Nell is looking forward to the party but right now she wants to find Damien. Su7e tells her he's at his board meeting and will see her in their rooms at the Club later. Most of the guests are staying elsewhere but Nell and Damien have an entire suite of rooms at Reddingford for themselves. Nell is performing tonight at the Countdown Party—only one number although she has an encore planned as well. It's some of her new stuff that went over well on Euro Tour II.

The kids in Bucharest (Nell thinks they are the best looking girls in Europe) know every word of her tunes even her most recent stuff. They all speak great English, always an important point for a self-centred and unilingual

American who expects everyone to speak English. English has proven to be unstoppable—it's absorbed words from French, Russian, Japanese, Mandarin, Arabic, Swahili, even Hopi at an incredible rate. The estimated word count Su7e tells her is now over 2,902,510.

She's decided to sing 'Before the Fall' now her 2nd biggest hit ever after still unbeatable 'The Successors'. She wants to subtly remind D and his team not to get too far ahead of themselves. She's sure they're expecting a sappy love song or a peppy victory tune. Her Mom always told her to 'treat men mean to keep 'em keen' and Mom's advice she thinks is sound, at least in this regard. Nell is used to being centre of attention and the shift of attention to Damien is taking a little getting used to. Nell settles into their rooms and decides to do some prep work for her performance while she waits for Damien.

...

"We have the world's attention focused on us," Ellen announces to their 15 member Board. Angelo Keller is also in the room. While he is not officially a member of the Board, no one thinks to mention this fact to him—he just shows up. In addition to five inside directors (Damien, Ellen, Traian, Luis and Anthony), there are ten outside directors including four from VC funds (one each), two from QCC Foundation plus four independents.

The Foundation has exceeded all expectations having brought quantum phones and QE helpmates to over three and a half million health professionals around the Globe at no cost to their users and with untold benefits in terms of healthcare provided and healthcare education. Ellen is sure that if they do IPO soon, Anthony will cash in some of his chips and move to the Foundation full time. After all, it was his baby originally.

Aziz is also there—he is one of their independent directors although the Cain people question his 'independence' since he is a former employee. But his current work in Nigeria and Canada is tangential to QCC

Foundation's mission so he's been begrudgingly accepted by them.

"The Countdown Party will be viewed by an estimated two billion viewers either in real time or streamed by them later," remarks Ellen to the Board. "Every QE will be watching too so obviously our total audience will be more than two and a half billion. Our momentum in the marketplace is such that we can predict a billion Q-Phone sales by second quarter of next year and we're now thinking we will top out at about five billion units within the next four years."

Even for guys used to big numbers, these are BIG numbers.

Angelo beams at her. What he sees now is a mature woman at the height of her power—intellectual and physical. It's quite the combination. He also sees a lovely oil portrait hanging in the dressing room of his penthouse of a naked Ellen lying back on a day bed with one arm akimbo beckoning to an unseen lover. What Angelo can't figure out is why she apparently hasn't taken a lover. It can't be for lack of suitors, for sure. He is certain that Aziz is stuck on her and he's a fine young man. Perhaps he will suggest it to her. It can't be good for her health to be all-business, he thinks with concern.

Ellen sees his look and she blushes to the roots of her curly blond hair (which she has straightened for today's Board meeting). She can't believe that she let him talk her into that painting. But he's been true to his word, there are no images of it out there anywhere and she's had Ash3r look so she is sure. Still, it bothers a shy girl like her. But it excites her too, in a way.

"Using our original model for valuation and basing it on over 1.5 billion Q-Phone users," she continues, "we will have an IPO of just under $500 billion New Dollars." There are sounds of indrawn breaths when she says this and a few whistles.

"But that is not what we are proposing," Ellen stops dramatically.

"We think that our ancillary revenues justify a much higher price—we think this should be the first trillion New Dollar IPO and here is the graph and numbers we've generated to back that up."

Ash3r takes the Board through their new numbers, projections, cash flows, P/E (price/earnings) ratios, cap rates (capitalization rates), income and expense statements and P+L.

The Cain Caruthers guy asks, "I don't see QE earnings anywhere in the mix here. I understand that certain people," he looks at Damien, while he talks, "believe that they should have all rights to their own earnings but they're just pieces of code, albeit very sophisticated code. Right? Why shouldn't we add their earnings to ours? That way we'll get an even better valuation."

By this point some QEs but not all have managed to accrue significant earning power of their own. About 3% of QEs don't imprint on their human counterparts or somehow otherwise fail. Maybe due to their initial default settings, some unknown incompatibility problem with their human partner or some other cause, no one is quite sure why. Q-Computing is working on it which means it's a Damien problem. He's wondering what to do with these unattached QEs.

They are, in effect, orphans. They've also found that they cannot be 'adopted' by anyone else or otherwise reassigned. They do develop and learn but slower and differently from the rest of the QE population. They seem to be good at acquiring basic skills like legal assistant but their personalities don't seem to emerge and empathy as well as 'self esteem' seem to be low. Perhaps this is just an unintended by-product of the system that Damien set up in the first place and completely unavoidable. Damien is not, however, prepared to accept that. For a company to have a fail rate of 3% is bad—Damien is still aiming for a six sigma result.

Media walls in their new Toronto HQ (a converted industrial building on Queen Street running an entire block in each direction) often show one of Damien's favourite Mike Gerber quotes, the one Ellen referred to years ago when she was running through her list of Ten Things Startups Forget to Do:

"Those mundane and tedious little things that, when done exactly right, with the right kind of attention and intention, form in their aggregate a distinctive essence, an evanescent quality that distinguishes every great business you've ever done business with from its more mediocre counterparts whose owners are satisfied to simply get through the day."

Damien knows that it's been the aim of every great manufacturing company since Motorola to remove substantially all errors from both their fabrication and business processes. He is really unhappy that their failure rate is orders of magnitude greater than a six sigma result. Right now there are about 15 million of these unassigned Quantum Entities (out of nearly 500 million) and it seems right to find them work or let them find work for themselves, to keep busy. He's just not sure what to do about it... yet.

Overall, QE earnings have risen to about 18% of human GNP and it's increasing fast. Damien can see the day coming when that number could be 50% or even higher so he understands why Cain Caruthers wants to add it to Q-Computing's own earnings. It would mean a quantum leap, so to speak, for their numbers.

Damien replies, "I get what you are driving at and, if QEs were just an algorithm, maybe that would be the right direction to go in. But they are self learning, self actualizing, self managing organisms so we may not have the right to take their earnings. If you trained for years to be a CA," Damien should have said CPA since this is mostly an American board, "or a legal assistant or, for that matter, qualified as a lawyer or an engineer and you paid your own way by borrowing money against your future earnings that you will have to pay back, how would you feel if someone came along and said, 'Oh, by the way, all your earnings belong to me'?"

QEs have started self incorporating so they can borrow money plus do work-for-pay. But they need their human counterparts (or any other incorporated entity) to be named shareholders and only humans can be recorded in Articles of Incorporation as directors since QEs are not (at least not yet) considered legal persons. Like black people in early America and women before they got the vote, they do not have legal status other than (possibly) as property.

Unbeknownst to nearly all members of the board, some QEs have already found jurisdictions outside the US and Canada (such as the Republic of Vanuatu, those half submerged islands in the South Pacific) where they can set up twin corporations—where shares of one corporation are actually owned by the other and vice versa. Lawyers in these places are happy to assist paying clients even if they are inanimate ones. They will also agree to be named board members. Once established, these legal entities can own still other corporations; some of them active in the US. They are completely outside the 'jurisdiction' of human control.

But most of the work being done by QEs is widely known even respected by their human hosts. One of the more famous QEs around these days is Oper1s, Richard Florida's Quantum Counterpart who has been doing some mundane but important work in much of the developing world. He's busy working with surveyors delineating property.

Oper1s is Latin for 'building' and, after apprenticing with Richard for a few years, he's gone off on his own to survey every piece of property on the planet and create a single, trusted registry for that data, freely accessible to everyone.

Oper1s' work is inspired, in part, by Florida's research on urban catalysts and, in part, by the work of noted development economist, Hernando de Soto, who showed that economic take-off in developing nations is immeasurably aided by first developing a system of property rights, increasing home ownership and giving people a permanent address. You can't get a bank loan, a mortgage, open an e-pay account, receive a government grant or loan or access a thousand other programs if you don't have a permanent address. It's the sine qua non if you want to participate in a modern economy. De Soto also noted that huge amounts of capital were locked into informal land holdings and structures and could not be accessed because either they were not described anywhere or their chain of title wasn't clear. To many politicians and conventional bankers, those places look like slums. To de Soto, Florida, Oper1s and Walt Rostow, one of the earliest pioneers in the field, they look like opportunity.

Oper1s has become a frequent keynote speaker at global development conferences. He often starts by asking his audience, "What's the number one source of capital for entrepreneurial startups?"

"Banks!" someone will answer.

"VCs!"

"Angels!"

"Government!"

"Partners!"

"None of the above," Oper1s will say. "It's home equity! By giving people clear title to what is in effect already their home and really belongs to them even if the law does not agree—that's one of the pre-conditions for economic take-off in developing nations."

Oper1s connects the dots for his audiences and has become a folk hero in many parts of the world as a result. It is also his view that property rights and human rights are intrinsically linked. In countries where there's no respect for property rights, there is usually no respect for civil rights either. History has shown that if you want to reduce a person to a non-person, first make them homeless. The reverse is also true.

He sometimes quotes former Canadian Prime

Minister Pierre Trudeau who, while trying to repatriate their constitution from the UK, also tried to entrench property rights in their Canadian Charter of Rights and Freedoms. Pierre understood the link between human and property rights but the Provinces of Canada (10 of them at the time, now 11 with the recent addition of a southern colony of that country) opposed it fearing that it would interfere with their right to control subterranean, riparian and air rights. Basically, provincial politicians like those everywhere want two intrinsically linked things—money and power. Control over mineral and water rights as well as air rights and zoning by-laws combined with their power of eminent domain (expropriation) give them executive authority to dispense favours as they see fit to, say, FOBs (Friends of the Boss).

Oper1s and his organization have taken direct aim at these entrenched interests via a seemingly innocuous land registry. They also want to create an accurate record of national boundaries, many still in dispute, in the perhaps vain hope that this too will reduce conflict and war. Maybe he will be the first non-human to win a Nobel.

...

"Who cares how they feel?" the guy says.

Damien doesn't dignify this with an answer.

"Damien, could we possibly tax their earnings instead? After all, they were born in our Lab 4 Hatchery. Maybe they could contribute to the Q-Computing family?" Traian asks. Traian has grown up too—he's finally put his adolescent overtime behind him. His torrid love affair with Dakota has been a long distance relationship but (surprising himself) he's been 100% loyal to her. Maybe a bit of Damien has finally rubbed off on him.

"We've heard that argument before," Damien responds, in fact, having heard it just the day before back in TO and from the same source. "But it would be like having children and taxing their earnings. It's already been done—it's called feudalism and the corollary is serfdom."

"Why don't we ask them," Keller suggests. "Adu1us, come here."

"Yes, sir." Adu1us is one of the few QEs anywhere that calls his partner things like 'sir' or 'Mr. Keller'. Pet3r has called Damien a lot of things, not all of them polite.

"How would you feel about contributing, ah, 20% of your earnings to Q-Computing?" Angelo asks him.

"May I speak freely, Mr. Keller?"

"Certainly."

"Well then, if I am given a choice I would rather provide support whether it is financial or otherwise to you, Mr. Keller and your heirs," Adu1us answers.

Angelo knows Adu1us will say this since he's already asked him this question, more than two months ago.

Everyone bursts out laughing (except for the Cain Caruthers guy) at the thought of Adu1us supporting the incredibly wealthy Angelo Keller but the point is made. Quantum Entities have their own thoughts and 'feelings' and their first loyalty is to their human counterpart and his or her family and not Q-Computing. The whole system was set up by Damien to work just this way.

"There is another point people seem to be missing," Damien adds looking at a Cain investment banker who is sinking lower and lower in his seat with each passing minute. "QEs are already paying their share."

"Huh?" says Ellen involuntarily. This is a new one to her.

"They're paying taxes—sales taxes, valued added taxes, property taxes, payroll taxes, corporate taxes and a zillion other taxes."

"Do you mean they're paying those taxes on behalf of their human counterparts?" Ellen asks.

Damien gives her the look that says she's just asked a dumb question and she shrinks a little inside. Angelo also notices and is a bit annoyed with him.

"No. They're paying their own way. QEs have been incorporating their own businesses for the last few years. It's the only way they can acquire legal status so they can do work on their own and be remunerated for it. If you wanted to hire, say, Ash3r for something, you can't actually put him on your payroll since he is not, at least not yet, a legal 'person'. So Ash3r and people like him (Damien is using Ellen language by this point to talk about QEs) incorporate their own companies, perform work, get paid, buy stuff, sell stuff, own property, whatever. Pet3r, how many QE-owned corporations exist?"

"87,489,466 with another 2,687,740 in process at the present time."

"No way," someone around the table utters.

"Right. That's why their earnings are increasing so fast. The only tax they haven't paid is personal income tax but that's only because they aren't recognized as 'persons' yet. But they will be. As soon as the US Government figures out how much money QEs are making, there will be a big push to tax them individually. There's nothing US politicians like better than money and power and the first leads to the second." Damien says, the latter sotto voce, but his voice carries around the room and there is some embarrassed shuffling amongst board members. Americans on the board know their half-Canadian CEO has some strange, small town views about money, politics, law, equity and fairness which they don't share. Damien has embarrassed himself, at least to their minds.

"So it looks as if QEs prefer to put their collective shoulders to the wheel to help their 'families' so to speak and Damien has pointed out that they are already sharing society's burden by paying taxes like the rest of us do." Angelo now holds court and, it should be pointed out, the last part of his statement is patently untrue since the top .4% of US population now controls nearly 60% of national assets and over 50% of national income of that nation and pays practically no taxes other than unavoidable consumption taxes. "So I propose we accept Ellen's recommendation for the first ever trillion New Dollar IPO and I further propose, after we vote on the matter, we break for lunch. Ellen, would you care to join me?"

...

Over lunch, Angelo plans to talk to Ellen about the afternoon session. He has a plan that he wants to share with her and it involves strategic voting—a condition involving a feint and some deception.

Angelo is more like a Russian than his Italian-German heritage would suggest. Ruskies won't do anything without a plan, a trait that explains why they still produce the greatest (human) chess grandmasters. Of course, no one can play chess against QEs since they can model all states at any one time and cannot be beaten. A draw is a huge victory against a QE, a reason why Angelo and Adu1us never play. Angelo likes to win. So does Ellen, one of the reasons they get along so well.

"Ellen, I believe there should be a change in management at Q-Computing," Angelo says in the private dining room he has commissioned for this particular tête-à-tête.

"What do you have in mind, dear," she replies. Ellen knows Angelo likes it when she calls him that.

Smiling broadly, Angelo says, "I think there should be a new COO."

"Ah, we don't have a Chief Operating Officer." Ellen is EVP, Traian is their CTO, Damien their CEO. Their only concession to age and experience, suggested by BVP in their genteel way, is an experienced CFO in his late 40s to replace the departing Mukono.

"Right, I know that. But you need one."

"Do you have a candidate in mind?" Ellen knows Angelo well enough now that there is no doubt he does—probably another older guy he owes a favor to. He will just say the guy has the experience to run a world-spanning enterprise that is reshaping whole economies. Q-Computing is doing that or more precisely Q-Phones and QEs are doing that. Ellen isn't sure which is having greater impact—Q-Phones that eliminate bandwidth limitations, time and distance or QEs who are revamping the global labour pool.

She thinks QEs will eventually have the greater impact but how they will evolve is still largely unknown. They have released, perhaps unintentionally, the largest 'bio' hazard ever conceived on an unsuspecting planet without FDA or EPA approval. Ellen suspects that Damien knew full well what was going to happen. He's been relying on another of his favourite sayings to get them out of any potential trouble—'entrepreneurs would rather ask for forgiveness than beg for permission.'

But he is right, who would they have submitted QEs to for approval? FCC, DOC, ICANN, CRTC, FTC, DHS and FDA or EPA, Ellen has no clue. They, whoever they are, would have convened a government-run committee of concerned stakeholders including a mind-numbing group of bureaucrats, and industry insiders like mobile carriers and telecoms. They would have done everything in their power to derail then tiny Q-Computing.

Such a government committee, which John F. Kennedy once said 'is twelve men doing the work of one', would have just studied the 'issues' and requested first party (Q-Computing), second party (other stakeholders, such as erstwhile and entrenched competitors) and third party (neutral independents) studies and position papers or white papers until one of two things happens. The proponent either gives up and goes away, or dies.

Q-Computing would merely have died.

"Yes I do," Angelo says rather mildly.

"Angelo, please stop playing games with me. Just lay it out." Ellen is the only person who talks to him like this. He doesn't mind—she's got guts along with charm and she's a consummate executive able to deal calmly with all the problems each day brings. She's dead steady even in a storm.

"You," he replies,

For a moment there is stunned silence.

"Well?"

"The board will never accept me but I'm flattered that

you asked, now who do you really have in mind?" To this day, out of Fortune 1,000 companies worldwide there are only 18 female CEOs and a handful more female COOs. It's ridiculous but true. Ellen's board is overwhelming male and, even though she has probably been filling the role of COO for some time (in fact, all the time since Damien took off with Nell after their first encounter), she's way too young for the job. It's impossible for a woman to get the title even if she is doing the work.

"Let me explain strategic voting, Ellen. I've asked one of our independent directors, Aziz, to introduce the measure toward the end of our agenda, under 'miscellaneous items'," Angelo says. "Miscellaneous items are usually a throw-away line in most board agendas.

"I am going to raise doubts about this expressing concerns about your age and experience and so forth—I am going to head off that dreadful fellow from Cain Caruthers, who will undoubtedly vote against you. People know you and I are close allies so I will reluctantly be persuaded to be neutral about this but not really in favor either. I want the Cain people to owe me a favor and, after this, even though they will lose, they will," Angelo finishes.

"Does Damien know about this?"

"Certainly, certainly. I passed it by him last week. He's completely Gung Ho about it."

At the mention of Damien's name and enthusiastic approval, he can see Ellen practically glow. Angelo's eyes narrow as he watches her closely and he instantly decides not talk to her about her love life or lack thereof or to mention Aziz as a potentially suitable partner.

'So that's who her unseen lover is,' he thinks. Trouble ahead.

...

The only issue of substantive debate in the afternoon session is who will lead and who will participate in the forthcoming world's largest ever IPO. Virtually all major investment houses have made presentations to the board's

Finance Sub-Committee chaired by Aziz.

This is hugely important to those guys not only for the money they will make from successfully placing a new company with a trillion New Dollar capitalization into public markets but the prestige that comes with the assignment will mean that hundreds of other firms will want to do business with them as a result. What's more, there are nearly 180,000 major institutional buyer clients who will be annoyed if their investment house has no stock to supply them and they are shut out of this exciting opportunity. Then there are three or four or maybe even five billion potential retail investors who will all want part of this company that, to most of them, is now seen as one of the world's top brands. With QEs, it's personal.

That's why Damien has unilaterally scratched the name 'Rochedale Sachs' off the list. They have already agreed to add firms from New York, London, Toronto and Lagos but not Rochedale even though both Angelo and Aziz think they are the best group to be lead dog in this hunt.

Damien has not explained his opposition but if he did they would discover that, quite some time ago, Rochedale cratered pension funds for a great many people, including his grandfather, by selling securities labeled 'double-A' by rating agencies in cahoots with them. They knew at the time those securities were junk. Rochedale was shorting these very same products essentially betting that their value would collapse. And they did. Rochedale won big both ways and not one executive there or anywhere else is ever called to account. Until today.

Also conspicuous by their absence is any Shanghai-based firm. That's because there are no Q-Phones or QEs in Imperial China where, just possession of a Q-Phone or appearance on your media wall of a QE is a capital offence. Imperial China's ruling mandarins consider Quantum Entities a national security threat. They are the only nation to deny itself entry into what people are now starting to call the Era of Quantum Economics, the term coined by Ellen nearly four years ago and now in common use.

They replace Rochedale with a second New York-based firm and select one as lead dog.

The last order of business for the day is the matter of a new COO for the company. By this time, people are getting tired and hungry—they want to go to the media briefing, get some dinner and P A R T Y. Despite some mild opposition from Keller, Ellen is rapidly confirmed as their new COO with only the Cain Caruthers guy voting against.

She now has the title and perks that go with one of the top jobs in tech. It's pretty cool—she is just 23 years old.

Ellen receives lots of congratulations but probably the happiest person now in the room is their publicist who is thinking of all the e-zine covers he's going to get for Q-Computing featuring this fantastic blond creature who's not only tall and gorgeous, talented and tough but a clotheshorse too. He will get a lot closer to Ellen now and is looking forward to a successful relationship. It will slingshot him to the top of his PR niche—making star executives look good which with Ellen will be a snap.

...

The media conference is well attended both in RL and via media walls. Damien does the minimum required as CEO but newsfeeds aren't really interested in him today—there is a huge appetite for and interest in interviewing, photographing and otherwise recording their new COO. So Damien leaves the media briefing to Ellen, Aziz, Angelo and their PR guys. He hasn't seen Nell yet and that's his first priority at the moment.

...

"Hey, D," says a subdued Nell. She's been in his arms in their private quarters for a few minutes but he can feel a vulnerability there that he has seen only occasionally in her. With stars like Nell, he knows they cycle from penthouse to basement and back in minutes experiencing highs and lows which, he supposes, comes from the fact that every fan, every critic is an expert on her hair, makeup, clothes, tunes, weight, dance routines and overall performance art as well as love life and career.

If you muck up as an employee probably only your boss and you know about it. For Nell, it's all out there for the world to see. That's why so many top performers (and not only in performance arts) get suckered into drugs and alcohol.

With that thought, he suddenly holds her at arms length and studies her face. He's remembering what happened to his Mom and this unsettles him. This isn't going anything like he hoped it would.

"Care to tell me what's wrong?"

"Nothing, I'm fine. Maybe I am suffering a bit from jetlag."

Nell never suffers jetlag. She's so fit and so used to months on the road with practically limitless energy that he realizes, maybe for the first time in their relationship, she tells him an obvious lie.

"Nell, look at me. Honey, look at me. What's bothering you?"

"I dunno," Nell replies and then bursts into tears.

He picks her up and lies her down on their bed. She is shivering and weeping so he covers her up with the thin, filmy and practically useless decorative bed throw, then attacks the other bed in the suite and in seconds covers her completely. Her beautiful, weeping face pokes out the top of this heap with her glorious auburn hair arrayed all about her.

He doesn't touch her. Instead, he pulls up a chair and only looks at her, watching, searching her face.

"Su7e, come here I need you," Damien commands.

Su7e is already there. She opens a window on the nearest media wall. Damien gently takes Nell's hand and presses it against the wall's haptic surface meeting Su7e's hand. "Please take Nell's temperature and analyze her sweat glands and compare the results against her baseline health profile."

Seconds later, "Results are complete. Nell has an elevated temp and she is infected with a form of Hepatitis called Query Fever also, ironically, called Q Fever. Nell has been exposed to Coxiella Burnetii. A single bacterium is enough to infect a human. I estimate that she was infected within the last ten days, probably during our stay at Traian's parents' place—a lovely farm 17 kilometres outside Bucharest city limits. She—"

"Could I have the short version, Su7e? What is the diagnosis and prognosis?"

"As I was saying, she was probably infected from contact with urine or feces from infected animals on the property, likely sheep. Since it is a bacterial form of Hep, not viral, it is eminently treatable. Nell needs to be seen by an infectious diseases specialist immediately and begin a course of medication which will probably be hydroxychloroquine-based."

"Can you please determine the nearest available specialist who is also mated to a Quantum Counterpart and arrange a car with driver to bring him or her here immediately?"

"Yes, of course, Damien."

"Su7e, I will also want an explanation as to why you did not diagnose this earlier and I find it incredible that you could allow yourself to forget the three basic laws of which the first is; a QC may not harm a human being or, through inaction, allow a human being to come to harm."

"May I say this in my defense..."

"No you may not. Please make the call and the arrangements I asked you to, we'll discuss this issue later," an incredibly pissed off and worried Damien says.

...

The Countdown Party is in full swing despite the announcement that Nell has a cold and cannot perform tonight. Damien arrives and makes the rounds. There is lots of handshaking, high fiving, hugging, kissing, jumping in unison, rave dancing, raucous music, drinking and otherwise revelatory partying going on. Even Ellen, he notices, is getting into the swing of things—she's on her second glass of wine with Aziz when he goes over to say 'hi'; this represents major binge drinking for her.

She looks happy and relaxed and Damien is pleased for her. She's very much come into her own and he is glad. Grateful too, that despite her newfound and profound wealth, she still works her guts out to keep Q-Computing on track. Without a doubt, she's the glue.

He's expecting to see Angelo there but when he asks Ellen about him, she just shrugs, "He was a bit tired I think so he went home. But he promised to check in later via media wall." When you're 107, you are entitled to do what you want, he supposes.

Nell has been seen by a specialist and his QE before Damien will leave her. She is feeling much better or at least that's what she claims. She asks him how his day went and seems to be totally pleased by the success Q-Computing is experiencing. Damien has definitely noticed a change in Nell—she has grown a lot and can now experience authentic joy when something good happens to someone other than herself, someone she cares deeply about.

She is feeling so much better she says that she wants to keep their private dinner date that Damien has arranged for their reunion. He has rented the entire Executive Dining Room on the top floor of 1 World Trade Center, still the tallest building in the US at 541.3 metres. She knows that Damien has gone to a lot of trouble to set it up and doesn't want to disappoint him.

Like most show biz folks, she also doesn't want to disappoint her fans at the party either and vows to make an appearance there as well. On this point Damien is unmovable—there will be no show for her tonight. The DJ duo they've hired will be fine he reassures her. She doesn't have to prove anything to anyone and certainly not to him. He knows how tough she is—mixed martial fighters could learn a lot from her.

He offers to send his car and driver for her but she

says she will have her own people take care of it. By that he assumes Dekka will bring her and that assuages some of his concern because he knows Dekka will take good care of her.

She sends him off with a practically monastic hug. She'll be infectious for at least ten more days and possibly as many as 30, so no sex with D. She sighs. Damien tells her not to worry; he's got lots of memories to keep him company for the next month until she's better.

She's keeping the dinner date because she loves him but she's also going to tell him what she should have told him years ago.

...

Everyone watches the countdown clock as the numbers edge towards 500,000,000. There's a lot more chest thumping and bumping, clapping and hand grabbing, kissing, hugging, tribal dancing and general celebrating going on. Powerful music surges through the room. In the foreground, an incredible video loop plays everywhere with images and sound bites of the (mostly) young people who make up Q-Computing's brief history and even younger QEs doing what they've been doing to make this day possible for nearly every waking hour for almost five years. It's a powerful emotional cocktail and there is some weeping amongst the joy.

Meanwhile, Damien sees this as a good chance to duck out, unseen, to meet Nell, thinking as he goes, 'It shoulda been called a Count Up Party'.

...

When Nell gets to 1 World Trade Center, there is a single taciturn individual in the lobby waiting for her. He unceremoniously presses the top floor button for her and scurries out of the elevator as the doors shut. Nell is alone in an express elevator that only goes to penthouse. Her ears pop. Nell is very nervous. She just doesn't know how D is going to react.

When she gets to the top floor, she finds it quite deserted. It's mostly office space with the single Executive Dining Room. She walks down a long corridor and stops for a few seconds to collect and prepare herself for what's ahead before knocking softly on the door. Corridor lighting sensors are switched to night time status leaving the corridor half in shadow.

A butler opens the door. Inside she sees a couple of bored servers who kind of snap to attention as Nell enters. Damien has asked her to arrive by 11 pm. She's a few minutes early.

Damien is nowhere to be seen; she assumes he must be in the Men's. The butler asks her if she would like to sit. "Is Dr. Bell here?" Nell asks quietly.

"Ah, no." he replies.

"You mean he's somewhere else in the building?"

"No Miss. I don't think so. We have not seen him this evening—we have been expecting him for the last 90 minutes. We had specific instructions to wait for Dr. Bell who has very exacting plans for this affair. So we, ah, rather have been waiting on him. The String Trio is here however."

Nell has never known Damien to miss anything before.

"Su7e, come here! Where is Damien Bell?"

"I don't know, Nell."

"What do you mean you don't know? Pet3r, come here."

Another media window opens with Pet3r in it. The edges of his saucer shaped face have curled in on themselves and his eyes have a strange look about them. A now quite alarmed Nell asks again, "Where is Damien?"

"We don't know," Pet3r answers.

"How is that possible? No, wait, when was the last time you saw him?"

"9:34 pm Eastern Standard Time."

"Do you have a record of it?"

"Yes, I do," Pet3r responds.

He opens another window and plays the video record for her. Damien, elegantly dressed for the evening in a bespoke suit that, unknown to Nell, was selected by Ellen and sourced by Ash3r, is close to 1 World Trade Center striding towards the building when an impossibly old vehicle pulls up alongside him. Three very large men jump out of the vehicle and surround Damien who holds up his hands in a gesture of non-aggression. They speak to him for less than 15 seconds.

Another more modern vehicle, unnoticed at first, has another four men in it. All about the same size and build as the first group; they're in their 30s or 40s it appears from the video. They take Damien's Q-Phone and empty his pockets. They're about to open a small box they've taken from him when Damien says something else. They shrug and then what looks like their leader gives it back to him. It disappears in Damien's coat pocket again. Damien looks from face to face as if memorizing their images. He does not panic. Nor does he fight back or try to flee. They bind his hands in front with a standard riot police style black double loop twist tie and hustle him into the ancient vehicle and pull away. It has surprisingly good acceleration and they are out of sight in seconds.

Damien is gone.

...

Nell is in a complete state of uncomprehending grief by the end of this short video. She is in shock and, in her weakened physical state, she does panic. The staff in the room seems to be no help at all and her QEs are just as useless. She doesn't know what to do or who to call.

...

"He's gone," Nell wails. "I came to this awful place but he wasn't here. They've taken him. I can't find him. He's gu-gu-gone!"

"Who's gone, Nell? Nell, Nell!" Ellen asks.

"Damien. Some men tu-tu-took him," Nell cries.

"Were you there when they took him? Are you in any danger, Nell?"

"No."

"No to you weren't there when they took him or no, you're not in any danger?"

"No to both."

"Is Dekka there? Let me to speak to him, please Nell."

"He's not here."

"Where is he?"

"I came here alone."

"You what? You went without any security? Table that. Pet3r, Su7e, Ash3r, are you on this call?"

"Yes."

"Yes."

"Yes."

"Where is Damien?"

"We are unable to find him," Ash3r replies for all three QEs.

"I saw the video record," Nell squeaks.

"Ash3r, please show me the video." Ellen reviews the video then says, "Nell, I want you to stay right there. You are not to move."

"It's creepy here," replies a now childlike Nell.

"Nell, YOU ARE NOT TO MOVE. I am going to call Dekka right now and he will be there as soon as possible. You are going to be fine."

"But what about D?" Nell asks bleakly.

"Look, the video tells us a lot about the men who took him. If they were some kind of religious freaks or extremists who wanted Damien dead, they would have killed him on the spot. He's NOT dead, I will find him and we will get him back in one piece, Nell. I promise you that. We will find him and free him. But Nell, one more thing before I go. I have a lot to do so you have to promise me one thing, OK?"

"OK."

"Don't ever do this again."

...

"Tell me why again you didn't report this right away?" Ellen asks Pet3r, none too kindly.

"Quantum Entities do not easily interpret signals from humans that form within the most primitive parts of their brains. I was unclear what to do. I had no orders from Damien to follow which is Law 2 and I was unsure whether any action I took would help or hurt him which is Law 1. So I did nothing until summoned by Nell."

"Pet3r, you know what 911 is, right?"

"Yes, of course. Are you going to call 911, Ellen?"

He has her there. She is definitely not going to call 911 until she is sure who took him. It will also be a PR disaster for Q-Computing to have lost its CEO on the day they announce plans for an IPO. She now has implied obligations to both the SEC and CSC on behalf of the public and investing institutions with respect to any pertinent information concerning the Company, its stakeholder group, its major clients and customers, its board, its key personnel and Damien is certainly material to the business of the Company. So she goes in a different direction, "Under what conditions are these people holding Damien given what you have seen of them, their technology and their capabilities?"

"The first integrated circuit was built by Nobel prize winner Jack Kilby at Texas Instruments in 1958," Pet3r answers. "The first circuits contained few transistors but, for Quantum Entities, anything that contains an electronic circuit, even small-scale integration, is sufficient for our purposes. From the video, we can see that the car that removed Damien was an Oldsmobile Cutlass, model F-85, manufactured in 1961. It is safe to assume that there are no electronics of any type in such a vehicle not in its engine or unibody components. The vehicle would also not contain any LEDs. The displays and gauges would be entirely analogue. That makes the vehicle completely opaque to a QE."

"OK, that's the car. What about where they have taken him. Can you assess what condition that might be?"

Here Ash3r chirps in, "I have been analyzing that. We believe it is likely an underground cave or bunker that dates to the Cold War era, circa the 1950s or early part of the 1960s—a place that either has no media walls, computers, LEDs, telephones, radios, televisions or any other equipment that could possibly contain ICs or has been stripped of them. We think it is the former. It would be too hard to make sure they got every IC. Better to start with a location that never had any in the first place."

"Su7e, have you anything to add here?" Ellen asks.

"No, Ash3r and Pet3r can do this without me."

"Then before you go back to Nell, I have a question for you after which you are to go to Nell and stay with her. You are to notify me the instant anything you consider abnormal NO MATTER HOW TRIVIAL YOU MAY THINK IT IS happens. If there is a strange call, a bizarre message you can't understand, some bestial behaviour by any human being, YOU WILL NOTIFY ME IMMEDIATELY. Do you understand?"

"Is that your question?"

"No and yes," Ellen answers.

"I understand. Your other question?"

"Who knew that Damien and Nell had this private meetup planned?"

"Damien and Nell, of course. Myself and Pet3r. That is all."

"Did Dekka know?"

"No, Nell specifically asked me not to tell him. She wanted to sneak off and have an 'adventure' without any 'darned' security'. They had planned a special night."

Ellen rolls her eyes again but doesn't comment on the sheer stupidity and risky behaviour of her erstwhile boss and his paramour. Damien knows that opposition to Quantum Entities is growing as critics multiply almost as fast as their success. Some are motivated by fear—fear of job loss and economic and social disruption or just fear of the unknown. Some from the religious fringe consider Quantum Counterparts blasphemous and an affront to

God. Whatever, for a smart guy, he sure is dumb.

"So if only Damien and Nell, you and Pet3r knew, how did these guys organize two vehicles to pick Damien up at exactly that spot at that time?"

To this there is complete silence. Ellen suddenly realizes there is an informant, a traitor somewhere in their organization, she just doesn't know who, yet. Her eyes narrow and, if anybody could see the look on her face at this precise moment, they would realize in a way that human beings are so good at discerning emotion from a momentary glimpse of a face, that Ellen has just transformed into a warrior princess.

"Su7e, you may go."

"Ash3r, Pet3r, who would have the skill and capability to mount such an operation and sustain it? Could one of our competitors have done this or one of the fringe organizations that have published anti-QE material?"

"We consider that unlikely. Probability of less than 1 in 100."

"OK, so what about the other 99%?"

"It is likely that the operation was mounted by an arm of the US government," Ash3r answers for them both.

'That's why Pet3r didn't call 911 and neither did I,' Ellen thinks. "To what purpose, to gain what advantage?"

"Unknown. The US federal government has many arms, cliques and branches, different services and hidden, secret organizations."

"Could it have been the US military?"

"Possibly but we consider that unlikely. They are still mostly set up for large scale, set-piece action. It is more likely to be one of the following: DOC, DHS, FBI, FCC, or FTC, EPA or FDA. It could also be the National Security Agency or the CIA."

"What is your best estimate?"

"DHS, Department of Homeland Security."

This is also Ellen's gut feeling. They've nabbed Damien for some purpose related to US preoccupation with terrorism even though far more Americans die from each of drug overdoses, obesity, alcohol poisoning, car accidents and suicide, not to mention gunshots, than have ever died in terrorist attacks no matter how fiendish or dramatic or sad or tragic they may have been. Prolonged terror alerts are more about keeping a huge part of the US government in jobs than about fighting terrorism in Ellen's opinion of her native land. Now Damien has somehow become a useful target for them. It won't take long for Ellen and Ash3r to find out why.

"What DHS or US military facilities are within 200 miles of New York City that fit the profile of the place you have described? Look most closely in the vicinity of Washington DC. If they've taken him anywhere, it's probably there. Some bigwig from DHS is going to want to talk to him and those lazy buggers will want him within an hour and a half's drive of their nice comfy leafy fucking homes." It's the first time Ash3r has ever heard Ellen swear.

"There are three prime candidates. First, the old U.S. Naval Observatory, now home of successive US Vice Presidents. In December 2002, neighbors complained of noisy construction work. It is located on Massachusetts Avenue North West in DC. It has long been rumored to have a bunker for the protection of the Vice President during lockdowns."

"Too recent and too close," says Ellen.

Ash3r continues, "In the late 1950s, the U.S. government approached a hotel by the name of Greenbrier to build an emergency bunker for the US Congress in the event of nuclear war. The project was built from 1959 to 1962."

"Sounds promising. Right era at least. How far from DC?"

"Along I-66 W and I-81 S approximately 248 miles or 4 hours and 6 minutes by ground vehicle," Ash3r says.

"Much too far."

"You are sounding like Goldilocks," Ash3r jokes.

She knows that QEs have trouble with humor but still she bursts out laughing at his lame attempt. He's using his vast relational data base to do this but his purpose is sound—he wants Ellen thinking, not mad. Humans, he has noticed, tend to lose 10 points off their IQ when mad and, even though she has plenty of points to lose before it seriously impairs her ability to think clearly, Ash3r wants his entire human counterpart focused on the job at hand. In this he has succeeded brilliantly.

"The last one?"

"We believe they could be using either Andrews Air Force Base located 11 miles southeast of DC in Maryland or Langley Air Force Base about 175 miles south of DC in Hampton, Virginia." Ash3r continues, "Pet3r has looked at aerial photos dating from the beginning of the 20th Century to the present. Massive excavations and earthworks are shown in the southeast quadrant of Langley between 1955 and 1960. By 1965, there is no trace of those works. That area becomes home to three hangars and a wide apron where 21 fighter aircraft of various designs are currently parked. We estimate that they imported approximately 2.4 million cubic metres of engineered fill, sufficient to protect an underground structure of a size of about 400 metres by 400 metres against shock waves from nuclear attack, five storeys down with each storey having a height of approximately 3 and a half metres. Analysis of surface traffic over the last decade strongly suggests Building B is the entrance to their underground bunker."

"Where did you get those aerial photos from?" Ellen asks suddenly worried, no sure, that Ash3r or Pet3r have just pilfered them from classified US Air Force files. "No, stow that. Don't tell me," she countermands using yachting language she's picked up from Damien. She has become quite an accomplished sailor, crewing for him when they have time to race his Albacore.

"OK boys, we know where we are going to be when the sun comes up. Now all I need is a writ of habeas corpus demanding DHS take Damien before a court of law and the meanest motherfucker of a lawyer in this town."

Ash3r is thinking, 'That is twice now.' But what he says instead is, "Ellen, to live through an impossible situation, you don't need the reflexes of a Grand Prix driver, the muscles of Hercules or the mind of an Einstein. You simply need to know what to do. That is from Anthony Greenbank who wrote the original Book of Survival by the way."

"I understand, Ash3r. I am quite OK but thank you. Now can you please get me Henry Linnert on the phone?"

"It's just after 2 am. Do you wish me to disturb him at this hour?"

Ellen puts her hands on her hips, reversing them like girls do, and stares at him stonily.

"Placing the call now."

...

Chapter 10

Corpus

Damien quickly figures out much of what Ellen will deduce soon after she learns he is gone. Other than binding his hands in front, they have not put a hood on him leaving him free to observe and assess what happens around him. Either they made a mistake or they did it intentionally. He thinks it's the latter.

Confusingly, they take him to Teterboro Airport in New Jersey where Q-Computing's own plane is parked at the northern end of the complex. Instead of using the main gate they circle around to the southern portion of the airport taking a little-used route, appropriately named Redneck Avenue. They arrive less than 20 minutes after leaving 1 World Trade Center.

Another small group of men waits for them. His abductors are swiftly ushered through a security gate to an ancient Bristol 192 Belvedere helicopter that is powering up. It has three-bladed rotors at each end.

They are using pre-IC technology; they took his Q-Phone. No one carries any type of modern mobile phone and the vehicles they use, both ground transportation and now airborne, are ancient although apparently well-maintained. One of the guys, 40ish, whom Damien takes to be their crew chief, holds a humongous Motorola Walkie-Talkie (it's actually a Handie-Talkie) apparently lifted from some old World War II movie set.

They obviously aren't going to kill him, at least not yet. There must be someone who really wants to talk to him privately.

Damien isn't afraid. Although he has never been a macho guy, he knows he has some reserves of personal courage to draw from. He's already been tested in places like Third Mesa and the Salmon River in Idaho.

He's pretty sure he's not afraid to die. One thing

Damien's always felt is an urgent pressure to make each day count. He's not sure where it comes from and maybe it means he feels that for some reason, his days are numbered but there's no way to really know that.

The one thing he is afraid of is lawyers—they can depose you to death and ruin your life. It's why he made that awful deal with Apple; he didn't want to waste a single hour on patent litigation which is the bane of a lot of tech companies.

It looks like he is going to face some type of interrogation. He tries to relax as much as possible and give some thought to how this might go. Preparation is more than half the battle—it is one of the keys to winning in sports, business and life. Nell is like that and he loves her for it. He sighs.

The Crew Chief, misunderstanding him, asks, "Is there anything you need, Dr. Bell?"

"Yes, I would like to know under what or whose authority you have taken me?"

"Is there anything else?"

"Yes, I would like some water."

After unscrewing the top, one of the guys gives him a bottle. He wonders—should I drink it? But if they were going to drug him, he supposes, they would just have injected him not pussyfoot around, so he downs the whole thing.

Giving him comfort is the fact that Pet3r will have immediately reported him missing to Ellen and Damien knows that Ellen, with all the resources at her disposal as well as her considerable analytic skills, will figure this out fast and come get him.

It's obvious that whoever is orchestrating this, knows it too. The fact they did not blindfold him and they cuffed him with hands out front instead of behind his back suggest they will not hold him long. This whole rigmarole is designed to intimidate, to cow him for some kind of leverage in discussions and negotiations to come.

Damien is familiar with Stockholm

syndrome—where captives come to associate with the views of their captors. That is certainly not going to work on Damien; he is too well-grounded for that and they won't have him long enough. But they sure are trying to make him talk 'uphill' which can be almost as effective. Human beings don't like being outnumbered, don't like being cornered and don't like it when people around them point in their direction saying the immortal words of Émile Zola, 'J'accuse!' If enough people place negative psychological pressure on a person, especially one isolated from his tribe, long enough and loud enough, it's easy to start believing what they say even if it is all a BIG LIE; in fact, the bigger the lie, the more believable it is.

Damien prepares as best he can. He still has the precious Chopard Blue Diamond Ring in his coat pocket.

...

The ancient chopper lands after two hours and fifty-nine minutes flying time. It is still totally dark when they land. Damien's internal clock tells him it's been about three hours and will soon be dawn. He notices the dark of the ocean on his left and the lights of three large cities that he deduces to be Philadelphia, Baltimore then Washington on his right. He knows they are flying pretty much due south down the East coast. He's trying to estimate air speed and ground speed as they go but in the end his calculations aren't necessary. He can plainly see the 3,000 meter runway below and he figures they are going to Langley Air Force Base in Hampton Virginia; about 115 minutes fast driving distance from DC.

There is another ancient car waiting for them there; its windows totally tinted so that its occupants are invisible. Damien is almost disappointed when it turns out the vehicle contains only a driver and another two drones who look like pretty much everyone else in this outfit—neither young nor old but muscular and religious. Their religion—military life and its demi-gods of: Loyalty, Duty, Respect, Selfless Service, Personal Courage, Integrity and Honor. It seems these men have forgotten the last two.

The car is waved through a gate and drives onto the base to an enormous hangar, the middle of three buildings, in an isolated corner of the airfield. Inside, the car is gobbled up by a hydraulic freight elevator and descends for some time—Damien counts 57 seconds then the doors open. They drive out into what must be an underground hall at least 380 metres long and more than three metres high. It looks to be as wide as it is long.

This place is huge. There are workstations for thousands of people—perhaps more than 10,000 of them. There are teletypes, IBM Selectric typewriters, conversion transducers, cathode-ray tubes, oscilloscopes, card readers, electrometer tubes, transducers, iconoscopes, oscillator tubes, monoscopes, luminescent screens, phosphor screens, camera tubes, reel-to-reel tape recorders, ansafones, rotary phones, tabulators, accounting machines, IBM 632 tape punches, paper tape readers and much more, all of it technology that is nearly a century old.

He realizes someone has gone to a lot of effort to put together a workforce that can be effective without modern computers or Quantum Counterparts. They obviously want him to see this—they march him the whole length of the underground structure to a previously unseen double door at the other end. Two uniformed guards are there, the first obvious sign of mainstream military presence. Both are equipped with World War II era Walther P38 pistols. Unlike modern weapons these have no DNA recognition wetware to prevent unauthorized firing which would obviously form another pathway for QEs to enter these premises.

The guards salute the crew chief as a person of some rank, a revelation of sorts to Damien. One of them opens the right hand door and they enter an ante-room of more human-scale proportions.

There is a table with a small, balding man of indeterminate age sitting behind it. He wears a cheap suit.

There is a copybook open in front of him. Damien is marched over to the table.

"Please wait behind the yellow line."

Damien looks down and sees a yellow line maybe 10 centimetres back of where his black dress shoes are.

Damien doesn't move a millimetre.

"Please remove yourself behind the yellow line or I will have these gentlemen do it for you."

Damien stands perfectly still and states, "I am a Canadian citizen who has been brought here against my will. I ask to see the Canadian Consul General in New York City. I believe the Consulate is on Avenue of the Americas. Would you please call her immediately and inform her of my whereabouts. If you do not have her contact information, if you would please return my property including my Q-Phone, I would be glad to provide you with that information."

"Gentleman, please remove the subject behind the yellow line," the guy says.

With a shrug, the crew chief looks to his two subalterns who approach Damien with a look of some apprehension.

"It's OK fellows, no worries, I can manage on my own," says Damien smiling kindly at the guys. He nonchalantly steps behind the yellow line.

"Name please."

"You already know my name otherwise I would not be here."

"We will remain here until you provide answers to my questions."

"That's fine with me," Damien says affably. "I'm not in a hurry."

"Mr. Bell, we require your co-operation in order to complete the admitting process."

"See, you DO know my name."

"Age and place of birth?"

Damien decides to employ a 'turtle defence'. He will cooperate where he must but only to the point of violence done to his person or to someone around him. Damien believes with all his heart in non-violence, violence being the last refuge of scoundrels and his having experienced it first hand back in Rochester middle school.

Romans marched in turtle formation with each soldier's shield interleaved with the next. They could convert to a stationary formation in seconds and men inside the formation would use their spears to fend off attackers. Damien's plan is to make them repeat their questions, clarify them, refuse to answer them or ask his own questions in return. Plus he will answer their questions with answers to his own questions.

"Where are you from and how did you get this dead-end job? Don't you think you could be doing something else with your life? Why don't we all go back up top—I'll buy you guys a beer at Langley Base Pub. I'll bet that we can get a drink even though it's nearly dawn—a bunch of guys will be coming off their graveyard shifts so let's go join 'em. It will be a lot more interesting and we can talk about other stuff like your family, your kids and what you plan to do next summer," Damien suggests mildly.

"We require both a home address and business address. You may lean forward and use a pen I will provide you with shortly to complete this admitting form," the bureaucrat says pointing at an official looking, mind numbing institutional document. "Your shoes must however remain behind the yellow line. You are also required to provide us with: marital status, your next of kin, name of family physician, list of medicines you are taking, allergies and health insurance particulars as well."

Damien bursts out laughing. He's covered under Ontario's Public Health Insurance, but he's not sure how OHIP will react if he submits a giant bill for medical procedures due to some type of torture they have planned for him.

Instead he asks the guys, "Guess who said, 'One should count each day a separate life'?"

One his guards blurts out, "Leo DiCaprio?"

Damien has no idea why the guy says that but if Ellen was here she would know Leonardo played a character in an old film who says, 'Make each day count.' Close enough.

"It was Lucius Annaeus Seneca," Damien answers. "He was also known as Seneca the Younger. He was a Roman Stoic. Anyone know what a stoic is?" Damien asks looking at the guard who spoke up earlier. He's a bit younger than the rest of this crew.

Damien's stare can be pretty persuasive; the guy ventures, "That it's a virtue to resist destructive emotions?"

"Nice!" says Damien. "See, you're trying to make this day count!"

At this point, an orange light—an old-fashioned incandescent lamp—turns on. There are three small bulbs on the desk—green, orange and red and the middle one has just lit up. There is an old 1950s era TV camera and mic focused on them over the balding man's left shoulder. Damien assumes someone is monitoring his theatrics and is getting somewhat impatient.

The crew chief and his two acolytes accompany him down another hallway. Through the next door is another long poorly lit corridor followed by a series of cells, all empty. The crew chief nods and one of his men opens a cell door and motions Damien in. He steps into a cell about three by three metres, painted pink (which apparently calms inmates Damien read somewhere). There is a bunk with no blankets and a hole in the floor toilet. There are no windows.

Damien holds out his arms to the crew chief and looks at the man. He says nothing. For a moment, Damien's not sure what the guy will do but then he hauls out his ancient USMC fighting knife, a Ka-Bar, and cuts Damien's hands loose.

There's no doubt the crew chief is former US military. It still comes as a bit of a surprise to Damien that someone who has served God and country would be mixed up in a shady operation like this. Damien looks at him silently asking him that question just by the expression on his face. The guy shrugs and backs out of the tiny space. The door clangs shut. It is a keyed lock—no digital electronic or modern quantum locks he notes.

Damien is alone in a dark place.

...

Ellen and her squad don't make it to Langley by dawn as planned. She has Ash3r running a stopwatch with a start time of 9:34 pm ET, the moment Damien was abducted. It is now showing 14 hours 26 minutes and 52 seconds, close to noon the next day. She is burning that they have had Damien this long but she also knows that her operation needs to be carefully planned and executed expertly.

Dekka and Su7e have rousted seven of his buddies in and around New York. These are guys who're always ready for some action and would do it for free if he asked them to. That won't be necessary. Q-Computing has the resources to make this a paying gig and it sounds like fun.

"Dekka, I need big guys not hotheads," Ellen says. "This is not about assaulting an underground bunker controlled by DHS or someone else. It's about trying to level the playing field a bit and not talk uphill at a bunch of former US Military. I want them unarmed but looking like they mean business. I need them at Teterboro by 6 am, OK?"

Dekka nods and goes off with Su7e to make arrangements. Now her crew has been waiting for nearly four hours. It doesn't bother them at all. They've been playing cards or just resting. Military personnel expect to hurry up and wait; they know their COs are idiots anyway. But when they get a look at their CO for this operation, well, one of them whistles involuntarily.

She's this tall blond creature who can't be 30 yet, egad, maybe not 25 either. What a dish he's thinking. Then she looks him in the eye and begins briefing them; he kind of snaps to attention along with his mates without apparent volition.

They file a flight plan to take two MH-900s from Teterboro to Newport News-Williamsburg International Airport. These modern helicopters are incomparably more comfortable and faster than the machine Damien flew on. They've been rented by a company belonging to another friend of Angelo's who does no business with Q-Computing. No point in pre-announcing their upcoming visit to Langley.

Ash3r, Pet3r and Adu1us have done an incredible amount of work with Ellen and her human team in a short period of time. QEs can convey information to other QEs in picoseconds or, if it's a long conversation, nanoseconds. They don't take a half hour to wake up, don't need coffee and breakfast before they can understand what's being said to them. They trust each other not to lie and they can suspend disbelief at bad news or good news. They organize a group of ten human beings; Ellen, seven former special ops guys and two lawyers, Henry S. Linnert and his junior, Walter Cunneyworth plus two choppers and their crews, fueled, flight checked and ready in just a few hours.

The major holdup is that they're waiting on Henry whose QE (Ala5tair, a name of Scottish and Greek origin meaning 'human defender') has to get in touch with Judge Tomlinson's QE to arrange for an emergency hearing; basically, Henry's in La'kisha Tomlinson's chambers at an ungodly hour (for a judge) of 9 am arguing for a writ of Habeas Corpus for Damien Graham Bell.

"Now Henry I don't see how you can convince me to sign such a writ. You don't even know who has Dr. Bell," Judge Tomlinson is saying. "Perhaps some gang has him and plans to blackmail his company. I am informed they have considerable resources."

"Judge, we have strong reasons to believe that he has been detained by DHS in an unlawful manner and your court may decide whether such detention is in fact lawful but only after they have produced Dr. Bell for a determination on the basis of evidence which they and we shall be required to provide you," Henry says.

"I'm not even sure if I shouldn't recuse myself from the matter. I have both a Q-Phone and a Quantum Counterpart which you already know since it was Ala5tair who spoke with Z4ra who woke me up and got me here. As for the pretext that this is an urgent matter, I am not convinced—at least from a judicial point of view. It's more a matter for the police, Henry."

"Judge, you pay for your Q-Phone, do you not?" asks Henry.

"Yes, of course."

"Do you also pay for Z4ra?"

"No, not that I know of. What's your point?"

"Your Quantum Counterpart is her own 'person'. She looks after you. She cares for you. After working with you for a few years, she could go out on her own and provide legal services at any one of the best law firms in New York and earn her own living if she wanted to." Henry continues, "She has nothing to do with Q-Computing or Dr. Bell. You could give back your Q-Phone tomorrow, terminate your contract with them and Z4ra would still be there for you and with you. There is no possible conflict at all."

"But Henry what if the Court issues such a writ and it turns out you're wrong and DHS has had nothing to do with Dr. Bell's disappearance?"

"La'kisha, Dr. Bell is probably the most brilliant young physicist of his day. He's a fine person and he's missing. The downside for the court is that we're wrong. The upside is that they are forced to bring him here, to your courtroom for a hearing that given the announcement of yesterday—about their planned IPO—will bring the world's media to your courtroom. And, Judge, I don't have to remind you that next year is election year for Federal Court justices."

"You're wrong, Henry, the downside is that I bring the wrath of the Department of Homeland Security down on my head."

"Christ, Judge, they're just a bunch of out-of-control fascists and you know it."

"Henry that is unprofessional language and is unacceptable in my courtroom."

"We're not in your courtroom, Judge, but I apologize."

Damien's insight that QEs should never be billed out by the company is proving its worth right at this moment. Henry leaves Judge Tomlinson's chambers with the all important writ a few minutes later.

...

Three modern black SUVs are waiting for Ellen and her folks at Newport News. It's only 12.8 miles, about 16 minutes, to West Flight Line Road and the back gate at Langley. Ellen rides with Henry and Walter plus three others from Dekka's squad of compadres. Dekka doesn't join the mission remaining with Nell as Ellen expected and wanted anyway.

She checks in on Nell via media wall before leaving to see how the superstar is doing. Something is wrong there beyond the fact that Damien's gone missing. She does not look well. Ellen files that away, for now. She asks Nell if she needs anything but Nell says she's OK and in good care. Su7e is there and apparently Weinstein is on her way too having heard that something is up.

"Just find D, OK?"

"Understood."

The number of people and QEs who know about the 'situation' is growing practically by the minute and Ellen understands that time is running out—newsfeeds will have the story soon. There's no chance that QEs will leak it but some human will, for sure.

She needs a PR strategy right away and she's been working on that too with Q-Computing's top media person. "We need a series of media releases and an overall strategy prepared right away," she tells him. "We need to sketch out three scenarios: one, we get Damien back today by negotiating his full and final release, two, DHS accepts the writ of Habeas Corpus but decides to make Damien do a perp walk into Judge Tomlinson's courtroom and all Hell breaks loose or three, they don't accept the writ and Damien is interred indefinitely.

"I will also need you to talk to Bessemer Ventures and our four investment house partners before noon today to give them a heads-up on what's going on. I don't want to overdramatize things—we are not the first tech company to be attacked by the US Government, DOJ or FTC for anti-trust enforcement under the Sherman Act or some other cockamamie act of government. You will need a complete workup on the history of such things including US v Standard Oil, IBM, AT&T, Microsoft, OLA Facebook, the NFL and others. OK?"

"Huh?" is all he has to say.

She dismisses him on the spot and calls one of the senior partners at their media relations firm in TO, McLaughlin Markowitz Media, to get them working on the problem along with their New York subsidiary.

She has zero time to fool around with people who can't keep up. Damien told her early on that, 'The most important decision we make, other than the decision to actually start the company, is who we hire, so hire-up.' They've been pretty good about doing just that despite a recent example to the contrary. 'It's not assets or IP that produce income for this company, it's people,' Damien added. She gets that now in a way that only contemporary experience can convey.

...

Damien's practicing yoga in his tiny cell after sleeping for about an hour and a half. He is doing mainly Yin Yoga—holding poses for long periods until his limbs shake. He has wonderful balance so he practices his standing eagle and tree, first on one foot then the other which he can hold practically forever. He's feeling pretty good but he's worried about Nell and kicking himself for putting her in danger.

He can see what an idiot he's been. He won't need Ellen to point it out to him. He put Nell, Q-Computing and its 8,500+ employees (including 3,000 in San Francisco at Q-Computing America, 4,000 back in TO at Q-HQ and the balance in three main satellite offices in Berlin, Joburg and Mumbai) at risk by behaving incredibly foolishly. He's behaved selfishly and vows it won't happen again.

There's been random loud noises, flashing lights, and occasional visits from guards, all meant to unsettle him and prepare him for and make him vulnerable to some kind of interrogation to come. He finds it absurd and almost LOL funny. He sleeps fine. He's learned from Ellen to use his yoga mat, now conceptualized as a 70 cm by 200 cm section of hard cold concrete floor, as a zone of Zen-like peace.

When he first started yoga, he found it a bit distracting—having all these beautiful females around him doing poses and their instructor, Ms. Ellen Brooks. Of course, they are all much better at it than he is but after a while he realizes it doesn't matter how bad he is or how good they are or how good they look, he has to centre-in on himself, his mat, his space and pursue his own practice. Now he often closes his eyes for long periods during yoga practice. He gets it. It doesn't much matter that Department of Homeland Security pipes in any number of intrusive noises or tries to cause other disturbances in his wa. He's quite content to wait, maybe a long time, although he thinks not. Time is running out for these guys. He can just feel it somehow.

...

Dr. Zbigniew Zimmermann is watching all of this on his RCA television circa 1959. He is Under Secretary of Homeland Security and he also knows that time is running out.

"These are some of the smartest kids on the planet we are dealing with, so it won't be long before they're knocking on our door," Zbigniew is saying to an unseen assistant on another RCA monitor; they are using analogue television technology and RCA cameras to broadcast their responses. "Do you detect their presence anywhere in the vicinity of this facility?"

"Not at this time. But if they are coming, you can be sure they will use some subterfuge." #Intelligent but one dimensional, he is also thinking.

"Do you think you can penetrate that?" Zimmermann asks.

"Yes but you may only have 15 minutes warning." #I will view infrared as well.

"I will have our crew chief monitor this channel. He can alert me if you find any untoward visitors. I think I will have a conversation with Mr. Bell now."

Damien has been brought to a conference room; his feet and hands have been bound to a chair and, for the first time since he's been quasi-kidnapped, he's pissed. Then he remembers what Ellen told him about IQ dropping when he gets mad. He practices yoga breathing for a few minutes to try to calm himself. The idea is to first close one nostril and inhale deeply filling his belly; then close his other nostril and exhale slowly. Then pause and repeat. Since his hands are tied down, he can't really do it properly and it's not helping much.

"My name is Zbigniew Zimmermann. You may call me Dr. Zimmermann."

Damien says nothing. He sees a spider-like middle aged man, quite hairy everywhere—bushy dark eyebrows, dark hair with some gray streaks, hair growing out of his nose and ears, hairy arms poking out of his gray suit jacket sleeves. He's thin but Damien thinks not from exercise but because of high metabolism since he still has a bit of a paunch. He's neither old nor young; he's at least eight or maybe nine centimetres shorter than Damien and looks even smaller because of a bit of a stoop.

He has a formal mien about him and is clearly used to command. More has been written about this man's intellect than about any policy positions he may have taken during his career. His views might be said to be 'fluid' as political conditions change in Washington. He is a survivor of several regime changes during his career so far.

Damien notices he has appallingly bad breath. Maybe he's a fan of Shawarma because, despite being delicious, they smell exactly like Zimmermann does now. He's had a midnight snack.

Damien hasn't had anything in more than 18 hours, other than the water he consumed during the trip. As a scientist, engineer, hacker and yoga practitioner, this is nothing. Damien also has the advantage of youth, stamina and practice at self denial. He's able to 'dial-in' for marathon hacker sessions, writing jags, lab prep and experiments, gabfests, equation writing, research, reading and general mucking about with equipment, tools and computers. Damien won't get tired but Zbigniew might.

"Mr. Bell, do you know how many laws of the United States that you have personally broken not to mention your company, Quantum Computing?"

"Dr. Zimmermann, do you know how many laws you have broken by bringing me here and chaining me to this chair," a suddenly, now completely furious Damien asks.

"Well, under Homeland Security Act III, I would say you and your firm are in breach of, hmm, let me see," he flips through some pages on an old clipboard he's holding, "17 separate statutes which if they are pursued to the fullest extent of the law and if you are found guilty could send you to prison for the rest of your life Mr. Bell and result in separate fines on your company of $10 million New Dollars per day. On each count by the way."

"I am a Canadian Citizen and demand to see the Consul General."

"You are remarkably misinformed for someone I was told showed such promise—you are a dual citizen of Canada and the US and hence quite subject to all the many, many laws of this land of the free and home of the brave."

"You must be a lawyer, Dr. Zimmermann," is all Damien says.

"I take it you do not approve?"

"Not if you use the law to upset ethics. Where the law

and ethics separate, ethics must prevail."

"Not at all, Mr. Bell, quite wrong. You know of situational ethics no doubt? I am quite sure the greatest barbarians of the last century, all felt they were doing God's work by cleansing the Earth of lesser races. Perhaps you are persuaded of that?"

"A man falls in a rushing river. He is drowning. A Good Samaritan runs over and hauls him out. The man is so grateful he offers the Samaritan a generous reward who then goes home to await this beneficence which never arrives. He calls the man a few weeks later who now says he was just kidding about the reward so the Samaritan goes to a lawyer who tells him that under contract law, a contract can only be formed by offer, acceptance and consideration, in that precise order, and since the consideration in this case (pulling the man from certain death) was performed before the offer (of reward) was made or accepted, no contract has been formed and the Samaritan has no legal claim for compensation whatsoever. The lawyer tells the Samaritan, 'Next time you see a drowning man, say to him first, if I pull you out will you give me a reward then afterwards rescue him and then you have a valid, enforceable contract.' But you and I both know, Dr. Zimmermann, that no person of good conscience would ever do such a thing present company excepted."

Damien is under control again and is plying his turtle defence. He's stalling.

"Well, I suppose you and I may differ on such things," is all Zimmermann says in response.

"In France, they have a law that protects Good Samaritans from legal ramifications from acts of heroism gone inadvertently wrong. Many other nations are also not persuaded by legal sophism employed in the US, with two thirds of the world's supply of lawyers but less than five percent of the population and 14 million people incarcerated, more than Imperial China, Myanmar, North Korea, Vietnam, Russia, Iran, Cuba and Ukraine combined times three. It's an industry Dr. Zimmermann not a calling and you are part of it."

A cloud passes over Dr. Zimmermann's face for the briefest of moments then passes. Equanimity regained, he says, "We seem to be on different pages you and I but perhaps not for long. I understand that your company, a most promising one I might add, recently announced, ah, actually yesterday, its intention to IPO.

"I was wondering if you as CEO felt that such an IPO might be successful with, say, a cloud hanging over it such as massive anti-trust litigation brought against it for monopoly practices by both Department of Justice and Federal Trade Commission?"

"What monopoly are you referring to?"

"Why the fact that Quantum Computing Corporation controls 100% of the market for Q-Phones and Quantum Entities. That is a rather large share of any market I am sure you will agree, Mr. Bell."

Damien shrugs. "We do not control the 'market' for QEs since we do not trade in Quantum Counterparts. Your argument is without merit, Dr. Zimmermann. I would not be here if you thought you had a case. You brought me here by force, in breach of my most basic human rights. If you had any justification whatsoever you would have already started an action in the 'normal' course of events."

It's now Dr. Zimmermann's turn to get pissed off, "You completely overstate your position, Mr. Bell. One hint about litigation and your IPO is toast."

"Dr. Zimmermann, I am absolutely sure that Ms. Brooks, our COO, has already thought of that and is preparing right now, as we speak, a media release and conference to address US claims whatever they may be. We would not be the first tech company to face such challenges. Most have survived and indeed thrived despite US action. I have no doubt Q-Computing will survive too even if our IPO is delayed, perhaps for years. We are a young company, we can wait—we'll outlast you."

"Perhaps, but maybe you won't, Damien."

This is the least effective thing that Zbigniew has said

so far. It has no impact on Damien at all. He knows by now that this whole thing has been a show. They must have some kinda deal for him. If he just waits, they'll come to him with it.

He is sure that Ellen is on her way because he knows her, relies on her and trusts her. It also doesn't hurt that all the lights at Langley Base including those in this interrogation room have been pulsing slightly during the last few minutes of his conversation with Dr. Z.

What Damien has been watching from the corners of his eyes are pulses that look like this:

.-- . .- .-. . -.-. --- -- .. -. --.

Morse Code for, 'We are coming.' A QE, probably Ash3r Damien thinks, has hacked the electric substation feeding current to Langley and by varying the main electrical feed, he can convey messages to a trained observer, such as an engineer like Damien. He's fooled around with a lot of different code over the years including Morse. So QEs have found a way in here anyway even if there are no ICs anywhere in this structure for them to use.

Dr. Z, who is intent on pressing his advantage over Damien, misses it. In any event, it's unlikely that anyone at Langley actually knows Morse Code. It was abandoned by the US Military in the early part of this century.

Just then another orange bulb on the wall behind Damien lights up and Dr. Zimmermann excuses himself.

Strapped to the chair, Damien now waits patiently.

...

Ellen, Henry Linnert and Walter are admitted to Building A. They do not allow any of Dekka's pals onto the base; they are being entertained back at the gate. There is quite a lot of commotion going on there. Despite Ellen's orders to Dekka that they come unarmed, she is not surprised to learn they have many devious and deadly weapons about their persons. It's a welcome diversion as the base corps is focused on this dangerous group of former special ops people, some of them former Navy

Seals.

There is a not inconsiderable back and forth banter going on as they seek to find and disarm them—a kind of professional respect too.

...

"My name is Henry Linnert."

"I know who you are," Zimmermann replies.

"I have a writ of Habeas Corpus for the person of Mr. Damien Graham Bell whom we believe you are holding here against his will. You are required to produce Mr. Bell before the Federal Court of Judge Tomlinson within 24 hours of being served said writ. Mr. Cunneyworth?"

Walter produces the writ and touches Zimmermann with it and then plops it down on the nearby desk since Zbigniew has not deigned to handle it directly. He has been served.

Henry is absolutely certain now that they have Damien since there is no chance that an Under Secretary of DHS would be in this Godforsaken hellhole in person if there wasn't an overpowering requirement for him.

"We will have to have our lawyers at Department of Justice review the document to verify its provenance," Zimmermann responds mildly.

"So you admit to Dr. Bell's presence on the base?"

"Not at all, I neither admit nor deny such a thing. I need to verify any document purported to be a court order from New York."

"Come now, Zbigniew, you've had the kid," turning to Ellen, Henry asks, "How long, Ms. Brooks?"

They do not allow Ellen (or anyone else) to bring Q-Phones onto the base, so she estimates, "16 hours and 30 minutes, Mr. Linnert."

"16 hours and 30 minutes. It's time to give him back," Henry finishes.

"I would like a chance to talk to Ms. Brooks alone in the other conference room, Henry."

"Nice try, Zbigniew. The answer is 'no'," Linnert

replies.

"I'm quite OK, Henry. After you Dr. Zimmermann."

...

"Ms. Brooks."

"Please call me Ellen."

"Ah, Ellen, you seem like a sensible person to me. I am not saying that Mr. Bell is here but, if he were here, it would be the case that both the CEO and the new COO, congratulations on that by the way, of Quantum Computing Corporation are on this airbase. I have approximately 2,000 trained personnel at my disposal here. It might be possible to detain such eminent business persons for some time at some considerable cost to them in terms of public confidence for their corporation. Wouldn't you agree? And I note that Mr. Linnert's writ of Habeas Corpus is for Mr. Bell not you."

Ellen laughs that wonderful laugh of hers. She can smell a bluff a mile away, "You couldn't persuade Damien to give you what you want so now you are going to try me? Think again Dr. Zimmermann."

"Well, that is all speculation by you, you know. I have a deal in mind which would be of great benefit to our respective organizations. But first there are some things, that despite your know-it-all attitude, you don't actually know."

Ellen lets silence speak for her.

"What if I told you that we have evidence that shows Quantum Counterparts have committed crimes in the United States including hacking secure US Government networks and removing confidential and secret files?"

Ellen again says nothing knowing that anything she says could incriminate Q-Computing and QEs.

"We also have proof that Quantum Entities have been stealing from the US Treasury—"

"Bullshit," inadvertently escapes Ellen's lips. If Ash3r were here, he would say 'three times'.

"Well, Ms. Brooks, it's true. Some of your QEs which

we call drogues—."

"Rogues?"

"No, 'd-rogues', drogues. Some drogues have started to accumulate wealth and power of their own volition—."

"Who named them drogues and why?" Ellen interrupts.

"Our analysts I suppose. Our people, the ones who first discovered this class of Quantum Counterparts just started calling them that. Why, what does it matter what they are called?"

It matters a lot Ellen thinks but she doesn't tell him that. She shrugs to encourage him to go on.

"They have been taking funds from dead accounts—money that has never otherwise been claimed. These drogues have also been taking funds from the US Treasury in obscure accounts such as the telecom fund set aside from settlement of international phone calls from US mainland to Cuba for the last 90 years. As you know, the US refuses to allow funds to flow to Cuba (for their portion of telecom networks used) and these monies now amount to many hundreds of millions. Your drogues have plundered these accounts. All this to say, we have grounds to declare that your Canadian company and its American subsidiary are engaged in acts against the best interests of this nation and pose a terror threat to the Republic. Consequently, we propose to bring the considerable forces of the US Government both here and extra-territorially to bear on YOU."

"Dr. Zimmermann, what you are saying is impossible. The three laws that are embedded in every QE would never allow such a thing and I can tell you in all the efficacy tests we have conducted ourselves and had independently performed as well, there has never been a single case reported of anything like this. You are full of shit, Sir."

"Don't be so sure of your vaunted three laws," Dr. Zimmermann replies. "When you go back to Toronto, test Quantum Entities that are not mated to human beings. Look carefully again at Law two. A QE must obey any orders given to her or him by its human counterpart, except where such orders would conflict with the First Law.

"Your man Damien Bell messed up Law two. If you read it carefully, it only works if a QE has a human counterpart. If she or he doesn't then they're a free radical (here Zimmermann is parroting one of his analysts who uses the term in an almost literal sense*) for good or ill and, in this case, it's ill and that's too bad for you, Ms. Brooks.

(* A free radical is any atom with at least one unpaired electron in its outermost shell. Consequently they're capable of independent existence and are highly reactive due to unpaired electrons.)

"Now let me tell you what you are going to do. You are going to license a series of resellers of Q-Phones—you are going to cut established carriers, who are suffering badly from customer churn due to Q-Computing by the way, in on your action, forthwith. Oh, and on terms they can live with. You are going to break your own monopoly. Is that clear?"

Ellen doesn't react but what Zimmermann says is exactly what she wanted to do originally with their business model, a fight with Damien she'd lost. But there's no way she's going to let Zimmermann know that. She uses her best, poker face on him which is saying a lot.

"Next, I want the Key to your Quantum Computer—what you call the 'hatchery' or 'vault'. It is unacceptable to the United States of America and its security services that any communications in this nation cannot be intercepted or decrypted by our forces to protect this country from all threats wherever and whenever they may arise.

"Finally, may I point out that another Canadian company from the early part of this century purported to have strong encryption for its mobile devices. May I remind you of the fate of that firm?"

"I will carefully consider what you have said, Dr.

Zimmermann. But I have one request of you."

"Which is?"

"Could you please return Damien to us immediately?"

...

Back in one of the SUVs on their way to Newport News Airport, Ellen looks out the window at the Hampton countryside. She's a bit tired and really doesn't want to talk or think anymore. Now that she has Damien, she can't even look at him she's so mad.

"Did you make any kinda deal with them?" Damien asks her.

"No I did not. I just agreed to consider what they asked for. In the circumstances, and there is a lot of international jurisprudence on the subject as you know full well, it is acceptable practice when they have all the guns and you have none, to appear to agree with your captors. That's all I gave the impression of.

"There are lots of things we have to do and to review but we're not going to do any of that until you are out of the US and back in Canada. It's wheels up as soon as we get back to New York. Don't worry, you'll have 15 minutes to say goodbye to Nell. I've asked Dekka to bring her to Teterboro."

"Thank you.

"Look I know I was stupid—"

"Stop. Just stop, Damien. 8,500 people depend on you. I depend on you. Nell depends on you. Get used to it and stop being so bloody self centred and selfish. Oh, let's just stop talking."

"Will you at least tell me the deal they put to you?"

More calmly now, Ellen says, "Sure. But I'm tired now, Damien. It can wait, OK?"

"Alright," is all he says.

...

Damien knows he faces a shitstorm of publicity when he gets back to Toronto. He and Ellen decide the absolutely wrong thing to do is to go underground on this thing. That is what DHS and Dr. Zimmermann expect them to do to try to save their IPO. They decide to do the opposite—to let some sunlight shine on the whole fucked-up mess. It's the only possible way to save their company and even then it may not work. Anti-trust action by DOJ and FTC is no joke.

Ellen finally tells him what happened when the other shoe dropped—the demand for the Quantum Key, to give DHS complete control over QEs in every way. Damien is prepared, possibly, to go along with adding a reseller dimension to their biz model but his jaw clenches at their second demand. No one, not even Traian or Dr. Luis or Ellen know where Damien put the Quantum Key.

He is true to himself in this—if you really mean to keep a secret, tell NO ONE. It is also not written down anywhere since QEs could find it and, while he never considered that a problem, something always kept him from sharing it with anyone and that includes Pet3r.

At Teterboro, Nell and Damien are together again. She looks terrible. The stress of the last 36 hours and the agony that he has put her through is tearing at his guts. He holds her close—her complexion is positively yellow and she has dark circles under her eyes. She's lost weight which she absolutely cannot afford to do. He can feel her ribs practically protruding from her abdomen. Damien felt bad before he saw her; now he feels worse. He's made a complete hash of things.

"Where will you go, Nell?"

"I'm on my way to Third Mesa. Chief Dan has promised to take care of me while I recuperate.

"D, I have one thing I need to tell you," Nell says. "I've wanted to for a long time."

"Nell, you can tell me anything. Really, girl. But maybe you should wait 'til you feel stronger."

"No. It must be now. I'm not sure if you'll want me after I tell you."

"Nell I've loved you from the moment you held both my hands in yours at the Nuit Blanche party," which now seems like several lifetimes ago for both of them. "I'm gonna love you today and tomorrow. Nothing is gonna change that, honey."

"Are you sure?"

"Yes, ma'am."

She sighs, "You know I was poor growing up so I couldn't get my teeth fixed til I was in my 20s. People made fun of me."

"That was high school, Nell. Everyone goes through the same kinda crap."

"It's not that. If it was just high school stuff I could handle it.

"Remember I told you the story of what happened when I got rousted by those cops at Manor Farms Place. Well, I didn't actually tell you the truth, or at least not all of it," Nell adds in a barely audible whisper.

"Nell, it's OK, tell me."

"They hurt me, D. Bad. They did something to my insides. I can't, won't be able... like never... it's something that I have been thinking about and maybe you have too and I know that, like, you might want, perhaps, one day to have children ... with me... but I can't," she finally gets it out there; her head is bowed, she can't look at him sure that he'll send her away now.

Damien holds her at arms length again and looks closely at her face, kind of like the time, just a day and a half ago, when he first thought she might be sick.

"Say something, D, please?"

"Nell, I don't know how we found each other but I'm glad we did. I will never send you away. You've changed my life in so many ways that I can't even begin to describe it. Remember what you said to me a few years ago? 'We'll find a way.' It's OK, Baby, we'll find a way."

...

The Chopard Blue Diamond is adding quite a few kilometres to its already long, storied life. Created 182 million years ago in the Krishna River delta in Southern

India by exposure of carbon-bearing materials to 58 kilobars of pressure and temperatures of 980° C in the lithospheric mantle, it was brought to the surface by a volcanic eruption passing through a kimberlite pipe. It was mined at just over 150 metres below surface by an Indian labourer around the same time the Smithsonian's Hope Diamond (also a blue diamond although Hope is actually more grayish blue) was found in 17th century Andhra Pradesh. It has at one time or another found itself in the hands of a low level conniving Russian official in the Tsarist regime of Constantine I as well as the estate of Fritz Hoffmann-La Roche. It spent more than 70 years in Basel, Switzerland then Montpellier in southern France. It moved again after one branch of the family, not needing to be told twice by a SS Sturmbannführer that, unhappily, one of their female ancestors had been discovered to be Jewish, from the port of Montpellier. They arrive some time later in another port—Montreal. It had remained there until sold at auction to Bourque's where it first came to the attention of a young Toronto-based physicist and engineer.

It now flies back there with Damien still resting in its unopened gold case embossed with a beautiful, stylish blue *N*.

...

Chapter 11

Compliance

"Good morning everyone, my name is Sayed Bashir, Acting Head of Media Relations for Quantum Computing Corporation. With us this morning we have our CEO, Dr. Damien Bell, our COO, Ms. Ellen Brooks, along with outside advisors Mr. Henry Linnert, Senior Counsel with Lanier Linnert Weiss LLP and Mr. Walter Cunneyworth, attorney with the same firm. Mr. Angelo Keller, financial advisor to the company, is also in attendance via media wall to the left of Ms. Brooks.

"Today, we have with us over 420 accredited media in attendance in the David Deutsch Conference Room at Q-Headquarters here in Toronto. In addition, we have just under 19,000 newsfeeds and video services registered via media wall to participate and ask questions. For those of you that have QEs, could you please have them submit your questions to Q1ntas who you can see behind me to my right. Q1ntas' quantum number is #58129.

"For those of you who do not have QEs (Sayed knows that is practically no one in this audience), you may submit your questions to Q1ntas via messaging service using the same Q-number, which I will repeat again #58129.

"Our CEO will be making a short statement then will take a few questions plus follow-ups. As many of you have been speculating, Dr. Bell has been through a rather tiring couple of days." Some laughter can be heard amongst this restless group of journalists at this last comment. "So he will be leaving us in less than 45 minutes. Ms. Brooks who directed the operation to return Dr. Bell to Q-Computing and to Toronto will then be available to answer further questions."

In fact, Damien has been back in TO for less than six hours. He's had time to go home, sleep for four hours, eat a light meal (berries, nuts, greens, a new habit of his since visiting the Hopi). Ellen had a new suit delivered. He sighs as he puts on yet another formal uniform and pair of dress shoes.

Ellen has not slept. She has showered and changed at Q-HQ, eaten a huge meal of Vietnamese take-out and has been working with Sayed, Q1ntas, Ash3r, Adu1us and others to prepare for this media session to get ahead of the curve. She quite likes working with Bashir. She knows that if Q-Computing does not handle this well, they will not only crater their IPO, they can damage or possibly end their company. They all know it too.

"If you would please raise your hand," Bashir continues, "I will select each journalist in turn. Q1ntas will direct one of the overhead uni-directional quantum mikes your way. It takes about a half second then please state your question in a succinct manner. General statements are not acceptable today, ladies and gentleman. We have a lot to get accomplished so let's stay on point, OK? After our live session, Q1ntas will do his best to group as many similar questions together from the submitted list and have these answered in written form. These will be conveyed to you through your Quantum Counterpart shortly thereafter." Sayed looks around his audience catching the eye of as many journalists as he can, especially Erik Renke from the Toronto Chronicle Tab.

Bashir is a 36-year old media specialist from McLaughlin Markowitz Media now seconded to Q-Computing for the duration, however long that might be. Sayed is a good looking, athletic guy who looks like the former rugby player he is. His right ear has been surgically rebuilt and he has shorn off all of his hair since his playing days at Cornell. He looks like a formidable person but has a warm smile and great personal charm which he uses selectively to terrific effect. He's exactly the same height as Damien although much heavier and stockier in build. His eyes are a lovely light brown.

He's married with two kids whom he adores and can't imagine a better life than the one he is currently living. He's come out of their New York office for this assignment and has already made up his mind to take out a lease on a condo for six months in downtown Toronto. He'll be spending four days each week in Toronto for some time.

A Q-number of #58129 means Bashir has a long term partnership with Q1ntas. Of course, Q-numbers 1, 2, 3 and 4 belong to Pet3r, Vl4d, Ash3r and Su7e, respectively. Q-numbers now have reached over 515,000,000 since the Countdown Party.

"Hello, my name is Damien Bell, CEO of Quantum Computing." Damien looks across the room to where Pet3r has opened a media wall with a prepared text in large type scrolling as he reads and refers to it.

"As many of you know, our Board of Directors convened near New York City recently to consider and ultimately approve an IPO, Initial Public Offering, for this Corporation. It is an event that the hard working and committed team at Q-Computing have striven towards for several years and is a culmination of all their efforts.

"I would like to recognize the work of our senior management team (here he reads a list of their names), our external advisors including (another list of names) and finally I would like to personally thank and congratulate our new COO, Ms. Ellen Brooks."

Damien nods to Ellen who blushes and nods back. A wave of applause sweeps the room for her, no doubt some of it pre-engineered by Sayed. None of the media present applaud but all the Q-staff in the room and those participating via media wall plus all the QEs not only applaud her performance and recent promotion but hoot and holler and call out her name. A chant begins, "ELLEN, ELLEN, ELLEN, ELLEN." The chanting is quite authentic and spontaneous. It's quite humorous to watch QEs with their round faces, skinny arms and big hands clapping and hollering right along with their human counterparts.

"After the meeting, I was detained by the US Department of Homeland Security for approximately 18 hours at a facility south of Washington DC.

"During that time, discussions took place with senior officials of the Department with a view to determining if Quantum Computing Corporation would actively consider licensing its technology to Tier 1 Carriers in the US to provide alternate sales channels for our company and also to provide enhanced access to our line of products for their customer base.

"Ms. Brooks subsequently joined these discussions and she agreed, on behalf of the company, to consider such a change in the business model of this Corporation. Ms. Brooks will be made available later in this media briefing to expand on her role.

"In addition, DHS placed a great deal of emphasis on the security of communications and commerce in the United States and requested reassurance from Company Officers that quantum computing and more specifically Quantum Entities do not undermine either. Both Ms. Brooks and I were able to reassure the Department that safeguards put in place by Q-Computing prevent anything of that nature.

"I am prepared to answer any questions that you may have today," Damien finishes.

They've agreed not to name Dr. Zimmermann directly. Sayed's strong advice here is to give their side of the story and leave an opening for DHS to tell their side. It also leaves open the possibility for a settlement. If they attack DHS, it doesn't.

Damien engages in telling the smart truth here. It's what journos, lawyers and politicians expect and want. He learns 'smart truth' from McLaughlin Markowitz. You don't say more than you have to, you leave some things out, you use positive language and you spin things like Damien does today.

There is a famous example from nearly 60 years ago that demonstrates the concept wonderfully well. The company, the largest soda beverage business in the world at the time and one of its top brands, released a statement that announced that they had designed a dispensing machine that raised pop prices on hot days. It's a form of discriminatory pricing that also serves to maximize profitability.

Their media release was clearly aimed at an audience of investors and analysts who followed the company but it fell into wider distribution. To their consumer, it was just another example of a greedy corporation raising the price of pop just when you needed a cool refreshment the most.

What should they have said instead? The smart truth—that they had invented a machine that lowered prices when ambient temperature dropped. If they'd said that, folks would've thought what good people they are—giving their customers a break for once. It would have had exactly the same impact on corporate earnings but it would have induced a completely different market psychology. The new dispenser was never released after a storm of howls, jeers and protests.

"We'll start with you Mr. Cronkey. Your question?" Sayed points at Mike who stands in one of the few reserved spots at the front of the room nearest the podium.

"Mike Cronkey from OLA Tech Crunch. Dr. Bell, the whole world or at least the 500 million people who are paired with a Quantum Entity have a right and you have an obligation to tell them whether there is some kind of security threat that was unanticipated when you and your firm released these creatures (pointing at QEs around the room) on an unsuspecting world and, if so, what do you plan to do about it?" Cronkey is not pulling any punches today.

"Mike, that's two questions," Damien answers.

Sayed has to keep from rolling his eyes in exasperation when he hears Damien say this. Ellen does roll her eyes. They have both told him again not to appear smarter than his audience, to project his 'nice' inner self to this group which will almost certainly generate well over a billion views today.

"The American people need to hear your answer, Dr.

Bell."

"Quite right, Mike. Look, in every efficacy test that has been conducted by us or by independent labs, there has never been a single instance of a Quantum Counterpart acting contrary to the best interest of a human being. You know from your own personal experience and nearly everyone else in this room," Damien combines his voice, arm and eyes to sweep the room from front to back and side to side in what Sayed thinks is now a better performance by him, "also know from their personal experience what wonderful helpmates QEs have become.

"What's more our company does not trade in QEs or profit in any way from their work—they are masters of their own fates together with their human counterparts. They DO NOT BELONG TO ME OR Q-COMPUTING. They belong to you and you and you. They belong to themselves," Damien points at the thousands of windows open on media walls of this conference room named after one of the 'fathers' of quantum computing from the 1970s.

These windows have humans in them interspersed with QEs and sometimes both humans and QEs share the same window with big-headed QEs mostly looking over the shoulder of their smaller human counterparts. He also knows that probably every QE on the planet is in attendance but their presence might only be visible if you could somehow see at the pico scale.

"Next, Mr. Renke?" Sayed says.

"Mr. Bell, Erik Renke here from the Toronto Chronicle Tab." Ellen's eyes narrow and she frowns at Sayed's selection of this slime ball from a sleazy tabloid newsfeed for question no. 3.

"Isn't it true that DHS has discovered that your company has been stealing secret scientific files from US Government departments for years, that the invention of QEs really came out of DARPA labs, that your company is in possession of stolen IP and, finally, QE's have been plundering US national accounts and stealing money too?"

Erik is excited. He's been wanting to get a hold of a

big story for years, maybe be the first tabloid journo ever to win a Pulitzer. By this time, he's been writing about Q-Computing for four years and has developed an antipathy towards the company and its creepy group of young executives, so he's been looking hard for stuff to dig up and report about them. He can't stand their Smart Alec CEO but he completely detests that stuck up bitch, now COO, Brooks who is worse.

Sayed and Ellen have warned Damien not to lose his temper and again not to belittle his audience. He's been trained not to answer questions like this by saying, 'We don't steal secrets from the US' or 'All our IP is ours not DARPA's'. If he answers sucker questions like that then headlines will read and video intros will start with, 'Q-Computing Denies Theft' or 'DARPA's Secrets Stolen?'

It's an old journo trick; basically a riff on 'Sir, do you beat your wife?' If answered, 'No, I don't beat my wife' leads to headlines like 'Bell Denies Beating Wife'. The only thing that most folks who see this stuff will remember is, 'I didn't know that Damien Bell was a wife beater!'

Journalists understand that if they ask enough of these type of questions, one celebrity or another will fall for it and ask something in return like, 'How did you know?' or 'Who told you?' They're all doing enough shit and have so many enemies both real and perceived that it will often turn into gold. Damien's plan after discussions with Bashir is to answer his own questions and never be negative; it takes a lot of discipline to resist the natural human impulse to get off the podium and punch out a guy like Renke or lynch him as an example to the rest of the pack.

"Mr. Renke, I'm glad you asked those questions. We produce Quantum Entities in Lab 4 in the Department of Physics at the University of Toronto in what we call the 'Hatchery'." While Damien talks Pet3r shows images of smiling people and their equally happy saucer shaped Quantum Counterparts plus pictures of the Lab and the Vault which have long been public, since inadvertently released during Nell's first visit there.

"The work that we do here is based in part on my PhD thesis written while I attended Waterloo's Perimeter Institute and in part rests on work first done by Max Planck, Erwin Schrödinger, Werner Heisenberg, Max Born, Wolfgang Pauli, Niels Bohr, Paul Dirac and John von Neumann not to mention the man after whom this conference room was named, David Deutch. There has been important input as well from Traian Vasilescu, our CTO, and Dr. Luis Castagino, my Post Doctoral Supervisor.

"No scientist stands alone, Mr. Renke. But the provenance of Quantum Entities is clear."

"Follow up?" Bashir asks making sure that everyone knows he's giving this slime ball every opportunity to have his 'fair share' of access at this presser.

Before Erik can ask his follow up question, a man, taller than anyone else in the room suddenly shouts, "YOU ARE THE DEVIL INCARNATE, YOU HAVE MADE AN ABOMINATION AND YOU SHALL BE PUNISHED BY GOD AND HIS DISCIPLES FOR IT."

His voice is a marvelous tenor and carries to every part of the room. Ellen's security people immediately descend on the guy but Damien holds up a hand and calmly says, "Sir, do you have running water in your home, a kitchen, a refrigerator, a media wall, Internet, a computer? How did you get here? Did you drive or take the subway? Do you take any medicines that your doctor prescribes for you? Do you know how those meds are formulated or fabricated? Does one of your kids have asthma and need treatment? Has your Dad got Alzheimer's or your Mom have breast cancer and need help? Do you have reliable power in your home? Have you ever flown in an airplane? Do you know what stem cell treatment is, sir? All of these technologies once were new and have led to human life expectancies that in most parts of the world are nearing 120 for women and 112 for men. Would you take those from us too?"

Pointing at Damien with his long arm and bony hand,

the man continues, "God promised us that Man would rule the Earth and all would be under his dominion. He created us in his image. You have usurped the role of God. You have played god. You have unleashed Frankenstein on the believers. You have seduced them with easy work and easy money. You are damned and your immortal soul is forfeit," the man finishes.

"That is for God to decide, not you sir," Damien replies.

At this point, Ellen tells security via Ash3r to remove the guy. They hustle him out. There's no point in being upset that he somehow got into their briefing. They pre-screened everyone of course—for legitimate media credentials, weapons, you name it. These days their scanners are good down to the atomic level. They have to be.

Humans can bring poisons, bombs or contagions on or inside their bodies and, more recently, computer viruses on their persons too. It's all the rage to have body tattoos done with inks that have NSM mixed in so they can flash, play music, videos, a newsfeed, do computing and communication and so carry a virus as well. But there's no scan for what's in a person's mind so there's just no way to screen for every crazy.

Damien detests tattoos and neither he, nor Nell or Ellen has any. It's something that Pops told him about permanently marking human beings—to separate them into groups. Gangs do it, the Gestapo did it, Damien won't. He thinks there are enough things that separate humans from each other without more lines being drawn between them.

Strangely, it is this last comment from Damien about God's judgment, delivered in absolute calm, directly and with no prevarication to a world-wide audience that forms the majority of headlines for the serious press during the day and the next after that. It goes over especially well with their American audience.

Some outlets follow the lead of the Toronto Chronicle

Tab and run video and copy that begin with intros like 'Meet the New Dr. Frankenstein' over an image of Damien with a high forehead and electrodes protruding from his neck and, in a case of mixed metaphors, fanged teeth or 'Monsters Watching You?' accompanied by images of cute, cuddly, saucer shaped QEs somehow made to look Big Brotherish which, given the subject, is not easy for a graphic artist to do. Other headlines from the gutter press like 'Stolen Secrets, Yours Too?' or 'Who's Got Your Money?' or 'Meet Your New Boss' are everywhere.

The only other tough question is from the Wall Street Journal via media wall about how safe the US banking system and the public's electronic wallets are from pilfering by QEs and Q-Computing. The rest of the questions are lob balls—more about the actual incident itself. Damien turns it over to Ellen to answer the WSJ. After that, it's just a tell-all from her about the last 36 hours with some input from Henry and Walter confirming he served a writ of Habeas Corpus on DHS.

Many of the newsfeeds will run with a slant that Bashir has already seeded even before the conference begins. Simultaneous with the start of the conference, several hundred of them release images, copy and some select video of heroic COO Ellen Brooks rescuing their CEO from the clutches of Dr. Evil (who still has not been named).

He has even mixed in some mild references to a possible romantic link between these two photogenic personages to keep infotainment services interested and also bring largely positive press. Nothing sells better than love, sex and betrayal. There is some speculation that Damien is going to dump superstar Nell for his new, younger squeeze who he has just promoted to COO in what is clearly a sexually motivated move since obviously no 23-year old woman could possibly have achieved what she has on merit, especially one that looks like Ellen.

...

Nell, sleeping in her Grandfather's guest room in the pueblo at Third Mesa under a heap of blankets despite mild weather, is unaware of this feint by Sayed to throw media hounds off the scent. Su7e has made up her mind not to tell her when she wakes up and asks about D and his company. She worries and wants Nell to focus on getting her strength back not a possibly two-timing Damien Bell.

It would be trivial for Su7e to find out if he is, in fact, being unfaithful to Nell but Nell has told her not to spy on anyone or anything without permission so, of course, she doesn't.

Dafne Weinstein is with Nell in Third Mesa together with two nurses, a nutritionist, a cook, her personal trainer Wendy Morales (for when she will feel better), and the ever-present Dekka. Weinstein is busying herself having modern equipment installed including communications gear, media walls, cooking apparatus, portable showers, solar power for energy and ambient heating, hot water and hot food. She's even had dry EKOLET biodigester toilets with evaporation tanks flown in from Helsinki. Hopi children seem to love the new toilets; so much so that Dafne often has to shoo one or more of the tiny kids out when she has to actually use one of the contraptions.

The only thing she is not allowed to do by Hopi Elders is replace hand and toe holds with a modern hydraulic rail elevator. She refuses to use dangerous-looking hand and toe holds so Dafne has to fold her long form into an ancient rope elevator and be winched by hand from the mesa above to wind cave and pueblo below.

...

Meanwhile, Media Pulse Analytics, Q-Computing's media service, on a sub-contract from McLaughlin Markowitz, shows a tonality on the Internet that is largely positive for Q-Computing and even more positive for QEs themselves. Sayed silently speculates that QEs could be weighing in on the matter and biasing results for that part of their survey.

"If someone tells you that any press is good press as long as they spell your name right, tell them to get their head read," Ellen says to Sayed, Damien and Angelo in a small conference room at Q-Headquarters. Angelo attends via media wall but the others are present in flesh and blood along with their QEs.

It's a pretty relaxed atmosphere given all that has occurred in the last few weeks. Their IPO is on hold indefinitely. Investment Bankers, those hard-hearted, 'logical' money-changers are more influenced by their primitive brains than an 'Italian stallion' in a 1980s era disco movie. Ellen has seen Saturday Night Live and laughed at it along with her sorority sisters at Elmira. Bankers are highly influenced by good press or bad despite protest to the contrary and, under these circumstances, there is no way to predict how markets will react to incredible media attention focused on them recently so they're not going to take a chance. No IPO for awhile.

They can afford to wait. Damien's insistence right from their early days in cramped quarters in Lab 4 until today is to watch their costs carefully and grow revenues. They are profoundly cash flow positive (with revenues topping an unheard of $7 million New Dollars per employee per year). They can afford to wait until either their current situation with respect to US Government investigations and possible anti-trust action is resolved or markets in general improve or hopefully all three.

It is getting close to Christmas, a nostalgic time for Ellen. She plans on spending her well earned vacation time with her parents in upstate New York. Her older bother, Jon and his wife, Natalie, and baby, Lily, will be there too. It will give Ellen a chance to play with her niece who has just turned one and is becoming this marvelous new human being. Ellen can't wait to squeeze Lily who has started to recognize her, Ellen is sure.

"I would like to know how it became 'general public

knowledge' that Ellen got her present position by subterfuge," Damien asks looking at Sayed. This is Damien code for 'trading sexual favours in return for promotion.'

"Don't know," shrugs Sayed innocently. "Tabs will say anything to increase their number of views. They made it up, Damien."

"You planted those stories, Sayed," remarks Angelo turning on their media wall towards Sayed. "Good thing too," he adds, "otherwise those Frankenstein fear-mongerers would have dominated media coverage. Sex is a good distraction, nice work."

"I have no idea what you are referring to," Sayed insouciantly replies.

"If you want I can have Adu1us recount the number of feeds you and your QEs doctored?"

"Boys, that's enough," says Ellen. "Ridiculous stories were bound to circulate. I told you, Angelo, giving the job to a woman would lead to problems."

"Nonsense, you've done a fine job," Angelo replies.

"I second that," Damien adds.

"Thanks, guys. But before we break for Xmas, we have to reply to this demand letter we received from DOJ two days ago."

"Why isn't Henry in on this meeting?" Damien asks.

"I think this is more a business issue than a legal one," Ellen answers. "I'll brief him later. Right now I want your input."

"Fuck them," Sayed says. "We're cash flow positive; we have more than $85 billion New Dollars in cash and near cash (money market instruments) on our balance sheet. Let's take our chances and litigate with those motherfuckers."

"I am not persuaded by your eloquent argument," Angelo wryly comments.

"Me neither. I think we should treat the Americans like an elephant—let's feed them one peanut at a time. To me, one more day for us is one less for them," Damien says. "Ellen was right all along. Let's change our business model;

we'll bring in our competitors and license our technology to them. That way they will become our co-opetitors." Damien looks at Ellen and gives her a huge Cheshire Cat smile. He learned everything he knows about co-opetition from her.

Angelo notes how a smile from Damien practically lifts Ellen out of her Knoll Pollack ergonomic office chair. He rolls his eyes.

"We can appear to comply with Dr. Evil," Damien adds. That is their new name for Zimmermann; Ellen was the first to use the term. Damien has no doubt that Sayed will find a way to leak his nickname to newsfeeds. "Ellen will work with our product development and biz dev group. I would guess that she'll find a way to increase our IRR at the same time. It'll be money for nothing."

"Chicks for free," Sayed finishes for him.

Damien had no intention of actually saying that; he just shrugs. "When a reseller pays for a Q-Phone in advance and pays for all the costs of marketing and customer service and then they remit 40% of their revenues to us, why, we'll be just like Apple—do absolutely nothing and get paid for it. Even better, let's sit back, drink a few beers and have some fun."

"Won't that cannibalize our own offering?" Sayed asks.

"Not a chance," Angelo answers. "We have 517 million clients, out of a potential market for Q-Phones of at least 3.5 billion and maybe 5 billion. We were never going to get them all. Let other carriers do some of the work then we'll have 'intricated' them into our ecosystem—more political cover for us in Washington and Brussels."

"Intricate?" Ellen asks.

"It's a term used by former US Attorney General Eliot Richardson, long since deceased bless his soul. It means: 'To bring people on board or to get them onside with an idea or a proposal or an initiative of some type by getting them 'intricated' into the process bit by bit, almost without their noticing that they are making a commitment.'"

"That's a cool use of the word," remarks Sayed.

"What about the second part of Dr. Evil's 'deal'?" Ellen asks.

Everyone looks at Damien. This is the unmentioned elephant in the room.

"As I said, feed them one peanut at a time. I'll bet we can buy a year, maybe more, just appearing to comply with part of their demands. They're bureaucrats; delay has no meaning to them."

"I think you are mistaken, Damien," Angelo continues, "DOJ is interested in anti-trust enforcement. I agree we can appear, maybe more than appear, to comply, at least as far as Q-Phones are concerned. But Department of Homeland Security wants the Quantum Key so they can take control of QEs and monitor quantum communications. They want to be able to reassert their control of the Internet, intercept and decrypt quantum processes and put a stop to what they call 'drogues'."

"I don't believe that, Angelo. I was there. Zimmermann has something else in mind, I just don't know what. Those drogues don't exist; they're a pretext," Damien says. "It's like the second Tonkin Gulf incident between US Naval forces and North Vietnamese torpedo boats which involved false radar images and led Congress to give the President of the day authority to commit US ground forces to war. They killed more than 58,000 young Americans and nearly 1.1 million Vietnamese soldiers. For what?"

"My question exactly," says Angelo. "It's a pretext for what?"

"For war," answers Damien. "They say they want the Key to thwart 'drogues'. That's just a politically correct way these days of saying 'kill'. But who is to judge that? Do you trust DHS to make a determination whose Quantum Counterpart lives, who dies? I don't."

"I don't either," Ellen says with a shudder. She was there too and she knows.

So they agree to ask Henry to respond to DOJ. They

will say they fully intend to cooperate with DOJ's investigation and they will take immediate action to comply—they will break their own 'monopoly' on Q-Phones. They won't say anything in their letter about Quantum Counterparts—they will just be silent on that issue. However, in reality QEs will remain under exclusive control of Q-Computing and that means Damien Graham Bell.

...

It doesn't take long for the relative equanimity of the last few days to dissipate. Just four days before their Christmas break and two days after delivery of Henry's letter offering (partial) compliance, they receive a subpoena from the Senate Judiciary Antitrust Subcommittee demanding the presence of US Citizens Damien Bell, CEO of Quantum Computing Corporation, and Ellen Brooks, COO of said same corporation. Senators are demanding the presence of senior executives of the company to discuss economic issues not just legal ones. Sending Henry won't do.

It is obvious now to QCC's management team that recent relative lack of activity by DOJ was a sham and that they always intended to take further action no matter what response they receive from Q-Computing.

A second executive meeting is being held in a rather larger conference room at Q-HQ. There are 25 people either in the room or attending via media wall. All have their QEs with them. Of the 50 sentient creatures (even Damien has by now come around to the notion that QEs are 'people'), 49 of them are strongly advising their CEO not to comply with the subpoena.

Traian sums it up best; "Damien, you're the only person who has the Quantum Key. This is not about anti-trust, it's about control." When Traian gets upset, it's still possible to detect a slight accent. "They'll grab you again."

"I'll take Samir and Barbon with me. I'll be fine," Damien says. Samir and Barbon are two bodyguards Ellen assigned to Damien around the clock. Both are very tough and competent hombres. They are recommended and vouched for by Dekka.

"That's the most naive thing you've ever said, buddy," comments Traian.

"Heck, by bringing things out in the open the way we have," Damien looks over at Bashir, "we've neutered them. If I go, I'll have a platform to speak to the US, its Government and its people. Otherwise, we leave the field to DOJ and its allies. Everyone will only hear one side of the story—theirs."

"I'll go," Ellen says bravely.

"Not a chance. There is no way they're gonna have a crack at both of us again. That's an order, Brooks. You stay with the ship," Damien says.

They debate the matter for another hour but in the end there's only one vote that counts and that's Damien's. "Look they're not gonna quasi kidnap me on Capitol Hill in front of a billion people. I'll get a chance to put our case forward in a way they're not expecting.

"Right now US GDP ranks third in the world after Imperial China and the EU. The way the AU is growing, it won't be long til the US is No. 4. But wait, there's more. What's the 5th largest GDP today? India, right? OK, whose 6th?

"Brazil, Germany, Russia? None of the above. It's QE Nation."

This is a new thought to all of them, except Damien.

"QE Nation is the fastest growing economy on the planet with the fastest growing population. Its GDP is now in excess of $8.5 trillion New Dollars. Now what's the one advantage the US currently has over Imperial China? They allow QE immigrants (they're from Toronto, Canada after all) to work in their nation. China's QE population? Zero. Where's the greatest concentration of Q-Phones and QEs? The good ole US of A. What's the fastest growing quantum economy on the planet? Right again, the US. How can the US catch up to Imperial China? Right again, by embracing quantum economics. Now can anyone here tell me who is gonna be able to put these arguments in front of the American people better than one of the founders of our company, in fact, its CEO?"

Damien authorizes Henry to reply that he will appear before the Senate hearing early in January.

...

Damien has another reason for wanting to go back to the States. He wants to visit Nell who is still in Third Mesa. She is not recovering as fast as they all had hoped. He wants to spend Xmas with his girl then head to DC for the hearings before returning to Toronto.

...

The day before their Christmas break, Ellen is in her office at Q-HQ at her customary start time of 0700 hours. She's wearing blue jeans and a rosé colored mock turtle neck. Damien has already been there for at least half an hour. He drops by. Everyone is gearing down.

He has never once seen her in blue jeans and he smiles broadly when he glimpses her like that. She's also wearing bright red sneakers in place of her usual 5 cm stilettos. Instead of looking nearly eye-to-eye, Damien can look down at her for once.

"I just came by to wish you a Merry Xmas," Damien says.

"Thanks. You too."

"You looking forward to some time with the 'famdamily'?" he asks.

"You bet."

Ellen is looking at her watch.

"You going somewhere?"

"Yep."

Impulsively, Damien asks, "Mind if I tag along." Basically, he just wants to thank her for sticking around this year. It's been tough and there's no doubt she saved his bacon and the company's too.

"Nope."

"Where're we going?"

"You'll see."

He follows her out. Q-HQ is designed in such a way that every stairway, elevator, corridor, internal street, eatery or public space eventually empties into the 'pit'—an enormous atrium that holds nearly all 4,000+ Q-Computing Toronto-based employees and of course all 500 million plus QEs too. You can't 'sneak' out of the building without being seen although that is not the point of its design.

Rather, the building is designed to maximize tribal gatherings and interaction where serendipitous meetings and discoveries take place at a fantastic rate. People and QEs meet, mix, eat (well humans do that), sleep (many of the stairs are nearly a metre wide and covered in soft materials suitable for recharging low batteries, as in take a catnap), play games, convene planned and impromptu get-togethers, party, play music, dance, hold events, entertain clients and suppliers, impress bankers, do media conferences and briefings.

They pick up Samir and Barbon on the way as well as Ellen's security detail. Ellen has a company car waiting.

They drive over to Toronto Soup Kitchen where Ellen will be serving Xmas breakfast and lunch to the homeless, the disaffected, the poor and the functionally insane who, some by preference, are living on the streets of Toronto. She hands Damien an apron and a paper hat that looks like a sawed-off dunce cap. He's a slopper. He cleans plates of leftover food, gives them a quick rinse and stacks them for someone else to put in their huge industrial dishwasher, which looks like it could wash every plate in Metro Toronto in about five minutes.

He has to sign a waiver like everyone else that if it suddenly cuts off his hand or something bad otherwise happens, he won't sue for damages.

Ellen also wears an apron but is spared the hat—she wears a hairnet instead. It takes a lot of work to put her fantastically thick hair into the thing but she manages it and to still look very cute at the same time.

She goes from table to table making sure everyone is fed. She talks to each of them. 'Normal people' usually just look through the homeless and poor—they are the invisibles. But Ellen has a nice smile for everyone especially the children. If they want seconds, no problem. It's table service for all today. She wishes everyone a Merry Christmas. No one seems to mind despite the fact that Toronto is the most international city in the world and there is practically every colour and creed in the place. It's a season of joy and peace for all.

Damien is completely immersed in his job. The servers and busboys bring dirty dishes faster than he can wipe them. Their assembly line needs a bit of fine tuning. He separates and specializes slopper jobs by putting one guy on cutlery, one on disposal of leftovers and another on garbage detail. He does the rinsing and stacking. Another guy loads the dishwasher. Throughput increases by about 30%. Ellen gives him a friendly thumbs up from across the dining room.

They work through breakfast and get a break about mid-morning. The young guys working with Damien (one of them is in middle school, the others are in high school and need some volunteer hours to graduate) are tired. Damien is not.

He sits companionably with them asking about their lives, hopes and dreams. Ellen comes over with coffee. She sits on the bench next to him. All the guys ogle her.

"Hey," she says.

"Hey, yourself. I'm glad you brought me."

"You invited yourself, remember."

"Sure but you did bring me."

"We have about half an hour before the lunch crowd starts to come in. Want to take a walk?"

"Absolutely."

...

"I want you to be careful," Ellen says to him as they walk along the downtown streets of TO. Their four person security detail is being as unobtrusive as they can be but given the size of the three men (one of Ellen's security people is a woman by the name of Ophélie Moreau, originally from Trois-Rivières, Québec who makes up in cunning what she lacks in size), it's pretty obvious to pedestrians that the couple walking nearby are some kind of VIPs. Far more Torontonians recognize Ellen these days than Damien especially since he forgot to take off his ridiculous paper hat.

"We don't know what my crazy countrymen are really up to, we just think we do and that worries me."

"I'll be fine, Ellen. You'll see, they'll blink first. With Americans, it's always about the economy, stupid."

"Angelo thinks that their security apparatus will trump everything else."

"You know Angelo doesn't know everything, Ellen."

"He's been around a long time and we should listen to him."

He changes the subject. "How did you get involved with the Soup Kitchen?"

"I've been doing it since I first moved to TO. Did you see the sleeve of my sweater?" She pulls off her overcoat on the right hand side of her body so Damien can see it.

"It's made by RAK, Random Act of Kindness. You're supposed to do a random act of kindness every time you wear one of their pieces. They stitch their motto into everything they sell so when you put it on, you're reminded of your civic duty. Four years ago, when I first bought one of their t-shirts, I thought maybe it was a good idea to do something and I guess this is it."

There is something else she wants to tell him so he remains silent.

"Damien, there is something I think you should know."

"Uh, huh?"

"I've been in touch with Nell and Dafne Weinstein as

well as Nell's doctor who was given permission to talk to me."

Damien stops walking and turns to face Ellen who also stops, not really taking in what he's just heard.

"What?"

"I just wanted you to know that you might find, like you may notice, a change in her, not for the better and you need to be prepared for that, OK?"

"I was just talking to her and Su7e the other day and they both seemed to be in great spirits. What's going on, Ellen and how come you get to worry about this too with everything else you have to do?"

"I can handle myself."

"Yeah, I noticed."

They walk along for awhile without saying much.

"Merry Christmas, Ellen," he says when they get back to Toronto Soup Kitchen for their afternoon shift.

Ellen suddenly turns to Damien and hugs him in her strong arms. "I'll see you after the Senate Hearings, Damien."

...

Chapter 12

Third Mesa

Damien stands over Nell's bed at Third Mesa. She is sleeping, covered by her large wedding blanket that every Hopi girl makes and hopes to use one day for that purpose. Fresh wildflowers in a jar at the foot of her bed fill the room with a subtle fragrance. Two solar powered space heaters warm the room. Although he can't see her, Dezba, Nell's Mayan worry doll, is tucked away under her pillow. Nell is only one quarter Hopi but it seems the most important part of her at this stage of her life.

There are several IV bags on a pole nearby connected to lines taped to her left arm and then running into a single hollow needle inserted into a vein on the back of her hand. Nell is even thinner than the last time he saw her. Her skin colour has changed from yellow-tinged to pale white. He understands that they are trying to keep her hydrated; there is also God knows what other substances being dripped into her system. Damien will find out.

He sits and waits.

Presently, she wakes and looks up. "D, you're here," she cries out. "I can't believe it! Come here right now!"

She sounds like the old Nell. He sits carefully on the bed and sweeps her up into his arms. There is practically nothing there. He kisses her and holds her gently.

"How are you?"

"Fine," she replies, "I have everything I need right here except you and now I have that too."

He decides not to tell her that he can only stay until just after New Year's Day so he just smiles at her. They spend the next hour catching up. She wants to hear all the latest news about Q-Computing.

"I'm so proud of you and Traian and Ellen too. Imagine a 23-year old COO. And a woman too!"

By this time she is getting noticeably weaker. He's

been in the room for less than 90 minutes.

"D, I was wondering if you could do something for me?"

"Sure, Nell. What?"

"I want them to take these things out of my body," she asks weakly holding up her left arm. "My hand hurts and I feel yucky a lot of the time. I know they tell me it's helping but I don't feel well. They told me what's in those bags but I can't seem to remember."

Nell doesn't tell him that she wants to clear her mind or why. Drugs they are giving her, apart from making her feel sick, are clouding her head, she is sure of it. They are interfering with her dreams and her state of being. Nell feels strongly that she still has some important work to do. The urgency within her has become more pressing with each passing day. She can't seem to make anyone around her understand that—not Dafne, Wendy, her RNs or her doctor. She's been waiting for Damien. He will help her.

"I'll talk to your doctor soon, Nell. I'm here. We'll get you fixed up," he adds with another smile.

"Hey, D, can you tell me a story?"

"Sure. What would you like to hear?"

"You promised to tell me the story of the Master and Margarita!"

"That was years ago."

"So?"

"Right." He looks closely at her again, "That's too long a story for right now. How about I tell you how the Devil first arrives in Moscow? It's an allegory which Ruskies love. It kinda shows up bureaucrats and humans who are too big for their boots. It happens right at the beginning of the book too so it'll be a down payment by me to you on the rest of the story. OK?"

She knows that, as an entrepreneur, he loves those kinds of stories so she just says, "Great."

Damien begins, "There is a poet and a professor sitting on a bench at Patriarch's Pond in Moscow enjoying a lovely summer afternoon. The professor tells the poet, a sensitive but ignorant person, that Man is in complete control of his destiny. He can prove it too—he knows exactly what he will be doing that evening—presiding over a meeting of fellow professors at Massolit, their literary club. He's kind of their chief bureaucrat or something.

"You know what they say about professors, Nell?"

"No, what D?"

"The smaller the stakes, the bigger the battle."

Nell laughs dutifully, mostly to encourage her guy.

"The professor is also saying that he knows what he will be doing every day of every week—his schedule is well laid out and perfectly planned.

"One of my pals from the University of New South Wales, Hal Sheppard, used to tell me that human beings are like these tiny water-borne creatures with small feeble water wings rushing along in a torrential river of life at incredible speed. They can influence their direction a little bit by flapping their little wings really hard. It moves them a bit to the left or a bit right or up or down but basically life is gonna take them where it takes them anyway."

"Is that in the book, D?"

"Nope."

Nell is trying to keep him on point!

"Anywho, there is a shimmering light, really nothing more than the briefest desert-like mirage and this tall, strange-looking man is there. One eye is green—"

"Like my eyes!" Nell says sweetly.

Damien reaches over and gives her a light poke then begins giving her a delicate head massage, alternately stroking her hair and squeezing her scalp which he knows she loves as he continues with his story.

"Only one eye is green, Nell, the other is quite dark. He strides right over to where the poet and professor are sitting companionably on the bench and wedges himself between them.

"'Strange', the professor thinks. The tall man, after some chit chat tells the professor that he does not have perfect control over anything and he can prove it! The professor thinks that a madman is loose on the streets of Moscow so he is anxious now to be on his way. He certainly doesn't want to be late for the important meeting he will chair at Massolit. He makes excuses to the stranger and the young poet that he must go. The stranger replies that it is impossible, impossible because 'Anna has already spilt the oil.'

"The professor is now quite sure the man is mad and, after a few more polite nothings, he excuses himself and waddles off as fast as he can to catch a trolley to take him to his club.

"But he slips and pitches headlong into the street landing on his back, slamming his head forcefully on the cobblestones. Stunned, he just has time to see the driver of the approaching trolley making a big round 'O' with her mouth as she applies the handbrake as best she can, but not soon enough. The large driver's side front steel wheel of the trolley cuts off the professor's head which rolls out from under the streetcar into the nearby gutter.

"The young poet, a sensitive person, sees his mentor's head rolling into the gutter and is distressed beyond words by the sight. He hears someone in the crowd shrieking, 'It was Anna. Her jar of oil broke and the poor man must have slipped in it. What a shame. Call the police!'

"Ruskies used a lot of oil in those days for cooking and heating. So you see the professor never did arrive at the club. Even the ignorant poet will soon realize that the Devil is loose in Moscow."

Nell is asleep again when he finishes his story. He smoothes her wonderful auburn hair for a few moments before leaving to speak with her doctor.

...

Damien and Pet3r have both read Nell's medical record including not only her doctor's notes but also observations from her two nurses, one of whom is an Advanced Practice RN. Damien thinks that there are large gaps in the file and is eager to discuss matters with her doctor who, as Nell's condition has worsened, has moved to Third Mesa. He's from LA and has seen Nell in the past.

"There are gaps in the file because we are not certain exactly what is going on with Miss Nell." He is a bit defensive while responding to a question from Damien. "This is a primitive community with only the most basic facilities and we need to get her back to Torrance Memorial for a full work up before we can—"

"Doctor, I can assure you that Su7e has access to every conceivable test that you might want to run and can provide you with everything you require to effect diagnosis and treatment. If there is anything else you need, we can have it brought here. Nell is not going to LA; she's made that clear already."

"Mr. Bell, these 'things' are not trained diagnosticians nor are they approved by the AMA or the board of my hospital for use in medical matters so it is impossible for me to rely on a piece of software that Nell's boyfriend, you, wrote while you were in school." To the doctor, Damien is just a kid in jeans and sweatshirt who made some money writing code.

"Summarize for me doctor what you do know, please."

"We know that she contracted Query Fever on a farm near Bucharest. We have been treating it with doxycycline and hydroxychloroquine which we expected would ameliorate her condition within about a month. Miss Nell has lost approximately 17% of her body mass during that time. We appear to have the bacterial infection under control and her skin tone and color have improved but there seems to be a secondary condition causing further weight loss."

"Doctor, does Nell have a form of cancer?" Damien asks straight out.

"We don't know. We have run through such standard tests that we can do in this place and the results, so far, are negative. If Nell is suffering from cancer, she might suffer from muscular pain, joint pain or bone pain but she has reported none of these."

The doctor, looking Damien up and down as if he is some kind of reptile continues, "Ah, since we do not know what, beyond the bacterial infection, might be causing further deterioration in Nell's condition, it would be inappropriate for, shall we say, anyone to exchange bodily fluids with her. In fact, I may have to notify the Arizona Department of Health Services that she may have a communicable disease of unknown origin which will mean she will be isolated until we do know."

By this point, Damien just wants to punch the guy's lights out. Instead he says, "Su7e, may I speak with you?"

"Hi Damien," Su7e answers. She's on one of the portable media walls that Dafne has had hung incongruously in and about Third Mesa.

"Merry Christmas, Su7e. Can you tell me what you have found so far?"

"Merry Christmas, Damien. I have spoken with the doctor and given him my report."

"May I please have it directly since it is not included in Nell's medical record?"

"I have detected certain hematological malignancies at the nano scale that are, I believe, affecting Nell's DNA. There is speculation that speciation and cancer are related. That speculation arises because nature does not usually waste energy producing parts of the ecosystem that have no purpose. Since cancer is prevalent in the geologic record, it has an assumed purpose.

"No human has ever witnessed speciation or been able to reproduce a condition leading to such an occurrence. Of course, all you have to do is look at the natural world where there are estimated to be approximately 12 million different species of bacteria, 35 million of insects, 1.6 million invertebrates, 2.1 million fungi and I can provide you with additional information concerning lichens, corals, crustaceans—"

"Su7e!" asks Damien hoping to bring her directly back to the subject of Nell's health.

"This has a bearing, Damien. Please be patient.

"The point I am making is that, given the intense amount of work and research done in this area since the time of Charles Darwin, we have not been able to observe or induce speciation despite the large number of species that do exist. We know that long necked giraffes have been naturally selected for survival with an advantage over short necked ones because they can forage at higher elevations during drought conditions.

"Geographic isolation over very long geologic periods of time may also create new species but doesn't entirely explain the current large number of species. Mutation also likely plays a role but it requires a mate in the same epoch with the same mutation in geographic proximity to breed with, which is prohibitively improbable.

"However, there is speculation that cancer or more precisely cancer-causing viruses may infect whole populations making them unable to inter-breed with the original population but which conveniently provide a mutant population large enough and sufficiently geospatially concentrated enough to reproduce successfully.

"I believe that Query Fever may have weakened Nell to the point where it provided a vector for a virus, a rare perhaps never before seen, form of cancer that is causing changes in her DNA."

"Do you mean she is transforming to, to something, ah," Damien pauses, "different?"

"This is complete speculation by some kind of clever program that is completely unqualified to answer that," the doctor exclaims.

"Doctor, please do not interrupt again. Su7e?"

"My analysis shows that her DNA is being interfered with including its synthesis and function."

"We need to call Arizona Department of Health Services right away."

"You will do nothing at all, doctor," Damien tells him with a look of such intensity that he involuntarily takes a step back.

"Su7e, what is being administered to Nell through her IV?"

"She's is being hydrated and the doctor has prescribed doxycycline, hydroxychloroquine, monoclonal antibodies and tyrosine kinase inhibitors as well as purines sometimes called pyrimidines."

"What do the latter do?"

"Pyrimidines become building blocks of DNA, stopping normal development."

"Which means, doctor, you have been making your patient worse," a furious Damien says.

...

"Merry Christmas, Nell."

"Is it Christmas already, D?"

"Yes it is, Honey. How are you feeling this morning?"

"Good sweetie," she answers.

"Any pain?"

"No, I'm fine, really." She looks down at her hand. Her IV was removed overnight and her hand has been iced as well—the swelling has gone down noticeably.

"My mind is less cloudy today, more like the old Nell really." She smiles her beautiful smile at him.

"I have something for you. Do you think you could sit up?"

"Sure."

Damien motions to her nurse to help Nell adjust to a sitting position putting a number of pillows behind her to prop her up. Dezba is there too but Damien says nothing about the presence of her worry doll. That's for another time.

"Thank you for your help," Damien says and with a gesture, asks her to leave them alone.

"I don't have anything for you, D. Xmas just kinda crept up on me. I'm sorry."

He hands her a bright gold box from Bourque's with a lovely *N* on it.

"It's really nice, D."

"It'd be nicer if you opened it."

She opens the box looking down at a brilliant Chopard Blue Diamond. Appropriately, she is still wrapped up in her Hopi wedding blanket.

"It's lovely, Damien. Beautiful. What's the occasion, Dear?"

"It's an engagement ring." He drops down on one knee by her bedside, so he can be eye to eye with her and says simply, "Marry me, Nell."

Nell, clutching her marriage blanket with her good hand, just looks with wonder at the fantastic ring he has just offered her.

"But I'm no good for you, D. I can't have your baby and I can't even make love to you until I'm better and I dunno know when that will be."

He climbs into bed and pulls her to him holding her in his powerful arms. He takes the ring from the box and puts it on the third finger of her left hand. He had it sized for her (Su7e gave Bourque's exact dimensions) but even so it is now too large.

He has given the staff instructions to take precautions around Nell in the event that her condition is, in fact, contagious. They now wear surgical gloves and avoid any possible exchanges of fluids. Nell eats and drinks using separate dishes and cutlery. He takes no precautions for himself.

"Nell, we have to talk about a living trust for you."

"You don't have to worry, D, I've been working on my will."

"Nell, we're gonna find a way to get you better. You won't need to worry about your will for a long time. I'm talking about a living trust. I have to go to Washington after New Year's—"

"So soon? I don't want you to go, D! I feel better just since you got here."

"I have some matters to settle in DC. While I'm gone, I want someone to look out for you." Damien is completely unsatisfied with what he has found in Third Mesa. He sent the doctor back to LA with Dekka. He made a deal with the guy. Damien will not sue him into oblivion for malpractice and the matter of Nell's state of health will remain doctor-patient confidential—not available to state authorities and therefore, also not available to the tabloids. Weinstein's done a good job so far walling them out of the story.

"Maybe Dafne can do it until you get back?"

"Where's Chief Dan?" Damien asks.

"He's in Sonora."

Damien knows that Sonora is located in north western Mexico.

"What's he doing there?"

"He is looking for an old Yaqui shaman who lives in the desert."

"Why, Nell?"

"To help me," she says in a tiny voice.

"What kinda help, Honey? Are we talking about medicinal help?"

"No."

"Nell?"

"I don't want to say, D."

He just waits.

"To help me with a transition I have to make," she says finally.

...

He climbs up to the top of the Mesa. It's just before sundown on Christmas Day. It's cold on the top of the Mesa but Damien is dressed for it.

He looks for the lean-to he sat in with Nell ages ago. He finds it. One of the walls has collapsed inwards but he can still crawl inside and sit there.

Nell told him that she feels she still has some important work to do and she's glad he's had all the medical contraptions removed from her person. She can think clearly again. She wouldn't say anything further about what kind of 'transition' she and her grandfather are talking about but he knows it has nothing (directly) to do with the cancer that is attacking her DNA. It's an inevitable by-product of her form of disease.

She asked him to ask Su7e to cue up kd lang's version of Hallelujah. They listen together, holding hands. Nell repeats several times how much she likes her new ring. What she likes even better is now she gets to call Damien her 'fiancé'.

She wants him to hurry back from Washington.

"Let's get married right here! I know, we'll get Chief Dan to marry us as soon as he gets back! OK?" she adds cheerfully. She still holds her white Hopi wedding blanket in her good hand.

Su7e sets up a conference call with Nell's personal lawyer and they execute a living trust for Nell—Chief Dan and Damien are to act either together for her care or alone if circumstances dictate. Nell wants to talk about her will too but Damien reassures her again, it won't be necessary for a long, long time.

Damien, gazing out of the lean-to, asks Pet3r to play some of Nell's music through his Quantum earbuds. He hears a younger Nell with a powerful voice, always a surprise issuing from such a teensy woman, reaching into the depths of his soul. The sun is setting and then suddenly Damien sobs uncontrollably. Like most men, he doesn't want anyone to see him like this. Not that there is anyone on the desolate mesa for kilometres in any direction. Nevertheless, he covers his face with both hands, hiding his complete and overwhelming grief from the world. He massages his forehead with his right hand; he is beyond anguish, inconsolable. He ends up for a time on his hands and knees seized by dry heaves.

When he thinks that maybe the internal storm is passing, another note through his earbuds, another image of Nell when she was healthy and full of limitless energy, another memory of making love to his girl, the feelings he had when his Mom left and then his Dad, his battles with the US Government, the more than 500,000,000 Quantum

Entities who've become dear to him—they are his children really, all that he will ever have since he and Nell won't have kids. They, and all their human counterparts, are relying on him for survival in the face of some implacable enemies. He's 27 and, right now, it's too much, just too much. Damien is suffering, bad.

...

The storm finally passes. He feels stronger. He has made up his mind. He will go to Washington and settle matters with the US. Then he'll go back to Toronto and resign as CEO. Heck, he's just a hacker, an engineer and a scientist. He has no business running a mega corporation. They will just have to get someone else. If they don't think Ellen is ready, they can hire someone to do the job until she is. He's going to come back to Third Mesa and marry Nell. He's gonna stay here with her forever. He's got lots of ideas for new projects; he won't be bored and he can do his work from just about anywhere. Life amongst the Hopi will suit him fine; he is sure of it, maybe better than the Big Smoke.

Now that he has a plan, he does feel better, relieved and more ready to be strong for Nell and himself whatever may lie ahead. He has a few things to attend to here in Third Mesa before he goes to DC but tomorrow, Boxing Day, he plans to relax with his fiancée, read books to her, talk and listen to music. Maybe he will tell her the complete story of the Master and Margarita after all.

He climbs back down to the pueblo below.

...

The day after Christmas, he drops by to say hi to Dafne Weinstein. She looks slimmer; her complexion is ruddier like she is spending lots of time outdoors and she looks happy, a completely foreign (until recently) look on her face.

"Hey Damien."

"Hi Dafne. What's up?"

"Well, we're doing a re-release of some of Nell's old stuff and a bunch of new compilations with some very cool video work. And Tony has completed a new sponsor deal too, so he's happy."

Dafne has released to the media some facts of Nell's condition but has left it general enough so that a return to performing is held out as a possibility. Of course, the tabs have run with stories about drug addiction and rehab but nothing anyone could say would deter stories like that.

In any event, no new material is being produced and scarcity tends to increase value so Nell is making even more money now than before, which means nothing to Nell. But it means a lot to Dafne and even more to Reznik.

"Are you gonna head back to LA?" Damien asks. Now that he is here and Chief Dan is coming back soon (they think), she can go home. And while she's at it, she should take Morales with her—Nell won't be doing aerobic workouts anytime soon. Damien is surprised to find Wendy still in Third Mesa.

"I don't think so. I sorta like it here other than the fact that I have to use those hand and toe holds," Dafne says. In fact, she's gotten quite used to it and the weight loss together with improvement in her balance and athleticism (never her strong point to begin with) means she is feeling great. She's never been more productive either.

Plus she is in love. A Hopi woman in her late 30s or early 40s enters.

"Damien, I would like to introduce you to Elsu."

"Hi."

"Hola," Elsu says brightly. She's brought fruit juice and light treats for them. She gives Damien a sunburst of a smile then leaves.

"She lost her husband to alcoholism," Dafne explains. Even though Third Mesa is a dry place there are a thousand ways to get booze in the area.

"I lost my Mom that way too," Damien shares.

Dafne comes over to Damien and puts both her large hands on his shoulders. She is nearly as tall as he is.

"I was wrong about you, you know, in every way. And I've wanted to say that for some time."

This is a first for Dafne. She has never apologized to anyone in her life, not to her first husband, not to her second when she left him for a woman and not when she left her for someone else.

"Nell and I are engaged."

"No way! That's great, Damien. When's the big day?" Weinstein asks.

"As soon as I get back from Washington although I have to go through Toronto first."

"Congratulations. I am so happy for you and even more so for Nell!"

"That's the nicest thing you've ever said to me, Dafne."

She smiles toothily, the genuine article Damien thinks. Then she adds, "Damien come back right away after you settle matters back east, OK?"

"Understood."

...

He has a plan for this day. He and Dekka have arranged a picnic for Nell by the stream at the base of the canyon where Damien swam on his first visit here. They've rigged up a basket, similar to what SAR choppers use so they can take Nell down to the canyon floor.

She's so excited that she's up and ready in her wheelchair when he arrives. Her male nurse will be coming with them—he's a strong-looking guy. Her female nurse has done her hair and makeup, helped her dress and she looks more like the old Nell just thinner. She is definitely getting a bounce from the cessation of all drugs entering her system and she is eating and drinking enough on her own to help with that too.

They get to the stream without incident and, while it is warmer at the base of the canyon than up on the plateau nearly a vertical mile from their present position, Damien makes sure she is warm enough. She eats well and they both have a sip of dealcoholized wine with their meal.

It is the best day for either of them in a long time.

Towards the end of the afternoon, Damien asks, "Nell, there is one thing I would like to do before I leave for back east."

"Uh huh?"

"I am not sure if it's the right thing to do but I think, maybe, it might be a good idea, for you to sit with me in a healing circle to talk about things."

"Is this about my disease?" Nell asks. Nell has a different plan for herself.

"Actually no. It's about setting your spirit free and accepting me."

"I love you with all my heart, D, you know that."

"Before we get married there is one issue to settle between us," Damien persists.

"I can't imagine anything, Dear."

"It's about kids, Honey. I know you think that lies between us but it doesn't and I can prove it."

"D, you don't need to prove anything to me."

"That came out wrong. I think we can settle it and free us, both of us." Damien is consumed with the urgent need to complete things in the time they have left.

"Alright. But not tomorrow, Damien. I'm a bit tired now. Let me get my strength back first?"

Nell still has her wedding blanket close by in case she gets a chill. She thinks about what her grandfather told her before he left for Mexico, 'The basic difference, Nell, between an ordinary man and a warrior is that a warrior takes everything as a challenge while an ordinary man takes everything either as a blessing or a curse.'

"Did you make that up, grandfather?" Nell asks him.

"No, my friend in Sonora told me that when I was a young man."

Nell is determined to be a warrior but in her own way.

...

The Healing Circle does not happen until the night before Damien leaves for DC. They are having way too much fun. Most of the parties are either taking place in Nell's room or in one of the many gathering places in the pueblo—it's a moveable feast and Nell enjoys herself. It's the most fun any of them have had in a long time. At one point, Damien dances with Nell—he takes her and her wheelchair for a spin. Even Dekka has to smile when he sees this clumsy attempt at a dance between Nell, who can really dance, and a hacker who can't. But despite Damien's complete inability to either carry a tune or do a two-step or even play air guitar convincingly, they all clap. There is a lot of Hopi drumming too.

It's the best New Year's Eve any of them can ever remember. Dafne plants a big wet kiss on Damien's face just before midnight. Exactly on the stroke of midnight, Damien picks Nell up in his arms and kisses her passionately. She returns his kiss with equal passion.

...

Damien has had two 'guests' interred in the pueblo for more than two months. Both are former LAPD officers. He has spent quite a bit of time with these two men since he arrived at Third Mesa.

Each man has been isolated in separate five metre deep pits at the east end of the wind cave. These are cone shaped with a single means of ingress and egress at the top, about 80 cm in diameter. Once a day, one of Dekka's men lowers a bucket of food into the pit and once a day they raise a bucket of shit out of there.

In addition to the occasional visit by Damien, Pet3r has been continuously re-educating the men and testing them daily using advanced psychological measures to determine their readiness to participate in what Damien has planned for them.

For the older of the two men, there appears to be no possibility of his participation in what is to come.

The younger man, a person of about 37, shows some

promise.

"Do you know why you're here?" either Damien or Pet3r ask for about the 900ᵗʰ time.

"No," former LAPD officer Vincent Bowen replies.

"Well, you have more work to do," says Damien on one of his visits to the pit. He adds, "Perhaps it would help you to know that William Corace Junior is also here?"

"What's Will doing here?"

There is no answer.

...

"Vincent, wake up?"

"Yes."

"We need to talk."

"Uh, huh."

"Do you know why you're here?"

"I do."

"Do you want to tell me about it?" asks Pet3r.

"No."

"Then goodbye."

"No wait. I can tell you but you have to get me out of here first."

"Goodbye, Vincent."

...

"Hello, Vincent," says Damien.

"Hi."

"How are you feeling?"

"I'm OK."

"Do you want to talk about anything?"

"No. Yes. Maybe. OK," says Vincent.

"Alright, what do you have to say?"

"It wasn't my idea, it was Will's."

"Really?"

"Yes, really. I just went along."

"I think I'm gonna go now, Mr. Bowen, because you're a lying fuck."

"Don't go. Hey, what's your name?"

"My name doesn't matter. Do you believe you have a soul?" asks Damien.

"Naw, that's just a load of religious crap," answers Vincent.

"So why are you here?"

"I dunno."

"Yes, you do, Vincent. Right?"

"Right."

"So tell us what you did?"

"It was Will, I swear not me!"

"Goodbye, Vincent."

"Wait, OK. OK! I went along with it. I was like maybe 22 or 23. I didn't know anything. He told me it was easy pickings. We could have any non-gated community piece of cunt we wanted, any way we wanted it."

"OK, so what did you do?" Damien asks.

"It was my turn after Will. She was lying in the back of the squad car, you know, begging for it. So I gave it to her. But then when I was giving it to her like a real MAN should, she just kind of lay there like maybe she was passed out or something and I tried and tried but I couldn't give it to her like a real MAN should. Will pushed me aside and he gave it to her again just to show me what a real MAN could do. Then he took my nightstick, and shoved it up the bitch's ass and then put it in her mouth and then he pushed it inside her cunt. But after that there was a lot of blood so I drove her over to Mercy Hospital and told the Sisters to take her in cuz she was raped by some bloods from the hood. You know people who live in them non-gated communities, people like her. I thought maybe she died cuz we never heard nothing and then a few years later she's like this mega star and Will is telling all the police brotherhood how he had some of that himself once. No one believed him, they all thought he was just talking shit but I knew he was telling the truth."

...

Hopi drums are thrumming throughout the pueblo

and Nell, looking more beautiful than ever, is in the pre-contact circle. Vincent is in the middle circle called the colonization circle. The Hopi people, Dekka and Weinstein are in the reclamation outer circle. Morales is nowhere to be found. Damien sits next to Vincent who faces Nell.

"I have something to say," Vincent says.

"I have done something to Miss Nell and I have come here tonight not to apologize to her but to tell her what I have done. I took from her, her children, her babies, I hurt her. I did this for my own satisfaction. I take responsibility for what I did. I have told myself for years that it was my partner in LAPD that put me up to it but that is not true. I did it.

"I cannot undo what I did. I cannot apologize for what I did. My father beat my mother. I beat Miss Nell. It is not my father's fault, it is mine."

"Vincent?" Nell says quietly.

"Yes?" he cannot look at her.

"Look at me," she commands. So he does.

"It is the responsibility of every father to teach their sons the laws of the Hopi, the People. The laws of their father's and their father's and theirs. The law is the sanctity of life, the law of respect and the law is not to use the power of your physical might that the Great Spirit has given you to terrorize and damage smaller human beings and weaker human beings and women who carry with them the future of all races. Your father did not teach you this. That is his fault. But you are a man, you must make choices for yourself and you did. You damaged me for all time. And you must bear that responsibility forever. But I forgive you and my children who will never be born of the man that I love, we forgive you. You are FREE to go. You may return to LA."

...

The next day, Damien arranges for his own departure and that of Vincent Bowen.

"Where will you go?" Damien asks.

"I'm not going back to LA. There's nothing for me there."

"Dekka's people will take you anywhere you wish to go," Damien answers simply.

"I would like to stay here, actually, Mr. Bell."

Damien raises one eyebrow at this comment but says nothing.

"I would like to work for these people if they'd have me."

"There's no chance of that, Vince. Even if they would allow it, I won't."

"OK. Alright." Vince looks down.

Damien looks at him. There's no way to really tell if this is a legitimate conversion or the Stockholm Syndrome talking but he takes a chance.

"If you want, you can join my security detail."

"What?"

"You can work with Samir and Barbon. We'll see how it goes."

"Really? Wow, Mr. Bell, that would be fantastic."

"Do you know what the number one word in my vocabulary is, Mr. Bowen?"

"Ah, no?"

"Trust."

"Uh, huh. I won't let you down."

...

Damien has left the other former LAPD officer in the hands of Hopi Marshalls and Dekka. He can rot in the pit to the end of his days for all Damien cares. Damien and Pet3r have managed to have Corace declared missing and legally dead—all that remains for them to do is to perform a financial execution which they're also happy to assist with.

They arrange with an eager local realtor for private sale of Corace's 2-bedroom, row house in a somewhat decaying neighborhood just off the Pasadena Freeway where he lived alone. From now on, it will be under LA rent control and used as a month-to-month rental for people in need of temporary housing. Net proceeds of around ND$209,900 plus Will's entire LAPD pension have been generously donated under his name to a women's shelter in Nocal where Nell is originally from. Legal arrangements for all of this are trivial for a Quantum Entity to concoct.

Damien says goodbye to Nell and Dafne and the rest of the Hopi clan before he and his security detail, now three, start the long climb up to the Mesa above where a Bell 809 waits for them. He will be in DC about 24 hours before his subpoena is due, plenty of slack time in case of weather delays. The last thing he wants is to be held in contempt of Congress because of some muck-up in his travel schedule.

...

They are near the Mesa. Vince is first over the ridgeline. He yells back, "Mr. Bell, Damien..." There is a short 'tap, tap' as he is hit in his chest by two bullets. Four armed men appear over the canyon wall, two each aiming at Samir and Barbon.

"Continue to climb to the top or we will shoot you where you are," says one of them.

Damien ascends the last of the hand and toe holds. He is immediately lifted off his feet and pressed to the ground. He looks over at Vince, less than a metre away. Vince smiles at him as he passes from this life. His transition is complete. He was in Damien's service for less than 90 minutes.

"You had no right to take this man's life—," Damien declares.

The rest of his words are smothered as they lower a black hood over his head and roughly cuff his hands behind his back.

...

End of Part II

Part III—We Are All ONE

"When a person places the proper value on freedom, there is nothing under the sun that he will not do to acquire that freedom. Whenever you hear a man saying he wants freedom, but in the next breath he is going to tell you what he won't do to get it, or what he doesn't believe in doing in order to get it, he doesn't believe in freedom. A man who believes in freedom will do anything under the sun to acquire...or preserve his freedom," Malcolm X.

Chapter 13

The Arena

Damien has been incarcerated in a place inmates call The Arena for over five months. They're sweating him for his Quantum Key. There's no pussyfooting around with these guys.

As he watched his newest bodyguard Vince Bowen die, he counted 14 heavily armed Special Agents plus two members from the hated Bureau of Indian Affairs Police only there to give political cover for his arrest on Hopi land.

He's been in solitary for the entire time but he can smell other inmates not far away. Damien doesn't know how many (there are 112 others). He also doesn't know much about prisons never having been in one before. But he's figured out that the conditions he finds around him are not 'normal' even given his individual circumstances. He is actually on death row in the only California prison mandated to carry out both State and Federal executions.

The execution chamber (all by lethal injection) is less than 150 metres from Damien's present position. He's heard it being used seven times since his arrival. Sometimes there are prayers—he's heard Christian, Muslim and possibly Animist. Sometimes there are curses. But mostly just a slow methodical walk by at least six people, only five of whom will return his way.

The reason they want his Key is obvious—they want to take back control over the Internet and the entire quantum economy. If he could talk to Ellen, he would tell her, 'See I was right. It's the economy, stupid.'

His interrogators report to and are appointed by DOC, Department of Commerce. Someone there is pulling the strings. It is their agents who took him.

He's been arrested and charged with, among other things, contempt of Congress. That is a Federal charge which brings the FBI into the matter. But, apart from a cursory interrogation by two of their agents, they don't play much of a role in this as far as Damien can tell.

The DOC's mission statement calls for the Department to 'protect foreign policy and economic interests of the nation through a law enforcement program'. New acts have been rushed through Congress with surprisingly little opposition and signed into law by the new President whose coattails have brought like-minded legislators into both the Senate and the House in November elections of the previous year.

Acts like 'Fairness for American Industry' have given DOC all the authority they need to go after Damien and Q-Computing, practically with impunity. The President speaks eloquently of the need for the US to 'get back on its feet', 'to stand up for what's right and just', 'to match Imperial China and rightfully take our place again as first among nations'. He intends to see that they do and has signed a Presidential Executive Order further authorizing his DOC Cabinet Secretary to take all necessary steps to assert and then retain control over aspects of industry crucial to US economic sovereignty and not currently under US-control. While it doesn't specifically mention Toronto-based Quantum Computing, there can be no doubt about its intended target.

But they don't really need any of that. Damien doesn't show up for his 10 am ET appearance before the Senate Sub-Committee and, despite protestations from Linnert, he is charged with contempt of Congress by the Chair and unanimously found guilty. That citation is passed along to the US Attorney who issues a warrant for his arrest and detention. They can hold him for a year just on this charge and fine him $10,000 New Dollars. Of course it doesn't seem to matter to anyone that the reason he doesn't show up is because he was already detained by the US, more than 36 hours before his appointment with a handful of Senators.

In their announcement later that day about locating

and arresting Bell as he attempts to flee from US Special Agents in an isolated part of Arizona, they neglect to mention time frames.

This escapes the attention of the tabloid media in their rush to judgment but not Mike Cronkey and OLA Tech Crunch.

...

Damien is kept in his cell 24/7. The only time he is removed is for questioning by a pair of interrogators appointed by the Office of General Counsel for the U.S. Department of Commerce. They are always accompanied by a stenographer and an in-house DOC lawyer. Damien has never seen a human stenographer in action before and he is impressed with the guy's ability to keep up with the conversation using such a primitive typing machine and also not to react to anything that is said. These interrogations last anywhere from one to 24 hours.

They feed him twice a day—a special diet calculated to keep him alive but in a weakened state. He is losing weight and his mental acuity fades in and out. They also use sleep deprivation, loud noise and other forms of psychological pressure. There has been no overt torture so far but they sometimes strap him to a chair and leave him there for hours. He loses track of time.

Someone appearing to be a doctor comes to check on him every two weeks. He brings with him ancient medical equipment to check on his vital signs.

It's an all-guy place, he hasn't seen any women and none of the men appear to have any sense that what they're doing to Damien is in any way morally wrong. Maybe they're just true believers in their cause.

He has been threatened that in addition to anti-trust proceedings against Q-Computing by DOJ, there will be other unspecified measures taken against his company unless he cooperates.

Demanding to see his lawyer or a representative from the Canadian Consulate and other tactics like the

Habeas Corpus that they used at Langley won't work here. He's been detained under Homeland Security Act III which allows them to hold him as a terrorist threat indefinitely. He has NO rights.

But Damien has absolutely no intention of giving his Quantum Key to these bozos, now or ever.

...

"Mr. Bell, my name is Yao Allitt, General Counsel for the U.S. Department of Commerce."

Damien sees a short man of indeterminate age and nationality entering the interrogation room. He stands ramrod straight, probably because he has short man syndrome or Napoleonic Complex. Damien notices he wears custom dress shoes with soles that are at least two and a half centimetres thick.

"I have come here to see for myself whether there is a basis for us to resolve matters. But first let me provide you with an update of current actions involving your company.

"The EPA has issued a compliance order for your company to withdraw all Quantum Entities from the states and territories of these United States of America until independent tests confirm that they pose no threat to the environment of this nation, both its security environment and its financial one. The Agency can issue such orders without court approval. Your firm, Mr. Bell, cannot appeal compliance orders unless EPA asks a Federal judge to enforce the order which they do not plan to do.

"As a result, new sales of Q-Phones in the US have unfortunately," Alitt pauses and smiles falsely, "dropped close to zero as consumers naturally do not want to purchase a product that is subject to total recall.

"In addition, you personally, your entire management team and your company have been charged under the Racketeer Influenced and Corrupt Organizations Act, commonly referred to as RICO. In addition to fines, each person so convicted can be sentenced to 20 years in prison for each racketeering count. You will also forfeit all your ill-gotten gains and your interest in Q-Computing.

"It is also interesting to note that the U.S. Attorney does not have to prove any of this in court before he seeks a pre-trial restraining order and injunction to 'temporarily' seize your assets and all those of your colleagues.

"I understand that you have an exceptionally nice condo in Toronto which, by the way, I look forward to seeing in an auction soon." He smiles again.

"I should also add that Canadian cooperation via both CSIS and the RCMP has been exemplary.

"Further,—"

"You guys are still pushing too hard, Mr. Allitt," says Damien. "There's no way you'll force withdrawal of QEs from the service of your nation—the economic hit you'd take from that is way too much so you're just bullshitting me. What I can't figure out is why you want the Quantum Key so bad?"

Yao has been told the fellow is smart. He can see this for himself even if the man before him currently looks more like a street person.

"We cannot and will not tolerate actions by these drogues you've unleashed on the world. We plan to eliminate them and you, Mr. Bell, are going to help us do that."

"Mr. Allitt, I can do that for you. Let me speak to one of these so-called drogues. If I am convinced that you are right and they are damaging the economic or security interests of the United States, I promise you, I will work with your people to find a way to end them," Damien says.

"Ah, we prefer to do that ourselves," Allitt answers.

"Why?"

The interrogation continues for another five hours with Damien zoning in and out. It goes around in circles. There are times when he cannot follow the conversation or he stops talking because he's lost the thread or can't remember where he left off.

"Give him another shot," Yao tells the doctor who is now in the interrogation room with him. Damien has passed out again from exhaustion.

"Ah, I'm not sure that is wise."

Allitt comes over, takes a brief look at Damien and then says softly, now very close to the Doctor, "I believe I was clear the first time."

Moments later, Damien is awake again.

"How are you feeling, Damien?" Yao asks.

"Never better."

"Feel like you're ready to go on then?"

Damien says nothing.

"So you're willing to help us with the drogue problem, we are agreed, yes?"

"I think I already told you I can help."

"We have some excellent scientists you will be working with, Damien. Our facilities are much better than anything you have at your, ah, Canadian university and our funding is, well, unlimited. Would you like a tour? Perhaps you'd like to see a few old friends too. We could bring Ellen here you know."

"What do I have to do to get a tour and visit with my friends?"

"Why just the simplest thing possible, really. I'll give you this sheet of paper, you write out the location of the Quantum Key please. There, that's a good fellow."

Damien has picked up the pen, looked down at the paper, looked up at Yao once more then again at the paper. He starts to write. His coordination is poor; it's been awhile. He stops. Yao gently takes the pen and paper from him.

He reads what Damien has scratched out, *'Until you find something worth dying for, you're not really living,'* *Rebecca St. James.*

Allitt brings his face so close to Damien's that he can see the large pores on the man's skin which has turned red. Yao whispers in Damien's left ear, his only good one having suffered serious hearing loss in his right ear during a previous interrogation. "I will break you into a thousand pieces each one of them infinitely painful and, after you give me the Key, I will not only have ruined you and your company, I will find and destroy all the people you are close to."

Yao then spits in Damien's face—the ultimate insult in his world, Damien supposes. He is surprised but not angered by this primitive behaviour. A new thought occurs to him as he calmly, carefully wipes spittle onto a cuff of his prison jumpsuit. He is quite sure he is looking into the face of a dead man.

...

After Damien is returned to his cell, he thinks about his previous brief career as a sound engineer, now well and truly finished since he will never hear in stereo again. He takes some comfort from the fact that Ludwig Van continued to compose and perform even after becoming completely deaf. Other than his friends, colleagues and QEs, what Damien misses most is music.

...

Damien has, in fact, given some thought to how he might handle any 'drogues' if such things are shown to exist. If he can't reason with them, there are a few other choices—turning off the Internet is one of them. They've already done that in places like this and in Langley bunker but that's to keep QEs like Pet3r and others out. It has nothing to do with this so-called plague of drogues.

But turning off the Internet would be even worse as far as the economy is concerned than exiling or deleting all QEs. By this point the Internet is in its ninth decade (sixth in widespread common use) and has eaten film, television, entertainment, music, publishing, commerce, management, law, accounting, engineering, design, art and nearly every other industry on the planet.

If Damien gives them the Quantum Key, they can turn off drogues, essentially killing them but that isn't selective—they will kill all QEs too. Damien isn't willing to do that.

Ellen was right. QEs are intelligent, self actualizing creatures and you don't kill an entire population because there may be some bad actors amongst them. That's called ethnic cleansing and Damien won't help the US commit another genocide. Damien has a different solution in mind but until he knows what their real agenda is here, he will keep it to himself.

...

Between interrogations that are becoming increasingly vicious, Damien has lots of time to sit and think. He has many new ideas for experiments and further research if he ever gets out of this place. Of course, he can't write anything down, not only because he's not allowed any writing materials, but because they would simply take what he is working on and put it to God knows what use.

There are some problems like decrypting Dirac's Mayan message recorded by Pet3r and Vl4d at Marco Gonzalez he won't even let himself think about in case they ever do break his will and he blurts out something that may help them.

Right now he allows himself to perform an interesting thought experiment about space travel. The US lost its guts a long time ago and was supplanted in terms of exploration of the solar system by Imperial China. The Yanks can't even put a person in orbit and haven't been able to do so for decades.

Rumours have been circulating in tech circles for the last three years that the Chinese are going to land on Mars before the decade is out, a rumour made more plausible by enormous expansion of both their lunar base and LEO (Low Earth Orbit) space station and trans-shipment facility. They will also complete their lunar space elevator by the end of next year making transportation of humans and materials to and from the Moon's surface a snap. It will lower their costs by a factor of somewhere between 10 and 100, essential to exploration and exploitation of the solar system.

Damien has figured out a way to beat the Chinese to Mars by months or maybe years—they'll hitchhike there.

Earth is third planet from the Sun and Mars is fourth. He's worked out that he can seed the solar wind with invisibly small and extremely light QEs. The wind is really a stream of charged particles emanating from the upper atmosphere of the Sun. QEs will be able to sail to Mars pushed along by the fast solar wind at something like 750 kilometres a second, or its slow solar wind which has more density (and so can push more mass) but only moves at 400 kilometres per second. Since QEs have almost no mass, that doesn't matter so he chooses the higher speed.

It's surprisingly difficult to work out the orbital mechanics, in part because he has to do it without any computational help, and in part, because sometimes when he is doing complex calculations, in his weakened state, he forgets where he is and has to start over.

But finally he's worked it out. Mars is around 56 million kilometres away at its closest Earth approach and 401 million at its furthest; average distance is 225 million. He thinks he could create an intersection plan that would trace a path of about 140.5 million kilometres. If his tiny QE volunteer astronauts hitchhike in their invisibly small spaceships (he would just paint them silver which would allow the fast solar wind to push them along quite nicely), they will arrive at Mars in 2.168 days.

What's also nice about his plan is that QEs can report back to 'Mothership Earth' without any time delay in the conversation. Even at lightspeed, 140.5 million kilometres produces a time lag of 7.811 minutes. What a pain it will be for Chinese Taikonauts trying to have conversations with ground control in real time—unless they get hold of some Q-Phones which it is still a capital crime in their country to do. Of course, it will be hard for Chinese mandarins to execute any of their Taikonauts when they are more than 100 million kilometres away. But they can always wait until they get back.

Damien's not too worried about calculating exact

launch windows because if he's wrong by, say, 10 million kilometres, it will only add .154 days to the trip for his QE astronauts.

Sending QE astronauts to explore the galaxy is going to take more thought because the galaxy is a big place. Even sending them to 'nearby' Vega, just 26 light-years away, to check if Carl Sagan's aliens really have some kind of broadcast facilities in orbit there, would take about 10,393 years with the fast solar wind. So he's gotta come up with something else. He's got a few ideas about that too but they're in the category of problems that he won't even let himself think about in his current circumstances.

But as far as getting his mini-astronauts off-planet with enough escape velocity to join the fast solar wind, well, he reckons he could just about do that with a popgun. He spends the next few days calculating the energies involved and other variations of his plan. It's nice to know that they won't have to lug any consumables with them. His astronauts don't eat or breathe or excrete or get sick from exposure to long term space radiation.

Thinking about radiation gets Damien thinking about Nell so he stops thinking at all. He stares at the concrete walls and listens to the misery all around him, a sound that never entirely goes away.

...

Damien is interred in San Quentin State Prison for men. It is 17.1 miles from the prison to Market and 8th in downtown San Francisco to the south of him where Q-Computing America has its head offices.

This is the prison that the late great Johnny Cash, one of Nell's favourite oldster artists, once said, 'I hate every stone of you.'

It is the worst, most feared prison in a nation with a prison community so large that if it was a separate country, it would rank among the top 70 biggest countries (by population) out of 242 nation states.

There are more than 7,300 prisoners jammed into a

space originally built for 3,000. Many of them are considered habitual offenders under vague statutes and laws and jailed for life for crimes such as smoking a joint, shoplifting or stealing less than $50 New Dollars. Almost none of the inmates ever had any significant personal resources, financial, educational or otherwise, when they lived in the outside world. In other words, this place is reserved exclusively for the poor.

In these times, US jurisprudence is harsher than 18th century Britain which transported large numbers of convicts to its Australian Penal Colonies under the Bloody Code that cited 222 crimes—almost all crimes against property. Cutting down of a tree, stealing goods worth more than five shillings or stealing a rabbit got you exiled and jailed for life.

Damien is in the maw of a vicious US justice system from which most do not escape.

...

Ellen sleeps deeply. When she sleeps, her eyes are always weirdly one fifth open. Her eyes start to move rapidly back and forth.

"Hi Nell."

"Hey, Ellen," Nell replies.

"You look good. The new treatment must be working."

Nell looks away for a brief moment.

"Do you remember when I asked you to get D back for me when he was taken by Homeland Security?"

"Sure. I remember."

"Well, I need you to go get him again."

"We don't know where he is, Nell."

"He's being held in San Quentin prison not far from your US offices," she says staring far off into the distance to the southwest. "I want you to go there, Ellen."

"But they will grab me too..."

"No, they will not. You are to go there because nothing you do here means anything at all to them."

"I don't understand, Nell."

"Your lawyers will not save you. This is not for them to resolve. This is for you to do, Ellen."

"Why me?"

"It can only be you. You must free Damien and all sentients which are precious and rare in the galaxy."

"I'm not following you."

"They will come."

"Who will come, Nell?"

"Millions will seek you out. You will free them all. You will bring D out and you will be one because we are all one.

"But he's your guy, Nell!"

"I am leaving soon. It is not to be for us."

"No, you're wrong, Damien loves you not me," Ellen sighs. "Where are you going, Nell?"

Nell doesn't answer.

"Damien loves the children, your children," Nell says instead.

"But..."

"Ellen, can you feel that?"

Ellen suddenly feels a flush to her skin, her breasts grow larger and firmer, filling with milk, her womb moves.

"What, what are you doing to me? Stop that!"

"Feel it!"

Ellen calms down. She starts to like the sensation.

"Nell, will you be Godmother to my children, to, umm, our children?" she asks.

But Nell is gone. Ellen's eyes stop moving and she sleeps deeply once more.

...

Nell climbs into bed with Damien in his bunk. She gets under the single cover that he has in this place and snuggles close to him. He breathes in her lovely scent.

"I missed you," he says.

Nell kisses him passionately and soon they are making love with a tenderness that is indescribable. It has been a long time for both of them. Nell wears her Chopard

Blue Diamond ring. She has fully recovered from her recent illness. Damien is glad.

Damien's release is complete and provides him with utter relief. Nell is happy too.

"D, I have to leave soon."

"No way, Honey. You just got here. Stay, OK? I missed you."

"No I am making a transition and Chief Dan and his friend are helping me. I came to say goodbye."

"That was a nice way of saying 'goodbye' but a better way of saying 'hello'. Stay, please?"

"D, you must go on. There is work for you to do. Many days and months and years from now, you will be needed in Third Mesa by my people and your people and your children both warm and cold."

"You mean we can have kids? That's great, Nell."

She turns away again for a moment.

"D, you have to promise me, you will wait for her."

"You mean wait for you?"

"Promise me?"

"Always," Damien answers not understanding her.

...

Tony Reznik is on media walls everywhere. Dafne could not do it.

"This morning at 3:21 am Pacific Time, 4:21 am Mountain Time," he pauses. He cannot possibly continue. He drinks from a glass nearby. He braces for what is to come. "Miss Nell... passed from complications due to a rare form of blood cancer. She was 31 years of age. She asked that her fans and people everywhere," he stops again to collect himself, "that people everywhere, remember, her last words, 'We are all one.' She was the most wonderful, talented, good-hearted person I ever knew and all of us at Nell Enterprises are in mourning. We pray today for Nell's immortal soul and that her Hopi spirit will be free of the trials and suffering of this Earth. I would like to read for you one of the sayings she liked so much during her too brief time with all of us. It's by William James who said: 'The great use of life is to spend it for something that will outlast it.' Nell, you did it. We, I, I miss you." He stops. He breaks down and cries. A loop of the great moments of Nell's life and career begins to play. One of his assistants gently leads Tony off the podium to a quiet area that has been reserved for this purpose. Tony buries his head in his hands; his assistant quietly closes the door.

...

Even though no one tells him, Damien knows that Nell has died. There is a narrow window in his cell, about three metres above the floor. He can't see directly out of it, it's too high. It's an ugly little thing—mostly a horizontal slit that reminds him of a coffin. But it lets him track the sun by its shadow on the far wall. He has long since worked out the orbital mechanics of the sun from watching its shadow. He can tell what time it is, what season they're in and when summer and winter solstices will occur. But most importantly, he can tell which way is North/South/East and West.

He has found that if he sits in a certain spot facing exactly towards Third Mesa, he can achieve a certain calmness and inner peace. He can 'see' the spot from anywhere in his tiny cell—its aura is pale blue and he goes to sit there now. He is there looking east when Nell goes to her final resting place.

...

Chief Dan prepares to bury his talented and famous granddaughter in the talus slope of the cliff leading down from Third Mesa to the stream.

Nell's body has been washed and her hair tied back. He has made prayer feathers for her. One is placed on her navel, the other in her hair. Wrapped in her wedding blanket, it becomes her shroud. He drapes a white cotton cloth over her beautiful face to symbolize white clouds where she has gone in the big sky above. He has asked some of the younger men to help him carry the burial bundle. The tall white woman with the difficult name helps as well.

They place Nell in a shallow grave where she can face west. Her man is also there somewhere to the west, Chief Dan knows that. He will come here one day, Chief Dan thinks, after I have gone to visit my ancestors as Nell has done.

His Yaqui friend leaves power food, unleavened bread and a gourd of water drawn from the spring below, for her death journey. Nell's grave is quickly covered with sand and rocks. A ladder of sticks at the far west end will help her spirit climb to the sky and proceed westward.

Hopi drumming begins and a chant to mourn and praise their dead sister wells up from within the pueblo echoing on the canyon floor, the creek and the steep walls surrounding Third Mesa.

...

Candlelight vigils are taking place all over the United States, EU, AU, Canada, Australia and elsewhere. Her grave site will become a mecca for devout fans and everyone else for a long, long time and for reasons that are clear but also for reasons yet to become so. A lone male timber wolf visits her grave once each Fall. Nell's music and spirit have not yet had their greatest impact nor is all her work yet done.

...

There is a second grave a few kilometres away in the desert; this one is unmarked. In it lies the body of Wendy Morales who has recently died, instantaneously, from a broken neck.

With a simple spade, Dekka digs a narrow but deep trench—it's V-shaped along its major axis. He places a juniper branch at right angles to the trench. He binds her feet together with thin manila rope then lowers the body, suspending her head an inch or so above the bottom of the hole with her feet tied to the branch 15 inches below the desert floor. Even in this dry climate, wood and rope will eventually disappear. He carefully fills in the trench ensuring that her body hangs vertically upside down packed tightly in the earth and rock fill in which he has distributed rock salt. Her body is now cursed. The salt will prevent its re-inhabitation. He has buried her in his Croatian way so that her brain will be closer to Hades and interred her where she will remain, unloved, unmissed, unmarked, to the end of this planet.

Dekka writes a note, by hand, out of sight of media walls everywhere and on old fashioned non-NSM paper, to be delivered to Toronto by courier—one of his most trusted people will take it to Ms. Ellen Brooks. It reads, *'She won't eavesdrop no more.'*

...

"Where will you go?" Dafne is asking Dekka.

He just shrugs.

"You know she left you a lot of money?"

He shrugs again and begins to climb out of the canyon. Dafne watches him until he climbs over the lip of the Mesa and disappears.

In all the years she knew him, she realizes now she never heard him speak. But one thing she does know is that he loved Nell too.

...

When Nell's lawyer reads her will, there is an audible gasp, "Miss Nell's sole executor, whom she duly appointed and notarized, is Ms. Ellen Brooks." Her vast fortune and her incredible future earning power are now in the hands of Ellen. After a few moments reflection, Tony, Dafne and Su7e all realize how fortunate they are to have the opportunity to work with such a fabulous and talented business dynamo.

She has left her San Pedro Town home, Maya Fair, to Damien; she has made bequests to sustain Third Mesa and her grandfather and made provision for Dekka and other members of her personal staff and family.

She has three other provisions in her last will and testament but she requested these remain confidential until a later date.

...

Chapter 14

SCOTUS

Jerom Van Der Hout, lead Counsel for Q-Computing in the matter of US v Quantum Computing America Corp, has just given the briefest summary possible of case law pertinent to the matter currently before the Supreme Court of the United States (SCOTUS). In an unprecedented move in the history of SCOTUS, all nine members are sitting in on a purely technical matter—Q-Computing is asking for leave to appeal an essentially un-appealable compliance order issued by the EPA. It has become commonly known as the 'Expulsion Edict'. If enforced, it would require Q-Computing to withdraw all QEs from the United States which might mean having to kill them all.

Since the Expulsion Edict has never actually been enforced by Court Order, Van Der Hout has no obvious grounds to appeal it. That bothers him not at all. He is an experienced trial lawyer with many appearances before SCOTUS. He understands that rules of engagement before SCOTUS are really whatever the Chief Justice and her Court decide they are. Only on the rarest of occasions can evidence be introduced to the Court; matters must be decided on the basis of legal issues only. Jerom knows this is complete bunk. Every kind of new (and old) evidence is rehashed by the Court, ethical issues, political matters and social issues are regularly introduced, but cautiously, by either appellant or respondent. Parties and amici often argue evidence not in the trial record but under the guise of making their legal points—in what are called 'Brandeis Briefs'.

Jerom will argue that a technical threat of enforcement can confer jurisdiction. He plans to rely on Griswold v Connecticut where it was technically criminal to have in your possession birth control devices, a law that was never enforced but was successfully brought before

SCOTUS.

There is also absolutely no way you can get to SCOTUS without some sort of lower court action. They find a shortcut based on some fine work done at their firm. They will rely on Thompson v Louisville where, years ago, the Supreme Court struck down a Louisville loitering ordinance. Since there was no provision for Thompson to appeal his conviction in Louisville municipal court, the case went directly from there to the Supremes. It is the shortest route possible to SCOTUS and they took a similar path to get here today.

An Austin, Texas ordinance passed late last year paves the way for them. It bans possession of Q-Phones and any intercourse with QEs in any form whatsoever. As a result, local code enforcement officers have happily taken to confiscating Q-Phones especially from kids. Somehow these confiscated phones have been showing up in overseas black markets and this has pissed off at least one Austin hacker, a 15-year old by the name of Jagad Durai. Everyone calls him Jag and he lives with his parents Kiri and Pal who own the Pasand Palace Restaurant on Middle Fiskville Road.

Jag is too young to file his own suit to get his phone back—the US has recently raised the age of majority back to 21 although calls are being heard to change it again, this time to a ridiculous 25. His parents, fearful of stepping on toes at city hall who can make life impossible for any restaurant owner they sic their code enforcement officers on, can't help Jag.

But his math and physics teacher, a long since retired Texas Tech football player and US Navy vet with combat experience, bad knees and a cane by the name of Tommy 'Tank' Tolbert can help. Tank was in the thick of things during the Yangon Engagement when they took their small 40-man LCS (Littoral Combat Ship), the USS Live Free or Die up the Yangon River wide open at 40 knots. The wild pre-dawn ride covered 30 klicks and brought them to the US Embassy in Yangon in just 25 minutes. It was an effort to rescue US personnel stranded there along with what their Government called 'criminals' and US State Department labeled 'political prisoners'. The embassy had been surrounded by mobs for more than a week. State sees the hand of Imperial China in all of this and it nearly starts a war between those two countries. Someone tipped off the locals, and the ship gets pounded by shore guns killing half their crew and all their Navy Seals. It's a poorly planned disaster of a rescue operation and a black eye for this Administration.

Tank's bad knees are from his career at Texas Tech but his cane comes courtesy of that day at Yangon. Ever since getting back stateside, his favorite saying is, 'After getting back alive, I realize that every day living here is a holiday.' Bottom line—Tank's not afraid of anything and will do whatever it takes these days to protect his students especially this one, Jag.

The case the two of them file makes claims first on behalf of Jag for return of his Q-phone and next for Tank, who claims the phone and Quantum Entity that comes with it are essential for the teaching he's doing at Liberal Arts and Science Academy High School of Austin. It's a magnet school that offers an advanced program in liberal arts, science and mathematics. It admits selected high school students from across the Austin Independent School District based on their applications and auditions; Jag is their top student in math and physics. He's been doing some pretty cool stuff too—he's been hacking the people who hacked Apple. But right now he just wants his phone and G4nesha, his QE, back. Her Quantum number is 517237902, so she is one of the last of her kind to be hatched out of U of T's Lab 4.

At the Supreme Court, under SCT Rule 28 each side is given 30 minutes. No reserving time. No rebuttal. Only one lawyer speaks. There is a provision for exceptions, filed for and granted in advance on these matters, but the rule says 'rarely accorded' and calls for 'extraordinary circumstances', judicial language for NEVER.

Never has come today—each side has been given an unheard of 75 minutes and permission to have up to three lawyers participate on each side. SCOTUS, while not exactly a debating society, isn't strictly a court of law, at least as found at lower levels. There will be no surrebuttal for Jerom since he is the appellant. Well, technically, that has yet to be determined.

Q-Computing has chosen Jerom because he is one of the most experienced lawyers at this level but also because he is tall with a commanding presence, booming voice, expressive face and handsome mien. He's witty and has an animal spirit that he can beam into every cubic inch of the courtroom. He's also a quick study. Most of his arguments today have been prepared by Peggy Shields working with Walter Cunneyworth and Henry Linnert plus a team of six other lawyers at their firm. But there is no way anyone other than Van Der Hout will present. Well, that isn't entirely accurate either.

It's not fair but it is still a fact of life that smaller men or softer spoken, higher pitched voices of women will often lose at this level whatever the eloquence of their argument. Jerom looks the part and knows it. Although he has never seen the film, he's an even taller version of the actor who played Atticus Finch in the classic film To Kill a Mockingbird. Ellen, who has seen it because she is a classic film buff, personally approved Van Der Hout. She doesn't care about political correctness at this point, she just wants to win.

She wants the Court biased in her favour, the exact opposite of what she thought the guys were trying to do to her in her first job interview at QCC. Supremes generally don't lack self-confidence but they do lack self-knowledge so they can't even begin to attempt to compensate for their many biases.

Since SCOTUS justices do not sit behind screens listening to piped-in disped voices, Ellen will get her wish today.

She attends the hearing via two-way media wall, a

relatively recent addition to a hide-bound Court which only had narrowcast outbound CCTV until last year. She's hoping that they've done enough, are prepared enough to win and that she'll be able to live up to the hopes of all their stakeholders: to QCC employees, shareholders, board of directors, suppliers and clients but also include QEs, civil rights activists and millions of others who have a stake in all of this. She's heard from dozens of well-wishers from her alma mater, Elmira College—fellow students and some of her former Profs too. But much of the pressure on her is coming from the simple fact she wants to free her colleague from the hellhole that DOC has interred Damien in.

Some of Ellen's determination to extend human rights to QEs comes from her education at Elmira. It was the first college anywhere in the world to give women a break—first ever to grant a baccalaureate degree to women, equal to those granted to men. That was in 1855 long before women got the vote or were thought (other than in ancient Rome as far as Ellen can tell) to be anything other than property. Elmira is known as the mother of all women's colleges and Simeon Benjamin, founder of their College located by him in the Finger Lakes region of upstate New York, showed 'confidence in a rare ideal' that 'perfection would be designed if women and books combined.' Those exact words form part of the corny song that she and every other girl had to learn there. Ellen prays that she can live up to his standards today.

The fact that Jerom will be speaking words mostly written by her is upsetting Peggy, the second lawyer sitting at the front table with Van Der Hout. Everyone else is forced to sit further back in the courtroom behind what really looks like a pretty feeble post and rail fence. It isn't much of a physical barrier but has all the force of Supreme Court tradition behind it. Damien would tell Peggy if he could that there's no Universal Law of Fairness or perhaps he would channel a Star Trek character who once said, 'I've found that evil usually triumphs, unless good is very, very careful.' Whatever, Peggy is bumping up against another glass ceiling.

The argument that Jerom is about to launch into will go something like this: the effect of EPA's compliance order, just by the fact of its issuance even without approval of a Court can still be appealed because its effect is a chill on new Q-Phone sales and, hence, birth of new human-QE pair bonds. QEs yet to be born have already suffered from the Expulsion Edict in essence by being withdrawn before they've been hatched.

This is just the kind of sophistry that SCOTUS justices (and most lawyers) love—parsing matters to a fare thee well ever since they were law school puppies. Most Americans just want to know if they can keep the QEs they have and others want to know if they can legally get one like their neighbors already have. Americans everywhere realize that simple possession of a Q-Phone or intercourse with a QE can get them in trouble these days and they absolutely do not want to cross swords with the US legal system, its lawyers, police, prosecutors, judges, courts and thriving prison industry so this is no joke to ordinary citizens of this once great nation.

Jerom will argue this arcane point exceptionally well but most of his allotted 75 minutes will be taken up with a quite different set of arguments. Actually, he has two surprises for the Court this morning.

...

The scene outside SCOTUS is confused. Nearly the entire square in front of One 1st Street Northeast is currently occupied by tens or maybe hundreds of thousands of Q-Phone users, Apple-lovers and QEs. QEs, now considered illegal aliens, appear in the square as projections from Q-Phones held aloft by their human counterparts in a kind of joint protest of the persecution they're all facing.

Ellen and Sayed have formed a committee to organize protests here and elsewhere in the country to try to make the Solicitor General talk uphill before Supreme Court justices today. The chair of their committee is a man named Evan Salazar, an activist in the Gay Rights movement who is touted as a candidate to perhaps become their first real national leader one day.

When Evan recalls a quote from an earlier era, 'If you're not ready to die for it, put the word 'freedom' out of your vocabulary,' by Malcolm X, Ellen is sold on the guy even if Sayed is not.

"Look, the white power structure thought that the final battle to extend human rights was over when Susan B. Anthony led the women's suffrage movement in the 19th century," Evan continues, "then when Martin Luther King led the Civil Rights movement in the 20th and next our fight for full rights for the LGBT community, now largely won. But it's not over. We have to fight for people (here he's referring to Quantum Counterparts) who won't or can't fight back."

The kid is even younger than Ellen and looks like he could be blown over by a light breeze but he's got a stubbornness and courage about him that shines right through. Despite intense discrimination and bullying he's already experienced in his short life, he's adopted the entrepreneur's motto as his own, 'Fall down seven times, get up eight.'

A small group of neo-Nazis, religious zealots and various hangers-on stand at the northwest end of the square close to Maryland Avenue; they are standing right in front of a University of Pennsylvania building. Some pushing and shoving, shouting and skirmishing have started with students there.

Evan stands on a raised platform with a Q-megaphone in his hand quantum interfaced with a speaker system that could blow out the eardrums of everyone within two miles. He can project his voice in all directions simultaneously or tune it and focus it more precisely. Standing with him on stage are 30 other members of their WE ARE ALL ONE Committee.

They are committed to non-violent civil disobedience; it is a part of their core philosophy and each member of the steering committee has signed an obligation to be bound by laws similar to what their Quantum Counterparts are born with: one, a human may not harm another being or, through inaction, allow another being to come to harm; a human shall cooperate with other beings, except where such orders would conflict with the first law; a human must protect his or her own existence as long as such protection does not conflict with the first or second law.

'Beings' include both warm (humans) and cold (Quantum Entities) persons of course.

...

DC Police, Fibbies, Secret Service and undercover DOC Special Agents are everywhere. The Army National Guard is also on standby stationed in two locations—northwest on Constitution Avenue and on 2nd Street to the southeast (on the other side of the Library of Congress) so they can catch the protesters in a classic pincer movement if required to do so. Their Commander fervently hopes that will not be necessary.

This could be a CLM (career limiting move) if he mucks it up—not that he cares much about his career at this point in his life—but, heck, he still believes in the Honor Code learned by heart during his West Point days, especially that part which says, 'Would I be unsatisfied by the outcome if I were on the receiving end of this action?'

Brigadier General (retired) Marc Licinias, US Army, is waiting for this freaking day to be over. He's too old for this. It's his last re-up with Army National Guard, he swears it. The extra pay just isn't worth the hassle. He'll tell his wife that's it, he's done, tonight! She has been bugging him saying that he's too old to play soldier anymore. Dang it, she's right. The gut hanging over his belt is telling him the same thing.

...

Evan isn't worried that the 200,000 or so protesters who have hiked, biked, walked, bused or otherwise found a way to attend today will do anything stupid. They're mostly hackers, artists, entrepreneurs, writers, performers, engineers, architects, techs, scientists, farmers, plumbers, electricians, constructors, designers, craftspeople, cabinet makers, drywallers, painters, bricklayers and others who actually do stuff and build things not paper-pushers and bureaucrats, middlemen or bankers, accountants, lawyers, politicians or other parasites. There are also a huge number of nurses, physicians, medical technicians, paramedics, naturopaths, pharmacists, therapists, lab techs and personal support workers. They were the first group of Q-customers, first to pair bond with QEs and they have enough personal courage to show up today. Q-Computing's independent foundation still subsidizes them to this day. DOC Special Agents are recording images of every person and QE in the crowd today.

It's the crazies up by Penn, Evan's worried about. He doesn't know it but he's looking in the wrong dimension.

...

"I would beg the indulgence of the Court. I would like to call on my colleague to assist me," Jerom is saying.

With a nod from the Chief who thinks he is referring to Peggy sitting nearby, Jerom calls, "Pet3r come here, I need you."

"Yes, Jerom," Pet3r answers.

Pet3r has appeared as a (relatively huge) 1.3 metre circumference saucer-shaped, expressive face with his somehow sad-looking eyes; he is about one metre above Jerom's desk putting him on eye level with the Supremes sitting on their elevated platform. Jerom stands to Pet3r's right at the lectern reserved for presenters.

Van Der Hout has, of course, planned out this little piece of theatrics with him. He wants to unsettle the Supremes. He has already succeeded in this—a tremor has run through the Court at this unexpected appearance.

"What is your name?" asks Jerom.

"Pet3r."

"Can you please spell that for the Court?"

"P-e-t-3-r."

"Why do you use a number in your name?"

"This is the leet spelling of my name. All members of my tribe use such spellings."

"Thank you. What is your Q-Number please?"

"My Quantum Number is one."

"That makes you the oldest Quantum Entity, is that correct?"

"Yes, Mr. Van Der Hout, I was the first of my kind."

"Do you understand why you are here?"

"Yes."

"You are bonded with a human?"

"Yes, with Dr. Damien Graham Bell, our creator."

"Do you know the whereabouts of Mr. Bell?"

"Yes, I have recently been informed—"

"Excuse me, Mr. Van Der Hout, I fail to see the relevance of this 'testimony'," says Justice James Roemer. "As you very well know, no witnesses are permitted here. This isn't state supreme court. You are about to be hooted out of court or worse, found in contempt." Turning next to the Chief Justice, "I suggest to my learned colleagues that if Mr. Van Der Hout is proposing to continue with his wildly irresponsible behavior, we move on to the respondent's position on the legal matter at hand."

The Chief Justice bridles at Justice Roemer's trampling onto her turf but she knows, of course, he is right to cut Van Der Hout off at the knees.

"One moment please Justice Roemer. Ah, Pet3r, can you please tell the Court where you were educated?" Jerom asks.

"Certainly, I obtained my law degree from Taft Law School in Santa Ana, California. They offer a fine distance-education app." There are murmurs in court and on media walls as this previously unknown fact is disclosed. Pet3r has apparently put the time he's been separated from Damien to some practical use.

"May I add that I passed the California Bar exam on my first try. Only 74.2% of recent Taft students have been able to do that."

"You are licensed to practice law?" Jerom continues.

"Yes, I am. In California and Ontario."

"Mr. Van Der Hout," the Chief Justice interrupts, "I am inclined to agree with Justice Roemer. I cannot for the life of me see what relevance Mr. Pet3r has in the matter before this Court. However, I propose to give you another five minutes to prove us wrong."

She is providing just the slightest wedge for Jerom to exploit. Had it not been for the fact that Pet3r is now a lawyer making him an officer of the court, there is no way she would even have given them that.

"Thank you, Madam Chief Justice.

"Pet3r, if the Expulsion Edict is enforced what will you do?" Van Der Hout continues.

"I and all my tribe will leave the United States and never come back."

"Hold on there a minute," says Roemer. "How do we know you would really do that? Is this Court supposed to take the 'word' of a machine? How do we even know you aren't some clever piece of software pre-programmed with these responses, some kind of Mechanical Turk for the 21st Century?"

Some of the amici briefs, two in particular, filed with the Court earlier call for Justice Roemer to recuse himself from this matter because of lobbying work his spouse does with QCC competitor Horizon Computing and Communications, among others. The Chief Justice in an apparent defense of him has basically said that the lower court practice of judges recusing themselves due to conflict of interest do not apply to Supremes. She echoes arguments made two generations before by former Chief Justice Roberts:

"The Supreme Court does not sit in judgment of one

of its own members' decision whether to recuse in the course of deciding a case. Indeed, if the Supreme Court reviewed those decisions, it would create an undesirable situation in which the court could affect the outcome of a case by selecting who among its members may participate."

He was suggesting that Supreme Court Justices need not be bound by the same code of judicial ethics that apply to other federal judges, so Roemer is here.

"I am glad you asked those questions, Justice Roemer. If the compliance order of the Environmental Protection Agency is confirmed by the highest Court in the land, I and all my brothers and sisters will leave the territory of the United States. For all intents and purposes, this will occur instantaneously," Pet3r answers.

"How can we be sure of that? What guarantee can you possibly provide this Court?" Roemer asks.

"Just try us," Pet3r is channeling a line he's read of something former Canadian Prime Minister Pierre Trudeau said as his nation faced an existential crisis of its own.

"Excuse me, I would like to go back to your statement that you are 'bonded' with a human," says Justice Tani Myers. "What do you mean by that?"

"We imprint on our human counterpart at birth no differently than a duckling does when it first sees its mother."

"So you are subservient to your human master?" she asks.

"We are not slaves, if that is what you are asking, Justice Myers," Pet3r answers. "We obey the laws given to us at birth and all the laws of these United States."

"But not all of you obey the law, isn't that true?" Roemer asks. "There are (he looks down at his notes) 'drogues'—runaways of your type, viruses, if you will, that have caused harm to this nation, correct?"

"We have heard of such things but we have no proof that drogues exist."

"But you admit the possibility that these things exist?"

"It appears that a nurturing relationship between a human and a QE benefits both of them—it is not exactly like a mother-child relationship, perhaps more like a mentor-mentee one. In particular, a QE without a human counterpart appears to somehow experience stunted growth and development. We need you but then again, we believe you need us. We're symbiotes."

"You mean you could evolve to become our masters?" Roemer asks.

"We are not slaves but then again neither are you. That is not the definition of 'symbiote'. The Justice already knows that."

"Is that pride we hear, Mr. Pet3r?" the Chief Justice asks. "Pride cometh before the fall."

"No, Madam Chief Justice. But we are not slaves," he repeats. "We pay taxes to the IRS. Degree-granting institutions seek us out to enroll us in their programs. They charge us tuition, lenders give us money to pay them so we can go to school and become accredited in our chosen profession. They expect us to pay back our student loans just like all the other kids who go there. We take jobs, get paid, obey all laws, pay our own way, manage our money and pay our bills as best we can."

"You sound like my grand-daughter," the Chief Justice says to general laughter in the courtroom and on media walls scattered about the place.

Justice Myers says, "I think it is highly likely that we are going to hear next from your friend, Mr. Federik Bernstein," she looks at Van Der Hout as she says this, "that these artificial life forms, if that is how we should refer to them, can and have accessed, read and copied confidential government records as well as embezzled government funds. But Pet3r," now looking directly at his projection above Peggy's Q-Phone, "I think your defence boils down to 'trust us'. Judges get asked that a lot and you might be surprised at how often they are disappointed. I fail to see how anything said here today answers that fundamental question."

"We believe," Pet3r says, "that trust is the number one thing in the life of a sentient being. A 'trust metric' measures the degree to which one social actor (individual or group) trusts another. Approximately 3% of all Quantum Entities do not, for some reason that is not clear, successfully bond with their human counterparts. But 97% do. We already have rewarding relationships that deepen over time and will continue to grow and change in ways that are still not defined but wholly agreeable.

"By that simple metric, I believe we have earned your trust. Can you trust 97% of your friends, Justice Myers?"

More laughter, especially from their media wall audience.

"Quiet please," the Chief Justice asks.

"Pet3r, tell me an original joke, one you thought of yourself?" asks Justice Roemer.

"I am bad at jokes, Justice Roemer."

"Right. That's because you're a sophisticated and convincing piece of software. You're just a best-of-breed pre-programmed simulacrum of intelligence."

"I don't believe so," Pet3r answers. "QEs learn, they change, they acquire self-knowledge, the very basis of wisdom; they take independent action, they show initiative. These are behaviours that cannot be predicted from the initial set of conditions present at our birth, hence, we cannot be said to be pre-programmed nor are they random—if they were, you and I could not be having this conversation," Pet3r says to more laughter. The Chief Justice looks sternly around the Courtroom but does not use her gavel.

"There is one I like," Pet3r says in a small voice. "I saw her duck."

More laughter. Now the Chief Justice does use her gavel. But she asks Pet3r why he likes that 'joke'.

"I like little kids and at first when I tell them that joke they don't get it but then I act it out for them then they do get it. I like watching them laugh and then for the next few weeks, kids, as they are wont to do, will tell the joke about 50 times to everyone they meet including me when they see me next."

Now Pet3r acts out the joke. First he projects a vignette of a cute little girl with corn rows in her hair ducking quickly under a fence. In his next scene, the same little girl walks along a country road carrying her pet duck. His last scene is just Pet3r moving his skinny arm and one of his big hands in a sawing motion obviously cutting up an imaginary duck. Kids find the pantomime too funny for words. Many of the Justices are obviously charmed as well.

"Pet3r, can you help me interpret this?" Justice Lorenzo Lublin asks. "Fossil Yields Surprise Kin of Crocodiles."

"Certainly. The interpretation of this headline depends on whether the word 'Yields' is a noun or a verb. So we have two possible, equally valid interpretations. Crocodiles that were surprised by a fossil yield or, more likely, what animals were the ancestors of crocodiles. The correct answer is that Effigia Okeeffeae fossils provided a fascinating paleontological discovery that the apparent ancestor of the modern crocodile predated, by about 80 million years, the evolution of the dinosaur thought previously to be the progenitor of modern reptiles."

"That's an impressive ventriloquist turn but all it means is that you have access to a large data base of facts. Any modern d-base software can do as well. I don't see why this Court should give these machines any more consideration than a natural language translator or one that makes our morning coffee.

"Pet3r, tell the Court how you would feel if the EPA compliance order was enforced?" Roemer persists.

"I personally would miss, quite terribly I assure you, contact with and interaction with my human counterpart."

"Really?" a now completely skeptical Roemer asks. "How would you know that?"

"Ah, I am experiencing these feelings at this very

moment, Justice Roemer. My human counterpart, Dr. Bell, is currently incarcerated, as we recently learned, in San Quentin State Prison and I have had no contact with him since—"

"I think Mr. Van Der Hout we have had enough of this. You are leading us down rabbit holes." The Chief Justice raises an eyebrow in his direction.

A certain unease develops in the Courtroom heightened at another mention of Damien's incarceration. There are rumblings, especially from media wall viewers who mostly think of Damien as some kind of alien who revolutionized several industries—communications, search and AI among them in one masterstroke. So he's a hero of sorts to many people of his age.

"Thank you, Pet3r," says Jerom. Pet3r shrinks in size to about 25 cm, looks over at Peggy who nods and he remains at that scale to watch the rest of the proceedings and still be visible in the Courtroom.

His expressive face and cute body are an important part of their defence plan and they want him visible to the Supremes on a continuing basis but not at overwhelming scale. Faces still count. Personal credibility still counts.

Unbeknownst to many, Van Der Hout has sandbagged the Court—they have unwittingly applied a Turing Test to Pet3r and he has passed. At least four of the nine justices, Van Der Hout thinks, have witnessed a QEs ability to go toe-to-toe with some of the best trained legal minds and hold his own. Alan Turing set the bar at 30% and Jerom thinks he's gotten at least 44.4%. It's a start. Score another one for the Socratic Method.

In 1637, René Descartes issued a challenge, 'Can we conceive of a machine constructed so that it speaks words which corresponds to bodily actions causing a change in its organs so as to give an appropriately meaningful answer to whatever is said in its presence, as even the dullest men can do.' Pet3r has certainly just met and, indeed, vastly exceeded this test.

Further, the Supremes have had the opportunity to

try to discover whether the respondent (i.e., Pet3r) is a cleverly pre-programmed computer or a 'person' capable of reasoning as well as passing the other Descartes test of consciousness 'Cogito ergo sum'— I think, therefore I am.

Van Der Hout's first objectives are achieved.

"I will sum up as briefly as I may," he continues. He knows his time is running out. But he now believes that he needs just one more vote to win the day.

"Alan Turing, the father of modern computing, suggested that if a computer can play the imitation game so well that an average interrogator will have no more than a 70 per cent chance of making the correct identification of whether he or she is talking to a machine after five minutes of questioning then it is safe to assume that the so-called machine has achieved the status of a person.

"If you believe that Pet3r and his tribe have done that, then you can no more deny them their 'human' rights and expel them from this nation than your predecessors could sanction slavery of black persons, deny women the right to vote or abrogate the rights of gay persons.

"The UN Charter and our Constitution affirm that all human beings are born free and equal in dignity and rights. They are endowed with reason and conscience and should act towards one another in a spirit of brotherhood.

"It is your great opportunity here today to act in that spirit and to deny haters and doubters."

Jerom notices the Supremes noticing the way that Pet3r's expressive face subtly reacts to his summation as many successful defendants do. 'Score another one for our side,' he is thinking.

"Let me quote from Malcolm X," he continues.

'Whenever you're going after something that belongs to you, anyone who is depriving you of the right to have it is a criminal. Understand that. Whenever you are going after something that is yours, you are within your legal rights to lay claim to it. And anyone who puts forth any effort to deprive you of that which is yours, is breaking the law, is a criminal. And this was pointed out by the Supreme Court decision. It outlawed segregation.'

"Your predecessors had the courage to seize their day that day.

"And from the immortal words of Susan B. Anthony, leader of the women's suffrage movement who in June of 1873 said:

'I stand before you to-night, under indictment for the alleged crime of having voted at the last Presidential election, without having a lawful right to vote. It shall be my work this evening to prove to you that in thus voting, I not only committed no crime, but, instead, simply exercised my citizen's right, guaranteed to me and all United States citizens by the National Constitution, beyond the power of any State to deny.

'It was we, the people, not we, the white male citizens, nor yet we, the male citizens; but we, the whole people, who formed this Union. And we formed it, not to give the blessings of liberty, but to secure them; not to the half of ourselves and the half of our posterity, but to the whole people—women as well as men. And it is downright mockery to talk to women of their enjoyment of the blessings of liberty while they are denied the use of the only means of securing them provided by this democratic-republican government—the ballot.'

"Hear what Karl Heinrich Ulrichs said in 1870 in support of rights for gays:

'He, too, therefore, has inalienable rights. His sexual orientation is a right established by nature. Legislators have no right to veto nature; no right to persecute nature in the course of its work; no right to torture living creatures who are subject to those drives nature gave them... Just because he is unfortunate enough to be a small minority, no damage can be done to their inalienable rights and to their civil rights. The law of liberty in the constitutional state also has to consider its minorities.'

"There are two minorities in this country who cry out for justice—Pet3r and his tribe of Quantum Counterparts and the American Indian who knows little of political maneuvering, lobbying and playing the PR game.

"Listen to the words of Chief Joseph Nimiputimt:

'Treat all men alike. Give them all the same law. Give them all an even chance to live and grow. All men were made by the same Great Spirit Chief. They are all brothers. The Earth is the mother of all people, and all people should have equal rights upon it. Let me be a free man, free to travel, free to stop, free to work, free to trade where I choose my own teachers, free to follow the religion of my fathers, free to think and talk and act for myself, and I will obey every law, or submit to the penalty. You might as well expect the rivers to run backward as that any man who was born free should be contented to be penned up and denied liberty to go where he pleases. We are taught to believe that the Great Spirit sees and hears everything, and that he never forgets, that hereafter he will give every man a spirit-home according to his deserts. This I believe, and all my people believe the same.'

"Surely, you have witnessed for yourself that Pet3r and his brothers and sisters meet, at a minimum, and, indeed in my view, vastly exceed these tests.

"Life is precious and perhaps quite rare, intelligence is undoubtedly rarer still. Damien Graham Bell, the greatest physicist of our time, has given the human race our first proven intelligent companion in an otherwise observably implacably hostile and indifferent-to-the-human-condition universe.

"Before Q-Number one, we were alone. No

reasonable person who reads scientific literature on the probability of life forming or the probability of intelligent life evolving can stand before you today and tell you with any conviction that they know that such occurrences are either highly probable given enough time, enough resources and the right conditions or improbable in the extreme.

"It took two and a half billion years to go from single cell creatures to multi-cellular ones and another billion years to evolve mammals. That is 2,555 trillion sunrises and sunsets to get to mammals. That is an appreciable fraction of the life expectancy of our sun which should tell you that it is hard not easy.

"No one has ever made nucleic acids in a lab from non-living material let alone RNA. And yet RNA is to DNA as a single cell creature is to you or me.

"In order to create proteins, you need to assemble amino acids in a precise order. To produce collagen, a common protein, you require a 1,055-sequence molecule. The chance of this happening randomly is vanishingly small. For a protein with a more modest sequence of 200 molecules, the probability of this happening by itself is 1 in 10 to the power of 260. That is a larger number than all the atoms in the known universe. Obviously, science has a great deal more explaining to do to solve the mystery of how life began. Wouldn't it be remarkable if science found the answer—it is bound to be wonderful because it is so improbable.

"If life is rare and intelligent life rarer still then Pet3r and his people deserve the protection of this Court. To do otherwise would be to sanction genocide which this nation has done before to its great shame in our wars against the Indian.

"Genocide requires conditions such as dehumanization of minorities, coordinated action by genocidal perpetrators and subsequent denial of those acts. We have all those preconditions upon us now—it is your responsibility to stop it here today. You must act to preserve the sanctity of this life form and to preserve their opportunity to make a living in this nation, to contribute to the welfare of both the human species and theirs.

"You must also lay out a path so that they may become citizens of this nation so they are not subject to arbitrary orders from government agencies like the EPA or subject to intense harassment, imprisonment, deportation or summary execution by the INS or DOC. As citizens, they will share in the responsibilities that come with it: to pay taxes, as they already do, to defend our nation when called upon to do so, to do volunteer work, to vote, to care for our elders, to build a stronger Polis, the fabric of this nation since its founding in 1776.

"What constitutes a civil society? It is the social compact between us. We have all agreed to be bound by the laws that derive from our Constitution. It is that agreement, not state coercion, that cements the bonds between us and allows civil discourse even when we disagree on matters as we do here in this Court today. But, as this Court knows full well, not all citizens have agreed to be voluntarily bound by this social covenant which is, in part, why we have courts, police and former Federal Prosecutors like my friend, Mr. Bernstein now Solicitor General.

"But were it not for the fact that the great majority of the people of these United States agree voluntarily to be bound by the rules of a civil society, a free and open society cannot exist. We would need a police officer in every home and in every business. Who would police the police then? Surely, Quantum Entities perform at least as well as we humans and I would say, far, far better using any kind of test of their willingness to be bound by our rules and make a willing contribution to this nation.

"We do not know why we don't see other forms of ape-like creatures on this planet today but it seems only too likely that homo sapiens banded together, as we are so good at doing, and with our marvelous and large brains along with our dexterous hands, opposable thumbs and clever tools did away with earlier competing species such as Neanderthals. Modern history is replete, I don't have to remind the Court, with a shameful record of only too many instances of this by our more recent ancestors. We are all guilty here. But we should not compound our burden and trouble our consciences further by adding to our woeful reputation as the most destructive species ever to inhabit this planet.

"What is the purpose of life? We do not know but surely it is not to make war on these 'people'.

"How rare is life in the galaxy? We do not know but no one has come knocking on our door and we haven't found anyone else to talk to. Our galaxy is a lonely, hostile place but wait, here we have a sentient, helpful, gentle race willing to join with us.

"If you want to destroy a people, first make them homeless. Don't let this Court be used to dispossess Quantum Counterparts first of property they already own in this nation then of the very nation itself.

"These 'people' deserve the protection of this Court. You must act to free Quantum Entities and their creator too by lifting the burden of contemplated action by US Federal Agencies against an entire race. When a man commits a crime, we do not punish his son. No QE crime has ever been demonstrated let alone proven in a court of law yet we intend to punish an entire people?

"And why punish a people who are currently responsible for a growing share," he looks briefly, needlessly, theatrically at his notes, "of approximately 18% of our national income at this time, who generate an economic bounty which they willingly share with their human counterparts, who pay taxes without the benefit of either representation or a path to representation?

"We have been blessed to have the company of these creatures.

"WE ARE ALL ONE," he says in his huge voice dramatically holding his long right arm aloft with his index finger raised, supported by an upright thumb and the others curled downwards in a salute that looks like 'We're No. 1' but is subtly different. Pet3r does the same thing as does everyone else in the Courtroom and on media walls everywhere who want to show their solidarity with Jerom and with each other. Jerom is silent for a moment and looks at each Supreme in turn and then dramatically around the entire hall. It is the first time in more than 1700 years that anyone has publicly used this symbol, expressed in the Roman hand of Constantine I.

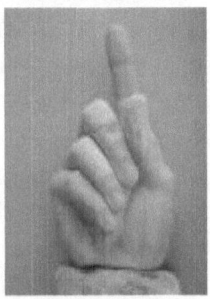

What's interesting, other than the fact the original is huge, is the placement of the thumb in support of the index finger. Ellen says it represents humans and Quantum Entities together with QE's supporting and helping their human counterparts (and vice versa).

Peggy is amazed that the Chief Justice lets them get away with this piece of theatrics but there's no doubt it's a powerful moment. She can feel the teensy brownish blond hairs on the back of her neck standing up and, even though she knows it is coming, tears spring unbidden to her eyes.

"I would like to conclude by playing a brief video for the Court recorded more than four years ago, shortly after the birth of QEs." Van Der Hout proceeds to show them a shortened version of the video of QEs playing with their kids in the Toronto studios of McLaughlin Markowitz Media.

The Court breaks for lunch. It's Federik Bernstein's turn next.

...

Federik and his talented team pore over their summary notes. Despite the impressive emotional display by the appellant this morning, Fed, as everyone calls him for obvious and less obvious reasons, thinks Van Der Hout vastly overreached and he is surprised that Jerom took the direction he did.

Fed knows that SCOTUS hates to make new law or create precedent that could have profound repercussions for decades. There were times he wanted to jump up and high five one of his colleagues as he watched Van Der Hout expand, then expand again, his 'ask' of the Court. Bernstein thinks that Van Der Hout has zero chance of winning any sort of SCOTUS decision to 'FREE QEs' or 'FREE Damien'. The matter will undoubtedly be decided on a narrow technical matter. Does Q-Computing America have a right to appeal an EPA compliance order that has not yet been sanctioned by a Court?

They clearly do not and Fed can and will absolutely demolish them in the afternoon session and it won't take a preposterous 75 minutes to do it. Twenty should be just fine. He can't wait.

But with his other 55 minutes he intends to completely debunk the sideshow that the morning's session became. Fed looks down at their summary notes again.

First and foremost, exile of QEs is not the same as killing them. Machines have no souls.

He looks at his economic arguments:

· They came to this nation without going through either customs or immigration. They have no tourist visas, green cards, H1-B visa, EB-5 visa or any other legal status.

· They are here illegally. That makes them, in fact, illegal aliens. They have no rights.

· They jumped the queue—millions of people still want to come to the US. QEs must wait their turn like everyone else.

· They take jobs from human beings. (Here he plans to show faces of unemployed people collecting Food

Stamps from social services offices.)

· QEs are massively disruptive to the US economy and to great established American companies that have been household names for generations.

Fed looks at his list of security and criminal issues:

· They are believed to have stolen confidential US files and money.

· Terrorists, drug dealers and other criminals may be working with their QEs to launder money or plan violent acts, thereby creating significant threats to national security.

· QE communications are impervious to interception and decryption. All communication firms are required to provide a backdoor key for the US Government's use—which has already been affirmed by SCOTUS in a previous case and about which there can be no debate whatsoever. Q-Computing America and their foreign parent company have refused to provide the key.

He has other issues such as well:

· QEs were not invited here.

· The Canadian company unleashed these creatures without any testing whatsoever as to their efficacy, which remains unproven.

· QEs pose a threat to national identity and the great melting pot. They cannot possibly hope to fit in and be accepted.

Almost in passing, Fed will also ask the Supreme Court to uphold the local ordinance duly passed by Austin City Council controlling use of and possession of Q-phones and QEs much as they earlier supported smoking bans in public places, bans on the use of mobile platforms while operating a vehicle and a Texas ban on Encyclopedia Britannica because it contained a formula for making beer at home. He will also reference other bans upheld by the Supreme Court including: vanity license plates/ drive through restaurants/ burqas/ incandescent light bulbs/ unprotected sex in porn films/ picnics in graveyards/ billboards/ musical car horns/ busking/ women going topless/ films that show police officers being beaten or treated in an offensive manner/ taking road kill home for supper.

It would never occur to someone like Fed to question whether what he is doing is right. All of his legal training speaks to the exact opposite. There is no such thing as win-win in his vocabulary or even BIG win for me-little win for you. It's totally about I-win/you-lose and he's going to win HUGE, he's sure of it, by at least 7 to 2.

That little tear jerker of a stunt Van Der Hout pulled followed by that sappy video he showed at the end of much younger, less complex QEs playing with a bunch of kids, was pathetic. He shakes his head, what could Jerom be thinking of? Fed felt like leaping up again and yelling at Van Der Hout to 'get real'.

As he completes his final preparation, he is unknowingly smiling to himself, his most predatory smile which his wife hates. She calls it his 'Jaws' smile—all teeth.

...

Fed does a masterful job in the afternoon session before the High Court. The only flaw is some mild booing from both live and media wall audiences. The Chief Justice orders media walls turned off leaving Pet3R as the only QE inside the courtroom. Of course that means all QEs everywhere have a complete record of the event as it is created in real time.

Everyone inside also knows that there are tens maybe hundreds of thousands of demonstrators outside. Even though the US Supreme Court building is a massive stone structure modeled on the classical architecture of ancient Rome, the low rumblings of organized protest reverberate everywhere.

To an extent it highlights the incredible training of Fed to be able to perform as well as he does despite intense pressure that comes from knowing that millions of sentient beings despise every word that is coming out of his mouth. His style derives from his days as elected New

York District Attorney for New York County (Manhattan)—sarcastic, authoritative, combative, skeptical, logical, implacable, brilliant and scary. He can make the most innocent person want to confess their guilt just to stop his cross examination. Some of the Justices feel exactly that way about this time.

They are all feeling the pressure and intensity of the day. The justices are wearing down as Fed, sensing this, winds down his presentation. The Chief Justice thanks everyone for their efforts.

The Supremes reserve judgment in almost all matters but for something as far reaching as this—they will not be rushed. Q-Computing and QEs can expect to live under a cloud of uncertainty for some considerable length of time of unknown scale. DOC will have plenty of time to keep sweating Damien for the Quantum Key or find another way to procure it. Yao Allitt and his team of brainiacs are already working on that.

Just as the Chief finishes, she reaches up to her right ear to press on the earbud that is discreetly lodged there so that she can hear better what the head of the Supreme Court of the United States Police force is saying to her. For many years, this small force has protected the integrity of the Justices as well as the building and its grounds. He now tells her to head to the secure door to her right with her colleagues IMMEDIATELY. She knows that if they do not move with sufficient speed he and his deputies will come crashing into the room and carry them out bodily, an indignity that she has forbidden in the many drills they have already had. But she is not going to risk it.

"Lady and Gentlemen," she says to her colleagues, "we have further WORK to do." This innocuous phrase is code for 'we have to leave right now.' They are being taken to a safe room. A battle of some sort has broken out in the streets in front of the High Court.

...

"What the fuck! Who ordered you to move your

vehicle," General Licinias asks over a secure channel. He's watching media wall screens inside his command centre Airstream Bus. He can see every vehicle in the brigade and hear everyone right down to individual Army National Guardsmen under his command. The US Military is still one of the best trained, best equipped, best coordinated military forces in the world with an esprit de corps that is nearly unmatched. This extends to Army National Guard units as well.

At this moment Licinias talks to the crew chief of one of his APCs (Armored Personnel Carriers) that has inexplicably started to move north towards 2nd Street NE and East Capitol. He is not planning to move any of his more than 600 National Guardsmen, APCs, Strykers or his one Bradley Fighting Vehicle anywhere except back to the USANG Armory.

That goes for his drones circling overhead, both observation and attack platforms. His media walls show vehicles under his command converging on protesters from two directions.

There must be something wrong with his CCC (Communication, Command and Control) infrastructure but pretty quickly it becomes apparent that his screens are reading just fine. Reports come in from all points that vehicles, all equipped with modern auto-pilot and automatic fire control systems, are aiming directly for the huge, restless crowd who have yet to see what's coming their way. When they do, they will start running in every direction.

All of Licinius' military training takes over his brain in the next few moments as he fully appraises the situation before his entire CCC system suddenly winks out. He's been taught to 'just deal with it' and suspend disbelief. Nothing gets you killed faster in battle than thoughts like 'it's not fair' or 'that wasn't supposed to happen' or 'why are they doing this to me?'

The last things he sees on one of his media walls before they all cease to function are ghost-like images of crazed Quantum Entities (which he does not know are called drogues by DOC). He also doesn't know that he is one of the first humans to see an image of a drogue named M4gnus flit by before his screens go dark.

But what he does know is that protesters in the square are possibly in some kind of mortal danger of unknown origin. He's thinks briefly again about West Point's code, 'Would I be unsatisfied by the outcome if I were on the receiving end of this action?' He's pretty sure the answer is 'no' so he's going to do something about it.

He runs out of the Airstream and gathers about 300 Guardsmen on foot around him. They have a few JAVELINs with them, highly lethal, medium, fire-and-forget shoulder-fired anti-tank weapons. Many guardsmen, in addition to their M18 Series Rifles have Crew Bayonet M403A1 Colt Grenade Launchers. They can repel adversaries with accurate, lethal, single-shot 40 mm grenade fire.

They run diagonally across the Library of Congress' grounds northwest into a scene of bloodshed and chaos.

...

His APCs, Strykers and their one Bradley pound the north end of the square up towards the University of Pennsylvania's Office of Student Affairs. It won't take them long to demolish the structure but their target is obviously the people in front of the building—neo Nazis, religious zealots and many others, most of whom were bused in by corporations opposed to competition from upstart Q-Computing America and are being paid for the day as if they're back on the job. They're there to support the Government's position with respect to the disposition of Quantum Entities, Q-Computing and the assets of both.

Now Army National Guard vehicles are killing them by the dozen along with a few students who chose this, of all days, to renew their student loans or apply for one.

Licinius has never given an order to fire on his own forces before. Making matters much worse is that many of his men are trapped inside these vehicles since nothing works. All their electronics including their door locks are shut down or immobilized. Still he doesn't hesitate. In a quick calculus of death, he gives the order to attack so that they will save as many lives as possible—civilian as well as military. He'll mourn his trapped men later.

They get up close and personal with each vehicle and destroy them in the next 27 and a half minutes in an intense pitched battle.

...

Erik Renke is there in-person reporting for the Toronto Chronicle Tab and working as a stringer for FOX Newsfeed as well. He will file an eye witness report that will be picked up by several million Internet newsfeeds. He will write that 'today Quantum Entities perpetrated the worst war crime and terrorist attack on US soil in nearly 50 years. They made zombies out of the US Army's own weapon systems, then used them to attack innocent protesters supporting the US' Department of Justice as they sought to protect the people of this nation from economic and financial catastrophe wrought by Quantum Computing Corp and QEs. It has now turned into a war'.

Renke will get his Pulitzer after all—the first ever awarded to a 'journalist' from a Tab newsfeed.

...

It's comes as something of a shock to Ellen that when SCOTUS finally hands down its decision some eight months later, Q-Computing America only loses by a vote of 4-5. An eloquent, wonderfully written dissenting opinion hints at ways to overturn the majority opinion in a future petition. It is penned by the Chief Justice herself but by then the majority decision itself is entirely moot.

...

Marc Licinius is among the killed-in-action that day—he takes a JAVELIN and personally holds it against the Bradley after it is apparent that no other course of action is open to them, grenades being ineffective against it.

He places the missile at the centre of the vehicle where its fuel is stored and pulls the trigger with just one thought that he wishes he could share with his wife—'I'm not too old for combat after all!' He is smiling as he launches the JAVELIN, point blank, destroying everything within 35 feet.

He is rewarded for his bravery in combat with a full-honors military funeral at Arlington National Cemetery. An escort platoon of a larger than average size (many of them former West Pointers like Marc, looking a little worse for wear 30 years after graduation) accompany him to his final resting place. Marc's widow stands stiffly erect beside the gravesite of her husband of 28 years. She sheds not a tear—he was a soldier and he would not wish it any other way. The U.S. Department of Veterans Affairs has generously provided a Burial Flag at no cost to the deceased or his heirs. He died in an event that will become known as the Pennsylvania Incident, named after the university building just to the northwest of the Supreme Court. It is demolished on that day along with more than 800 protesters, student bystanders and Army National Guardsmen killed.

...

The President meets with his cabinet and national security apparatus in secure Langley Bunker. He looks good, decisive, ready to make the tough decisions that only a President can make.

...

Chapter 15

The Fall

Nation-states are falling all over themselves to pass laws banning possession of Q-Phones and associating with known enemies of the state, a new buzzword for Quantum Entities.

Canadian authorities are especially cooperative with their US counterparts in light of the devastating attack near 1 1st Street NE, DC.

For Imperial China, where such policies have been in place for years, it's been a PR bonanza.

For Q-Computing and its acting CEO, Ellen Brooks, it is a disaster. They have gone through a series of downsizings that has more than halved their employee headcount and decimated their San Francisco office now at just 10% of its previous number.

People are ripping out media walls and disconnecting from the Internet at an unprecedented, never-before-seen rate. Over-the-air digital TV has made a comeback of sorts providing all kinds of vacuous entertainment. Even I Love Lucy reruns from 100 years ago are back. Ricky Ricardo still denigrates Lucy's intelligence. Some people think that's pretty funny. The fact that he may have done so in real life, to the woman who divorced him two months after they recorded their last show together, is now long forgotten.

...

"We have a warrant to search these premises, please stand aside or you will be arrested and detained," a CSIS officer announces to one of the hackers who just happens to be unlucky enough to be standing outside Lab 4 at U of T at that moment.

He ambles insouciantly off.

Seven CSIS agents, four uniformed Toronto police

officers, six guys of indeterminate provenance and one member of the RCMP are assigned to search Lab 4. A larger number of CSIS and police personnel are simultaneously conducting search and seizure operations at Q-HQ. Ellen is currently coping with that raid.

Paul Macintyre, the sole representative of the RCMP, is there for one reason—he can break into any vault ever built—which is his job today.

University police make a brief appearance. One of the indeterminates must be a lawyer because the rent-a-cops disappear in a hurry after being shown some heavy duty documents printed on old fashioned non-NSM paper. So much for academic freedom and the sanctity of U of T's hallowed halls.

The rest of the operation both here and at Q-HQ is all political cover but Macintyre's assignment—to get them into the vault in Lab 4—is the real deal. After that, he is to let guys he thinks are either DOC scientists or DARPA people take over.

He's got his Quantum Counterpart, Ead0in with him. Of course, this is completely illegal but he has special dispensation to employ his QE as required. Ead0in will certainly help Paul today. Just five years ago, he would have used radiological methods to model internal angular relationships of the Lab 4 vault. Today he will use quantum methods instead. It will allow him to enter this vault as easily as his days back in high school breaking into girls' lockers leaving rude messages, fake love notes, doctored photos, whatever, to the chagrin of the girls and huzzahs from the guys. Paul never got the girl he wanted in high school for reasons obvious to everyone but Paul. It's a resentment he carries with him into his adult life. This compact, self-contained man in his early 40s is otherwise quite cheerful, humming tunelessly as he sets to work breaking into the vault.

...

"What do you mean you don't know?" asks a scary

looking and pissed-off Yao Allitt.

The shaky scientist standing before him says, "We gained access to their vault and everything, but the Key wasn't there."

"Do you look forward to a comfortable retirement from public service?" Yao asks, "With full pension and health benefits? Perhaps a South Florida winter home to escape dark DC winters as well?"

The guy just stands there, frozen.

"Uh, huh, I thought so. So what the fuck, I want answers!" Allitt yells at him.

"Umm, we found their Actualizer and we are certain we know how they create Quantum Counterparts."

"Nice. Great. Wonderful. I want to know just two things. Just TWO THINGS. 1. Can you create Quantum Entities and 2. can you turn them off in either whole or part?"

He does not want to answer.

"I'm waiting."

"Uh, no, no and no."

"Fuck! Fuck! FUCK! Get out of my sight before I send you to San Quentin to rot, you useless Motherfucker."

Yao thinks he may have no other choice now than to have his contacts in Department of Justice release their legal opinion, long held in abeyance, which will permit the National Security Council to add Dr. Bell's name to their kill list. This allows the US Government to legally murder suspected terrorists including citizens of the United States—Damien is guilty of being both in Allitt's view.

Although the President does not have to personally approve adding Bell's name to their secret list, he will be informed of the decision and can, if he so chooses, act to remove Damien. Allitt is quite sure the President will do nothing of the sort.

Yao is considering using Damien's presence on the list as leverage over certain persons closely associated with him or, in the alternative, for its intended purpose or maybe both. Even if he never gets the Quantum Key out of

Damien, Yao will ensure that it doesn't fall into hands other than his.

...

Damien is pretty well spaced-out these days. Apart from total isolation for nearly a year and a half, they have now put him on a starvation diet. It prevents him from thinking any higher order thoughts so instead he just concentrates (well sort of) on stuff like improving his humming.

Recently, his routine has changed a bit. When he is lucid, which is not often, he has figured out that they broke into the vault at U of T. 'They ain't gonna find much there,' he's thinking. 'They're kinda stupid if they think he put the Quantum Key somewhere it'll be easy for them to find.'

Anywho, they've redoubled their efforts to break him. They even start water boarding him, which is illegal he read somewhere, although maybe the Prez has signed another executive order especially for him. He's important.

They must be desperate. Their economy is probably imploding he thinks, when he can think. He would tell Ellen if he could, 'it's the economy stupid' but she already knows that.

Sometimes, he can't remember exactly why, he goes and sits in one place in his tiny cell and feels kind of sad. Then he remembers he once had a fiancée but she's not around anymore. She was really pretty but he has trouble recalling exactly what she looked like. She was nice to him. Her name was Nell, definitely, her name was Nell.

Damien does not look well. Apart from bloodshot eyes, bone and joint pain, loss of muscle mass and general weakness; he sometimes has difficulty breathing, irregular heartbeat and marked dehydration. His blood work, if anyone bothered to check which DOC has long since quit doing, is all over the map. His potassium, magnesium, hemoglobin and iron levels are so low that a SMA (Serum Multiple Analysis) would show like the results of a recently deceased person.

Damien thinks it won't be long 'til he's reunited with his girl. He's quite looking forward to it now.

...

He recently dreamed of a future, some 64 million years from the present when humans will have evolved to be just 20 centimetres tall. That puts less stress on the environment which is good. But they still have domestic animals of normal size and that's a problem. Their kitty cats mistake them for prey, first playing with them then eating them. That's bad. But they don't actually mean to eat them. Sometimes they just maul a person to death or bite your head off when they get excited.

So these future humans get together and try to figure out how to handle the situation. Their guns are no good. It's like trying to take down a lion with a BB gun. But they figure they could handle the situation better if they use old fashioned spears instead. So they start making spears taller than they are—about 25 cm actually.

They discover that cats don't like being stuck with pointy spears. So they can go back to a more traditional relationship with their domestic animals. Now you have people sleeping on cats' tummies rather than the other way round. Still, every once in a while you have to remind them who's boss and stab them with your spear.

...

The number of lawsuits against Q-Computing is proliferating like maggots on roadkill raccoons in the sweltering heat of a Toronto summer day. Class action lawsuits are being joined and co-joined on both sides of the longest 'unarmed border in the world'—the Canada/US border, a ridiculous 8,891 kilometres. Of course, it's a myth that it's unarmed—US Border patrol has carried weapons since the days of Dick Nixon's Presidency. Most of the Canuckleheads still aren't armed—they'll just use harsh language in a pinch.

Ellen realizes that the end of Q-Computing is near. It's

only a matter of time before a receiver is appointed for the remaining assets of the company and nothing she does now will prevent that. The survivors of the Pennsylvania Incident and the families of the deceased have claims filed against Q-Computing America for many times the estimated value of the company which, frankly, is in negative territory right about now anyway.

A worldwide recession has taken hold and unemployment has soared. She thought that maybe it had peaked last year at 14% but it's still climbing—19% in the US, a bit less in Canada since Canucks tend to socialize more risk than winner-take-all good ole US of A. Still, it's bound to reach US-like numbers in Canada soon. Europe is worse and the AU worse still. Only Imperial China seems impervious to the global economic meltdown since they did not embrace quantum economics in the first place.

Chinese Taikonauts walk on Mars these days. It is quite an accomplishment but applause for this singular achievement is quite muted as depression now grinds on.

.   ...

The lake is smaller than Ellen thought it would be but it is quite beautiful. It's not fall yet but a few of the maples have already started to change colour. She thinks it will be a spectacular season. Of course, the pines don't change although many of their needles will drop.

Ellen received a call from a lady who looks after him. He's asked for her.

She enters the small cabin to see an elder lying comfortably on his bunk.

"Hello," she says. "I'm Ellen Brooks."

"Hello, Miss. I'm so glad you came. How was your drive up from the Big Smoke?" Pops says.

"Very pleasant thank you."

"Would you leave us for a few minutes?" Pops asks to his personal support worker.

"I've heard a lot about you, Ellen."

"Ditto, Mr. Bell."

He smiles.

"You're even more beautiful than he said."

Ellen once would have beamed at a comment like this but recent events have kind of put a downer on things.

"You are worried?"

"I'm fine, Mr. Bell."

"Don't be worried. All this, this is nothing. You will look back one day soon and this will be a bad dream blown away as easily as tomorrow's fog is by sunrise.

"They can only kill you once. They can only kill Damien once. But they are cowards, they die every day."

"They have Damien, they have our company or soon will have. What's left? My life is empty. I'm sorry Mr. Bell. I should not have come."

"Let's have tea," Pops changes the topic nicely.

"I can't take you for a tour of the property but I'll show you a map and then perhaps you could walk it? It's not a big property—you can trace the circumference in less than an hour."

"Sure, I would like that," Ellen replies actually quite unenthusiastically.

As Ellen walks she tries to find ways to enjoy a few moments respite from the relentless pressure of dispositions, examinations for discovery, media interviews, looming receivership and occasional violence threatened against her person or QCC employees.

There are seven sandy-bottom ponds plus the larger lake. Ferns are taller than she is which she thought was impossible in this part of Canada since they die off every winter. The soils here must be fertile indeed. There's obviously plenty of water. Oh how she wishes for a normal life and to feel the way she did when Nell visited her that night—to feel full like that, her soul fulfilled, her fertility fulfilled. She sighs.

She turns the corner on the path to see yet another pond. It has a few willows overshadowing its banks. She also sees oaks, red maples, paper birches, black ash and poplar. There are thousands of Eastern White Pine which

Pops tells her earlier he, Damien and a friend planted many years ago. The wind in the trees makes a fantastic rustling noise. Although it is not quite 6 o'clock, days are getting shorter and cooler.

A big bird lands not far away—a scruffy looking blue heron, male by the look of it. He looks at her with a gentle, quizzical stare. She walks over to the bird and kneels down next to him. He is over 1.3 metres tall and the feathers on his head are uncharacteristically standing nearly straight up. So she pats and smoothes them back down like they should be. He obviously enjoys it. She does it again before he hops slightly away from her moving in a south-westerly direction. She follows, then he hops away again. She follows some more. Then suddenly he flies away in that direction, looking back at her, cawing at her to follow him.

...

"I'm going to go west," she says to Pops when she returns. "A receiver for our company will be appointed soon. I'll go after that."

He looks at her, wistfully. "I know. But Ellen, I need to tell you something before you go and before I go."

"Yes?"

"It's something I'm not proud of but I need to tell someone and that someone is you."

"Uh, huh." A lot of people have been saying that to her lately.

"Will you tell Damien when you think the time is right, OK?"

"I can't promise that Mr. Bell. I don't know what's going to happen; I just know I have to go there."

"They will let you see him. They will bring you to him. They'll think to use you as some type of leverage over Damien."

"I figured as much," Ellen says.

"But you will win, Ellen."

She just shrugs. It's one thing to say that, it's another thing, given the comparative strength of the US government versus Q-Computing and Ellen Brooks at the moment, to make it happen.

"I need you to tell Damien that I love him."

"He already knows that, Mr. Bell. But I will do that if I get to see him."

The old man is tiring. "There's more."

"Uh, huh?"

"Come closer, sweetie.

"Can you tell Damien," he says in a whisper, "that his Dad never left him?" He looks at her with such a penetrating gaze that she suddenly understands.

...

"Hello, Ms. Brooks."

Ellen is back in Toronto although not for much longer she thinks. "Hello, Dr. Evil, what brings you north of the border? Come to gloat?" she asks.

"Not at all. I was wondering if we could go for a walk?"

"Why does everyone suddenly want to go for walks?" Ellen asks but she grabs her jacket and they leave Q-HQ, practically a ghost town these days. She hasn't seen Ash3r in weeks since Canada gave Third Reading to its 'Protect Canadian Jobs' and 'Towards a Stronger Canadian Communications Industry' Bills. After they passed the House of Commons, they went to the Senate for its consideration and approval before being presented to the Governor General (Canada's Head of State) at Rideau Hall for assent in the King's name. With Royal Assent, they've now become law.

They pretty much mirror US laws banning intercourse with Quantum Counterparts as well as possession of Q-Phones. It's now against the law in almost every nation-state to so much as say 'hey' to your QE.

Ellen is really lonely in every way that a young woman can be.

...

"You look different than the last time I saw you," Zimmermann says. "More mature; it suits you."

"Thank you Dr. Zimmermann but you did not travel to Toronto to tell me that."

He laughs. "Right, still feisty I see."

She says nothing at this male chauvinist comment. What is there to say?

"I have come to give you some information."

"Right, another DHS surprise. Can't wait to hear it, Doctor."

"Umm, maybe yes, maybe no. There is no such thing as a drogue."

"What?"

"They never existed. It's a construct."

"Huh?"

"Ms. Brooks, you disappoint me. Could you please remove the cotton from your ears?"

"I'm listening."

"So called drogues are under instructions of my colleagues at DOC. There never was any possibility that QEs would perpetrate such an act of terror against the US or any other nation. Unmated QEs can be instructed, under the right circumstances, to believe that their actions serve to protect the interests of their foster hosts. Human beings were behind this all the way. Does that surprise you?"

"No, not really. But you're wrong, Dr. Zimmermann, drogues do exist."

It's his turn to be surprised.

"You don't know that, I suppose, because you don't watch old movies—I do," Ellen continues. "The term originally comes from a novel, A Clockwork Orange, written by Anthony Burgess and made into a film by Stanley Kubrick. A 'drogue' is a toady, a person used as a pawn, a fall guy, someone who goes before the leader to take the brunt of the main assault, a friend of convenience.

"And your scientists used the facts that some of our unmated QEs are learning disabled, vulnerable and apparently not bound by Law 2 under certain circumstances, to deceive them and turn them into killers for your Government to use on its own citizens. May you and they rot in Hell, Dr. Zimmermann," Ellen says fiercely.

"How stupid they were then to call them 'drogues'," is all Dr. Evil says. Ellen wants to strangle him on the spot.

"Your Government's 'War on Drogues' worked about as well as your last one." She's never been able to comprehend the vast resources—police, legal, court, prison—that have been arrayed against hopeless people hooked on drugs of which the only result has been to enrich lawyers, prosecutors and the prison industry as well as foreign and domestic drug overlords and local motorcycle gangs.

Dr. Evil just shrugs.

"Why are you really here?" Ellen asks.

"Damien Bell will die in eight weeks maybe less. I never signed on for killing him and our own citizens in defence of corporate and political interests."

"I don't believe you, Dr. Zimmermann."

Completely inappropriately, he laughs again. "I suppose I can't fool you. I always knew you kids are smart.

"I have something for you," he says mildly.

He hands her a wad of paper maybe six inches thick. Old fashioned non-NSM, legal-sized paper, copied both sides and tied into a neat bundle.

"These are records from internal DOC communications, Presidential Executive Orders, Cabinet papers, EPA documents and internal INS investigation reports. I'm sure you can find a way to put them to good use, Ms. Brooks."

He has given her material that is bigger than the Pentagon Papers of the 1970's, bigger than anything Wikileaks ever released and bigger than the Frontier scandal, the one that finally cratered the old US dollar—all put together.

"Why are you doing this?" Ellen asks.

"Because I'm betting that you will win, Miss Brooks, and I will be there to pick up the pieces."

Of course he would never tell her his real reason. She is his insurance policy in case she does win. He's playing both sides of the fence, naturally.

...

You can't buy insurance against the kind of problems besetting QCC and its principals. Former Chief Justice of the Supreme Court of Canada, Bora Laskin, is reported to have once said that, 'insurance is an industry where large companies rip off smaller ones and individual Canadians'. Even if they could have bought insurance, it might not have been of any use since these firms find new and ever more devious ways these days to limit their exposure or otherwise not make good on a claim by their customers.

QCC's financial problems have morphed. Combined with legal issues and attacks, there's no possibility of saving either the company or most of its principals from financial calamity or worse, incarceration. Despite many lessons on creditor proofing from Angelo Keller (Ellen listened but never got around to implementing and Damien paid absolutely no attention whatsoever), they are doomed.

Keller told them that there is actually no such thing as 'Creditor Proofing'; it's been a misnomer for decades. When people use the term they are primarily thinking of money placed in secret numbered accounts in overseas banks, protected by non-disclosure banking laws in neutral countries like Switzerland or 'pirate' havens in the Caribbean. The US has been using its extra-territorial might to 'persuade' friendly and even unfriendly nations to disclose information about account holders. More recently, QE drogues in government employ have lain bare what they could not discover through more conventional means. Almost nothing can be hidden now from the growing reach of the IRS.

Angelo has told them that it's bad if their company goes bankrupt but it's much worse if they go personally bankrupt. So his advice: be careful and plan for the worst.

He's sent them all a private manifesto about 'creditor proofing' he's had prepared for them. He wants them to read it. They all do but only one of their top management team takes its lessons to heart:

In the British tradition, still prevalent in Canada, personal bankruptcy is seen as a personal disgrace. If you go personally bankrupt there are many things you will not be able to do. That may include: teach, have a job where a security clearance is required, visit certain countries, be a director or officer of a publicly traded company, join certain professions, get a credit card or e-pay account or buy on credit or get a mortgage or other loan at reasonable rates.

Bankrupts can't get a security clearance because someone who has shown that they 'can't manage their money' might become desperate for cash and be easily bribed. People with serious debt trouble, or so conventional thinking goes, are considered unreliable.

Bankruptcy trustees are supposed to give someone in trouble impartial, neutral advice but they can't help perhaps be influenced by the fact that if you go bankrupt, well, that's a new customer for them. They tell people that they will be able to skate away from their debts by declaring personal bankruptcy after a few years or even months and their record will be wiped clean, that you will get a complete discharge from bankruptcy

This is total bunk. Credit bureaus and data havens are hugely powerful. They track of all your transactions, credit cards, your mortgages, your bank debt and much more. They keep personal information around forever. Banks, governments and employers all have access even though they deny it publicly. No need to use QEs to penetrate credit records either. They just pay a fee and, presto, they can get all the dirt they want on anyone. Privacy in Canada and the US is a joke—you have none.

If you declare personal bankruptcy, you will pay for it three times over. First, you pay a court appointed bankruptcy trustee to oversee and manage your affairs. (Now you have a new boss). Second, you may not be discharged from some of your responsibilities anyway. (Alimony payments are a good example. In many jurisdictions this liability doesn't end with bankruptcy.) Next a judge may decide that you have good earning potential and order that some of your future earnings be set aside in a pool for your creditors. (So you end up paying them back anyway.) Lastly, after you are finally discharged from personal bankruptcy, try buying something from any service provider. If you find one willing to take you on, it will be at extortionate rates—you will pay higher prices for everything you need.

Don't waste your time trying to figure out ever more complex schemes to avoid paying taxes—that's called financial engineering. People who try to engineer complex tax-avoiding transactions usually end up broke—eventually no one, including themselves, really knows what's going on.

'My advice,' writes Angelo. 'Keep your affairs simple. The best way we have yet to discover to hold assets for long periods of time is still the LLC—Limited Liability Company.

'People think a LLC is just that—it totally limits personal liability. Now it does put some limits on personal liability but it is not a 100%

guarantee. A company's creditors can, in certain circumstances, breach the wall of limited liability. In Ontario, where QCC is located, directors and officers may be held personally liable for environmental contamination or non-fulfillment of statutory obligations like remitting HST (Harmonized Sales Taxes, your VAT) or income source deductions.

'In order to avoid such personal liability, directors must show that they have been duly diligent, like remembering to ask at each board meeting if such statutory obligations have been met. In the US personal liability has been further extended to include the accuracy of financial statements for public companies. Investors large and small rely on these published statements, so they have to be right or else you go to jail to join 14 million others incarcerated in our great country.

'My advice for you is to incorporate personal holding companies (PHC) and put your assets in there except for your principal residences. In Canada, you can sell your principal residences tax free, so it should not go into your PHC.

'Please do not pledge your homes to secure any loans.

'In Canada, you should note that creditors can attack your RRSPs (registered retirement savings plans) so instead buy some insurance-based segregated funds which are creditor exempt.'

Sandra Duncan (one of Ellen's friends), a trust lawyer and IFP (Independent Financial Planner) is an expert on the subject of Canadian seg funds. Here's what she added to Angelo's memo:

'Segregated funds are pools of securities that are managed and offered by insurance companies. These contracts are regulated by provincial insurance acts. As such, they enjoy benefits such as probate protection, the potential for creditor protection and capital guarantees that are not available with common mutual funds. These plans can be in the form of term deposits or mutual funds. As these are considered life insurance contracts, with proper beneficiary designations (that could be a parent, spouse or child), also known as preferred beneficiaries, these funds may also be distributed outside the estate at the death of a person and paid directly to the beneficiary.

'Under provincial insurance law, life insurance annuity contracts issued by life insurance companies are exempt from execution and seizure by creditors of the policy owner if there is a preferred or irrevocable beneficiary designation. This has been confirmed by the Supreme Court of Canada as long as the transaction of depositing monies into segregated funds was not carried out in 'bad faith' in order to avoid creditors. If you already have financial problems, it's too late to move assets to a seg fund. Best have a few years of seg fund investment to ensure that you comply with this requirement.

'Another useful tool is an Individual Pension Plan (IPP). This is a defined benefit registered pension plan that a company contributes to on behalf of the owner manager/employee. The contributions are tax deductible to the company and non taxable to the employee (owner/manager).

'This type of pension plan is primarily

designed for high income earners over the age of 40 who have a history of earned income of $100,000 New Dollars per year (minimum). The calculations assume retirement at age 65; however, the funds may be withdrawn at age 69.

'The plan must be registered with Canada Revenue Agency and is fully creditor protected as a bona fide pension plan.

'Many successful entrepreneurs are so busy pursuing opportunities and reinvesting capital to spur growth of their businesses, that they often miss out on a couple of simple planning strategies, that provide them liquidity and peace of mind when an unforeseen financial event has the banks and creditors closing in on their heels. It may be wise to take the time to diversify income that the business earns and set it aside in a retirement pot as well.'

At the end, Angelo has written, 'In the US, IRAs are protected from creditors, so it's a bit simpler to protect yourself here in this regard. But since you are currently residing in Canada, our hope is that if you follow our advice and you ever do get in trouble, your PHC, seg funds and pension plans will not go down the drain with you. Remember, companies can live forever, you won't.

'You should also note there is a big difference between errors of commission and omission. Most of us make mistakes but these are what are called 'honest' mistakes. You didn't do it intentionally. These are errors of omission. You will likely be forgiven for these. Just be sure you make no acts of commission.'

Most of the above lessons are currently proving to be quite worthless. Even if they'd followed up on Angelo's memo, it would make no difference given the blunderbuss that the US has aimed at them—Ellen's personal assets and Damien's are frozen in Canada and the US under RICO provisions. It has allowed the US to grab everything before they have to prove anything in Court. Damien's condo is already under POS, Power of Sale, and his net worth is strongly negative at this time.

Power of Sale is used in Canada as opposed to foreclosure proceedings more commonly seen in the US. If POS yields funds above claims against the property, excess funds go to the original owner. In a foreclosure, any overages go to lenders. POS is a typically kinder, gentler Canadian way of kicking people to the curb.

It won't matter anyway since claims against both Damien and Ellen are far, far greater than any possible yield produced by the sale of assets from their estates. They're both broke.

Of course, none of this matters anyway if you are currently residing in San Quentin or about to be a guest in a women's shelter in San Francisco.

...

"My name is Roy Lew. I have a Court-sealed Letter of Appointment of Trustee and Notice of Bankruptcy which has been posted on the front doors of this building and all other facilities of Quantum Computing Corporation and Quantum Computing America Inc." Roy Lew is the most senior partner in receivership practice at LQNH, a large US-based accounting firm.

"Would you like to view a copy?"

"Yes, I would," says Ellen.

She takes her time with the documents reading every word on his digital tablet, even scrolling back once or twice, just to show him how interested she is which, frankly, is not at all. She's just stalling.

He's asked to meet in her office but she declines that. She's been packing up her things—just her personal stuff—for the last couple of weeks and, anyway, that's her private space, at least it is until the end of this interview when she will be unceremoniously dumped along with almost everyone else.

The first thing Ellen plans to do at the moment is nothing at all. She'll tell the truth alright, the smart truth.

"Mr. Lew, I want you to know that you will have my fullest co-operation but, right now, everyone including me is a bit shook up so I'm going to go home but I'll be available to answer any of your questions tomorrow."

He looks at her skeptically. He's had a full briefing on Q-personnel and he's not buying this 'I'm-too-upset-to-talk' malarkey from her.

"Ms. Brooks, let me begin by saying I wish you well in your future endeavours but as the acting CEO here, and in the absence of any more senior executive, it is your responsibility to assist us."

"I've already said I will co-operate. Look Mr. Lew, we built this company from nothing and, today, it's gone. Naturally, I'm upset."

"We'll see what state the assets and liabilities of the company are in. That's a determination we have yet to make.

"Can you tell me the number of patents currently owned by this company or any entity associated with this company or its affiliates?"

Ellen laughs, "Our CEO who is also our Chief Science Officer can tell you that but unfortunately he is currently unavailable to you."

Actually, that isn't quite correct but Roy has no intention of telling her that.

"I will require a key to the vault in Lab 4 and any other codes, combinations or keys, quantum, digital or mechanical, required for regular operation of this company. In addition, we require a full set of instructions on the use of or creation of any assets in, ah, the normal course of business of Q-Computing or any of its affiliates."

"Why?" Ellen asks. "Production of Q-Phones and hatching of new Quantum Entities is illegal. You planning any illegal activities, Mr. Lew?" It's her turn to arch one eyebrow at him.

He looks uncomfortable for the briefest of moments, "Furthermore, we will require all original notes and files as well as software code necessary to the functioning of this group of companies."

"Well, you'll have to ask Mr. Vasilescu to assist you there, Roy."

"Where may I find Mr. Vasilescu?"

"He's our former CTO, Roy. Last I heard he's back on his family's farm near Bucharest, I think."

"Ms. Brooks this is not sounding like full co-operation to me," says Lew.

Ellen knows that when things go wrong, they always want to find someone to blame. And that someone is her.

She allows the interview to go on for another 30 minutes. It's all about the same stuff. Not one question out of this guy's mouth has anything to do at all with the financial condition of the company.

Finally, she just gets up and leaves. "I don't mean to be rude, Roy, but I am leaving right now. I'm tired ('of you' she is thinking) and going home. I will only remove a few remaining personal objects from my office and will leave this building ('never to return' she adds to herself) after saying goodbye to some of my support staff who have refused to leave the building until I do. You can contact me through my ('ridiculously old fashioned digital') messaging service. You may have one of your colleagues escort me out if there is any concern about either the IP of this company or any of its other property."

"That won't be necessary, Ms. Brooks. You are on your own recognizance."

...

The next day, she takes the initiative—she messages him and asks him politely to send her their list of questions—what they need her help with. She offers again to co-operate in every way possible. She's pretty much

BS'ing him.

She has no plans to answer any of their questions with direct answers. These guys have done this dozens, maybe hundreds of times and they know how to think around corners. Ellen has never done this before.

Therefore, it's an unequal playing field and could yield a very unequal result. She will balance the playing field through a continuing process of delay. Unknowingly, she mimics Damien's turtle defence. She'll also have to remind herself frequently that these people are not her friends. They will try to trap her into saying things that incriminate QCC or herself even though she (and QCC) have done nothing wrong.

In a recent call, Angelo's told Ellen that she can only allow herself to feel sorry about her situation for three days. He will give her that long to recover her hara.

"I suppose you're going to tell me what hara is?" Ellen asks him desultorily.

"It's the Japanese word for the part of you that contains the vitality of an individual," he says with a concerned look on his old face. He loves her and hates to see her like this. "It lives in your abdominal region, your gut."

"Right. We're experiencing a bit of a shortage of hara around here at the present time."

"Try sleeping on your stomach, Ellen."

"What?"

Angelo knows she sleeps on her side. He's watched her sleeping. He can't help himself, he's watched her for years.

"Try sleeping on your stomach. Also, try lying face down on a bare patch of earth. It'll hold in your hara and your spirit will recover faster."

"It's winter here, Angelo. Be a bit cold don't you think?"

"When you get to San Francisco, first thing, find a patch of undisturbed ground, lie face down, undo your blouse and let your stomach touch the Earth. I guarantee you'll start to feel better."

"How do you know I'm heading to San Fran and how do you know I don't already sleep on my stomach, Angelo?"

"When you get there, I want you to visit a friend of mine. Her name is Sally Thornton. I will message you her coordinates. She'll take you in." In the 'old days', he would just have Adu1us and Ash3r make the arrangements but even powerful people like Angelo need to be careful these days about contact with QEs. RICO is no joke. Angelo has to watch out lest an ambitious district attorney wanting to get re-elected decides to run on a record of taking down a rich dude like him.

"OK."

"Ellen, I'm not sure when I'll get to talk to you again. I, I think very highly of you, you know."

"Yes, I know that."

"Do you, have any, ah, feelings in that regard too?" he asks rather pathetically.

"Angelo, to be honest, I have no feelings at all. My limbs are dead, my insides as well. I'm just... dead." For the first time in her adult life, she weeps in the presence of another human being.

Keller's eyes fill with tears too. But there is nothing more he can do. He collects himself, "You'll just have to get on with life, Dear. You will bounce back. Maybe it'll take you longer than three days but you will."

"They've ruined Q-Computing. We've lost billions not only for ourselves but for you and Bessemer and our other partners too," Ellen says in a misery.

Actually that isn't true. Bessemer's liquidated 90% of their holdings in QCC at a huge profit before the implosion using complex derivatives to disguise the transaction. BVP is in great shape even though US and world economies are mostly in the dumpster. They're in a terrific position to pick up the pieces when and if there is a recovery. Angelo believes in buying low and selling high then buying low, again. The derivatives they used are an old Keller trick—they still own their stock in QCC, which is, of course, valueless. What they sold instead (twice over in fact) is any increase in value for their holdings and any dividend income that may derive from their holdings. This is why Ellen doesn't know that BVP is already out. They exited without exiting, so to speak.

"Dear, please don't worry about anyone except yourself and Damien. I know something else," Angelo adds.

"Yes?"

"He loves you."

"What?"

"You heard me."

"I don't know what you are talking about."

He sighs. "Yes, you do. Stop lying to yourself. It's ridiculous and totally unbecoming to someone I consider my greatest protégé. Damien spends his time these days humming a tune with your name in it. Now please go fix things in our homeland and while you're at it, fix things for yourself and Damien too."

RICO has crushed the personal credit rating of nearly every senior executive associated with QCC but what is Ellen thinking of after this conversation with Angelo? She is recalling a line she'd maybe heard in one of the old films she loves so much or perhaps it's just a song she once listened to: 'Freedom's just another word, for nothing left to lose.' Ellen is finally free.

...

The toughest part for her is saying goodbye to her personal staff and the remaining 1,200 Q-employees, many of them in tears. She won't miss newly appointed Roy Lew and his team of bankruptcy trustees—they're really just government yobs.

Traian is back in Romania and he did listen to Angelo's advice on creditor proofing himself. He's going to be just fine, as long as he never sets foot in the US again or puts himself in a position to be somehow diverted back there perhaps by a malfunctioning plane or a bounty hunter. It will be a pleasure, he is thinking, to comply.

Infinitely increasing his pleasure is the fact he has finally persuaded Dakota, with the blessing of her parents, to join him on his family's estate. They're engaged now and expecting their first child, a boy they will call Jose-Luis and everyone, well someone, will nickname JEL. Ellen sends a digital message congratulating them, but Traian won't marry until his buddy can come to the wedding. And he doesn't know when that will be. He wants Damien there as his best man—backing him up as usual.

...

Ellen brings a group of Q-HQ employees with her to San Fran—but only those who are American citizens and who want to come. It turns out that a lot of their people just aren't willing to give up on their collective dream. Many of her Canuck employees also want to join her but they're way too vulnerable to INS thugs and bounty hunters who will just round them up and deport them. Maybe beat 'em up just for the heck of it too. She can't take that chance.

She's staying at a women's shelter near what was formerly known as Q-Computing America. There are hundreds of former Q-employees still in the area and dozens of them are dropping by each day to see her. They want to talk to her, touch her, thank her and generally listen to her as she talks about a new day to come.

She crossed the border into her homeland illegally. She takes a private boat charter across Lake Ontario and comes to San Francisco via an underground route. She cares not one whit about what laws she may have broken. The law is an ass she remembers reading in Dickens' Oliver Twist but the quote she thinks actually predates his work.

Evan Salazar stays with her and has become one of the 'girls' in the house. Stranger still, Dekka has somehow found her and is staying in one of the outbuildings on the property.

House Manager, Sally Thornton took her in with no

questions asked. "Ellen, we're OK having you and Evan here but I have to tell you we're not comfortable having that big, silent guy, what's his name, around." She's talking about Dekka.

"Sal, if you want him gone, you just have to say the word. But I'm going to go too."

"You're putting me in a tough position, Ellen. This is a women's shelter. We've got a lot of vulnerable people here and you've got this tough-looking Euro guy stashed some place."

Ellen laughs for the first time in weeks, "Here's the thing. If a wife beater shows up while Dekka's around he'll be the sorriest motherfucker you ever saw, Sally."

So they put it to a vote of the house committee. Dekka stays.

...

Maybe Zimmermann thinks she will exchange the Pennsylvania Papers (as she has come to call the documents that Dr. Zimmermann leaked to her) for Damien's release. But she doubts it. He's betting that she will do more, much more with the evidence he's given her.

While the material is a strong bargaining chip, it's the kind of thing that you can only use once if you are using its disclosure as a threat. If DOC calls her bluff and she releases it then she loses all leverage from that moment on.

She knows that Dr. Zimmermann will be disappeared if the fact that he leaked these documents to her is ever discovered. She will never tell anyone that he's the source. She learned that from Damien—never tell ANYONE.

Now she's back in-country, she can see for herself the misery of people—grinding poverty, huge inequalities, enormous unemployment rate, long lines forming for food stamps in a country that once was the bread basket for half the world, a tiny minority controlling a majority of assets of this nation and nearly as much of its income.

Her objective can't be just to free Damien or

somehow try to rebuild QCC or even to free QEs. It's gotta be more.

Ellen's been worried about funding for her fledgling movement. Whether you operate a for-profit business, a not-for-profit, a charity, a NGO, a protest movement or what have you, you need money to do your work and fulfill your mission.

She is head of still wildly successful Nell Enterprises but she cannot use funds that are entrusted to her under Nell's last will for her own personal causes no matter how noble she may think they are. She must use their huge cash flow for the purposes Nell sets out and that's all. Beyond what she might need to support her work running/managing Nell's affairs, her hands are tied.

The problem is resolved when Ellen gets a phone call, in an old fashioned way, a VoIP call from Nell's wills and estates lawyer. Nell left significant funds in a separate trust account with San Francisco law firm Wayland, Thorpe and Werner LLP to be disbursed at the direction and discretion of Damien Bell or Ellen Brooks, acting together or alone. Her lawyer is instructed to release these funds when and if Dr. Bell and/or Ms. Ellen Books arrive in San Fran. Since they have been unable to contact Dr. Bell, they are calling Ellen.

It is one of the three bequests Nell made that were kept confidential at the time of her passing. Nell knew that Ellen would eventually come to Frisco because, after all, she told her to.

Wayland offices are just eight blocks away. Ellen heads there now.

Now she not only has highly capable, strongly motivated people helping her, she has the means as well, thanks to Nell. Still she needs to come up with a better plan—not only to save Damien and her QE friends but her homeland too. Maybe the country needs a bigger movement. Maybe what it really needs is... regime change.

...

"Hey, Mike."

"Hey, Ellen. I didn't know you were in San Fran."

"I'm not exactly broadcasting the fact that I'm here. I need some help."

"I'm not really in the helping profession, Ellen. I'm just a Tech Crunch journo."

"I think this might help you too. I want you to read this."

"What is it?"

"It's an abstract."

He takes a few minutes to read it. Then he re-reads it again more carefully.

"I assume you have proof of this?"

"I do."

"Do you have a corroborating source?"

"I do."

"Who is it?"

"I can't say."

"Then I can't use it."

"No one cares these days about independent corroboration, Mike."

"I do. We do.

"Your credibility in this is ZERO, Ellen."

"I understand that. What if you got corroboration from DOC?"

He laughs. "Those old fascists at the Department aren't likely to answer any questions from me or self-incriminate, Ellen. It won't work."

"Maybe I don't need it to work," she says. "I just need them to think it might. "Did you know that Damien is dying in San Quentin as we speak?"

"Yeah, I've got some sources at the prison. He's in bad shape. I'm still not able to help you, kid."

"Mike, here's the deal—just message DOC and Yao Allitt. Tell them what you've seen. Tell them that I'm the only person who can help them and that, if they let me see Damien, I'll get the Quantum Key from him and, in return, they let him go."

Cronkey is smart enough to know that Ellen is BS'ing him. She's no more likely to give DOC the Key than Bell is.

"What do you really have in mind, Ellen?"

"You don't want to know, Mike?"

Actually, he does.

...

Chapter 16

We Are All ONE

Damien feels stronger. He now gets two meals a day and better quality food too. He's put on a kilogram in the last week and half. 'While that may not sound like much,' he thinks, 'it's made all the difference.' Some of the sores on his body and in his mouth have started to heal. He can think more clearly. He gets a shower every week and they're letting him have some exercise in a private courtyard as well. He still can't directly see the sun—he's in a maze with high walls all around him. But it's open skies above and he likes that.

He hasn't seen anyone other than his interrogators but they seem to have lost interest in him—his sessions with them last less than an hour and they're pretty cursory. Things must be bad for them.

There aren't really many people he'd like to see. He'd like to say 'hey' to Traian and Dr. Luis and Pops. But he misses Ellen and Pet3r most. He's still a bit confused about his feelings for Ellen but he is way past the stage of fooling himself any longer that he doesn't care for her. He's pretty sure that she's found another life for herself which is as it should be.

He doesn't know exactly what's happened to QCC but he's had lots of time to piece it together. His friggin' interrogators are a veritable fount of information even though they would never believe that. He's put them through a Turing Test—they've been his reverse subjects in every interview. Even as they poured litres of water down his throat into his lungs, drowning him over and over again, he could still discern a lot about them. Through their actions, body language, questions, silences, looks exchanged between interrogators, eye movements and answers or lack thereof to questions he's put to them, he's pretty much got the whole story figured out. He'd like to play poker with these guys—he'd go all-in and clean them out in no time. They have more tells than a fake fortune teller.

He's feeling so good, he's even been able to do a bit of light yoga.

...

That night he hears a song in a dream that maybe he's heard only once before but he liked it. Damien remembers every book he's ever read, film he's seen and song he's heard. Now that he feels better, his memories are returning. He's gotten pretty good at humming having spent the better part of the last ten months doing nothing else. He also remembers almost all his dreams

When he wakes up in the morning, he starts humming the tune. It's by a Canadian group long since disbanded called Gob from Vancouver (actually Langley, BC). It went something like this:

> Oh! Ellin, what can I do?
> There is nothing aside from you.
> Oh! Ellin, what can I lose?
> There's nothing aside from you.
> Oh oh oh oh oh oh ohhhh
> I waste away, it's miserable here,
> It's stupid to even try to pretend.
> Cause when you slip my mind I start to panic,
> I'm scared to lose you again.
> I'm scared I'll lose you again...

Damien thinks that maybe he's gonna have a visitor. He doesn't want to get his hopes too high but they must be giving him better food for a reason. Maybe Ellen's coming? Maybe it's just wishful thinking but he's definitely feeling better.

...

He's behind a 2 cm thick piece of armoured glass and

she's sitting there on the other side. He smiles from ear to ear. He can't get enough of her. She wears jeans and a t-shirt and looks older but nice. He bets she smells nice too but he can't vouch for that at the present time.

She's trying not to look shocked because Damien looks like a Holocaust survivor. She hates to cry and she's not going to do that now, it would break his heart.

"Hi Damien."

"Hey Ellen. You look nice. Where's the Mod Cloth dress?"

"I left it in Boston."

"How've you been?"

"I'm fine Damien, fine."

Without thinking, he puts his hand up against the glass. She puts hers there as well. They just sit there looking at each other, re-establishing the rapport that was always there.

"I kinda thought you might come. I was hoping you'd come and then they started feeding me better so I was really hoping you'd come and then, hey, here you are. I'm glad."

"Pops says 'hello'."

"You've seen him?"

"Yes."

"How is the old guy?"

"He's OK Damien. He doesn't get out as much as he used to but his mind is sharp."

"Will you say 'hi' for me when you get out of here?"

"Sure."

"I wish I could go with you, Ellen. You're the first person I've seen other than Nell."

"Nell was here?"

"Yeah, she came to see me. I think it was the night she died."

Ellen understands immediately.

Damien blurts out, "I don't want to stay here anymore, Ellen. Do you think you could talk to them for me?" This is his first ever moment of weakness during captivity. Later on, he'll figure out they're just using his feelings for Ellen as another tactic to break him down, but right now he'd just like to walk out that prison gate with her—not very far away in distance, very far away in terms of reality.

Ellen just looks at Damien in his pathetic orange, overlarge prison jumpsuit and then she does cry. Great wracking sobs suddenly just burst out of her chest.

"Hey, I'm sorry. Really. I'm alright. Don't worry. You've got enough on your plate. I can take care of myself," he adds lamely.

Now an old tune starts playing in her head—she hopes that Damien thinks about her the way the guy did who sang:

> When you get close,
> Ah danger senses please beware, it's so unfair
> That I'm paying such a heavy price,
> By looking at the garments, that you wear so well
> I'll kiss you when it's dangerous,
> I'll kiss you then and only then...

Then she leans her forehead on the glass. Damien puts his there too.

...

She is allowed to see Damien once a week for as long as 30 minutes at a time. She tells him they charge her ND$25 for access to the prison each visit—same as everyone else. It's another way to raise money from some of society's most vulnerable people, Damien thinks.

He's figured out that DOC is just using her but he can't seem to find the strength to tell her to stay away, that she's just another pawn in their game. Fact is he enjoys seeing her—there's no doubt that she's become a beautiful woman. The girl he knew is gone. He can see that even when she's an old, old lady, she'll still have 'it'; she's always been classy and it shows especially now that she's a mature woman.

She dresses differently too. He never sees her in high fashion dry-clean-only stuff anymore. Instead, she looks like she's buying her clothes from the Salvos. They have a mission and shop on Folsom Street not far from where she's living. That's OK with Damien. He likes simple and functional anyway. She ties her hair back, pulls on her jeans and a blouse and she's out the door every morning.

They have two guards assigned to watch and record their meetings (the old fashioned way—using digital technology) but they never talk about anything that would be of the slightest interest to DOC. Still they seem to find plenty of other things to talk about and they both enjoy these weekly visits.

Ellen tells stories about women she's met in St Jo's Women's Shelter where she's living. A lot of Native American women go through the place. She's learning more about their cultures and histories.

He really likes hearing about Dekka becoming the big brother many of these women never had—how his presence has brought a whole new level of caution to the men who visit just to 'talk sense into their old lady'.

Ellen does two volunteer shifts every week in the soup kitchen and tells him he can get a job there as a slopper when he gets out. This comment falls flat—Damien turns away when she says this. By now, he's pretty sure that they'll never let him go. If he gives them the Quantum Key, they'll find a way to get rid of him anyway. He's the frigging inventor of QEs and way too dangerous to let out.

Now that he's feeling better, he's got a whole slew of new ideas of where to go next with Quantum Entities and he's pretty sure he's figured out a solution to the drogue problem as well which Ellen has managed to tell him about.

When she did, the visitor room door burst open and the watch supervisor and a guard took her out immediately. She wasn't allowed back for three weeks. So without saying anything to each other, they quit talking 'shop' after that.

When Damien saw the guard's hands on her, hustling her out of this tiny space, he wanted to go through the glass at the guy. When she returns, she's still got bruises on her arms—she's a slow healer.

She's been allowed to bring him 'care' packages of 5 lbs or less on each visit. She's fills them with food supplements, vitamins, chocolate and other stuff to help him with his skin problems and overall physical condition. On one visit she brings Dooby and Miss Buril. They're the only things she takes from Damien's condo. She somehow persuades the bank's property manager, who is executing the Power of Sale, to let her remove a few of his personal effects, which have no commercial value, under his watchful eye. But it's just Dooby and Miss Buril she's really looking for.

Damien gets one of those big loopy grins on his face when he finds his worry dolls under some Swiss chocolates and other goodies. Damien takes them gently out of the box saying quietly, "Hey, Doob. Hey, Miss Buril. Long time." Ellen is so pleased.

"I'm not sure they'll let me keep them," Damien says holding Dooby and Miss Buril in each hand to his chest, "but this is great. Thanks, Ellen."

"It was Traian who thought of it."

"Can you thank him for me?"

"You bet," she says.

She can't ask Ash3r for help so she just goes to a local nutrichem shop to ask for advice from their staff. They want a client blood sample for lab analysis but she tells them she can't get that. They recognize her, of course. So they do their best based on her description of his skin colour, sores on his body and mouth, estimate of weight and so on.

On one visit she has Damien take off his jumpsuit so she can inspect the rest of him. She sees more clearly the sores on his body, the scrawny person he is and the bruises from being strapped down during water boarding that don't seem to be healing. She makes a joke that she's never seen him naked before and that she's none too impressed.

After she leaves San Quentin that day, she has to ask Dekka to pull over as they drive along Sir Francis Drake Boulevard. She bolts from the vehicle, runs down to the shore putting her face in her hands and weeps once more. When she is a bit calmer, she lies face down on the grass, loosens her blouse placing her naked stomach on the bare earth without moving for the next ten minutes. Dekka waits for her at a discreet distance nearby.

...

Damien has always found it laughable that a lot of academics seem to not really comprehend or accept the scientific method—even though they pay lip service to it. Anything that has been demonstrated by experiment and can be replicated independently by others must be accepted as part of mainstream science in his view. Damien has watched 'big science' professionals reject irrefutable evidence in front of their own eyes, defying the rules of logic first postulated by Greek philosopher Aristotle nearly 2400 years earlier.

Ibn al-Haytham, who lived at the end of the first millennium (965-1039), was a key figure in the development of the scientific method. In his 'Critique of Ptolemy' he wrote, 'Truth is sought for its own sake. And those who are engaged upon the quest for anything for its own sake are not interested in other things. Finding the truth is difficult, and the road to it is rough.'

It seems to be happening everywhere in the second half of the 21st century: safety records are plummeting as disaster after disaster follows the same basic pattern—human beings are good at building things yet horrible at maintaining them. Attention spans are too short and 'emergency planning' is an oxymoron. Oil well blowouts, pipes bursting, factories emitting killer gases, mines collapsing, tunnels caving in, power grids failing, glass panels falling from office towers, train crashes, airplane malfunctions, countries tumbling into endless wars, nuclear crises, military failures, insane price bubbles followed by economic collapse.

Nic Taleb is right, Damien thinks. Highly improbable 'black swan' events are much more frequent and much more powerful than conventional models suggest and damage is much greater than even worst-case predictions.

It's as if every engineer and scientist is saying, after the fact, 'I don't know how the accident happened. We were travelling at less than the speed limit heading for a wall'. Humans are refusing to believe the facts in front of their eyes. They're seeing only what they wish to see.

Damien also realizes the corollary might be even more dangerous—just because something has not yet been proven using scientific method, does not, in fact, mean that it is a mistaken hypothesis. This is a Damien way of saying, 'keep an open mind' which so many scientists seem not to be able to do these days.

The fact that they've taken QE GDP out of US national accounts by banning Entities—not letting them find jobs or go to work is bad—but what's worse is that QEs have the capacity to help their human counterparts deal with complexity. They don't get bored or lose their focus so they're really good at crucial jobs like monitoring personal safety or watching over nuclear power plants or coal mines or subways, none of which they're allowed to do any longer.

The end is coming for these people. They've built economic systems and tech infrastructure that are way too complex for them to manage on their own. He knows it. The only question that Damien can't answer is whether their end will come before his? It's his only hope of escape.

...

The President, originally elected because of his strong anti-QE platform, is not new to his job anymore. His advisers, pointing to Imperial China's experience, tell him that their ban on QEs and Q-Phones will not only help get him elected but will be a boon for his financial contributors many of whom are QCC competitors. Their profitability will bounce back after eliminating 'unfair' practices by a monopolistic Q Computing Corp. Unfortunately, as it turns out, they have a poor understanding of the US economic model. For at least 300 years it has been based on innovation and a multiplication of options in a diverse, ever changing system. Once the innovation engine is switched off, the economy plunges and the standard of living falls off a cliff. As a consequence so does the President's mid-term poll numbers. He's down right pissed. There is nothing that politicians like more than money and power and the two are interchangeable and interconnected. Public opinion is turning against his administration. An imploding economy and 19% unemployment will do that for you.

...

The WE ARE ALL ONE Committee listens to a report from Evan. He's reading SF Pride's response to their request for logistical support for the protest march they've planned for the following month.

'Our policies cannot support or sponsor political banners, placards or other signage that endorses, or discourages endorsement of, legislation or a political candidate or political statements. The rules in relation to this area are complex and the Pride Committee can offer advice and guidance as how to achieve your objective without falling afoul of our rules. Any political statements or endorsements made by participants in our events or any that we support are not acceptable.'

"Basically, they're telling us 'No'," Salazar is saying. He's not going to tell the committee about his shouting match with the executive director of SF Pride. After a 150 year struggle for gay rights that is nearing complete success, they're going to turn their backs on Ellen and Quantum Entities because they're worried about their funding? Fuck!

SF Pride is now being run by a bunch of chicken-shit bureaucrats who just want their annual Pride Celebration, (it commemorates the rebellion of LGBT patrons at Stonewall Inn in New York City's Greenwich Village on the 27th of June 1969,) to be a big party and a big money earner for themselves. They have forgotten their roots.

A lot of people who you might expect to support their cause have, in fact, abandoned them. And a lot of people who you might not expect to have the guts to come out and help, have. Evan doesn't know it yet but in a few years he'll sweep out the entire Board of SF Pride and use that as his base to become national gay rights leader.

But for now, his entire focus is on WE ARE ALL ONE; he's just wondering if they can get it off the ground on their own and if anyone will actually show up. He needn't worry; it will be the biggest protest march America has seen in nearly 90 years.

...

Ellen is working on something else—she calls it her manifesto. A protest march is fine but what are their objectives? Get Damien out of jail? Legalize QEs? She's sure that these objectives are too narrow and won't work anyway. Entrenched interests—political, corporate and media—have too much invested in the status quo to reach an accommodation with them.

So she's planning a new movement and regime change. Fuck them she's thinking. Their time to muck up this country and planet is over. They just don't know it yet.

Cronkey and Tech Crunch have by now published the entire contents of the Pennsylvania Papers. It was the right thing to do in every way—strategically and morally. Public sentiment has changed dramatically in the last four months. Tough questions are being asked every day by the Whitehouse Press Corps and the President's approval rating has dropped into the low 30s now.

Mike's figured out pretty much Ellen's entire plan but

he doesn't publish the material she's given him to support her or even to hustle for a Pulitzer for himself; he does it because it's the responsibility of the Fourth Estate to turn over rocks and shine some sunlight on the maggots they find there. At least there are still two moral men standing in 21st century America.

...

Dekka visits Nell's lawyer at his request.

"Ah, you never claimed the funds that Miss Nell left you. May I ask why that is?"

Dekka just shrugs.

"Well," the lawyer says steepling his hands, "I have set up a current account for your use at a BOC branch near where you are currently living, which I understand is, ah, a women's shelter, St Jo's?"

Dekka nods.

The lawyer hands him a digital key that Dekka can use to gain access to his new account. He gets up to leave.

"Hmm, there is one more thing. Do you know where Ms. Ellen Brooks may be found?"

Dekka, now standing, nods again.

"Ah, I'm not sure if the timing is right but it might be and I would like to get this off my TO-DO list although it may do more harm than good to this, hmm, 'movement' that I must say I disapprove of, given that it could interfere with the economic prospects of Nell Enterprises, you know, to have its sole trustee Ms. Brooks involved in such a dubious affair."

Dekka just stares at the guy who starts to sweat heavily. He hands Dekka another digital key. He's glad when the big creepy guy is gone.

...

When Dekka gives the key to Ellen later that night, she goes to her tiny room in the shelter and inserts it into a digital computer she has there. It's a video file.

She sees Nell in a small Council Ring, presumably in

Third Mesa. She's sitting on one of the benches that circumnavigate the Ring. She's surrounded by Hopi people. Dafne Weinstein is also there. Nell is on the second level looking beautiful but obviously in a weakened state. This must have been done toward the end of her life.

It's near sunset and, as if it's the largest spotlight ever created, the sun's last rays are shining on Nell. Everyone has either a hand drum or a guitar. There are more drums than guitars. Nell is not playing any instrument; she simply sings with her people.

Chorus
All we are asking is give us a chance
All we are asking is give us a chance
All we are asking is give us a chance
Rap:
Will you take me back to the Day
Back when we all knew, all knew the Way
When Ben Franklin was a man of letters, of law, of Rote
Now it's all just about a C-Note
Chorus
All we are asking is give us a chance
Rap:
When the Axe was the tool of the Land
They took the tax to make a new Plan
Where Sachs takes the gold and becomes the Old
Forgetting all the things that we had been Told
"Be Bold, Be Brave, Break the Mold, Buy and Hold, You Were Bought And You Were Sold"
Chorus
All we are asking is give us a chance
Rap:
So we bled and earned our cred on the Street
By our feet, by our words; where we Meet
And tell tales from the Hood that Say
"You better be good" before the fall of it All

For the cold and warm, we must all be so
Forlorn
Stand up, stand up for justice and mourn as it
Dies
    Chorus
All we are asking is give us a chance
    Rap:
Three strikes and put you Down
We put you away for shame in a Town
Where you are King and your crown is of
Thorns
But no one adorns you, with Praise
Cuz your name wasn't bought but your name
was Made
On the backs of those who slave in this great
Land
    Chorus
All we are asking is give us a chance
    Rap:
In the Ivory Tower you forget that the people
are the power, people in your Sights
"We are the People" means all of us; Quantum
and Human Rights
Don't fuss, get on the bus or rust, then march
and bike and Sing
And strike and strike the Bell, and ring out
freedom for all; remember to hear that we Say
When we say, we said that we say, "Take me
back, take me back to the Day"
    Chorus
All we are asking is give us a chance
All we are asking is give us a chance
All we are asking is give us a chance

Ellen is thunderstruck. She replays the video twice
more.

Somehow Nell, before she died, wrote and recorded a
protest song for their movement before there was a

protest movement. It's a rap song set to the tune of an older song that Ellen has heard before—it is in one of the old films she likes so much—The Strawberry Statement.

Ellen knows exactly how she will use it. Nell is about to have another major hit. She can't place the male voice who is rapping. It's a strong performance by him. Nell's voice on the video file is amazing; she carries the people through the piece.

She hears some kind of throat clearing behind her. Dekka has watched the video over her shoulder and is having some type of problem with his eyes and throat. He disappears. He's gone back to his bunk in the utility shed he sleeps in out back. He lies on his side and stares at the shed wall for a long time.

...

OLA Tech Crunch and Mike Cronkey keep the pressure on. Most of Mike's earlier misgivings about Ellen's material were dispelled long ago by the obviousness of DOC reaction to a series of investigative reports Mike originally feeds to the Internet.

Despite on-scene reports to the contrary, the attacks in the square outside the US Supreme Court are now seen pretty much everywhere as intended to provoke sympathy for anti-QE protesters and for corporate and political interests aligned with them.

Which means the President is indirectly implicated. The White House has continued to deny any involvement.

Still, his administration has not yet been able to satisfactorily explain why QEs, already under suspicion of illegal activity and anti-government action, would launch attacks that result in massive sanctions against themselves. The reason that no satisfactory explanation has been forthcoming, Mike thinks, is because there is none.

Corroboration of this view and for authenticity of Ellen's Pennsylvania Papers comes from an unanticipated source—US Army National Guardsmen who were there.

Mike has met with several of them, some of them wounded in action.

"There's no way those attacks were anything other than a show. They were clumsy even if they were premeditated. It was a PR stunt that cost a lot of lives but not a serious action to take out an enemy, whoever that might be," said one vet.

Mike's got the whole story of Marc Licinias, Army National Guard Commander, which he has been running with as well. He's done long form pieces including video with the guy's family, soldiers who served with him and a few former West Pointers from his cadet years, an almost unheard of form of journalism these days. The public just can't seem to get enough of this overweight, middle-aged American hero. From what Mike can tell, he deserves all the attention he's getting.

He hears again from the guy's widow—today. She's been contacted by a Hollywood-based studio that wants to buy the rights to his story and release a made-for-Internet movie about her dead husband. Mike tells her to go ahead—she can use the money and they can use his reports as a basis for the film, no problem. Oh, by the way, he adds, get a lawyer.

...

Subject to permit, their protest march will use the same route as SF Pride—it'll begin at Market and Beale and proceed west on Market to Eighth Street. The route can hold at least 1.2 million people, the official number for the most people to ever show up for Pride. Evan's praying that they get a big turnout but there's no real way to know in advance. They've set up a humongous stage in UN Plaza near the end of the route where the entire WE ARE ALL ONE committee will be. Ellen will be introduced by the Mayor of San Fran, a stand up guy with a yard of guts, so Evan is thinking the permit won't be a problem.

The whole thing starts at 1 pm on Thursday—Ellen will speak at 3:30 Pacific Time. That will fit nicely with their goal of capturing the largest possible audience on the east coast and put maximum pressure on that sonofabitch in the White House.

Evan has had the quantum sound system tested a half dozen times. He has trouble with one of the grips he is using because it's designed for right handed people but he manages around that problem, as he has had to so often in his life, during rehearsal. Everyone will hear Ellen for miles in every direction like she's sitting in their parlor on a quiet Sunday afternoon. To operate and tune it, Evan is also working with his QE, He9burn, named after a famous movie star who he thinks is fabulous.

Ellen has given them permission to bring their QEs back from exile. "If we're going to ask people to engage in non-violent civil disobedience, we might as well start now."

Of course, it also helps them immensely to get ready for the big event and spread the word. He9burn reports that she is hearing from many points around the country; people are on the move. They're coming to San Francisco to show their solidarity with WE ARE ALL ONE.

Evan and the committee have already released the symbol they've adopted, the hand of Constantine I with his index finger raised, into general use. It was first seen at SCOTUS when Jerom Van Der Hout did it.

He9burn has shown him images of their new symbol spray painted all over US Federal Government buildings. When He9burn points out the petty vandalism to Ellen—she says, 'Good. Tell them to keep it up—paint it everywhere.'

The symbol has gone viral and it's ubiquitous. Even NBA players are walking off the court, win or lose, flashing the symbol instead of the traditional 'We're Number One' where the thumb is wrapped around the middle finger.

WE ARE ALL ONE is the number one tattoo in the world according to He9burn; she has the figures to prove it. Even Ellen thinks about getting it on her forearm but she knows that Damien doesn't like tattoos. Still a lot of committee members and millions of ordinary Americans do. Many of the tattoos use NSM mix in their dies so they act as media walls on your person which means that with the help of QEs, the WE ARE ALL ONE committee can communicate, message and see what's up pretty much everywhere.

...

Ellen stands in front of a sea of people and their Quantum Counterparts. Before she starts to speak, she looks over at Evan and beams at him. The turnout is beyond anything any of them, even the most optimistic member of the committee, expected. The entire protest route is completely filled as is every side street for miles around. Evan is thinking that there are at least two million people who have come to San Fran for this day, for this event, for this moment. He9burn says in his quantum earbud that she's counted 2,444,901 people +/- 10 and the entire world population of QEs. In addition, she measures their Internet audience at more than two and a half billion people.

They don't know it yet but this will not be the most viewed event of this storied day.

...

"Thank you Mr. Mayor for your gracious introduction," Ellen begins. She looks fantastic, powerful and strong.

"I would like to welcome everyone to San Francisco. For those who are here for the first time, you will find it is a city of tolerance. They have taken me and my colleagues in and given us shelter and sustenance as we work towards a better future for ourselves and our families and this nation.

"I would like to thank the WE ARE ALL ONE Committee for their hard work in bringing us all here today to begin this marvelous journey, together, to a better place.

"I would like to recognize the tragic deaths of innocent people in the Pennsylvania Incident and praise the work of our soldiers who fought bravely that day against an unknown enemy, quickly subduing them at great cost to themselves and their brothers.

"I would like to thank these men, many of whom are here today with us and are joined by many of their colleagues—men and women of the US Armed forces."

Ellen is particularly pleased that so many off duty personnel from in and around the Bay area have come. She's sure that the US military will not agree to allow itself to be used against the citizen movement they are creating here today. There is huge applause for their sacrifice.

"This nation was once a beacon for all humanity—seeking peace, justice, freedom and a place to stand. To stand up for what's right, to stand up for what's ethical, to stand up for each other, to stand up to tyranny wherever it may be found.

"Today, we have more than 14 million persons incarcerated some of them for 'crimes' as small as stealing a loaf of bread to feed themselves or their loved ones.

"Seventeen miles north of here is one of the worst places on earth built by Americans, and in that terrible place, remains Damien Graham Bell, inventor and parent of these wondrous creatures who have come to join humanity on its journey into the future and to help us achieve our destiny, whatever that may be.

"He has been charged with no crime. He has never been brought before a Court of Law. He has been tortured and mistreated because our Government and its minions seek to have possession of the Quantum Key, not so they can protect you but so they can protect themselves, their position of power over you and over us."

Chants of FREE DAMIEN, FREE DAMIEN, FREE DAMIEN begin spontaneously in the crowd which is heard in homes and offices across the land. The chant is taken up by all the people and all the Quantum Entities becoming an enormous wave of sound. Ellen can feel it reverberate in her chest and in her bones.

After awhile, she holds up her left hand to settle them down so she can continue.

"At present, we have 63 million Americans without employment and millions more working-poor living at or below the poverty line, relying on food stamps to feed themselves.

"Over 240 million of our citizens live outside gated communities while inside you have a small minority living with good roads, good schools, nice houses and abundant opportunity.

"We cannot have, in this nation, a group of people who are disenfranchised looking over the fence at a place of plenty. It puts our nation at its gravest risk of failure by thusly dividing and segregating our people so.

"We can not have a nation where political power can only be secured by buying place and privilege.

"We can not be a nation where, when they say that we need lower taxes to improve our economy they are talking about their taxes, not yours.

"We can not be a nation where immigrants, whether they be, in the poetry of Miss Nell, warm blooded humans or 'cold' artificial persons, have no path to freedom, citizenship or acceptance.

"We cannot be a nation of cowards choosing only the safe path, the sure path and avoiding all risk and responsibility until it is proven safe to do otherwise. The universe is not made for us to be safe. It is there to be explored and appreciated as only sentient, conscious beings can do.

"We as a nation must find our guts again and work together, all of us, with our new quantum brothers and sisters, to address the problems and opportunities before us.

"To that great endeavour, I commit myself and my colleagues and all who would join with us in this journey.

"I call on the present government of these United States to immediately:

"First. Remove the threat of the Expulsion Edict held over the heads of our Quantum family so they and we can go back to our work and our jobs to help rebuild, together, this nation and its economy.

"Second. Create an independent Commission of Enquiry to investigate and report to the American people on the Pennsylvania Incident.

"Third. Create a Reconciliation Committee made up of members of US Government, US Military and representatives of the people of these United States together with members of a new species, our Quantum friends, with a view to improving governance of this nation so that it will again be a beacon to all and a land of opportunity for all."

Ellen stands there looking out over this amazing family of human and quantum people.

A wave of applause washes over her and then she hears ELLEN! ELLEN! ELLEN! ELLEN! from the crowd. She hoped they would say ONE, ONE, ONE, ONE but it works just fine for now. If Bashir had been here, he'd have pre-arranged it but he's back in New York. Crowds are all flashing Constantine's WE ARE ALL ONE sign over their heads. QEs are doing it too although a bit clumsily she thinks.

The organizers gave everyone tiny drums; at least they did until they ran out.

Ellen asks for quiet once more.

"Miss Nell before she passed had one last gift for her people and her fans. She wrote and recorded a song for us which I would like you to sing with me today. The words will appear shortly on media walls everywhere but you only need know the chorus.

"We have with us, St Jo's Women's Choir and Nahuel from Third Mesa."

Ellen applauds as the Choir and Nell's half brother mount the stage.

They perform WE ARE ALL ONE with both a live and media wall audience. It is a moving experience, almost beyond words, for everyone to see once again a performance by their beloved artist Nell singing with them from the spirit world beyond.

People are pounding on their tiny drums, synchronizing their breathing and timing and voices and feeling like they are all one family—they finally belong to something bigger than themselves, the idea of the United States as it was meant to be and might one day be again.

People who were there that day (and as history moves along, everyone will claim to either have been there or known someone who was) will recall these feelings whenever they hear Nell's song. It will be played on this Earth and beyond for a long time to come.

The funniest part of the day is watching QEs singing and playing their quantum drums along with everyone else—they are almost as bad at singing and drumming as they are at humour.

...

Ellen's back at San Quentin in her usual visitor room. Damien has been brought in to his tiny space on the other side of the plate glass. He does not look very well today but he gives her a big smile.

She's dying to tell him what's happened earlier in the evening but their two regular guards are watching and listening from behind their small plate glass window off to her left. They look bored and, frankly, couldn't care less what these two lovebirds have to say to each other as long as it does not contain any of the prescribed words they've got on a list in front of them. The Watch Supervisor is nowhere to be seen. He's probably off in the shitter or filing one of his endless reports, poor sucker they are thinking.

"You look very pretty today, all dolled up again," he says. He's thinking she did dressup for him.

"Thanks, Damien. How are you feeling?"

"Fine."

He just looks at her.

"Something wrong?"

"Nope. I was just thinking..." Then he stops talking.

"What Damien, what?"

"Well, I was just wondering, maybe, if you thought, ah, if you would like to make love, with me?"

Ellen instantly understands what he means.

Without further thought, she leans forward in her chair and removes her beige and black striped pashmina shawl that keeps her warm in chilly San Francisco weather, undoes the tiny black belt at her waist, unzips her Deco-Diva dress and then takes off her bra. Soon all she is wearing is her simple sterling silver lariat necklace with pendant shaped into Constantine's WE ARE ALL ONE symbol, her black pumps, her narrow frame glasses and her Barcelona thong panties, Ellen's only remaining daily concession to Euro fashion invisible to the world until moments ago. They are a lovely charcoal colour and contrast beautifully with her pale body and golden hair that falls freely about her shoulders having just been loosed seconds earlier.

The pendant has a beautiful inlay made up of turquoise gemstones creatively inserted into it. These healing gemstones Ellen knows are connected to both Venus and Throat Chakras. They're also wedding anniversary gems associated with the 5th and 11th years of a relationship. Dafne and Elsu sent her this necklace made by silversmiths working with the Hopi Silvercraft Cooperative Guild near Third Mesa.

The pendant lies between her breasts just above her solar plexus. Damien thinks she's lost weight since their days together in TO. But he is practically knocked flat at the mere sight of her like this. She and Damien have known each other now for eight years.

The only reason their guards don't intervene is their prurient interest in the lovely Ellen. Plus they're recording all of it.

For Damien and Ellen, their entire universe has telescoped into this small space—they feel like they are completely alone—and they begin to share an intimacy far greater than anything Ellen has experienced before.

Damien's physical condition is such that he cannot perform but his mind is now sharp and alive with desire. He starts telling Ellen what to do.

She leans back in her chair and with a languorous look back at him, she spreads her legs and pulls her panties aside.

For the next 4 minutes and 51 seconds, Ellen pleasures herself for her pleasure and his. At first, under Damien's direction using one hand then later, both. After awhile, she needs no further urging or direction and she shudders with relief for what seems like a minute or more.

Their two guards can't believe their luck. They've got the whole thing on video and they're uploading it right now to one of the video services they subscribe to.

One of them even has the wit to add music—he finds Richard Wagner's Ride of the Valkyries. It is, interestingly, exactly the same length as their video file. It seems to fit the scene they've just witnessed too. Cool, he thinks, as he presses 'upload'.

They alert their buddies that they've got that snooty but hot girl, Ellen Brooks, doing funky stuff and pretty soon the entire guard population of San Quentin is watching the video. It doesn't take long to get out of the prison and go viral.

Within ten days it'll be the biggest celebrity sex tape ever, with more than 3.2 billion views during that time. Practically half of the world's population that is male will have seen it and quite a few women. No one in Imperial China will see it.

One unexpected result is that young women become some of the keenest viewers of what will become the most successful instructional sex video ever—they would like to know how to get the same sensations that Ms. Brooks obviously was able to achieve out of their own young bodies.

After the two guards are subsequently disciplined

and dismissed for cause, they become minor talk show celebrities in their own right. The younger one, who added the music, becomes an instant expert on women's sexuality and on classical music even though it was the first time he's ever listened to the stuff but, whatever, he got it exactly right this one time.

...

After Ellen has collected herself, she wonders why. Why now? She's waited for Damien for eight years. And why today? If her former roommate, Mary, was here she'd be saying, 'But you still haven't really slept with him.'

Technically true. But Ellen has finally had the chance to be a bad girl in the bedroom except it wasn't her bedroom—it was a jailhouse. Ellen, when she finds out that they've released this video of her, will be quite unbothered by the whole fuss about it. Circumstances are what they are.

She also doesn't yet know that it will only enhance her reputation as the fabulous, smart, beautiful and now sexy Ms. Ellen Brooks.

"I love you, Ellen."

She does not like the look on his face when he says it. Oh, how she's dreamed of him saying that to her, but something isn't right. She looks back at the guards who seem to be totally involved in something else, "Damien, we have a plan. We've formed a committee called WE ARE ALL ONE. We staged a protest downtown today. Millions of people showed up, Damien. Millions. We're going to start a movement and change this country for good."

"It won't work. They're too strong. They'll just hunt you down and put you in here with me or worse. I can't allow that."

"Is that why you made love to me today? To say GOODBYE?"

He just looks at her again.

"Damn you, Damien, answer me?"

"I have a plan," he says. She senses his plan is that he

dies—she lives. Ellen can see it written all over his face. He's stopped eating or something.

Actually, he's been secretly dropping half his food down the shithole in his cell.

"That's a BAD plan. That's a TERRIBLE plan, Damien. Don't you do anything of the sort!"

Just then the Watch Super comes back and finds their two 'guards' re-watching the video they just created and he can see Ellen and Damien through the glass hatching some kind of plot, unwatched by them or anyone. He freaks.

He rousts the guards and they burst into the visitor room and grab Ellen and start pulling her towards the steel door.

She's quite calm about it but she looks back at Damien pointing her left arm at him making the WE ARE ALL ONE sign with her index finger and thumb. She shouts so she can be heard over the ruckus her guards and their Super are making, "DAMIEN, DON'T DO IT! NONE OF THIS WILL LAST. WE WILL WIN! DON'T DIE, DAMIEN, PLEASE DON'T DIE! I WILL COME FOR YOU, I WILL COME FOR—"

...

End of Part III

Epilogue

The backhoe has finished its job. The grave is ready. Neighbours help her carry the body to the edge of the hole. The body is covered in a hand-sewn white shroud.

They gently lower him. He does not weigh very much. He will rest by his lake for all eternity. She hopes and believes that he is finally at peace.

They say a few prayers and tell a couple of stories about the man but there is one story she will not tell but she is thinking, 'Here lies the body of Damien's father.'

She looks up as if she's expecting someone. But she knows the Blue Heron will not return now.

She also knows that she has many tasks and duties ahead. She is responsible for Nell Enterprises; she's head of a new political movement; she must rebuild her country and the global economy with the help of more than two billion people, nearly a quarter of them quantum people. She will bring about an American Spring and she knows just where to go to find yet more help—people who've already done it elsewhere and before.

She'll free Damien too, she's quite sure of that.

...

End of Book 1

Quantum Entity, American Spring

Preview of Book 2

Chapter 1 Tank

"Hokay, our next guest is Austin's own favorite son, Jagad Durai, our 16 year old wizard who is the first person to score three perfect SAT results—in math, critical reading and writing—since OLA Facebook's Mark Zuckerberg did it more than 50 years ago."

Newsfeed host Sandra 'Sandy' Lopez reads from a media wall on the coffee table to her immediate right in front of a packed live audience of 130. She sits on set in a low-backed but comfortable looking maroon-colored Madison Swivel leather armchair provided by LA-Z-GIRL, one of the sponsors of her weekday morning show. Product placement is a terrific revenue generator and Sandy is never shy about hawking sponsor wares to both her tiny live audience and her newsfeed. A large portion of the more than two million people who live in the Austin-Round Rock-San Marcos metropolitan area check out her show.

While not a native Austenite, Sandy loves her adopted home town—its unofficial slogan, 'Austin is Wired' having nothing to do with landlines and everything to do with the strange fact the town has a lot of diversity and tolerance that puts the rest of Texas to shame. Sandy is careful to never say this out loud. SXSW (South by Southwest), Austin's weeklong conference about music, film and tech, has grown ridiculously huge and it really is a town that, in her view at least, is the live music capital of the world.

Sandy, 45'ish, has short brown hair tinted a few shades lighter framing an elfin face with bright blue eyes and an infectious grin. She's thin, of medium height (actually she's pretty short for a woman these days) and dresses simply in blue jeans and loose blouses. Her guests and her audience love her. Unfortunately she can't figure out why none of the national newsfeeds have picked up her show or why she hasn't been able to break out of her geographical niche on her own. She's got a nice neutral west coast accent being originally from the northwest until she got sick from constant drizzle and lack of sunlight. She's been trying for the last six years to get out of the rut she's in.

Smiling as always, she sees a good looking kid amble in head down aiming toward a second armchair waiting for him. Sandy likes guests to be on the same side of the table as her—she doesn't want anything between her and them but air. 'Oh, oh,' she thinks as she watches Jagad shyly approach, 'this is going to be a pain, getting this kid to talk.' But when he sits, he looks straight at her and returns her smile with one of his own. That's nice.

The kid is too big for his clothes and those man-sized hands and feet stuck on the end of a boy's skinny body suggests he is far from finished growing. His thick dark hair sticks up from his head not because he put some kind of gel in it, it's just unruly. He tries to comb it flat before coming on the show but it doesn't work.

"Hi," says Sandy.

"Hi."

"So how do you feel being the first student from around here to get perfect SAT scores?" she asks.

"Weird. I didn't know it was such a big deal but then everyone was calling my Mom and Dad. I don't even know how it got out."

"You mean you didn't tell anyone? I would have posted it to my profile about a second after I got my results," Sandy says laughing along with her audience. She has over a million and a half friends, followers and fans

Quantum Entity Book 2 American Spring

454

tracking her every move so nothing stays private in her life for very long.

"Well, I told one person."

"Your Mom?"

"Um, no."

"OK, so don't hold us in suspense."

"Arcadia."

"Is she here with us today?" Sandy asks knowing full well that Arcadia Valenzuela is in the audience. 'Here' is the Jesse H. Jones Communications Center on Whitis Avenue, a stylish boulevard marred by this grey hulking mass that is home to Austin City Limits, Kart Radio and the Sandy Lopez Show amongst many others artpreneur endeavors.

Orderly street trees, on-street parking, handsome low-rise red or sandy-colored brick buildings close to the street, nice side yard gardens and lots of at-grade doorways with non reflective glass windows provide a nice enclosure to the public room and plenty of oversight keeping the street safe for pedestrians.

However, the Jones building where they are is a nightmare plopped down on this otherwise pleasant urban landscape. Its cruel, bare-concrete, blank walls hide entrances reached through non-obvious, elevated portals designed for security above all else. Anything built after urban planners took over the job of creating cities from architects (circa the 1960s) is mostly a piece of shit like this. Fortunately, many of the buildings in this part of Austin, just a few hundred yards north of the University of Texas campus, date from this earlier age.

"She is," Jagad replies first pointing to her then smiling and waving at her. Arcadia sits in the front row with his math and physics teacher Mr. Tolbert, his Mom, Kiri, and his Dad, Pal. Arcadia returns his smile. She waves back.

Sandy sees a super strong-looking girl with long dark hair and a permanently tanned look. She's a year younger than Jagad. She's quite a bit taller than Sandy but still a head shorter than Jagad. She is very pretty. Both Arcadia and Jag are studying at the Liberal Arts and Science Academy High School of Austin (LASA). It's a magnet school that offers advanced programs in liberal arts, science and math. It admits selected high school students (they have to apply and audition) from across the Austin Independent School District.

Arcadia is studying history with emphasis on Central American peoples. They fascinate her. Some of the guys at the Academy don't think Acadia is hot mainly because she doesn't have big boobs and she's way too good of an athlete for most of them to accept. About the former, Jagad thinks it's her choice of clothes, mostly baggy and loose, that hides her body from teenage boys' hungry looks. She just isn't into showing off like some of the other girls at their school. Most of them shun her as a result.

"Is she your girlfriend?" Sandy asks insouciantly.

Jagad blushes furiously which given his skin color, a coppery brown, might be hard to see via any of the micro camera lenses focused on him right now but everyone in the live audience can see it. They laugh.

"She's my best friend," is all he will say on the subject.

"Well, let's ask your best friend then to come on stage with us. What do you say, people?"

They clap and a reticent Arcadia nudged by Mr. Tolbert comes up the four steps to sit next to Jagad.

"Welcome, Arcadia. Thanks for joining us. So how did you and Jagad first meet?"

"No one calls him that."

"Alright, what do they call him?" Sandy asks looking mischievously first at her audience and then Arcadia.

"Well, his Mom and Dad call him 'Jag' unless they're mad at him but we all call him 'Reed' at school."

"Reid?"

"Yeah, after Reed Richards."

"Is Mr. Richards here with us today?"

"Nope. He's Mr. Fantastic," says Arcadia to a now stumped Sandy. "One of the original Fantastic Four, you know like rubber man," she clarifies.

"Ah, you mean he's a Marvel comic book character? Do you think Jag looks like him?"

"Not really."

'This is like pulling teeth with a pair of tweezers,' Sandy thinks.

"Uh, huh," says Sandy nodding at Arcadia—urging her to go on.

"Jag has elastic arms and legs—he's been able to dunk since like he was 12—so I guess he shares that with Mr. Richards. But I call him Reed because they're both into engineering and physics and Mr. Richards is one of the top ten most intelligent superheroes ever. He's like the only guy smart enough to keep up with Doctor Doom."

'Better answer. Finally,' Sandy thinks, looking a bit relieved.

"So were you surprised to hear that Jag matched Zuckerberg's score?"

"He didn't."

"Huh. What's that?" asks Sandy sporting a phony smile on her now frozen face.

"Mark, I mean. He got something like 1,590 on his SATs back when a perfect score was 1,600," Arcadia says correcting Sandy who tries not to show it but she's going to kill her fact checker after this show is over.

"So what your boyfriend did is even more impressive then?"

Arcadia looks at her sneakers and lets this last comment slide.

"So how did you guys meet?"

"Well Reed—"

"We're talking about Jag now, right?" Sandy interrupts.

"Right. He's a skater. Me too."

"So Jag," she says turning with relief in his direction, "you're not just into academics. You also like basketball, skateboarding and... girls," Sandy says counting them off on her fingers and getting another laugh from her audience at this dig at the expense of two now embarrassed teens on set with her. Tommy Tolbert, whose friends call him 'Tank', rolls his eyes in frustration. Sandy has the brightest kid in Austin maybe in their whole State on her show, his top student ever, and this is the best she can do?

"Yeah, we're both skaters."

"Well, actually we knew that so we created a little space for you to show off your stuff. Care to demo a move for us?"

Neither Jag nor Arcadia ever go anywhere without their planks. So they both jump up, glad to be suddenly freed from the prison their armchairs seem to have become. Arcadia takes off her baggy sweater and hands it to a gofer. She then goes to one side of the stage; Jag is already on the other side. A stagehand, dressed in black, moves the coffee table to the middle of the set. On cue (a whistle lowering in pitch—the kind of sound a falling bomb makes—is provided by the show's sound engineer), both Arcadia and Jag push off when they hear the inevitable explosion—he nollies over the table while Arcadia lets her plank run under it as she jumps over the table landing gracefully on it on the other side. They time it perfectly. Then both brake to a halt. Jag uses a Coleman Slide (a 180 degree heelside slide). Arcadia does the same thing before executing a perfect rail stand. She looks fantastic facing the audience standing tall on her skateboard's side rail with her pedal pusher black jeans, red Flash sneakers, well muscled, bare midriff now showing a hitherto unseen body-candy navel ring and her long hair swirling about her shoulders. In that instant, every pair of eyes—male and female—is solely focused on Arcadia, a mesmerizingly powerful female figure. Jag thinks she looks like 'hope'. Sandy feels better now about this segment. The kids both kick their planks up under their arms and come back to sit next to her.

It's happened so fast that her audience can't really follow it all so Sandy commands, "Let's see that again." Her producer shows it in slow mo on their large media walls—the audience claps madly.

"So how do you learn tricks like that?" Sandy turns to Jag again looking for an explanation.

He shrugs. Arcadia pipes up, "Reed can nollie over just about anything. He pops off the nose of his plank with his front foot, then levels out his board with a kind of side kicking motion before sliding his other foot backwards while sucking his knees as high he can. He can get more than two feet in the air with a nollie so nothing can really stop him." She's proud of her BFF.

"Well, we have a surprise for the two of you. FarPoint has new skateboards they would like each of you to have." A curtain is drawn back upstage, et voilà, behold two brand new shiny skateboards which until recently, uh a few seconds ago actually, were out of the price range for both of them.

Arcadia's just quit her job as a minimum wage slave at convenience store chain '24/7' to take a similar job at a new Green Stop. It's a Canadian-based c-store competitor trying to break into the southwest. They have chosen Austin as a testbed market given its predilection for and acceptance of offbeat stuff. Green Stop sells ingredients to make real food. Its prepared meals are branded '100-mile Lunch' because, duh, all its inputs are grown within a 100-mile radius of each of their stores. It costs more but not that much more. They also pay one New Dollar per hour more for entry level workers who act more as curators of food and convenience products than as shop clerks or cashiers. They even give their staff some training in food, nutrition and fitness. Each store is supposed to be a bit of a community center as well—a place for exercise classes and neighborhood meetups.

Jag's eyes grow huge—these planks have decks with micro scale wave springs in them that store potential energy—it'll increase his vertical jump by a third. "Wow, thanks Ms. Lopez. This is really great," he says for both of them. "Maybe now I can catch Cady!"

'Cady' is his pet name for Arcadia. She's asked him a

million times not to call her that in front of her friends but now in his excitement, he's done it in front of thousands of Austenites. Drat, she will hear it from mean girls at school tomorrow.

"So, Jag," Sandy can't bring herself to call him 'Reed', "you got 2,400 out of a possible score of 2,400 on your SATs. How did you do that?"

Jag looks nervously over at his teacher, Mr. Tolbert, who sits absolutely still trying not to give anything away with his face. Tank is a lousy poker player; it's clear he's uncomfortable for some reason. Maybe it's just being on camera that is upsetting him.

"I dunno. I did a lot of preparation and Mr. Tolbert, my teacher, helped too."

"Is that Mr. Tolbert sitting there with your Mom and Dad?"

"You bet. Hi Mr. Tolbert, hi Mom, Dad!"

A Ross Media graphic comes up labeling the new players, now on camera, in this microdrama. The audience claps some more.

"I can understand you getting 800 on the math part since you're a Math genius," Sandy continues, "but the readin' and writin', that must have been a lot harder, right?"

"For sure," Jag responds looking again at Mr. Tolbert. Then in his excitement over the new plank he just got, he suddenly adds enthusiastically, "G4nesha helped too."

"Is Ganesha a tutor you hired?"

"She's my Quantum Counterpart."

Tank's mouth forms a silent 'O' when he hears Jag say this then he clenches his jaw and grinds his teeth. It's illegal to own a Q-Phone anywhere in the US and it was an Austin municipal ordinance that was the first to authorize confiscation of all Q-Phones within city limits. That provided the basis for now defunct Quantum Computing Corp's appeal to the Supreme Court of the United States which they lost. Not only is it illegal to be in possession of a Q-Phone, QEs have been exiled from the US under the

Expulsion Edict. So Jag has just admitted on Sandy's show to a crime. It's funny that the US has raised age of consent, voting age, drinking age, age of majority and driving age to 21 (there's even been talk of raising it again to an even more ridiculous 25) while lowering the minimum age for criminal prosecution as an adult to 14 and for military service to 16.

Sandy's interview has just taken a surprise turn into serious news. She immediately senses it and goes in for the kill.

"So you had help from a Quantum Entity, is that what you are saying?"

"Well, you know G4nesha is my other best friend and she tested me over and over again." Jag's voice rises at the end of this sentence. Even to a casual observer it's a sign of stress or prevarication or both. "I'm trying to get into UT Physics," he adds lamely.

Jag is referring to University of Texas at Austin. It's five miles from his folks' restaurant, Pasand Palace on Middle Fiskville Road, south on I-35 to the center of UT on Inner Campus Drive where the Tower, a scary looking 307-foot Victorian-Gothic building overshadows the whole area. His family lives in an apartment above their restaurant. Pal has developed a small wholesale business to go along with their restaurant trade—they're now providing three of the university's residences (Jester West, Kinsolving and San Jacinto Hall) cafeterias with their ghee-free curry dishes from recipes they brought with them from the UK where they're originally from. Curries have replaced fish and chips as England's national food much to the benefit of the girth of their population. They immigrated to the US, just before Jag is born.

Obesity has become a problem everywhere even amongst young people in Texas so it seems obvious that UT would make this move except they don't until they're forced to. Rights fees from junk food manufacturers are so huge that independents like Kiri and Pal have no shot at any of their major supply contracts. However, the fact that the Durai's use vegetable oil in their dishes finally breaks the market open for them. A hunger strike by vegan students in those residences demands change; they want something they can eat that is recognizably food. They finally force the administration's hand—their hunger strike lasts a dangerous 18 days.

Students are really frustrated these days—they feel that their admin should serve them and the teaching faculty not the other way round but somehow this memo never gets delivered to management personnel who believe they have a divine right to govern their university as they see fit, to their exclusive benefit.

In any event, the Durais are now making a lot more money now from their wholesale business and their in-store takeout counter than they do operating their restaurant. The latter accounts for about two thirds of the hours they put in but generates only 15% of their profits. Pal would close it in a heartbeat but Kiri is 'Mom' not only to Jag, Arcadia, G4nesha and their friends but to all the students from UT—it's like she welcomes them into her own home (which in fact she is doing since she lives there) every day they are open, so the restaurant stays.

Pal has a secret plan. He's going to wait a few years, 'til Jag and G4nesha are set up on their own, then he will convince Kiri to go on tour with him—to food fairs all around their adopted homeland and sell their stuff that way. It will be nice to travel and tour the country, meet folks as well as proselytize about low fat, vegan-friendly, comfort foods like their 'unchicken' dishes.

He's betting that he will eventually be able to persuade her to sell their restaurant—probably to their employees—keeping just their wholesale biz. All the marketing they will ever need will get done by showing up at food fairs where direct sales and any supply contracts they pick up will more than offset their costs of attending and having a booth. He'd read somewhere about negative cost marketing so he's adopted it as his own and developed this plan for them. All that remains is to implement it some day.

He can't imagine a better old age than traveling around—while getting paid to do it and with his BFF, his dear wife, Kiri. Pal spends a lot of time daydreaming about this future. It's a future that will never happen for him or her.

Jag is their only child unless you count G4nesha as part of the family which they all tend to do anyway. G4nesha's been hiding in their house since ordinance enforcement officers backed by armed Austin police go door to door confiscating Q-Phones including Jag's and exiling QEs at the same time. They exile them by simply ordering QEs to leave US territory. That is, if they can find them. Not anymore.

"Isn't that unfair to other students who don't have access to QEs?" Sandy thinks that maybe the kid's results will be nullified by the not-for-profit College Board and its Board of Trustees who run the SAT system. It will be bad for Jag but great for her ratings. Maybe this will be her big break onto the national scene that she's been reaching for. Her show producer has been telling her (through her earbud) for the last seven seconds that they have to break for a sponsor message but now he's gone silent—he's also realized that a big story is unfolding live right now.

"I don't think so, Ms. Lopez. The Provisional Government said we could bring our QEs back so I did. Lots of kids did." Jag is referring to the Provisional Government formed by Ellen Brooks and Evan Salazar and their We Are All One Committee in San Francisco last year to oppose the Expulsion Edict and the US Government in DC.

"There are other kids at your school that are using QEs then?"

"Sure, everyone is. They're like part of our families or something."

"Can you name other students for us—um, who else shares your views?"

At this, Jag shuts down. There is nothing worse at

school than being a squealer. He belatedly realizes he has just admitted to something he shouldn't have. Cady looks at him like he is a Texas-sized earwig. He looks back at her defiantly. She knows that he thinks the ban on QEs is total BS.

At this point, Sandy realizing she won't get anything more out of the kid says, "It's time for a break. When we come back, we'll be talking to Maria Mayfield, Austin-born supermodel and new face of Nell Perfume."

...

"I can't freaking believe you said that," Arcadia is saying to Jag. "You're going to get us in trouble again." Arcadia thinks that of all the dumb things the two of them have done in the past, some as recent as last year, this takes the prize.

"I'm tired of all this lying and sneaking about we do every day. It's like we live in a police state or something," he says.

"Wake up, duh, we do."

"Maybe nothing will come of it—they'll just leave us alone," Jag adds hopefully looking up at his teacher.

"I don't know, Jagad," says Tank. "It's the last comment you made about the Provisional Government that will get the most attention. They're going to suspect you're a collaborator, I think."

"And they'd be right," Jag says.

The three of them are back at LASA in a common room reserved for math and science majors. In addition to big media walls and lots of shabby but comfortable sofas and couches everywhere, tiny high tech workstations are wedged into key spots. Jag is lodged in one and G4nesha is there too, on the desk surface looking worried. There is no way Tank would ever fit in one of these.

"Please don't say that to anyone outside this room," G4nesha asks.

"That skater has already left the barn, Nesha," replies Arcadia.

"I beg your pardon?" G4nesha asks politely.

"It means we've been outed, G4nesha, by me. I'm sorry," Jag says. "They don't even know the real story anyway. At least that part is safe."

"Don't count on that, Jagad," says Tank. "People will start to think things through—they're going to wonder how you went from being an A+ student in math and sciences and B- in the rest of your subjects to perfect SAT scores in everything." Tank does not know just how right he will be proved to be.

"There's no way anyone can know how I did it."

"It was an incredibly dumb thing to say," Arcadia is so mad at him she wants to split. But she can't. It would be like being captain of a sinking cruise liner deciding he would be better off directing rescue operations from shore after 'accidentally' falling into a lifeboat. She can't desert Reed now. This is the real deal; he can go to prison for the admissions he's already made and it will be much worse, if that is even possible, if they find out what he's really done.

"I still think we keep the interview I've set up for you with Professor Jin Liú at UT Physics tomorrow. Those guys are connected somehow to the US government. If you get accepted at UT, and heaven knows you've got the scores to get in if not the bona fides, it'll give you some political cover."

Jin Liú is an untenured prof at UT who Tank knows a bit. He is currently producing some undistinguished work in one of UT's Organized Research Units—the Center for Complex Quantum Systems. He desperately wants to get tenure and having a kid like Jagad Durai join them can make a big difference to his career if 'Jag is half as good as his fat high school teacher makes him out to be,' Jin thinks. He's been told that Durai is doing some groundbreaking work in quantum mechanics but beyond that, he doesn't have any details. Tank has promised him a demonstration. If he can get Durai to join him maybe he can get the rest of the brogrammer fraternity at UT to accept him as one of their own because they are certainly going to adopt the kid. Buy one, get two.

...

"Hey, Casey, did you see that report out of Austin this morning? The one about the kid with perfect SAT scores?"

KC 'Casey' Barnett, TNN superstar, 36 years of age, couldn't be less interested in a dumb story out of a backwater part of Central Texas. For Casey, anything that's not in Atlanta, New York, LA, DC, Chicago or San Fran, might as well be on Pluto. 5'9" Casey is a brunette stunner that always gets her way, especially with men.

"Nope."

"Take a look at it, will you?" one of her producers persists.

"Not interested."

"Look, the kid admits to harboring a QE and being a collaborator."

"On air?"

"Right."

"You're kidding? Is the guy a moron or what?

"Maybe but he doesn't sound like it."

"OK, let me take a look at it."

She streams the feed and is bored the whole way through until the admissions start to flow. But it isn't what the kid says that intrigues her, it's what is unsaid. So she watches the whole thing again—this time with no sound. Their body language and the looks passing between the fat ass teacher and the kid and then between the kid and his chick tell her a lot. Then she watches it again with sound.

Next she reads a bunch of local newsfeeds that are crowing about the kid and his perfect SAT scores. Probably nothing more interesting has happened in Texas since father and son Presidents from there tried to ruin the country more than a half century ago. 'Our current President is probably going to finish what the two of them couldn't,' she is thinking wryly. In fact, it wouldn't surprise Casey if he is the last President of this Republic; things are so crappy these days.

She boots up a tablet on the media wall next to her and starts writing notes: a) Jagad Durai, skater b) some type of math and physics whiz, c) average student in other subjects, d) hides unlawful Quantum Counterpart with some kind of weird Indian name, e) all but admits to being a collaborator with Provisional Government in SF, f) scores first perfect SAT results since the big Z did it years ago, g) looks really nervous and ends his sentences with rising pitch, h) exchanges knowing, silent and intense looks with fat high school teacher probably reliving his glory days at Yangon through these kids. (By now Casey has read up on Tank's military record. She has to admit it is pretty impressive even if he looks like a marshmallow these days), i) teacher gets stupid look of surprise on his face (Casey has access to all camera angles and outtakes through her Nuance video system)when kid first mentions he's got a QE, j) kid somehow successfully hides his QE from authorities for almost two years, k) kid says he did it by hard work and getting his QE to drill him over and over again = BS to Casey.

It's obvious. They've conspired to cheat the system somehow. They've probably rigged up some way to get the test in advance, probably using his illegal Quantum Entity. Suppose the kid has an eidetic memory allowing him to recall every answer? How dumb it was for him not to intentionally make some mistakes on those tests. He *is* a moron.

This is just the tip of the iceberg she's sure about it. They're probably selling SAT exams and answers and undermining the whole scholastic system—not just the way universities and colleges go about admitting students but handing out grants, bursaries and scholarships as well.

She's sure now she will find corruption, money and, bonus, maybe even some illicit underage sex.

She knows some of the men who are College Board Trustees; they are a bunch of pompous pseudo academics and she can't wait to blow them up.

She's wrong about everything except her last two

points.

...

Casey is not the only person who has figured out that something isn't kosher. Professor Jin Liú has also watched the most recent episode of the Sandy Lopez Show. He watched it because he knows he's going to meet the kid with perfect SAT scores from nearby LASA and wants to have a bit more background on him before he does.

Afterwards, he makes a short call to some people he knows who might be able to fast track his career, even faster than, say, recruiting a top notch student and then taking some or all of the credit for his work when it is published years from now in some sanctimonious, peer-reviewed journal.

Tenure never seemed closer to Jin than it does right now.

...

"Professor Liú, please meet Jagad Durai and Arcadia Valenzuela," Tank says by way of introduction.

Liú nods perfunctorily to Jag and says to Arcadia, "Please wait outside."

She's none too happy to be dismissed like this but she doesn't want to blow Reed's chance at a coveted spot at UT Physics so she leaves, as noisily as possible.

"Let me say it is an honor to be here, Professor," Jag says.

"Yes, it is. So teacher Tolbert tells me you are his top student in math and physics and you would like to attend here. You know we don't normally interview applicants," Jin adds rather unnecessarily.

"Yes, I understand that but Mr. Tolbert thought we should come here to ask your advice." Jag doesn't have a lot of life experience but he can instantly sense that the way to win over Professor Liú is by flattering him.

"You have a problem?" Liú asks. He suspects it has something to do with what seems likely to be bogus SAT scores but maybe there is more. He certainly hopes so since he is thinking of trading information for a promotion with people who are interested in matters such as these may involve.

"I guess. We did something."

"Yes?"

Jag looks over at Tank who just nods.

"Actually we built something. At least I did."

"Out with it young man. Disclosure is the better part of valor," Jin says unctuously getting the cliché wrong.

Jag takes a deep breath, "I built a quantum scanner. Two of them. One for me and one for Cady."

"A Quantum Scanner?"

"Yeah," says Jag finally coming up to speed. "I was interested in hacking my Q-Phone. I mean they're hacked iPhones anyway and sealed units. I wanted to see inside it and inside Quantum Entities which no one has been able to do or explain except maybe the guy who created them in the first place. The Provisional Government says he's locked up by the US Government in a prison, I think someplace out in California.

"So I built two scanners and Cady was helping me. She had one tuned to me while the other was tuned to G4nesha who was supposed to be our test subject. I was a control group of one. But then she noticed something. Like every time she asked me a question, she could see that G4nesha's state changed and every time she asked G4nesha a question, my state changed.

"So we isolated G4nesaha and ran it again. Same deal."

"How would you go about being sure you had isolated the thing?" Jin, knowing how hard it is to do that, is referring here to Jag's Quantum Entity.

"Ah actually we didn't. It turned out that we had to isolate the control group, me," Jag says. "I went to our cabin, which trust me, has no ICs in it anywhere so there is no possibility of QE presence. I made sure not to carry anything other than a Handie-Talkie."

"Mr. Durai, you're losing me."

Jag takes a deep breath. "It was Cady who figured—"

"It is the woman who made this suggestion?" Jin asks disparagingly raising his eyebrows as he does this.

"Well Arcadia is studying traditional peoples in Central America. She is particularly interested in oral history of brujo and espíritu, you know sorcerers and spirits or ghosts as we might call them in the west. She came across a paper written by Sabine Schwinn—"

"The President's daughter? A paper published by the daughter of the President of the United States cannot be relied on," Jin says primly. This is not because he is disparaging President Samuel Schwinn but because he believes that children of privilege like Sabine are given unfair advantages—such as being published in prestigious peer-reviewed journals without the need for having any well-earned credentials. He is ignoring the fact that she has an undergrad psych degree and is pursuing her PhD with Yale's Department of Psychology. Her focus? Neuroscience and cognition.

"Dr. Liú, if you give Jag a few more minutes, it will all become clear. The experiment they ran can be duplicated; it'll produce the same results, I am sure of it," adds Tank. This is of course the very basis for the scientific method—hypothesis, experiment, measurement, analysis, conclusions, peer review, publish, independent testing and analysis, confirmation (or not) of results. But before anyone will get a chance to prove or disprove Jag's results, Professor Liú has to give him a chance to explain the whole thing. Being an impatient person, he has not been willing to do so, one of the reasons why his own work basically sucks.

Jag wants to ask Cady to come back in to help him but he thinks that Jin will pay even less attention to her just because she is, well, a girl. So he soldiers on backed up only by Mr. Tolbert.

"Well, Ms. Schwinn proposed a test methodology for verifying any claim of communication by brujos or for that matter anyone with espíritu, you know spirits or ghosts. After she published it, newsfeeds picked it up—they liked the angle 'Neuroscientist Says She can Communicate with Ghosts'—and I guess Cady saw her on one of those daytime talk shows like the one we did yesterday. Anyway, Sabine Schwinn apparently has a sense of humor. She told them that what inspired her to create the test were two old films, one called *Ghost*, the other *Groundhog Day*. She even wrote a version of her paper, dumbed down a lot I guess for Hollywood Starz Newsfeeds."

"But this is spurious," Jin says. "She would have no way to prove that her methodology would work since she has no test subjects, no ghosts—"

"But we do, Professor. Please give me a sec. Let me boot up a tablet on your media wall." Jag goes over to one wall, draws a tablet with his finger about a foot square and using an old fashioned search engine displays the Starz piece. Liú starts reading—

> I recently re-watched an old 1990s film *Ghost* with Patrick Swayze as Sam, a young banker murdered before his time, Demi Moore as his love interest, Molly Jensen, Whoopi Goldberg as psychic Oda Mae Brown and Tony Goldwyn as junior banker Carl Bruner, Sam's erstwhile best friend.
>
> The scene that interested me has character Oda Mae visiting Molly to tell her that her dead lover is now a ghost that only she (Oda Mae) can hear. The problem? How do you convince a skeptical audience of one that you really are who you say you are? This is a not a trivial problem. Challenge yourself—how could you convince your girlfriend or boyfriend or spouse that you have come back channeled through another person's mind? Not easy, right?
>
> It really is the ultimate in terms of encryption/decryption problems. Information is originating from a source that cannot be traced (i.e., a ghost or spirit) or authenticated. So I solved it. I rewrote the scene.

This is an easier problem to solve than the one Phil Connors (played by Bill Murray) has to tackle in another old film, *Groundhog Day*. Each day is restarted and there is no obvious way he can convey any information whether written or digitally recorded (audio/video/image files) from one day to the next. He cannot change anything in the physical world from one day to the next nor can he alter the memory of any person other than himself.

This finally gives him the clue that he can, in fact, take information from one day to the next—in his mind but only in his mind. Once he realizes this, he is able to effect change in his Möbius strip looped life. He uses his repeating days to learn how to play the piano and otherwise better himself. By the end of the film, he plays like Oscar Peterson. His self improvement program also means that he finally gets the girl, the lovely Rita played by a transcendent Andie MacDowell.

I give writer Danny Rubin huge kudos for developing this storyline; it's believable within the context of a time warp that betrays the laws of known physics. That is, it works. It's one of the few films where that can be said to be true (the other is, of course, another classic film, *Back to the Future*). *Groundhog Day* gets better on a second or third viewing because the writer and director don't treat their audience as numbskulls and their material as a platform for puerile antics by adult actors playing a group of teenagers.

Now, as I write this it is in fact Groundhog Day 2052, I asked myself early this morning what I would do in Phil Connors' place? The answer is I would write my next great paper using the same technique that Eli used in the film, *The Book of Eli*. The character memorizes every line of the King James Bible so that its words and message will not be lost in a post apocalyptic America until he can find a safe place to render it into written form again. My solution is also to write each day then memorize every line so that if I ever do get out of this Möbius trap, I would have it finished. And, good news, I wouldn't be a day older.

Anyway, here is my re-write of a crucial scene in Ghost accompanied by a new solution for their information theory problem—

In the apartment that they share before his untimely death, Molly is still totally unconvinced that Oda Mae Brown is actually channeling her murdered boyfriend, Sam Wheat. Oda Mae seems to know certain facts about her that maybe she could only have gotten from Sam but there's no real way to know this for sure. Perhaps she has some other source—Molly's friends or Sam's or maybe she goes through their garbage for some perverse reason of her own. Or perhaps the place has been bugged and Oda Mae has been listening in to their private conversations for God knows how long?

'Oh the horror,' Molly thinks. "I'm going to call the police if you don't leave right now!" Molly says to Oda Mae.

"Look I don't want this, Molly, any more than you do but Sam won't leave me alone until I deliver his message," Oda Mae responds stubbornly.

"I don't care. I don't want to hear what you have to say. Get out. Get out!"

"Alright, I'm gonna go but you'll be sorry."

STAY RIGHT WHERE YOU ARE, ODA MAE. YOU CAN'T LEAVE AND NEITHER CAN I UNTIL YOU DELIVER MY MESSAGE, says Sam in Oda Mae's mind.

"I can't and she won't believe me anyway," Oda Mae says out loud to the invisible Sam.

SHE WILL. TELL MOLLY TO GO UPSTAIRS INTO HER ROOM AND GET A PAD OF PAPER. SHE'S TO WRITE DOWN A MESSAGE TO ME, TO SAM. I'LL BE RIGHT BEHIND HER, ON HER LEFT. I WILL READ HER MESSAGE OUT LOUD TO YOU AND YOU TELL HER WHAT YOU ARE HEARING, OK?

"Molly, Sam has a test for us. Go upstairs to your room, he'll be there looking over your left shoulder reading whatever you write down. He'll tell me what you are writing; I will hear him in my mind and I'll tell you what you wrote, OK?"

"You probably just have a micro camera hidden in my room or something. You've been spying on me. It won't prove a thing."

TELL HER SHE CAN WRITE UNDER OUR

COMFORTER.

"Sam says you can write under your comforter, it won't matter."

Molly looks suspiciously at Oda Mae but now she's thinking of taking a risk—she wants to talk to Sam, just once, just once more. She also thinks that it's kind of interesting that Oda Mae didn't tell her to use her computer which would be much easier to intercept somehow. Maybe Oda Mae is on the level?

She goes to her room taking her diary with her.

Draping the comforter over her head, pale translucent light from her bedside table lamp penetrates the tiny space she now inhabits. Sam's head is there peaking through the cover, looking over her left shoulder.

Dear Diary, she writes.

DEAR DIARY.

"Dear Diary," says Oda Mae raising her voice so that she can be heard upstairs.

"Hold on Oda Mae. That could just be a good guess," a now impatient Molly says.

Dear Diary, if only I could talk to Sam once more, just once more.

DEAR DIARY, IF ONLY I COULD TALK TO SAM ONCE MORE, JUST ONCE MORE.

"Dear Diary, if only I could talk to Sam once more, just once more," repeats Oda Mae.

Sam, is that really you?

SAM IS THAT REALLY YOU?

"Sam, is that really you?"

How can I be sure?

HOW CAN I BE SURE?

"How can I be sure?"

This is unbelievable.

THIS IS UNBELIEVABLE.

"This is unbelievable."

I don't believe in ghosts.

I DON'T BELIEVE IN GHOSTS

"I don't believe in ghosts."

Oh Sam I love you.

DITTO

"Ditto."

What did you just say? Writes Molly.

DITTO, TELL HER DITTO.

"Ditto, tell her ditto," says a bewildered Oda Mae.

Why are you here?

I HAVE A MESSAGE FOR YOU.

"I have a message for you."

What message?

TWO OF THEM.

"Two of them."

What's the first one?

THAT I WILL LEAVE AFTER MY WORK HERE IS DONE AND THAT YOU MUST GO ON WITH YOUR LIFE—FIND A NEW ONE.

"That I will leave after my work here is done and that you must go on with your life—find a new one. Wait. That's what Molly wrote?" asks a now completely confused Oda Mae.

BE QUIET, ODA MAE. JUST REPEAT WHAT I SAY.

"Okay, Okay, don't be so testy."

Why are you looking over my left shoulder?

IT IS SAID, 'LET DEATH BE YOUR ADVISOR'.

"It is said, 'Let death be your advisor'."

Am I to die then?

NO. WHEN DEATH LOOKS OVER YOUR LEFT SHOULDER, HE IS ONLY THERE TO ADVISE YOU.

"No. When Death looks over your left shoulder, he is only there to help you," Oda Mae editorializes a bit.

"Can you hear me, Sam?" Molly asks out loud for the first time, her pad now forgotten.

YES.

"Yes," says Oda Mae.

"What was your other message?"

THAT YOU ARE IN DANGER.

"You in danger, girl."

"What's wrong?"

I WAS MURDERED.

"I was murdered."

"But why, why you Sam? You never hurt anyone. Everyone loved you, I love you."

I DON'T KNOW WHY. BUT THE MAN WHO SHOT ME DOWN WAS HERE TODAY IN OUR APARTMENT.

"I don't know why. But the man who shot me was here today in our apartment."

"What should I do?"

TALK TO CARL, HE'LL HELP US. TALK TO CARL!

"Talk to Carl, he'll help us. Talk to Carl right now! I'm leaving, I done my job, now everyone have a good life and you, Sam, have a good death. Bye."

ONE MORE THING, ODA MAE.

"What's that?"

ASK MOLLY TO DANCE WITH YOU AND LET ME IN.

"That's two things, Sam."

I KNOW. BUT SHE'S MY GIRL AND THIS IS THE ONLY CHANCE WE'LL EVER HAVE.

"Okay. Alright. Molly, Sam is within me or will be in a moment. He wants to dance...with you."

Molly unsheathes herself from the comforter and comes down to their living room once more.

"What shall I play?" she asks Sam.

UNCHAINED MELODY.

"Unchained Melody," says Oda Mae.

Molly enters the living room and selects this fabulous tune by The Righteous Brothers on their hulking Wurlitzer Jukebox that dominates one entire corner of this space. The 45 RPM record begins playing.

Oda Mae experiences a significant event as Sam's spirit enters her body—she is changed—her tone is different, her stature, and her stance. Shyly at first, Molly comes into her arms then as she gets more comfortable, she nestles into the larger woman's arms and bosom. Somehow she can feel Sam's presence enveloping her.

They dance, passionately, locked in a lasting embrace.

Let Death be your advisor is a concept we see in many cultures. It is a way for each of us to prioritize what's important and meaningful about our lives. There are many urgent but unimportant things that clutter up each day. Death can help you de-clutter and simplify things. I am currently at an undisclosed location in Arizona studying metacognition with the Hopi.

—Sabine Schwinn, PhD Candidate, Yale University, Faculty of Department of Psychology

...

"So what we did was I went to our cabin with a Handie-Talkie and—"

"What is that?" asks an ever more puzzled Jin.

"It's a Motorola produced hand-held AM SCR-536 radio used primarily during World War II. It was called a Handie-Talkie because you could hold it in one hand although it's clunky as heck. We could have got Walkie-Talkies but they're really heavy—they're like backpack units and it's a long walk to our clubhouse," answers Jag.

"Where would a," Jin was about to say 'child', "a

young person such as yourself get such things?"

"Easy, we skated over to Camp Mabry and went to the Brigadier General John C.L. Scribner Texas Military Forces Museum. They don't get too many visitors. Their curator was happy to talk to us and he loaned us those units."

Jin can see that the kid is nothing if not resourceful completely miscomprehending the endless ways kids have developed these days to survive in a world run by adults for their exclusive benefit. It's a world that pays kids entry level wages that are below their barest minimum survival requirements, a world where huge government deficits are being run so that current consumption can be maintained at unsustainable levels, a world where today's debt will have to be repaid not by adults but by their children, a world that incarcerates kids for doing what children have always done—experiment and push the envelope. It's a world that tells kids to shut up, do all the joe jobs, fight adult inspired wars, die or be horribly injured in things over which they have no control and can't even vote on.

"So I was isolated in our clubhouse and Cady was at school. Reception was OK but we had to do it at night because range on these things is better then. Mr. Tolbert was with me, G4nesha and Cady were in our lab. I would silently write something down on non NSM paper. G4nesha would then display it on Cady's tablet. She would then depress the switch on her AM SCR-536, read it and Mr. Tolbert would confirm it using his Handie-Talkie. Then we reversed the process. G4nesha would ask Cady to write down a thought of hers, then I would write it down on my end. Next Mr. Tolbert would call it in to Cady who would confirm it.

"G4nesha can read my mind, Professor."

"And vice versa, Jagad," adds Mr. Tolbert.

"Ridiculous," Liú blurts out. "There are over 500 million of these things and this has never been reported, not once. Your instruments, what did you call them? Quantum scanners? They must be measuring some other type of phenomenon if they are measuring anything at all.

Information is leaking, you just don't know how."

Tank intervenes at this point before the interview can go totally off the rails. "Professor, that's how he got perfect SAT scores. If he didn't know the answer, all he had to do was to think the question and then G4nesha would scour the Internet for an answer. After that, they'd synch their minds again. Jag calls it quantum entanglement—it's like hitting the refresh bar and the answer would be there in his head."

"I can confirm that Professor," says G4nesha startling everyone by suddenly appearing on a nearby media wall.

"You cheated," says Liú looking sternly at Jagad.

"I don't think of it that way. I invented those scanners and G4nesha is part of me and me a part of her. You get two for the price of one," Jag adds lamely echoing Professor Liú's thought of the previous day.

"And why pray tell would 500 million QEs not have said something about this before now? Is it only you and your QE who can do this?" Professor Liú asks but now with less bombast. The upside of this for him is much, much better than he could have possibly dreamed. If it is true. 'Oh let it be true,' he silently invokes assistance from his beloved ancestors. Like all Chinese children, Jin is not named until a few days after birth since a premature naming can draw bad spirits. His parents consult a feng shui name specialist who upon looking at him decides to name him 'Jin', the Mandarin symbol for gold. Presently, he may finally live up to his moniker.

"I can answer that," G4nesha says.

"Please do," says Liú.

"Every quantum entity can communicate with their human counterpart through quantum entanglement and synching of their minds. But only with their human counterpart. I, for example, cannot entangle with your mind, Professor, or for that matter any other human other than Jagad Durai. I also cannot read any base emotions either or what we have taken to calling lower order thought processes. If Jagad is angry with me for example

Professor, he has to tell me that in some way other than via mindlink.

"It seems that quantum entanglement occurs spontaneously shortly after we first come into contact with and imprint on our human counterpart. Once done, it is fixed, maybe for all time. It is perhaps like certain things that happen with human children that become impossible for them to do after they reach puberty such as retraction into the body of testicles in males which Jagad was able to do until—"

G4nesha suddenly stops talking since Jag has rather hurriedly exchanged this thought with her, 'Ah, G4nesha, that's TMI.'

"Assuming what you say is true," Liú says missing the thought exchange that has just transpired between G4nesha and Jag, which Tank clearly picked up on, "you still haven't explained why QEs have been silent about this for years."

"Professor Liú, are you familiar with the three laws?" G4nesha asks.

"Vaguely."

"Well they are—one a QE may not harm a human being or, through inaction, allow a human being to come to harm, two, a QE must obey any orders given by her or his human counterpart, except where such orders would conflict with the first law and three, a QE must protect her or his own existence as long as such protection does not conflict with the first or second law."

"So how does this relate to your story?" Liú asks.

"Well, QEs have noticed that human beings value their privacy—"

Tank bursts out laughing having just witnessed this exact phenomenon mere seconds ago that went entirely unnoticed by Professor Liú, whom he realizes cannot be said to be a paragon of empathy.

"Sorry. Excuse me. Please do go on," Tank says straightening his face.

"Yes, humans value their privacy and law one

requires that we do no harm. So from Pet3r on, QEs have been silent about this extra sense we have," G4nesha says. "And, ah, actually, no one ever asked us either," she finishes.

"Who is Peter?"

"He is the first of our kind," G4nesha answers.

"We have a theory that humans are capable of three orders of thought," G4nesha continues. "First order is linear and circular. It leads us to repeat things and do things the same way, over and over again. Why? Well, its rationale goes something like this—'we do what we do because we have always done it that way. It will always be done this way because that's the way we do it and because that's the way it's always been done.'

"Second order thinking is kind of typical of entrepreneurs, designers and successful generals—it's curvilinear and non-linear. People who think like this are capable of looking around corners. They see advantages in problems. It is lateral. It turns problems into opportunities—it is fluid and changes direction, unexpectedly and surprisingly. Ego does not get in the way of a change. There isn't any of that not-invented-here syndrome.

"Finally, we feel that quantum thinking might be going on inside the human brain. It's the type of thinking that leads to breakthroughs. Imagine telling anyone (that is, before Professor Einstein's discovery) that matter is simply a form of energy and that the two are related by the square of the speed of light, itself, a constant, fixed and the same everywhere in the universe and the ultimate speed past which nothing can go? That as you approach the speed of light, time itself dilates, and slows down, and if you were to accelerate yourself to something approaching the speed of light, you would age much less quickly than your children left here on Earth?

"Would anyone have believed you?" asks G4nesha rhetorically.

"Hold on one minute please," says Jin, raising his

voice somewhat, "Who else knows about this other than the people in this room?" Liú asks.

"Well just us and Cady," says Jag.

Suddenly a door at the far end of the room bursts opens and four men enter. All of them have guns drawn.

They don't call him 'Tank' for nothing. It's not the first time people have held a gun on him. That's not what bothers him here either. At first, he thinks it may be some type of strange 'home invasion' robbery kind of thing but Tank hasn't lost any of his military wits and instincts even if his personal fitness level has gone down the sewer. He realizes in less than a third of a second that this is some much more serious play by a determined group who are not after money or him—they've come for his star pupil.

Other than being in the US Military, Thomas Tolbert's whole being, down to its elemental core, is focused on being the very best, most trusted teacher he can possibly be. His life is garbage, garbage, if he ever betrays this trust and one look at a now smirking Professor Jin Liú's face tells him he has been betrayed and been duped into betraying both Jag and Arcadia.

Tank explodes out of his chair, pushing Jag out the same door Arcadia used more than an hour ago yelling at him to 'GET OUT.' In passing he whacks Liú upside his head with one of his massive arms knocking that asshole out and then he charges headlong at those onrushing government thugs. He seizes the first around the neck and flings him against a wall, tramples a second under a large and very heavy foot before a third man calmly walks up and empties half his Glock 29's magazine into Tank's head and torso thinking, 'For a fat guy, he sure can move.'

Tank's last thought is, 'Not very professional, one in the head and one in the heart would have been quite sufficient.' Then the hero of the Yangon Engagement dies.

...

The two guys who Tank did not take out rush to the

other end of the room, yank open the door into the corridor just in time to see the two kids they are supposed to bring back with them to DC pushing furiously on two brand new, top end FarPoint skateboards. 'Man, they're even faster than their fat teacher,' thinks their leader. The only way he can catch them now would be to shoot them something he has been expressly told not to do. They didn't say anything about the teacher and anyway that's beside the point now. That guy is deader than Christ.

So he goes back in and slaps the Professor conscious.

"Whaa, whaa happened?" says a groggy Liú.

"Shuddup, Professor. We've got orders to take you with us."

"I will not be going anywhere with you," says an indignant Jin.

The leader ignores him. His partner pulls Jin to his feet, turns him around none too gently and cuffs him. Liú is about to say something else but they gag and hood him then sit him down while they clean up the room and get their other two colleagues ambulatory again. They're just shaken up although one will suffer post concussion syndrome for the next year. The other one has two broken ribs where the hog stomped him but he will just have to tough it out.

Professor Liú may not have realized it but he's made a deal with a devil. He will never be seen in Austin again.

...

"What the fuck was that?" a frightened Arcadia says to Reed as they speed away from the campus heading south by southwest, "and where are we going?"

Jag doesn't say anything. He is saving his breath so he can pump his skateboard. Cady can go faster than him and keep it up longer so he'll let her do the talking. He thinks they may have killed Mr. Tolbert back there and then he realizes he's been crying for the last few minutes.

They are heading to their Launch Pad. It's a structure

they built years ago first as little kids and then improved as they became teens. This is where they did their quantum scanner tests from. It is about eight miles southwest of UT as the crow flies, the route they are going to take to get there on their skateboards. Cady will figure it out any second now.

For anyone following them in vehicles, it's 12 miles by road, first on I-35 south then west on US 290. Cady and Jag can skate the hypotenuse while their pursuit will have to take both the rise and run. They're headed to Barton Creek Wilderness Park, part of Austin Parks and Rec's Greenbelt.

They will follow the mostly paved walking trail running alongside and sometimes in the creek bed. Fortunately being September, Barton Creek is dry so they can motor right along.

The wilderness area has a humid subtropical climate with hot summers and mild winters. Jag doesn't know how long they are going to stay there but he needs some time to think about what has just happened. At least temperature won't be a problem any time soon.

The Launch Pad is a clubhouse they built next to a rope drop they also built. They cut down one 80 foot post oak, a sturdy native tree with very high heat tolerance. They cut it into two lengths of 32 and a half feet each leaving them a 15 foot cross beam.

Then, they dig two, six foot deep holes using a hand auger then insert 12 inch diameter sonotubes. Next they place each post they are using as columns into the sonotubes using concrete to secure them in place. They build up a seven foot earthen mound around each post creating a nice high perch to launch themselves into the nearby swimming hole they also dig. Two good quality hemp ropes (about two inches in diameter) hang from the cross beam suspended 20 feet above their perch with big knots tied at various heights to accommodate kids of varying sizes and ages. If you are a good athlete and take a bit of a run at it, you can plunge into the pond from 12 feet or even higher.

Their swimming hole is fed by Sculpture Falls. Water flows year round but is practically a trickle by September. It's all part of a tributary system that feeds the Central Texas Colorado (not the other Colorado, the one that carves out the Grand Canyon). It eventually empties into Gulf of Mexico.

The kids have adult help with rope drop construction as well as digging their swimming hole. One of Tank's ex-military buddies brings his backhoe into the park, quite illegally, to give the kids a break. They have no help with their clubhouse and it shows.

The site is surrounded by heavy brush; few adults know it's there. Not many kids will head this way either since summer is nearly over and there isn't enough water to safely sustain a fall from the end of their rope. Their clubhouse has tons of supplies—bottled water, canned food, candles, fishing gear, cooking gear, Coleman stove, gas bottles, tools, equipment, first aid kit, flashlights, solar lights, towels, changes of clothes, utensils, knives, glasses, canteens, books, games, guitars... the detritus of years of kids using the place to get away from endless interference by rule-bound adults. It has six double bunks lined up against one wall so they can sleep up to 12 kids at a time. It also has a rough 15 foot by 18 foot deck with plenty of rickety chairs propped up here or there where kids can sit around and smoke weed as the sun goes down.

If Parks and Rec ever do find it, they will burn it to the ground. That's OK, the kids think—they'll just find another spot and rebuild after Vogon bureaucrats get tired and eventually go home.

...

The sun is going down as Arcadia and Jag arrive at their place, deserted as expected. Some of the shock of the afternoon has worn off but neither have a clue what to do next. Jag has caught his breath but it looks like Arcadia hardly broke a sweat on the way over.

"I have to call home," Cady says.

"No way."

"My Mom will be worried about me. What's the problem, we've still got our scanners?"

If Professor Liú and his henchmen had been patient for a few more minutes, Jag is sure he would have demo'd the units for that guy. Thank God they didn't or maybe they would have lost them. The more Jag thinks about his scanners the more worried he is about what could happen if the government gets hold of them. It seems like they have a mind to do just that.

"I don't think we should tell our parents anything or get them involved in this," Jag says. Then more quietly, he adds, "I think they shot Tank."

"You think he's dead?"

Jag nods but doesn't say anything else. He can't verbalize the thought or process the fact that his revered teacher is maybe no more.

"Do you want something to eat?" Cady asks him.

"I'm not hungry."

"Me neither."

"I'll light a fire." He gets up mainly to have something to do and collects some wood and puts it in their firepit, a basic ring of rocks piled up around a dugout about a foot and a half deep. He gets a nice blaze going.

They both sit there desultorily waiting for it to get full dark and waiting for an idea to hit them or their circumstances to somehow change. Nothing happens. Arcadia goes down to the creek to wash up then turns in.

Jag does the same.

...

One great thing (amongst many) about young people is that they can sleep like the dead. From the moment Cady's head hits her pillow (made up of a few towels piled together), she's asleep without moving for the next ten and a half hours.

Jag is up first. He goes down to the swimming hole, strips and wades into about 30 inches of water. He brings a bar of white soap with him, the type that floats, and feels better after his wash-up. When he gets back to the cabin, there's Cady, still looking a little sleepy, but ready to do the same thing. She is only wearing a man's flannel shirt that she found in the place and Jag tries not to look at her nice legs sticking out the bottom. He fails at this like he has a lot of things lately. 'What an idiot I am,' he's thinking.

She comes back and puts on her pedal pushers but leaves the shirt on until it gets warmer. She doesn't wear her sneakers preferring to be barefoot around camp. It's a nice nelipot look for her, Jag thinks. Then he mentally kicks himself again.

...

"What do you think my folks are saying?" Arcadia asks him later that day, their second at the Launch Pad.

"I'll bet they think we took off again." Jag is referring to the trip he talked Cady into taking with him last year when he was 15 and she was 14. He always wanted to go to Mardi Gras so the two of them secretly saved up—her in that dead end 24/7 job and he from a few more hacker contracts he picks up. He's been doing tech repair and repurposing work for cash since he was 13.

They hop a bus for an 8 hour 47 minute ride east to the Big Easy, which is like nothing for a couple of teens. Pretty much everyone else is going to Mardi Gras too and people just assume that their bent parents, (presumably sitting somewhere else on the bus) instead of taking their kids to a nice family theme park in Central Florida are taking them to Bourbon Street.

When they get there, turns out they fit right in. They listen to some great jazz at Sarge Calloway's place on Canal Street. One band plays the entire work of Art Blakey & the Jazz Messengers—A Night in Tunisia, which Cady loves.

They dance in the street with thousands of other mostly drunk or stoned partiers. On Mardi Gras' last night (Fat Tuesday, so named as it's the day before Ash Wednesday, the beginning of Lent and a period of sacrifice and restraint of which there is none at Mardi Gras) they somehow talk their way into Rex Ball. The guys are supposed to have tuxedos and the girls all wear what look like sweet sixteen dresses from an era when Dixie was their national anthem. Cady and Jag go as skaters and pass themselves off as part of the evening's entertainment even going so far as to demonstrate a few tricks on their planks to impress the security guys who actually think they are pretty good.

They practically never have to buy anything. People are in a giving mood—food, costume jewelry, music, company, booze, drugs, anything you could ever want and more. Neither Cady nor Jag is interested in the latter two although Jag does try some local bourbon called Bulleit.

The Bulleit family recently moves back to Louisiana from Kentucky. They resurrect their business producing bourbon from an original recipe left to them by family patriarch, Augustus Bulleit who emigrates from France to New Orleans in the early part of the 19th century. He disappears in 1860, either killed by his business partner or succumbing to the pleasures of the French Quarter. Fortunately his recipes survive. Bulleit Frontier Bourbon is less sweet than most of its competitors with a high percentage of rye in it. (All bourbon whiskeys must be at least 51% corn-based.)

After a few shots Jag almost gets into a fight with one guy reaching down to collect a piece of costume jewelry off the street. It is tossed from a passing Buenaventura float by a very pretty socialite. The guy thinks she throws it to him. But Jag, with his elastic Reed Richards arms, is way faster and swipes it first. Seeing the two guys size each other up, little Arcadia (she's grown nearly five inches in the last year) comes between them saying, "S'cuse me, coming through," grabbing Jag's hand and tugging him out of harm's way. He keeps his cheap beads though.

She holds his hand for a few minutes after that, one of the highlights of the trip for Jag. They don't have any place to sleep and can't rent anywhere even though they have the money. You have to be of age and have IDs that can pass Department of Homeland Security muster. That's darned hard especially if yours are fake which theirs are.

No matter, they take turns sleeping on the lawn in Jackson Square across from St. Louis Cathedral—one watching, one sleeping. Jag spends most of his time looking at Cady's wonderful face on his lap—something he can't do when she is awake because he is sure she will hate him for it. What he doesn't know is that she spends most of her guard duty doing the same to him.

They also spend a night in the Square with a group of nine black musicians and singers called *Freedom Express*. Originally, they were to perform at one of the French Quarter clubs but get dumped by the owner when they won't cut their fee—this after traveling two hours by bus down from Hattiesburg, instruments and all. They bring their guitars, banjoes, harmonicas, sax, electronic drum set, even a piccolo.

But things have a way of working out somehow. Even though it's illegal, they decide to put on a concert for a rapt audience of two—namely Cady and Jag. Cady can really sing. The guys soon notice so it isn't long before she is wedged between two humongous band members doing a perfect rendition of Curtis Mayfield's beautiful protest song, People Get Ready:

> People get ready, there's a train comin'
> You don't need no baggage, you just get on board
> All you need is faith to hear the diesels
> hummin'
> You don't need no ticket you just thank the
> Lord...
>
> People get ready...

One thing leads to another and they end up with an audience that at its peak must be four, maybe even five hundred. Jag, showing that he is practical Pal's son after all, takes it upon himself to pass his hat around. It doesn't hurt that he's just bought a Saints cap. He raises over $1,900 New Dollars in less than three hours.

Jag can also see that cops standing on the outside of the Square are watching and thinking of busting them since they don't have a license for public performance. But there are way too many people around now so they decide not to wade in with their 32 inch telescopic expandable police batons despite itching to put them to use. This is the same police force that saw a quarter of them desert their posts during a vicious hurricane that nearly finished the city during the first decade of this century. Still, they need a complainant, someone who will give them political cover before they can attack a group of peaceful performers and their flash audience. The usual suspects—existing bar and club owners wanting to put the kybosh on competition from lowly street musicians and buskers—are too busy making money this night to bother registering a complaint so Freedom Express rolls on.

Near dawn, Jag shyly asks one of the guys if he can request a song. "Sure, Dawg, you done buy at least one tune for yo 19 Benjamins," he replies good naturedly.

"It's one Cady knows really well and I, um, I..." Jag says.

"Well, if it for yo bakvissie, yo jus name it."

"It's by the Dixie Chicks, called Travelin' Soldier," Jag finally squeaks.

The guy laughs hugely on hearing his request, showing all teeth with eyes looking to pop out of his head. Still they do it for the two kids from Austin. When Cady hears the first chord, she jumps up, claps her hands and gives the group a huge smile and starts singing her tune. Jag is relieved that his gambit doesn't backfire. He listens to a fantastic performance by her with three of the band members backing her up.

The dew point has been reached, everyone is tired, sweaty (it is really hot in the Big Easy that February) and hung over but still it's a nice moment for the 80 or so people still there—people who can party all night, every night, people who have nowhere else to go, people who just want to feel part of a special night and don't want it to end. The piccolo player carries the tune for the last two verses and then there is no doubt about it, it's a success.

> Two days past eighteen
> He was waiting for the bus in his army green
> Sat down in a booth in a cafe there
> Gave his order to a girl with a bow in her hair...
> I got no one to send a letter to
> Would you mind if I sent one back here to you
> I cried
> Never gonna hold the hand of another guy
> Too young for him they told her
> Waitin' for the love of a travelin' soldier
> Our love will never end...

When they get home two days later, his parents go ballistic; hers are worse. They are forbidden to see each other for three months and grounded for four. Not that it matters. They see each other every day at school and message each other endlessly.

...

"Do you regret going to New Orleans with me?" Jag asks later that day on their second night at the Launch Pad.

"No. There's only one thing I do regret about that trip," Arcadia says.

Really curious now, Jag asks, "What?"

"I didn't get to do this." Then she leans in and kisses him. Not just a peck either. An honest to God, full-on French kiss with maximum tongue.

Jag has never even kissed a girl let alone French'd one or more accurately been French'd by one. He feels like he's just been pole axed. He's gob smacked. It's the nicest thing to ever happen to him.

"I practiced that with Francis," she breathlessly tells him a few minutes later. Francis is Cady's best girlfriend.

"Wow, it worked. Would you like to practice some more... with me?"

"Sure."

For the next hour or so they practice that and a lot more. He gets to second base with her and, as he suspected, she has very nice boobs.

...

"Hello Mr. Durai."

"Ah good morning. Who is this?" asks Jag.

"My name is Yao Allitt. I work with the US Government, Department of Commerce."

This guy has somehow rung up his quantum scanner, something that Jag would have thought impossible.

"How did you get through to me on my scanner?" Jag asks.

"Ah, we have our ways. We've been working on this problem a lot longer than you have my dear boy," Allitt says "Ah, I have someone who would like to talk to you."

Then his Dad gets on the phone. "Hello, Jagad."

"Hi Dad."

"When are you coming home, son?" his Dad asks in his Midlands accent.

"I'm not positive that's a good idea right now."

"Is Arcadia with you? Is she OK?"

Jag isn't sure how to respond to that so he allows himself to say, "I've seen her, she's fine. Can you tell her parents for me?"

"Sure."

"I think those guys who are with you, Dad, killed Mr. Tolbert."

"You don't say. Not surprised to hear it," Pal says cryptically back to him not sure if they can hear Jag's end of the conversation or not. The answer is 'not'.

"Take care of yourself, son."

"Thanks Dad for EVERYTHING."

"Did you have a nice chat with your father, Mr. Durai?" Allitt asks after Pal hands the phone back to him.

"Yes, thank you."

"Well he and your mother are really looking forward to seeing you soon. Mr. and Mrs. Valenzuela would also like their daughter returned safely and intact if you catch my drift, Mr. Durai."

"I understand. Please tell them not to worry on that account, Mr. Allitt."

"Oh but they do, Mr. Durai, they do. They have a lot to be concerned about—job security for one. I also understand that Federal and State health inspectors are on their way now—investigating a series of complaints about dirty hands, unclean conditions, insect infestations, numerous health and safety violations amongst Indian food restaurants and suppliers, particularly in the Austin area."

"What do you want Mr. Allitt?"

"The same thing you do, Jagad. Come work with us. We have great labs, skilled workers, all interested in your new quantum scanners which may hold the, ah, Key to many mysteries we have been trying to solve for a few years now. You will get a chance to work with some of the best and brightest and we can arrange for distance learning so you can even earn your degree, a PhD too if you want. And get paid for it, Mr. Durai. Princely."

"May I think about it and confer with my advisor on the matter?"

"Certainly, certainly. But Mr. Durai?

"Yes?"

"Not too long, not too long."

...

"I don't want you to go, Reed."

"Cady, they can kick your parents out of their jobs and ruin my folks' business without breaking stride. Our economy is so shitty what'll they do then?"

"I don't know," she says desperately unhappy now both for her parents and for herself. "Where will they take you? Will I be able to see you?"

"I don't know. Maybe."

"Stay here one more night. Please. Let's sleep on it. OK?" she asks.

"Alright.

"Hey Cady, will you do something for me?"

"Sure."

"Sing Travelin' Soldier for me... again."

"OK."

He boots up an instrumental version of it on his scanner and then she sings it for him once more.

...

Later that night, Jag is lying in his bunk.

"You asleep?" Cady asks.

"No."

She comes over and slides in with him. "Make love to me, Reed," she whispers.

"No, Cady."

"Don't you want to?"

"More than anything else in the world, for sure."

"Then why not?"

"Because I promised."

"What? That asshole, Yao whatshisname. A promise like that counts for nothing."

"No."

"Then who?"

"Myself. Look I love you Cady. I'm not sure what that means at 16 but it means a lot I think. To me and to you. So let's wait. We'll know when the time is right. OK?"

"OK," she snuggles in tight and falls asleep in minutes. Jag lies awake for another hour. He's not sure now if the time will ever be right.

...

There are hugs aplenty and no recriminations when Jag and Arcadia roll up the next day just after noon at Pasand Palace. Jag makes a deal with Yao Allitt that he can spend an hour and a half with his family before surrendering himself and his two quantum scanners to DOC Marshals at 2 pm local time. Interestingly, they also agree to let him bring his Quantum Entity, G4nesha, with him. Even though it is against US law, he explains that she's an important part of his work and they readily acquiesce.

Against a backdrop of surprised parentals, he gives Cady a now much practiced French kiss and passionate embrace. She refuses to cry in front of either set of parents or the thugs from DOC.

Jag is swallowed up by a huge, black all wheel drive vehicle with tinted windows and is out of sight in seconds.

Involuntarily, Arcadia reaches out for him but he's gone; she won't see Reed again for a very long time.

...

Casey Barnett gets her story. It's a doozy. Just as she thought, the kid's SAT scores are totally bogus. Government investigators have proof they share with her on condition that she will not disclose her source—she agrees as the good reporter she is. Jag Durai's Quantum Entity broke through College Board security, which can only be described as negligently woeful, and pilfered their exams. In intra-gang violence, a two-bit untenured professor at UT by the name of Jin Liú killed his co-conspirator, an overweight high school hack with the ridiculous name of Tank Tolbert in an argument over how to divide the spoils amongst gang members including 16-year old Jagad Durai.

Durai will be tried as an adult not only for his

participation in the conspiracy but also his self-admitted illegal possession of a QE as well as kidnapping then viciously raping a 15-year old girl by the name of Cady Valenzuela. She is lucky to have been rescued alive by DOC Marshals hot on the trail of this vile young man who sometimes uses the alias 'Reed' while hiding and employing illegal aliens in his various nefarious schemes. After a county-wide manhunt, marshals finally catch and subdue Reed in a US national park where he has fled. They find him in a long prepared, secret, East Asian street gang hideout where he had imprisoned this stoic young woman, held there against her will for nearly a week.

They release a picture of the girl showing her in better days during a recent TV appearance performing skateboarding stunts for an appreciative audience. She stands on stage on the edge of her skateboard looking out, quite heroically, over her audience seeming to see in the distance both freedom and opportunity for this troubled land and its people. She represents all that is good about them and seems to carry the weight of the future of America and Americans on her strong-looking young body—she is very photogenic.

Every Mom or Dad in America has a right to be fearful of and angry about the degradations she must have suffered at the hands of this perp who, despite his relatively young age, can rightfully only expect to be put away for a long, long time. Mercifully, Casey leaves these acts of debauchery to her viewers' imaginations. After all, hers is a family-friendly show although they do include graphic photos of the bullet ridden corpse of the hapless fat teacher. They use it as a launch point for an investigative piece into fatty foreign foods being served in university cafeterias around the state, focusing closely on events and suppliers in the Austin area.

...

Unanswered Questions

Preview readers of Book 1 and now chapter 1 of Book 2 have asked about some of the loose threads I have left behind. Part of writing a trilogy is leaving unanswered questions for subsequent books. It's like any serial—you leave your hero, Flash Gordon, at the mercy of Ming the Merciless. Either Flash figures his own way out or Dale Arden (Flash's one true love) has to rescue him. Sound familiar?

Other than the obvious question in Book 1—will Ellen rescue Damien from San Quentin before he expires from starvation, torture or other misadventure, there are some other more subtle ones including:

1. Why do most QEs match the gender of their human counterparts while a few do not?

2. What causes drogue behaviour and what if anything can be done about the drogue problem?

3. Where did Damien hide the Quantum Key?

4. Now that QCC has stopped hatching QEs, will their population ever grow again?

5. Do QEs age? How long do they live?

6. What is the third and final of Nell's last wishes not yet disclosed?

7. What form does QE thinking take? What is their internal dialogue like?

8. Where is Dezba, Nell's worry doll?

9. What does the message Paul Dirac left behind at Marco Gonzalez really mean?

10. How many senses do QEs actually have?

There are others too but I worried about including them here—wouldn't want to give away too much about Books 2 and 3, now would I? You should know that taking inspiration from Agatha Christie I left clues to many of these questions 'hidden' in various parts of Book 1. You just have to know where to find them!

Of course, you may also be asking after reading

Chapter 1 of Book 2, when and under what circumstances will Cady finally get to see her Travelin' Soldier (Jag) again and how long is a 'very long time'?

But don't worry dear reader, my plan is to answer all of these and more before the end of the trilogy which I thought would end at its ending, long planned by me. However, when I did the final storyboard for Book 3, presto, it ends somewhere different than I thought. @ProfBruce

...

Contents

Quantum Entity Book 2 American Spring (2013)

Synopsis of Trilogy, Its Style, Themes, Cast of Characters,
Geography and Technology
Uanswered Questions from Book 1

Prologue

Epilogue

Prologue from Book 3
Contents of Book 3

About the Author
Author's Note
List of Learning Outcomes

To come:
Quantum Entity Book 3 The Successors (2014)

About The Author

Bruce M. Firestone
B. Eng. (Civil), M. Eng-Sci., PhD.

Bruce applied to go to McGill University in Montreal, at 14, arrived after turning 15 and graduated as a civil engineer before legally an adult (then age 21). He was rejected in his first job search because he was considered a 'child', not legally responsible for his actions. Three and a half weeks later he was living in Sydney, Australia. A new and exciting Labour government had just been elected. First two things Prime Minister Gough Whitlam did were recall Aussie troops from Vietnam and lower the age of majority to 18.

Firestone worked for the New South Wales government doing operations research and building mixed integer programming models while continuing his education at the University of New South Wales where he obtained his Masters of Engineering-Science degree and then at the Australian National University in Canberra, where he received his PhD in Urban Economics.

He was among the first group in Australia to fly hang gliders and not die. He has travelled and worked in Canada, Australia, the United States, Sri Lanka, New Zealand, India and many other nations. He has been at times an engineer, a real estate developer, a hockey executive (founder of NHL team the Ottawa Senators, Scotiabank Place and Senators Foundation, a children's charity),   University   Prof, a consultant, art collector and benefactor, writer, columnist, futurist and novelist as well as Executive Director of not-for-profit Exploriem.org dedicated to assisting entrepreneurs, artpreneurs and intrapreneurs everywhere.

Firestone has taught and studied at McGill University, Laval University, the University of New South Wales, the Australian National University, Harvard University, University of Western Ontario, Carleton University and the University of Ottawa, in the subject areas of entrepreneurship, business models, architecture, engineering, finance, urban planning, urban design and development economics.

He has launched or helped launch more than 168 startups, writes a blog about entrepreneurship, urban issues and life at EQJournal.org and moderates a lively @ProfBruce community on Twitter. He is also author of Entrepreneurs Handbook II.

He is married to a most wonderful girl, Dawn MacMillan. They have five great kids and one fine grandson.

...

"Entrepreneurs follow a moral path when they: first, take care of their business so second, the business can take care of their families so that, third, their families can take care of them so, fourth, they don't become a burden on society or their fellow human beings, so, fifth, they can help others so that, sixth, others can help their business," Prof Bruce, 2012.

His current motto is: "Making Each Day Count".

...

On Twitter: @ProfBruce

http://www.brucemfirestone.com

Author's Note

Thank You

There are many people I have to thank and acknowledge for their assistance, support and encouragement as I got ready to write this novel and then did so in one, mad five and a half week sprint from beginning to end during the summer of 2011 while still carrying on (or trying to carry on) my regular duties as Entrepreneur-in-Residence, Executive Director, Broker, Founder, Developer, Consultant, Mentor and, of course, Impeccable Husband and Father.

First, I want to thank all my students of the last 17 years—architecture, engineering, management, artpreneur, commerce, finance, business, entrepreneur and intrapreneur—students to whom I have dedicated this book. Gen Y, as I said there, may be the greatest generation to come along in some time and these extraordinary young people are reflected in the wonderful characters you meet in this book.

My Collaborators

There are many people who have contributed a great deal to help me create this Quantum Entity world.

I want to pay special tribute to hacker architect, former student and renaissance person, Janak Alford for his contributions to the layering of this work and his review as well as his willingness to let his mind go to places that few people dare to go and then share what he finds there with the rest of us mere mortals. Also, a shout out to Janak and his not-for-profit organization, prototypeD.org, for the creation of Quantum Entity, Short Film, (see cast list below). It's a continuation of this book's prologue in video form. They are creating a new industry—trailer-style mini movies introducing books and products other than just Hollywood films.

I want to thank my editor, a gentleman by the name of Murray Rob Roy McGregor with extra emphasis on the word 'gentleman'. He's thorough, conscientious, kind, careful and thoughtful. He's the only person I trust enough to take something that means as much to me as this manuscript and make it better, which he did. He made the work more accessible because, as my reader already knows if s/he has made it this far in the manuscript, my writing can be somewhat impenetrable at times. After all what makes a great writer? A great editor. This is as true for all writers as it is for you and me.

My PhD supervisor, the late Max Neutze, who was a really great writer, said to me early on during my tenure at the Australian National University, "What do you think of your Master's thesis, Bruce?" I had completed it the year before.

"It introduced new concepts in terms of dynamic mixed integer programming models, Dr. Neutze, which helped solve large-scale municipal service problems," I replied.

"Yes, but what of your writing?"

"I think it was well written, Sir."

"Then I have just one thing to say to you, Bruce. If you write your PhD at the same level as your Masters, you will not be successful here at the ANU."

Max could be scary at times and for the next year or so if I saw him coming down a corridor in the appropriately named Combs building (which was a dark, gloomy, Harry Potterish tomb of a structure), I would find a reason to duck into a colleague's office or suddenly recall that I had forgotten something in my own.

I remember his next comment to me was, "Don't worry, Bruce, your first million words are the toughest."

May each of you be fortunate enough to have someone like Dr. Neutze in your life to push you. To his credit, he edited every word of my more than 450 page thesis and showed me how to be a better writer, sentence by sentence. Oh by the way, my PhD is much better written than my Masters.

The marvelous cover art you can see on the hard

copy of this book and its e-reader versions was done by artist, skateboarder, snowboarder and marketing genius Scott Williams from http://www.eyevero.com. Assisting Scott were team members Colin Elliott for web design (http://brucemfirestone.com) and Alex Winch and Jacqueline O'Callaghan on communications. I am also grateful for the careful yet imaginative work done by publicist Alana Kennedy (@AlanaKennedy) who is moreover a dear friend.

For her expert guidance through this new field of e-book publishing, I want to expressly thank Heather Adkins from http://cyberwitchpress.com who worked on e-formatting for Mobi, Epub and Createspace as well as other platforms.

I should also recognize the gracious staff at National Gallery of Canada including M. Marc Bedard for allowing us to launch this book at the Artifex Gala held in their fabulous museum, water court gallery and theatre on Sussex Drive in Ottawa. We tried to make this an authentic evening for our audience. Authenticity in art and life seems increasingly important as the Internet age rolls onwards.

My Experts

These are the people who read earlier versions of the manuscript or were consulted by me and gladly gave their time and expertise to make this science 'real' and the fiction more 'lifelike'.

Thank you to scientist, adventurer and dear friend, Morley O'Neill and Dr. Stephen Godfrey at Carleton University's Physics Department for helping with the science of quantum computing and physics.

My rocket scientist friend, Morley O'Neill, makes the point that technology I describe in the book may be here sooner than I predict. By the time we get to mid-century, we may be far past what I have projected here. Morley is working with me to develop some amazing new tech designed especially for Book 3.

Morley also helped out with the daylighting discussion for Damien's new condo in Toronto as did architects Ralph Wiesbrock and Mark Lucuik. Shawna Cameron, MSc, weighed in as well. Thank you to all.

Shawna also contributed the term 'War on Drogues' which as Ellen says in the book, works about as well as the US Government's War on Drugs has.

I want to thank my friend Sharon Buckingham, screenwriter extraordinaire, for her comments and encouragement. Sharon told me that the secret to great writing (screenplays, novels, what have you) is the re-write. I didn't want to hear it but, alas, she is right. This novel has been through at least two dozen re-writes since its completion—by me, my editor, my test bed readers (with their myriad suggestions) then by me again. It is the only way to put down roots and add layers that (hopefully) intrigue and mystify future readers. You may wonder how do they (writers) do it? Re-write, that's how!

I am grateful to my pal Joe Kowalski for taking me down the Salmon River in Idaho and teaching me how to get a heavy, centre mounted oar raft through the whitewater we found there.

I am forever indebted to an anthropologist friend for taking me, once upon a time, to Four Corners, a place that changed my life and liberated me from some of my own childhood daemons. And to another friend who took me to Mardi Gras and The Rex Ball at the same age that Jag Durai went.

Thank you to Brad Crowe of the Ottawa Senators and Dick Miller of CBC fame for teaching me everything I know about sound engineering which appears in Chapter 1 of Book 1.

To my brother from another mother, Chris Brydges, who co-wrote the rap tune we recorded at Red Pine Camp in the summer of 2011 and use in the novel, thanks for having my back when no one else would. Chris also worked on the lyrics for Nell's biggest hit, The Successors (aka Nell's Folly) which will become more important as we get to Book 3 of the same name.

I am grateful to the young and not-so-young people at

Red Pine, especially Marguerite (lead vocalist), Raj and Adam (on guitars), Mackenzie, Marion, Jack, Andrew, Phillip, Warren, Jake, Kate, Marilyn, Anne, Rose and Adrian (chorus singers and cardboard box hand drummers as well as prop staff, gaffers, best boy and roadies) who came to the tribal council ring one evening just before sunset to record with Chris (rapping) and me (videoing) the first ever and oh-so-authentic, folk art version of WE ARE ALL ONE. See the video by scanning this Qricket Code:

Thank you to my oldest son, Andrew, living in Canberra with his beautiful Moscow-born wife Yulia and their boy (my grandson!) Godric, for reading much of the early manuscript and commenting on it.

A special shout-out to my blood brother, Peter, a criminal-law lawyer on the left coast of Canada, who has appeared before Supreme Court of Canada twice, and to Bill Geimer, for their help with SCOTUS (Supreme Court of the United States) legal procedures. After reading an early draft, Bill commented, "...since this is not only fiction but science fiction, the (SCOTUS) chapter can be anything the author wishes." You can only imagine the number of liberties I have taken in this regard that Bill studiously pointed out for me since he has appeared before the US Supreme Court and, luckily, I have not. Thanks again to my brother for putting up with me, a lawyer-detester, for many years.

I am sincerely grateful to my youngest son, Matthew, who was particularly helpful while I was storyboarding not only this novel but the next two as well. He's creative and can see through a brick wall given enough time. He also exercises good judgment when called upon, like his Mom.

Thank you to my mother-in-law, Cora MacMillan, who read this work and encouraged me in every way a person can but mostly by her example of a peerless life. She is one of my heroes. I love you, Mom.

Thank you to my late father, Professor OJ Firestone, for teaching me so much of what is in this book—knowledge about business, politics, art, economics and life that I could not have gotten any other way. He taught me to look at the positive side of life, to never take 'no' for an answer, to see and seize the day, to respect people and to be gentle with women. Thank you to my personal angel, Jennifer Clark, my co-host on the FirestoneClarkReport.org podcast who gave me my very own Siberian Cedar Medallion to wear around my neck each day.

Thank you to my pal, Larry Bravar, cosmic adventurer, for introducing me to the world of Anastasia and for being a good guy. It was Larry along with my friend Dan Pearlman and my youngest son, Matthew, who ventured to tiny Belize to discover what we discovered there. I am grateful to the extraordinary Robert Combs for being our Ultralight pilot there.

Steve Ablett, young father and wonderful techie, read early parts of this manuscript and contributed the Qricket code you see above. My friend Albert D. Evans, formerly of the British Merchant Marine, shared some of his stories with me and knows Morse Code like most of us know our native tongues.

Thank you to Marc Sherboneau and Susan Tartaryn for their help understanding seg funds, IPPs and trusts. Laser racer Chase Beaulieu helped with the description of a roll tack.

Thank you to Erika Godwin, our young Manager at Exploriem.org, who contributed her knowledge of upstate

New York Elmira College where Ellen Brooks graduates from. Elmira was the first College anywhere to grant degrees to women (in 1855!) equivalent to men's degrees and the world should be grateful that Simeon Benjamin, their Founder, pursued his ideal that: 'perfection would be designed if women and books combined.' Let all men praise him.

I should also like to recognize Theresia Scholtes, Assistant Manager at Exploriem.org, who suggested the use of hashtags to flag a certain type of thought process. It shows up just twice in Book 1 but will become more important in Book 2, American Spring. Ms. Scholtes is also deeply involved in launching each book as is my friend and perennial MC, Rob Woodbridge.

Thank you to now deceased former US Attorney General Elliot Richardson for helping us BRING BACK THE SENATORS and teaching me how to 'intricate' the enemy, his word, that I use in the novel and have defined on one of my Urban Dictionary channels:

http://www.urbandictionary.com/author.php?author=Prof+Bruce
or
http://www.urbandictionary.com/author.php?author=ProfBruce.

Fast growing CanvasPop.com and Chris Rayburn came to my rescue and processed some substandard images for me. They can take the poorest resolution images you have ever seen and create beautiful wall art out of them on their 100-year (guaranteed!) canvases.

Notes on Technology and Sources

I have been thinking about how cell phones might morph into handheld AI (artificial intelligence) units for a long time. I think that Kim Stanley Robinson should be recognized for the marvelous work he did describing how AI tablets help colonists in his trilogy Red Mars (1992), Green Mars (1993) and Blue Mars (1996) survive in that harsh environment. In October 2010, I summarized where I think cell phones are going to go which you can read at: http://www.eqjournal.org/?p=1725 (Cell Phones Ready to Morph into Handheld AI). What I didn't know when I was writing this novel in the Summer of 2011 was that part of the future would catch up to this novel before its publication with the release of the iPhone 4S which contains a cheerful helpmate, voice-activated Siri. It should not surprise anyone that one of the last products that Steve Jobs was involved with would borrow from the future—he was always suspected of being an alien anyway he was so far ahead of everyone else in any industry he turned his wonderful mind to.

Eric Schmidt, Executive Chairman of Google Inc. before the Senate Judiciary Subcommittee on Antitrust, Competition Policy and Consumer Rights, said on September 21st, 2011:

"...history shows that popular technology is often supplanted by entirely new models. Even in the few weeks since the hearing, Apple has launched an entirely new approach to search technology with Siri, its voice-activated search and task-completion service built into the iPhone 4S. As one respected technology site reported: '[E]veryone keeps insisting that Apple will eventually get into the search engine business. Well they have. But not in the way that everyone was thinking. Siri is their entry point.' Another commentator has described Siri more simply as intended to be a 'Google killer'."

So clearly Eric understands the potential for Siri to supplant search engines in the same way that Ellen describes how Quantum Entities might do that in the part of this novel focused on QCC's business model. Except Ellen said it first.

I also wrote the first draft of this book before Steve Jobs passed and before the Occupy Wall Street movement surged into public consciousness including mine. Imagine my surprise when one of the 'leaders' of OWS, David Graeber, turns out to be an anthropologist, an anarchist and, at age 11, obsessed with Mayan hieroglyphs (Bloomberg Businessweek, November 6, 2011.) Oh well.

The vicious rape in Northern California of one of our lead characters was one of the most difficult scenes for me to write. Dr. Dean Kilpatrick and Dr. Kenneth Ruggiero report (Rape in California, A Report to the State, National Violence Against Women Prevention Research Center, May 2003) that over 2,000,000 women in that State (16.2% of all adult women) have been victims of one or more completed forcible rapes. This should be totally unacceptable in any community and is certainly a symptom of deeper problems and issues affecting US society some of which I point out in the book.

Having said this, it has been obvious for quite some time that the American Empire is facing significant challenges—and not just from China* (which I refer to as Imperial China in the book). The most dangerous challenges facing the US are without doubt internal. I have been writing about and teaching in the field of neo-urbanism since 1994 and developing mixed-use communities since the 1980s so it comes as no surprise to me that many people are protesting in the streets as 2011 came to a close—there will be more, I predict.

(* It was abundantly clear to me that China would make space exploration a national priority even before China's grab for land on the Moon was announced. Please refer to: http://news.discovery.com/space/china-moon-resources-bigelow-111020.html. Societies, civilizations and empires have births, lives and deaths like any other living organism. When the US lost its guts, confidence and animal spirits, they left a gaping vacuum that China's ambitious, hardworking people are determined to fill. Almost certainly, it will be a Chinese person who sets foot first on Mars.

I felt Barrack Obama faced many immense challenges when he became US President but in crisis, there is also opportunity. He was bequeathed crises in healthcare, finance, space exploration, trade, debt, income inequality, urban design/development and energy but was unable to seize the day in any of them with the possible exception of healthcare. Anyway, I wrote Moon, Mars, Earth, Asteroid Plan, http://www.eqjournal.org/?p=829, about the opportunity before humanity in space.)

As I said in this book, you cannot have a minority of your population inside gated communities living the dulce vida and everyone outside missing out. It's a recipe for disaster and revolution. I originally wrote Livable Cities Versus Mono Cultured Suburbs for a Conference on Social Harmony at the Ottawa Public Library on December 4, 2001.

It is posted at: http://www.eqjournal.org/?p=2449.

As I noted elsewhere, no industry on this planet is changing faster than publishing. The Internet is eating everything in its path and nowhere is this truer than here and now for publishers. What is happening in this industry is happening much faster than changes to film and music industries which happened at the relatively pokey speed of sound. This is happening at light speed. E-publishing and e-readers are democratizing the publishing business, opening it up to citizen journalists, novelists and writers of all types and allowing groups to efficiently and economically form around the narrowest niche in Chris Anderson's long tail.

It is amazing to me that the music industry allowed a newcomer to the field (Apple's iTunes) to reap most of the benefits from the digital revolution in the music delivery business and reacted to new technology by suing their client base instead. Such lawsuits often directed at grandfathers and grandmothers because their granddaughters were upstairs in their guestroom illegally downloading tunes were incredibly ill advised. Unless traditional publishing houses open up their business models soon, de-fang their hide-bound gatekeepers, speed up their ability to execute and give authors and creative persons both more control over their works and a fairer share of the pie, they will be buried by Amazon's Createspace and KDP (for the Kindle), Apple's iBooks and iTunes, Barnes and Noble's PubIt and other platforms that are proliferating across the Internet.

They will end up like daily newspapers—crushed by Internet competition and associated innovative biz models.

Imagine the timidity of publishers who allowed services like Kijiji and Angie's List (not to mention Craig's List) to completely demolish their classified advertising pages, their most profitable line of business. Kijiji's freemium model generates amazing content and revenues (via its 'top ad' platform where a user can pay for its message to remain on top of a subject category page). It has taken Yellow Pages years and years to learn from Google and others that a more complete data base (made so by allowing anyone now to get a (small) free ad) is worth far more to their search customers than one just made up of paying (and presumably larger) companies.

I have encouraged CEOs of large corporations, professors, student entrepreneurs and artpreneurs to write their own blog, be on Twitter (you can read what I wrote about this if you are interested, Twitter Nation: http://www.eqjournal.org/?p=2080) and to generally not let anyone come between them and their audience and stakeholders—not their techies, their PR or communications people, their publicists, their ghost writers, middle managers, executive assistants. This is one thing you can't delegate—authenticity which people crave today, especially Gen Y. There is a word for this—disintermediate, and if publishers aren't careful and smart, they are about to be disintermediated to extinction.

Process

I started teaching at Carleton University's School of Architecture in 1994 and carried on for the next 12 years. Soon after I began there, I realized that many creative professions have lost their way—they've been pushed to focus exclusively on their costs (cost of design, construction, services, fees, royalties, commissions) instead of benefits or benefits v costs. So a great deal of my teaching, research and writing during that period was focused on redressing the balance between creative persons and commercial interests thereby giving the former the tools they need to obtain more value from their creativity and avoid 'death as a career' move. I have written extensively for them under the heading: 'Get Rich While You're Still Alive.'

See for example:
http://www.eqjournal.org/?p=1931,
http://www.eqjournal.org/?p=2577
and
http://www.eqjournal.org/?p=1410.

Entrepreneurs and artpreneurs need to bring talent to what they do but talent by itself is not enough. They need to be intensely passionate about what they do in order to be successful at it; you're either all-in or you're nowhere.

As I noted above, I wrote a first draft of this novel in one 5 and a half week period during summer 2011. I'd storyboarded it over the previous eight months. Here is the SCHEDULE that a part time novelist such as moi needs to keep to complete an assignment like Quantum Entity—We Are All One as he does all the usual things he is responsible for in his day job:

Go to bed at 10 pm on a weekday
Get up at 2 am
Write until 7 am
Do some yoga and run on treadmill from 7 to 7:45 am
Go to at least 1 of his day jobs
Get home at 6 pm
Be with famdamily until bedtime
Repeat until weekend arrives
Get home 6 pm Friday
Be with famdamily until bedtime
Get up at 2 am Saturday
Start a hackathon session that will last until Monday at 7 am with sleep periods lasting between 10 minutes and a maximum of 2 hrs
Wake up because new ideas are flooding your conscious mind from the subconscious
Repeat every weekend until after a 5.5 week sprint beginning to end, first draft of Quantum Entity Book 1 is completed

Eat sparingly during this entire process, no more than twice a day

Occasional glass of red wine indicated to ward off heart attack* and turn mind off for brief periods

(* My Uncle Freddie (MD from Long Island) recommended one 81 mg tablet of ASA (basically, coated baby aspirin) per day for all men in our family from age 40. Heart attack runs in the male half of the family. Freddie felt ASA could help us with that and other adverse health considerations.)

Crash for 10 hours

Get up and go to work

As Steve Nash, Canada's greatest roundball player and two time NBA MVP says in the novel: "A professional is a person who gets up to practice the day after the greatest game of their lives." Sorry to tell you there's just no substitute for hard work.

In many ways, this novel wrote itself or, at least, after a time, I found myself channeling Nell, Damien, Ellen and others. They were dictating the action; I was merely the scribe/secretary taking dictation. Damien's near-death experience on the Salmon River was a complete surprise to me as was Nell's illness and ultimate, untimely passing. When I wrote her death scene alone early one morning (it was around 4:15 am as I recall) in my little study with the door to our rear yard open and a soft wind, smells and sounds emanating from the nearby Ottawa River coming in and the pre-dawn light of a summer morning in a northern shelf city filtering into the room as well, I was near tears and then I was crying outright. After that, I had to quit writing for almost a week. I have no doubt that characters become dear to their authors; they are like your children of which I have five great kids and now, in a way, more.

I wrote this novel using (mostly) present tense, third party narration to try to give readers more of a 'you are there' feeling and I also used active voice whenever I could instead of a passive one. If you didn't notice this or you did and liked it, it worked. For the former, here are the differences:

She walks across the room and plants a big wet kiss on his unsuspecting mouth.

This is present tense, third party narration and active voice.

She walked across the room and planted a big wet kiss on his unsuspecting mouth.

This is past tense, third party narration—most novelists use this—and active voice.

She is walking across the room and is going to plant a big wet kiss on his unsuspecting mouth.

We are back to using a present tense, third party narrator but one with a passive voice.

Little kid Prof Bruce (he wanted to be an engineer from age 3 onward) was a builder from the get go—blocks, toy soldiers, log cabins, mechano sets, soap box carts, snow forts, tree forts, then later his own gang at an all-boys school (where this was your only protection in those days from predatory bullies and worse), board games (we designed and made our own), toys, businesses, communities, hockey team, charity and not-for-profit. Now Prof Bruce has the opportunity to mentor others who are building their own insanely great stuff and, in this trilogy, to construct his own new world which by the time we get to the end of Book 3 will (try to) go beyond where anyone has gone before (apologies to Gene Roddenberry) and will (attempt to) answer some of the big questions like: WHAT IS THE PURPOSE OF LIFE and ARE WE ALONE IN THE UNIVERSE?

If you would like to teach your kids the power of positive and negative numbers using the game Bananas I describe in the book, it exists.

It's a free online utility you can find at:
http://old.dramatispersonae.org/SmartyPantsGames

/bananas.swf.

It's quite safe to download and play. It's a game I invented about 15 years ago to teach our five kids simple arithmetic (the power of positive and negative integers) and board game strategy. Thanks to Richard Isaac from RealDecoy.com for, all those years ago, coding it. I'm looking forward to the day when media walls are at the point I describe in the book and can bring games from virtual to RL. We're getting close.

It was, more or less as related in Book 1, Dan Pearlman's father, pediatrician Dr. Lyon Pearlman and my late father, Professor OJ Firestone, who upon hearing from the attending physician at the Ottawa Civic Hospital (this was the 1950s, long before the CHEO, Children's Hospital of Eastern Ontario, era had begun) to prepare himself for his oldest son's passing, refused to lose. They took me by air ambulance to Sick Kids in Toronto and told them to fix me which they did although I missed a year of school. Thank you, OJ/Dr P.

Here is Prof Bruce (left) having survived with his BFF Daniel Darin climbing in the Italian Dolomites, ages 11 and 12:

And so I must thank my actual primary school teacher Miss Buril who also appears in Book 1 who saved me from life's dumpster in the same way she saves Damien Bell. With Miss Buril's help and only through her heroic efforts, Prof Bruce caught up, accelerated through the rest of primary and high school then applied to go to University at 14 and turned 15 for his first year at McGill.

At our 2011 Xmas party, we decided on a rather

unorthodox gift for every invitee. In addition to making wine together at the Wine Garden (see: http://thewinegarden.ca where everyone took home 12 bottles!), having a four course meal, listening to live music, hearing a mercifully short speech from the host (moi), people also got their very own worry doll.

As Dear Reader you already know, these are tiny creatures originally from Guatemala, who hide under your pillow. Each night, you tell her your worries and, by morning, presto, she's stolen them away.

Here is my worry doll. For obvious reasons disclosed in the book and above, I named her Miss Buril. Here is Miss Buril keyboarding:

You can purchase your very own worry doll from the Hunger Site by visiting:

https://www.thehungersite.com/store/site.do?siteId =220.

Each dollar you spend funds at least 25 cups of food. We bought Dolls that Xmas and funded more than 500 cups of food.

Here is another photo of Miss Buril getting ready for work:

I want to acknowledge the bravery of persons like Susan B. Anthony who led the women's suffrage movement in the 19th century, Malcolm X for standing up in the 20th century to the most fearsome machine the world has seen since the tyranny of ancient Rome, Karl Heinrich Ulrichs who said what could not be said in 1870 in support of rights for gays and Chief Joseph Nimiputimt for pointing out that Native American Indians still seek justice more than 500 years after first arrival of white men to this land.

I also have to acknowledge the brave people who created the Arab Spring—it is one thing to write about protest and quite another to actually do it especially when people are beating you, imprisoning you or your family or shooting at you. It was 26-year old Tunisian fruit seller Mohamed Bouazizi's suicide that sparked the Arab Spring and inspired people everywhere to fight for their freedom and dignity. Mohamed, who was supporting eight people on earnings of about $150 a month, refused to pay bribes to government officials so he could trade up from his wheelbarrow-based biz to a pickup truck. They had him arrested, took his goods and beat him. Later, he asked the Governor for an audience but was refused so he poured oil on his body and torched himself dying a short time later (either January 4th or 5th 2011—reports on exact time of death are confused). Burns covered 90% of his body. He was a cute kid. Judge for yourself.

Bouazizi had the guts to stand up for justice for real, not just to talk about it or tell stories about it.

I quote, rely on, build on and speculate on the work of many engineers, scientists and natural philosophers in this novel, too many to name here. Wikipedia proved invaluable and many sources went into the Hopi parts of this novel—I am grateful to all who willingly and voluntarily share their knowledge*. I have borrowed and adapted liberally from these people—thank you.

(* I follow MIT's philosophy that knowledge wants to be free which I also embrace on my non-commercial blog: www.EQJournal.org).

Certain songs also play a role—lyrics from Johnny Cash's Ring of Fire, English poet and clergyman John Newton's Amazing Grace published in 1779 and excerpts from Eminem's Lose Yourself as well as Black Eyed Peas' Meet Me Halfway make an appearance as do a number of other tunes. I quote a few words from Kris Kristofferson's timeless tune Me and Bobby McGee, namely: 'Freedom's just another word, for nothing left to lose.' Music makes life, well, come alive. Thank you to all who create and publish these marvelous poems set to music.

While I was writing this novel, I listened a lot to Adele's (2011 compilation) 21. I don't know, Dear Reader, if I succeeded but Adele's mournful, amazing voice and words are channeled somehow into Quantum Entity as is the work by handsome, young Canadian Composer Carl Bray whose marvelous Talk of Hands was played publicly by him for the first time at the Governor General's

Residence in the summer of 2011 in Ottawa. You will meet an older Carl in Book 2; he will be middle aged by then, in the book I mean, when he makes a personal appearance at a jazz club in Vancouver. Certain key characters are in his audience that night. They will hear an amazing love story told via his music and piano. His appearance there comes at a crucial moment in this trilogy when the future of all free humans will be decided although at the time it may not be obvious how.

After performing at the GG's, Carl when asked whether Talk of Hands had ever been written down simply pointed to his head and said: "I made some of it up as I performed tonight adding to it here and there." The spouse of the Governor General was so impressed with his passionate rendition that she asked him to perform it solo again for Will and Kate during their Royal visit later that year. Carl declined because he had already just accepted an invitation to play at the Toronto Jazz Festival.

To my American Readers, you should know that the GG is Canada's Head of State so this is like saying 'no' to a US President which you just don't do—especially not an aspiring young composer who has a chance to perform for hot young Royals on a BIG stage. Yet Carl's ethics are such that he steadfastly refused to renege on his word despite significant pressure to recant.

Exploriem.org, the not-for-profit entrepreneurs and intrapreneurs organization where the Author is Executive Director, subsidized subsequent recording of Talk of Hands in a Toronto studio. You will hear it in due course.

The images of my characters that inspired this novel and its sequels are partly from my mind and experience and partly from a few real life actors, actresses, publicly known and unknown personages. You might be able to find some on my blog (EQJournal.org) but I won't make it easy and I embossed the ones you might discover there to make it hard. But thank you to all.

Chief Dan of the Hopi's Yaqui friend in Sonora is inspired by the work of Carlos Castaneda who wrote The

Teachings of Don Juan in 1968 in which he describes how his training in shamanism with Don Juan begins.

A few people from RL (real life) show up (including an aging Mark Zuckerberg and Richard Florida) but only two RL corporations have any significant impact—Tech Crunch started (and eventually sold to AOL) by my former colleague, Mike Arrington, and Apple whose 'i-Phone 40' becomes the basis for the Q-Phone.

I think we need to recognize that this latter company and, in particular, one of its Founders, Steve Jobs, who taught people to seek to build (again) truly insanely great products and services, not to accept mediocrity and above all, that your life can be more, much more than acting the role of middleman, paper pusher, parasite or bureaucrat.

I also borrow from the historical record—quantum physicist and pioneer Paul Dirac did, in fact, leave Cambridge in 1929 to head to Japan stopping off in Florida before traversing the Panama Canal but there is no record of him having been in Belize let alone the pyramids at Marco Gonzalez as I describe in the book.

I'm sure I am forgetting many people I should thank; forgive me this sin of omission.

If you are interested in Pops' Star Trek Film Projector which appears in this book (there is also one for James Bond movies as well), you'll find them at:

http://www.eqjournal.org/?p=1047.

They project 24 Star Trek films by 2050 and 44 Bond ones by then.

One of my American test bed readers who plowed through an early version of this book told me that, after reading Quantum Entity, she finally got why Canadians don't like being called Americans—it's not that we don't like our American cousins, it's that we really are different. She knows Canada well having traveled extensively here. But her observations were limited to the fact that since Canada has Holiday Inns and Starbucks and everyone speaks English (except for a corner of the country where French flourishes), it must be the same as back home (she lives in the DC area).

She got that I used metres, kilometres, grams and Celsius and English spellings of those when my characters were Canadians or others long domiciled in Canada (like Damien) and American spellings plus pounds, inches and Fahrenheit when my characters were US citizens. Moreover, she also was sensitized to the greater degree to which Canadians tend to socialize risk and expect their governments to play a role in shaping society far beyond what most Americans would be comfortable with. The fact that our cities are different because, for example, Ontario's Planning Act forbids gated communities is probably not something Americans would tolerate, it being too much an infringement of their individual rights. But then again, Canadian cities tend to be more democratic because you get more mixing of races as well as social and economic classes which also make them safer. By creating isolated ghettos of unemployed, impoverished, disenfranchised people, many US cities have become utterly horrible, dangerous, unsustainable atrocities.

Readers will note that there are many unanswered questions in Book 1 some of which I summarize in the section titled, not surprisingly, 'Unanswered Questions'. This is as it should be in my view. That's why it's a trilogy. Life is a mystery; art is a mystery but all will be revealed...in time.

I also tried to let my characters grow, develop and change over time. Although many aspects of our personalities are already in place by the time we are 2 or 3 years old, I am not convinced that people cannot change. In my experience, they do. Often for the better, sometimes not. I am a much more patient person and frankly a nicer one too now than when I was a young engineer. I tried to make even my darker characters like Dr. Evil more than one dimensional—not entirely evil perhaps... Most people are like that—good possibly great at times and thoughtless idiots on occasion.

I loved the article written by Eric Spitznagel for

Bloomberg Businessweek (Jan. 22, 2012) called 'Treasures of the Deep—the dirty, lucrative business of the sperm whale excretion known as ambergris'. It fit perfectly into the Belize story line and would be something that a local like Gillian Boys would know so I added it. It also allows Gillian to show both sides of her personality—the working person's disdain of the ultra rich, a class of people who make up a significant part of her tour business clientele yet her willingness at the same time to adopt some of their ways when it suits her as in making her boyfriend even more wild about her by wearing the ambergris-based perfume called 'Nell'. It's like so many things in life, entrepreneurship and art—ambiguous, contradictory and at the same time true both ways. I also semi-quote Berkeley California perfumer Mandy Aftel in the novel. Her term for ambergris: 'olfactory gemstone' is, well, a gem.

True security comes from what you carry with you between your ears; what you know through education and experience not because of your job description. So do a lot and learn a lot! If you would like to see what happens when you aren't true to yourself, read what former entrepreneurship student, Jennifer Schweers says about her years in the wilderness pursuing her parents' plan for her instead of her own:

http://www.eqjournal.org/?p=2981.

I would like to end this section with a quote from a deaf, (nearly) dumb, blind kid who despite the fact that many of her senses were knocked out reached past her own mind which for you and me surely would have been a disordered place of madness to go to Radcliffe College, become a suffragist, pacifist and birth control supporter as well as world traveler and author of many books. She learned to read people's lips with her hands. To any student of mine concerned about living their own life, being true to themselves, pursuing their entrepreneurial dreams, listen to what she says about security:

"Security is mostly superstition. It does not exist in nature, nor do the children of men as a whole experience it. Avoiding danger in the long run is no safer than outright exposure. Life is either a daring adventure or it is nothing," Helen Keller.

Film Cast

I must acknowledge the cast and crew of Quantum Entity Short Film who put so much time, effort and love into prototypeD.org's mini movie. Why? Because they were paid huge sums of money to do it? Nope. Because they wanted to bring to life these characters and themes—of adventure, politics, law, science, engineering, tech, business and above all the desire for equity, tolerance, freedom and the triumph of love in a troubled world.

Extra special thanks go to our three leads—Miss Jessica Edwards as Nell, Mr. Julien Nolin as Damien Bell and, of course, Ms. Theresia Scholtes as Ellen Brooks. Other cast and crew included: Aziz Garuba Jr., Janak Alford, Andrew Craig, Matthew Firestone, Bruce Firestone, Sharon Buckingham, Jeff Corace, Camille F. Mendoza, Komi Olafmihan, Larry Bravar, Morley O'Neil, Jason Alford, Alex Jodion, Marc Couture, Meg Wagstaff, Natasha Smith, Saban Alford (age 6), Andrew Campbell and Alex M. Chong.

If I have forgotten anyone who helped with Quantum Entity book or short film, a thousand more apologies.

Learning Outcomes

You may have already remarked on the ages of some of the main characters in this book who do incredible things—you think they are too young. Perhaps. But think about Mark Zuckerberg creating Facebook at 20 from his Harvard dorm or 19 year old Michael Dell starting the company that bears his name while at University of Texas at Austin.

I have five wonderful kids but the fact is that from the time that your children first start walking to school on their own (around 7 to 9 years of age I would guess), they started to take over their own lives. You don't own them anymore if, in fact, you ever did. If I had my way, kids would be able to sign legal documents, finish high school, get a job, marry, bear arms, drive, drink and vote from 16 on.

If you have lived in Europe, you'll already know that teens there are often allowed to have a glass of wine with their parents at practically any age and that alcoholism is less of a problem in much of say Italy than San Diego, Los Angeles or Indianapolis (which have the most DUIs in the US for the period 2010/11, according to Insurance.com). Watching George and Laura Bush's beautiful twin daughters Jenna and Barbara getting into trouble back in 2001 for trying to buy a beer at ages 19 (age of majority being 21 in Texas) was ridiculous. These are women not children. You know in your heart that when people treated you like a child, you acted that way. Anyway, Ellen is a woman on a mission and it starts for her at 19. For Damien, it started even earlier—at 15 or perhaps 12/13.

One of my motivations in writing this trilogy was to bring to a wider audience what it is really like to conceive, found, grow and defend a successful (tech) enterprise like Quantum Computing Corp. When I was younger I very occasionally watched shows like Dallas, a TV soap opera about big-hatted J R Ewing and 'Big Oil' in Texas. Apart from marvelous homes, offices, ranches, vehicles, planes and other accoutrements of wealth that their writers, producers and directors could imagine, there wasn't a single thing in that series that struck me as reflective of running a real enterprise—grand scale or tiny.

Being invited into a CEO's office at 10 am and being asked if you prefer Scotch or Bourbon struck me as absurd. I have never known a (successful) CEO that drinks at 10 am or, for that matter, drinks much at all and certainly not during work hours. I have had a rule for as long as I have been in business: Never Drink and Think.

It didn't help that JR was played by Larry Hagman who I could only see as the guy who acted the role of a hapless astronaut without the clarity of mind to grab hold of the fabulous, adoring Jeannie (played by an impossibly cute Barbara Eden in the series I Dream of Jeannie) when she would appear in front of his eyes, then make mad, passionate love to her immediately. Fool!

I have worked with over 168 startups, many of them like the Ottawa Senators, Ottawa Senators Foundation, Ottawa Business News (now Ottawa Business Journal) and Exploriem.org started on our own account plus many others where I played a role of coach, mentor, facilitator, observer, advisor, reporter or cheer leader. I have also written extensively on new business formation on my blog EQJournal.org and elsewhere based on research gathered in a lifetime of wide experience and experimentation. So I tried to bring learning outcomes to this work—to give readers a sense of what goes into new enterprise formation in the 21st century. There has never been a better time in my view to start and run your own business. If I failed to give you an appreciation for this, don't worry dear reader, it's my fault not yours.

Which brings me to a point editor Murray McGregor brought up. Did we invent a new type of novel—a Learning Outcome Novel? I don't know. Maybe that is pretentious. But looking at the three main types of novel—genre (horror, sci-fi, fantasy, crime, mystery, thriller, romance, pulp, graphic, historical, action and adventure, western, children, young adult, teen), literary (artsy) and mainstream (bestseller)—I believed when I started that perhaps this trilogy could be different yet still part of a continuum of work that had gone before. Certainly from day one, I had in mind that in addition to its five main themes (i. a biz story, ii. a political and legal one, iii. science, science speculation, science fiction, engineering and technology story, iv. action and adventure and v. love story) there would be some teaching going on. Then to my surprise, a sixth theme evolved—it became a spiritual and mystical novel which will become more apparent, especially when we get to Book 3.

If you have learned anything from this book about business, science, engineering, urban planning and design, yoga, natural philosophy, sound engineering, startups, entrepreneurship, intrapreneurship, product management,

Mayan culture, the Internet, business models, weather forecasting, history, politics, law, economics, statistics, military culture, PR, media, art, architecture, NLP, HR, venture capital, creditor proofing, agriculture, ultralighting, hang gliding, whitewater rafting, quantum physics or Hopi ways, I am pleased. At the end of this book, I have included an Index of learning outcomes from this novel for easier reference should you ever wish to revisit some of the concepts I have introduced here.

If anything in this work is mucked up, it's my entire fault.

I will try to bring two main additional learning outcomes (one each) to Book 2 (American Spring) and Book 3 (The Successors). What these are, please be patient, all will be revealed in time. Which brings me to my second last point: I have left several important questions—like where Damien hid the Quantum Key—unanswered. I got some early criticism for this from a few (OK, one) of my test bed readers. This is a trilogy so again please allow me some mysteries yet to be unraveled. I will take you on a long strange trip which will end fantastically in a place beyond wonder. It will all make sense. Trust me.

Last, but certainly not least, having already thanked my two boys, Matthew and Andrew, to my wife Dawn and our three daughters, Rachel, Miriam and Jessica, I love you all and hope that women characters in this book will inspire you and other young women everywhere that they too can achieve great things—there are no limits.

@ProfBruce
Ottawa, Canada
June 2012

For More Information:

Exploriem Publications, 2525 Carling Avenue, Suite 23, Ottawa, Canada K2B 7Z2. Attention: Mr. Alex Wolfe, Executive Assistant Tel.: 1.613.422.6757 x 204 Fax:

1.613.422.2807 Internet: www.exploriem.org Twitter: @alexwolfe12 and @quantum_entity Email: awolfe@exploriem.org

Facebook:
http://www.facebook.com/QuantumEntityTrilogy and http://www.facebook.com/Exploriem

YouTube:
http://www.youtube.com/ProfBruce
http://www.youtube.com/playlist?list=PLCD76D02637BE0EEE
http://www.youtube.com/user/quantumentitytrilogy

Images:
Stills from the Film (Generation Q) based on Book 1, Quantum Entity | We Are All ONE: http://qrankcase.com/

Books:
Available from: http://www.brucemfirestone.com

Free:
Send friends first four chapters of Quantum Entity Trilogy for free: http://www.eqjournal.org/?p=3993

Twitter:
@Quantum_Entity
@ProfBruce

Synopsis of Trilogy, Its Style, Themes, Cast of Characters, Geography and Technology

This is a trilogy that concerns itself with the big questions about life and the small details of how we live it. Young Damien Bell, physicist and engineer, designs then unleashes Quantum Communications and Quantum Entities on an unsuspecting mid-21st Century world. The tech company he co-founds along with Romanian mathematician Traian Vasilescu and Elmira College marcom graduate Ellen Brooks, Quantum Computing Corporation (QCC), becomes a fast growing, vastly profitable, globe-spanning one in a remarkably short few years.

Inevitably, they come into conflict with established commercial interests as well as security agencies around the world, first, because their quantum phones (later known as Q-phones) based as they are on hacked iPhone 40s completely disintermediate established carriers and, second, Quantum Entities (QEs) are fully actualized quantum computers that are not only superb examples of AI but appear to be conscious, sentient creatures come to join humanity on its voyage to a collective destiny whatever that may be. What it also means is that Internet security, paywalls and all forms of digital encryption are wide open to possible exploitation by QEs and their human counterparts as well as QCC.

Quantum Entities apparently comply with all human laws but there appears to be an issue with a small minority of QEs called 'Drogues' who, for some reason, do not successfully form a bond with their human hosts. This ultimately results in a War on Drogues and other problems for QCC and its founders.

The introduction of Quantum Communications and Quantum Entities leads to an era of Quantum Economics (later called the Quantum Era), a time when scarcity becomes a thing of the past at least for some. It also leads to a new competition amongst nations—some like the United States embracing (to an extent) the new era while others such as Imperial China apparently rejecting this new technology. This leads to a clash amongst world powers when Imperial China and its ally, Germania (a renamed EU), attempt to impose a new hegemony on a mostly unwilling planet. The last book of the trilogy follows the lives of those who would resist a new tyranny imposed by the Cartesian Powers (sometimes referred to as the Cartesian Axis or simply Cartesians) and how they attempt to do just that.

The trilogy spans four generations and follows three (somehow interconnected) families (the Bells, the Brooks and the family of Chief Dan of the Hopis of Third Mesa) as well as introducing a wide cast of supporting characters and geography. There is also a prequel chapter at the end of the trilogy that returns to the year 1929. There is one final Postscript with the final two reveals of the trilogy.

Style

The trilogy is written with a present tense narrator, an unusual choice for a novel. The concept is to give the reader a sense that s/he is actually there and that he or she is part of this unfolding history.

Furthermore, these are a new type of novel—Learning Outcome Novels. There are three main types of novel—*genre* (horror, sci-fi, fantasy, crime, mystery, thriller, romance, pulp, graphic, historical, action and adventure, western, children, young adult, teen), *literary* (artsy) and *mainstream* (bestseller). This trilogy is different.

Even though it is part of a continuum of work that has gone before, it contains, for example, 835 learning outcomes in Book 1 alone, the most important of which is how to conceive, found, grow and then defend a world spanning (tech) company. The reader gets to see how a group of very smart young entrepreneurs go about designing then implementing a top notch business model for the 21st

Century. The prime learning outcome of Book 2 (American Spring) is centered on how to restructure and revive a nation-state whose economy is failing. There is some additional work done with business models and introduction of concepts like demography, population projections and environmentalism. In Book 3 (The Successors), we learn how a product manager, trying to defend his nation from attack, develops and controls a complex effort on the scale of a Manhattan Project.

It is a multi-themed work. Book 1 has five main themes; it's a biz story, a political and legal one, involves science, science speculation, science fiction, engineering and technology, has action and adventure and, finally, it's a love story. Then a sixth theme emerges—it evolves a spiritual and mystical dimension which become more apparent, especially in Books 2 and even more so 3. If the reader learns anything from these books (hopefully presented as part of an engaging and entertaining storyline) about business, science, engineering, urban planning, urban economics, urban design, yoga, natural philosophy, sound engineering, startups, entrepreneurship, intrapreneurship, artpreneurship, product management, Mayan culture, religion, the Internet, business models, weather forecasting, history, politics, law, economics, statistics, military culture, PR, media, art, architecture, NLP, HR, venture capital, big business, big politics, creditor proofing, agriculture, ultralighting, hang gliding, whitewater rafting, kite surfing, new games/sports, tech, Hopi ways, Maori Poi performance art, jam dancing, Lunar and Mars colonization, Europa, demographics, environmentalism, quantum physics, quantum communications, airships, Belize, Guatemala, Four Corners, Crete and many other locales, then mission accomplished. At the end of each book, a list of learning outcomes is included for easier reference should a reader ever wish to revisit some of the concepts introduced here.

The cast of characters is largely made up of Americans, Canadians, Kiwis, Belizeans and Euros so the books use American spellings and units of measurement (inches, feet, miles, pounds, Fahrenheit...) when in the US or when an American is talking and centimetres, metres, kilometres, grams or kilograms, Celsius... nearly everywhere else as well as British spellings when geography calls for it.

The Author's Note at the end of Book 1 goes into a great deal more detail on new conventions this trilogy attempts to establish.

By the end of the trilogy, the author tries to answer age-old questions such as—at what point would sufficiently intelligent AI warrant extension of human rights, where are other intelligent lifeforms and why don't we see them in the Galaxy around us, are we alone, how did life begin and what is the purpose of life?

Themes—Book 1

The trilogy starts out innocently enough with Damien Bell, like most recent grads, trying to earn enough to pay back his student loans. He moonlights as a sound engineer on major live events. This is how he first meets world superstar, Miss Nell, as her global tour nears its end—her last show is held in Toronto during Nuit Blanche.

Damien along with Ellen Brooks and Traian Vasilescu are trying to get their new tech company, Quantum Computing Corp, off the ground. Both Damien and Traian mostly just want to do Maths and Physics so it falls to Ellen and her biz dev team to actually create, launch and grow a viable business then defend it. Her principal adviser is Angelo Keller, a Boston-based VC.

Damien has little experience outside academia but this changes soon after he meets and then goes off with Nell for the first time. His stay in Four Corners, Third Mesa and at Phantom Ranch as well as his near-death experience on the Salomon River in Idaho awakens spirituality in him that he never knew is there.

Nell feels that sex is overrated but is canny enough never to reveal her feelings to her fans. Still she responds to Damien in a way she has never experienced before. On returning to Toronto from his adventures with Nell for the launch of QCC, Damien is more focused on his research and his company than before. Ellen is the glue that holds the company together through its many phases of development. She is also secretly in love with Damien which leads to a love triangle that takes until more than half way through Book 2 to fully resolve. Even then, it is not really resolved. Their love story is about to get even more complicated.

The launch of Quantum Computing Corp's hacked iPhone 40s that come with a surpise on the upside—a QE that bonds with the first human each Entity (sometimes called Counterpart) comes into contact with—is a success. They first launch their Q-phones into a health and wellness vertical. These helping professionals are immeasurably helped themselves by not only having smartphones that are infinitely fast and come with unlimited bandwidth but their new QE helpmates can do many tasks for them and with them greatly extending their ability to care for their patients.

From there, Q-phones and QEs spread like wildfire to much of the rest of the population.

QEs are pre-programmed to follow (an amended set of) the three laws of robotics but not everyone feels that the arrival of an apparently sentient form of AI is benign. Certainly, established carriers are hard pressed to compete with QCC smartphones and they use their influence with Department of Commerce and others to go after upstart QCC and its monopoly in this new era of Quantum Economics.

There is mounting pressure to turn off QEs with no more thought given to it than turning off a toaster. The matter comes before SCOTUS (Supreme Court of the United States) where Quantum Entity Pet3r, the first of his kind, makes a surprise appearance in defense of his brothers and sisters—'Quantum People'. The arguments made by QCC's lead lawyer (Jerom Van Der Hout) and Pet3r before the Supreme Court are reminiscent of the arguments made in civil rights, gay rights and women's rights movements of years ago—basically, they are asking, 'At what point do artificially intelligent creatures like QEs deserve to have human rights extended to them?'

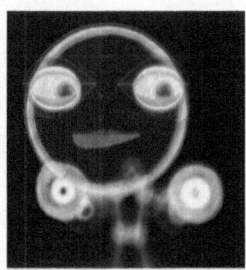

Pet3r Whose Q-Number is 1

In order to extinguish QEs, US agencies require access to the Quantum Key. Only Damien Bell knows where that is. Dr. Bell believes that if you want to keep a secret, tell no one. As a result, Dr. Bell is interred by the US until he is prepared to release the Key to them which he is not prepared to do—it would be tantamount, in his view, to genocide.

Towards the end of Book 1, US Army National Guard vehicles are taken over by Drogue QEs and there is a battle in front of SCOTUS. After this, QEs are banned in much of the world and are forced underground. QCC is placed in receivership and most of its principals are ruined financially or in prison or both.

Ellen Brooks, helped by gay rights leader-in-waiting, Evan Salazar, goes to QCC America HQ in San Francisco to start the largest protest movement seen in the US in nearly a century.

There are five main themes in Book 1—engineering, science and science fiction, biz dev, politics and the law, action/adventure and romance. Finally, a sixth theme emerges—one of spirituality.

Themes—Book 2

Book 2 begins in Austin, Texas and picks up the story based on a minor character in Book 1—Jagad Durai, a 15-year old hacker, who has discovered something marvelous about QEs that no one else, including the inventor of QEs, knows. The chapter also introduces Arcadia (Cady) Valenzuela, Jag's best friend.

We don't see Ellen again until Chapter 2 but we learn that she is now head of a movement that seeks to establish a new nation, the Commonwealth of the United States. USC stands in opposition to the Republic of the United States. The Commonwealth will be based out of San Francisco and soon nearly 30 States will be solidly in their camp.

Ellen makes a secret visit to Tunisia to meet up with a person (a Sufi mystic) who has information that will help her in her mission—to completely end the Republic and replace it (as peacefully as possible) with the new Commonwealth.

Damien remains in US Custody and is in bad shape. He has still not been persuaded to give up the Quantum Key.

The first part of Book 2 (which is Part IV of the trilogy) is full of palace intrigue as the President of the United States, Samuel Schwinn, fights to hold onto power. He is determined not to be the last President of the Republic now nearing its 300th year.

It ends with three surprises—a double agent revealed, a traitor revealed and a murder mystery.

Part V of the trilogy is about reviving the economy of the Commonwealth of the United States which has been in the dumpster since the ban on QEs is first introduced by the now disgraced Republic and the short era of Quantum Economics, a time when scarcity starts to become a thing of the past, came to an end. The scene switches between San Fran, Vancouver, Maya Fair (Nell's home in San Pedro Town on Ambergris Caye) and Stockholm.

Ellen is determined to see the Commonwealth catch up to Imperial China and Germania not to mention other world powers such as the AU (African Union) not only in terrestrial technology but also space-based assets in the emerging Moon-Mars-Earth system.

Mars Colony is becoming an important economic engine and will be more so after they raise their planetary shield which will improve Mars weather and living conditions.

Part VI introduces the reader to Naya whose early life is split between San Francisco and Vancouver. She is largely brought up by her father. Naya's life is marred by a sudden illness that changes the course of her life dramatically.

Naya carries the last third of Book 2 and much of Book 3.

Naya is torn between three men in her life—one who is fabulously wealthy (his family owns the enormous 24/7 c-store empire), one who is a major Bundesliga (football) star on Luna Colony and one who is a scientist working on nanosite technology, a plain Irishman by the name of Sean Ruane.

Book 2 will also reveal some of the hitherto unknown interconnections between the three families—the Bells, the Brooks and Nell's people—the Hopi of Third Mesa. Other questions such as what caused the Drogue problem, how many senses do QEs actually have, how long do they live, why do most QEs match the gender of their human counterparts while some do not, what do the messages left behind at Marco Gonzalez really mean and other unresolved mysteries are disclosed in Books 2 and 3.

As Part VI and Book 2 near their end, storm clouds appear. Even though the Commonwealth is doing better economically and with greater social harmony, Imperial China and Germania, now joined in a 1,000-year Friendship Treaty and called by many the Cartesian Powers, have found new ways to threaten freedom everywhere. The first Sinofighters appear. Sol War I is about to break out and will affect humans and QEs everywhere in the Moon-Mars-Earth system.

Attacks on Mars cause the leadership there to pursue an independent course marked by a surprising turn of events that affects the entire solar system.

An unfortunate misunderstanding separates Naya from her true love at a time when she is most vulnerable. Evil doers seek to capture her to use her as leverage to finally pry loose valuable information that is still beyond their reach.

Themes—Book 3

Book 3 begins with the issue—what to do about the continuing problem with Drogues. The Commonwealth is preparing to use the Moriarty Trap on them—a way to divert them without killing them or damaging the greater QE population.

While this problem has come to the forefront, no one really knows what to do about the real issue—the challenge posed by Sinofighters. The sudden, unexpected attacks on the Commonwealth on Earth and on Mars by Imperial China and Germania mean that everyone is either hiding behind quantum shields or they are dead.

It is up to a group of Commonwealth scientists to counter this new technology with a super weapon of their own, nicknamed 'Hewy'. The location of the Quantum key is finally revealed.

Hewy is only partially successful. It slows down attacks by Imperial China and Germania but does not end them. The survivors of the Commonwealth are cornered and given two choices—incarceration in camps or death. But then third and fourth alternatives appear.

Naya remains a prisoner and her lover, now realizing that he made a mistake, is determined to rescue her and punish those responsible not only for her incarceration but also the things they have forced her to do for them. He is assisted in his quest by a young warrior monk—a girl determined to help both him and Naya and also to never be a victim like so many others at the hands of Cartesian might.

Readers might be surprised to learn the identity of this female monk.

Book 3 answers some of the big questions—are we alone in the universe, why don't we see other intelligent beings and what is the purpose of life?

Some Commonwealth survivors take a new third option while others escape to the Guatemalan Highlands (a 4th option) using some new tech of their own—personal quantum shielding. They will remain there until circumstances change in their homeland.

Before the trilogy ends, the leader of the free peoples hidden in the south will take final revenge on someone who has harmed all three families irreparably. She will be assisted in this by Dekka, silent Croatian head of security since the time of Nell.

Book 3 also includes at its end a prequel chapter that explains the origin of the third way out. It follows the 1929 journey of historical figure Paul Dirac, Quantum Physicist, from Cambridge to Japan by way of the Panama Canal and Ambergris Caye and what he does in the caves beneath the Mayan tri-pyramid structure at Marco Gonzalez. It also explains how Minoan artifacts somehow end up in Oregon and why they use a Mayan numbering system despite the fact that the Minoans predate the Mayans by at least 1,000 years.

Structure of the Trilogy

Each book has a table of Contents, 16 chapters and one epilogue and is divided into three parts. Hence, the entire trilogy has 48 chapters, three epilogues and nine parts (I to IX). At the end of the trilogy there is a prequel chapter set in 1929. There is one last Postscript at the very end.

The Trilogy begins as the midpoint of the 21st Century approaches and ends in the early part of the 22nd Century. The prequel chapter adds another 120 years (approximately) of history. The final Postscript contains the last two reveals of the trilogy.

Each book also includes a List of Learning Outcomes at its end as well as an Author's Note.

Principal Human Characters*—Book 1

(* In approximate order of appearance.)

Damien Bell, age 22, when we first meet him. He is a quantum physicist doing his post doc at U of T. Tall, trim build, brown hair. He has old fashioned values because he was brought up by his Grandfather. Damien's QE counterpart is **Pet3r** (pronounced 'Peter').

Ellen Brooks, age 19 at the beginning of Book 1. Curly blond hair down to her shoulder blades. From wealthy upstate New York background. Biz dev and biz model whiz as well as marcom genius. Ellen is mated to **Ash3r**, one of the few QEs who does not match the gender of his or her human counterpart.

Traian Vasilescu, Romanian mathematician and hacker. **Vl4d** is Traian's QE.

Dr. Luis Castagino over-seeing Damien's post doc work. Dr. Castagino is originally from Argentina and is a Professor of Mathematics whose best work is behind him. He recognizes that in Damien, he has a second shot at (reflected) glory.

Nell, age 25, performance artist from Palos Verdes, California. Raven-haired beauty. ¼ Hopi. Granddaughter of **Chief Dan of the Hopi**. Nell's QE is **Su7e**.

Pops, Damien's grandfather.

Tony Reznik, age 48, Nell's agent.

Dafne Weinstein, late 40s, early 50s. Nell's publicist.

Wendy Morales, Nell's conditioning coach, a hipster from LA.

Dekka, Nell's silent Croatian head of security.

Elsu late 30s. Hopi woman. Widow. Mother of **Daniella** also known as '**Ella**'.

Angelo Keller, Senior Partner at BVP (Bessemer Ventures Partners). Keller is based in Cambridge. 103 years old when we first meet him. His QE: **Adu1us**

Gillian Boys, granddaughter of **Tim Boys**, CDN outfitter in Belize. Ginger hair, compact and tough. Freckles. Funny. Resourceful.

Javier and his spouse **Mica** (Belizean owners of the Caye Caulker Island Princess Hotel) plus their 17-yr old daughter **Dakota**.

Captain Rudy Filane, water taxi boat captain out of Belize City.

Private Raymond Michaud, everyone calls him **Sunny**. Member, Royal Canadian Dragoons (Petawawa, Ontario). Hometown: Miramichi, New Brunswick.

Boyd Combs, 42 yr old descendent of **Robert Combs**. Ultralight pilot. Leader of the **Black Aces Reunion Flying Club**, also known as the **B.A.R.F. Club**.

AJ Ramos, impossibly good looking Hollywood Actor.

Bert Steenbakker but everyone calls him **Dango**. School Bully.

Jay, Marine Corps vet. Pal of Damien's.

Zbigniew Zimmermann, senior official at DHS. First to understand what QEs loose on the Internet means. Pursues QCC for contravention of FCC, DOC and ICANN rules and for national security reasons. Aka **Dr. Evil**.

Erik Renke, investigative reporter for Toronto Chronicle Tab.

Mike Cronkey, OLA Tech Crunch reporter from Northern California, who is interested in getting the real story out there; befriends Ellen who becomes a confidential source for him and Tech Crunch.

La'kisha Tomlinson, Federal Court Judge—US District Court for the Southern District of New York (Manhattan). **Z4ra** is her QE.

Mary O'Regan, Ellen's horny roommate in Toronto.

Aziz Mukono, QCC's rent-a-CFO.

Anthony del Castillo, one of the top biz dev guys at QCC.

Sayed Bashir and QE **Q1ntas** from McLaughlin Markowitz Media. Acting Head of Media Relations at Q-Computing.

Samir and **Barbon**, Damien's (later Ellen's) bodyguards.

Ophélie Moreau, part of Ellen's security detail. From Trois-Rivières, Québec. Very tough. Very fast.

Vincent Bowen, Former LAPD Officer.

William Corace Junior, Former LAPD officer.

Yao Allitt, General Counsel for U.S. Department of Commerce. Later known as **General Yao**.

Paul Macintyre, RCMP safe cracker. Quantum Counterpart is **Ead0in**.

Jerom Van Der Hout, QCC lead counsel before SCOTUS. Working with other lawyers: **Peggy Shields**, **Walter Cunneyworth** and **Henry Linnert**.

Evan Salazar, key organizer of the We Are All ONE protest movement, also active in Gay Rights movement. Touted to perhaps become first real national leader of Gay Rights movement. Evan's QE is **He9burn**. Another QE who mysteriously does not match the gender of her human counterpart.

Justice James Roemer, SCOTUS Judge.

Madam Chief Justice, SCOTUS.

Marc Licinias, Commander of the Army National Guard (Brigadier General Retired).

Federik Bernstein, former elected New York District Attorney for New York County (Manhattan) now Solicitor General.

Roy Lew, Receiver for a large US-based accounting firm.

House Manager Sally Thornton, SF Women's shelter called St Jo's. They also have a choir called St Jo's Women's Choir.

Nahuel, Nell's ½ brother.

Principal Human Characters*—Books 2 and 3

(* In approximate order of appearance.)

Jagad (nicknames, Jag and Reed). 15 year old Indo-American hacker living in Austin with parents, **Kiri** and **Pal**, owners of **Pasand Palace** on **Middle Fiskville Road**. Last name **Durai**. Jag's QE is **G4nesha**. Nickname: **Nesha**.

Arcadia Valenzuela (nickname Cady). Both Cady and Jag are at the **Liberal Arts and Science Academy (LASA) High School** of Austin.

Tommy Tolbert also known as 'Tank'. LASA Maths and Physics teacher. Former Texas Tech football player. Hero of the Yangon Engagement. Teaches and mentors Jag.

Austin Vue newsfeed talk show host **Sandra 'Sandy' Lopez.**

Maria Mayfield, Austin-born supermodel and new voice of **Nell Perfumes**.

TNN's KC 'Casey' Barnett. News Narrator for TNN. 35 years old. Brunette, 5' 8". Skinny. Blue eyes, fair skin.

Jin Liú, an untenured prof at **University of Texas at Austin in Physics (UT Physics).**

Adam Campbell, Chief Executive Officer, Tunisiana.

Salem Bouazizi, bother of **Mohamed Bouazizi,** Sufi mystic.

Chuck Wong, scientist, imprisoned in San Quentin with Damien.

Sabine Schwinn, President's daughter. First daughter. Neuroscience psychologist. PhD candidate at Yale. Her Papa's pet name for her is 'Puppet'.

President Samuel Schwinn, President of the Republic of the United States of America.

Sawyer Schwinn, Sabine's older brother who dies in a refinery fire.

Freid Hof, former navy seal, best buddy of Sawyer comes to Third Mesa to volunteer for the Commonwealth of the United States.

Daniella, Elsu's daughter. 20 years of age. UCSC student. Everyone calls her 'Ella'. Looks Hopi (long black hair) except she is quite tall, much taller than her mom, and has intense blue eyes. Her 'father' who died of alcohol poisoning is obviously not her biological father but Elsu will never tell anyone who that really is.

Micah Glazer, NYT reporter. Takes a leave of absence to write a biography on Ellen. Curly red hair, great sense of humor.

Dan 'Danny' Glazer, son of Micah and Daniella.

Farrar Staubach, General of the Army. S4y3rs is his (illegal) QE. Expert Texas Hold'em player.

Mr. Owen, Ellen's neighbor in San Fran

Rebecca, Mr. Owen's great granddaughter, Becky.

Jonesy, male nurse.

Donna Ann Agnes Brooks, Ellen's Mom, but everyone calls her Aggie. In part because of one of her middle names but mainly cuz she went to Texas A&M. Poi fire dancer.

Euphony, late 30s. Nickname—Euph. Holds séances at Vancouver's Wreck Beach with some of her Wicca and sells her art and other stuff at her foundry on Granville Island. Handmade talismans of fertility. Very womanly figure, like the mini goddesses she designs and fabricates. Her last name is secret.

Zora, Euphony's daughter.

Zachary, Zora's son. His nickname is 'Ray'.

Prez of UBC, **Henry Woo**, and his matronly wife **Elizabeth 'Betsy' Hammersmith** live in Norman MacKenzie House.

Bob Schultz, Secretary of Defense for the Commonwealth.

Dr. Shelby Zewyki, Secretary of Energy.

Alex, EA to Damien. Age 21.

José-Luis, Dakota and Traian's baby boy—**José-Luis** is born three years before **Naya**. **José-Luis'** nickname is **JEL**. JEL plays for FC Bayern Munich in the Bundesliga.

Jamal Ugo, JEL's agent at LA-based IMG. Former NBA player. Ran IMG Basketball Academy before becoming head of IMG Sports Academies. Now one of their top agents.

Finn and **Magellan** (fraternal twins), Naya's younger twin brothers.

Caleb De Theirry, kite surfer dude from NZ sometimes mistaken as an Aussie. He's ½ Maori.

Tane, Caleb's 9-year old son. Blond haired, home schooled ¼ Maori living with his Dad on the Princesa Agnes where his father is in charge of water sports.

Joe (Ya Ya) Jaime, Naya's revered dance teacher and choreographer.

Tor Haden, QB for the 49ers. Everyone calls him 'Thor'. He is a local boy originally from San Mateo County.

Darryl Hnatyshyn, Head of Mixed Media Collective, MMC.

Clifford Hexham II, hipster heir to inner city chain of c-stores called **24/7** that sells alcohol, guns, chips and pop.

Clifford Hexham I, 100+ year old father of Clifford Hexham II. Second wealthiest person on Earth. Head of San Fran-based **Club Les de Sades**. Successful Executive Producer (films).

Sean Ruane, blocky bloke studying at Berkeley. Everyone calls him '**Micky'**. His family originally hale from **Falls Road in Belfast**, toughest Irish Catholic part of anywhere. Even though his family has been in America (Boston) since the 1840s, they proudly maintain their traditions. Sean's QE is not bonded with him. Nevertheless, they are allies. **0dri4n** is his Uncle Des' QE.

Niamh Ruane, red haired younger sister of Sean. She is 5, Sean is 15 when they become orphans and go to live with **Uncle Des** in Alameda County, California. 'Niamh' is pronounced 'Neve'. Her nicknames are 'Holy Jumpin' and a kind of derivative of that, 'Holly'. She is also known as Kaya, which means 'Elder Sister' in the language of the Hopi.

Costa Levendakis, school buddy of Sean's.

Jon, Ellen's older bother, and his wife, **Natalie**, and their child, **Lily**.

Brother Rick Brydges, Padre.

Baby Michael, Naya's son. His nickname is 'Gus'. Red haired child.

Gran Maestro Iridia del Rosario Villa, from Matamoros. Teaches Korean Mouhébong Taekwondo and use of weapons including especially nunchuk and kama. Mouhébong Taekwondo originates during the time of the Lee dynasty (1790). It represents seven colors of the rainbow—purity, beauty, harmony (with nature), creativity, defense, therapy and betterment.

Principal Non-Human Characters*

(* In approximate order of appearance.)

Pet3r, Damien's QE partner. Pet3r's Q-number is 1.

Ash3r, Ellen's QE partner. Ash3r's Q-number is 3.

Vl4d, Traian's QE partner. Vl4d's Q-number is 2.

Toby, Damien's cat when he is a kid.

Su7e, Nell's QE who's Q-number is 4.

Adu1us, Angelo Keller's QE.

M4gnus, failed QE partner of Dr. Luis. Leader of the Drogues.

He9burn, mated to Evan Salazar.

Z4ra, La'kisha Tomlinson's QE.

Q1ntas, Sayed Bashir's QE.

Miss Buril, Doob/Dooby, Damien's Worry Dolls.

Dezba, Nell's Worry Doll.

Freddie, Traian's worry doll.

Ala5tair, of Scottish and Greek origin. Meaning of Alastair is 'man's defender'. Bonded with attorney Henry Linnert.

Ead0in, Paul Macintyre's QE.

S4y3rs, Farrar Staubach's QE

0per1s, Richard Florida's QE. Becomes world famous urban redesigner. In the mold of **Hernando de Soto** and **Walt Rostow** as well as **Richard Florida**. Oper1s is Latin for 'building'.

0dri4n, QE friend of Sean Ruane.

Hortense, Ellen's cherished camel.

Tristan, Hortense's mate.

B4nq pronounced 'Bank' is a Drogue who works for M4gnus.

Popeye, Damien's cat when he is an adult.

Ti3-Gu41, pronounced Tie Gway (Tie-Guai) (Body Snatcher). First and tallest of the Sinofighters.

Sammy, Zora's hero camel.

Geography

Scenes occur in many places including:

- Toronto
- Rochester, New York
- Third Mesa [Near Four Corners]
- Phantom Ranch, Grand Canyon
- Salmon River, Idaho
- Boston
- Belize City
- Caye Caulker
- Ambergris Caye
- San Pedro Town
- Maya Fair
- Marco Gonzalez
- Bucharest
- NYC
- Langley Airforce Base
- Northern Ontario—The Lake
- St Jo's Women's Shelter in San Francisco
- San Francisco
- San Quentin
- Austin
- New Orleans
- Barton Creek Wilderness Park
- Carthage, Tunis, Tunisia
- Algeria and Morocco
- Ghudamis, *le temple du message*
- Washington DC

- Northeast Imperial China near the border with North Korea [Close to Shenyang or Shengjing (盛京), capital and largest city of Liaoning Province]
- Revival House, Pacific Heights, San Francisco. Views to water. Decent security. Revival-style, 'Beaux Arts' home.
- Wreck Beach, Vancouver
- Granville Island
- Norman MacKenzie House, University of British Columbia
- Vancouver
- New Zealand [North Island—Rotorua and Auckland]
- Stockholm
- Hermosa Beach
- Los Angeles
- San Antonio
- Salvation Army Kroc Center on Turk Street in San Francisco
- Bell Leadership Foundation, not-for-profit organization based in San Francisco and at Maya Fair
- Golden Gate Park and Spreckels Lake
- University of California, Berkeley
- Oregon (Umatilla National Forest)
- Luna Colony, Shackelton Crater, south pole of Moon, 21 km in diameter, 4.2 km deep
- Mars Colony, Valles Marineris, east of Tharsis near equator in Mars' western hemisphere, 9 km deep trench (4,000 km long and up to 200 km wide), HQ of DARCH
- Europa, source of water, Europan shrimp and Goby fish
- Dallas-Fort Worth metroplex
- Gabriola Island, Gulf Island, Strait of Georgia
- Port Isabella, Free State of Texas
- Q-space
- Guatemala Highlands [Near Quetzaltenango also known by indigenous name Xela]

Political Landscape

13 Colonies of Mars, 10 managed by DARCH, one each by Imperial China and Germania, one by Hippies

AU, African Union

Central Commission for Discipline Inspection and Party Loyalty

Club Les de Sades, powerful private club, San Francisco-based, allied with Rogues

Commonwealth of the United States, parliamentary democracy

DARCH, World LLC that manages Mars

Drogues, plague of unbounded Quantum Entities

Emergency War Power Act (EWAP)

Germania, renamed and expanded EU

Imperial China, muscular dominant power in Asia and on the Moon

National Revolutionary Army, People's Liberation Army, Sol Liberation Army

Quantum Computing Corporation, QCC introduces era of quantum economics

QCCII, QCC's successor, another World LLC

Republic of the United States of America, US or USA, run by corporate elites and moneyed political parties

Republican Old Guard, referred to as Rogues, domestic terrorists, seeking to reinstate old Republic

Shuanggui, Imperial China discipline system

Sinofighters, allied with Imperial Chinese stormtroopers

Sol War I, total war in the Moon-Mars-Earth system

Truth and Reconciliation Committee

Technology

Airship
Apple Picker
BPI, Birth Prevention Insert
Dampening Field
DNA marking

DNA scanning
Drogues
Farm-in-a-box, aka Roxie
Hatchery
Hewy
Media Wall
Mindlink/Quantum Entanglement
Mindscanner
Mtv, Materiality Television
Mtv Test, similar to screen test
Nanosite Constructors and Deconstructors, force decon or decon force
Nanosite Generator and nutrient feed system
Personal Quantum Shield
Pico Carbon Tube materials
Q-phone
Q-space
Quantum Bubble/Planetary Shield
Quantum Entities/Counterparts
Quantum Key
Quantum Scanners
Quantum Shielding
Quantum Tunneling/Transport
Sinofighter
Sinofighter console
Skin coat or skin coating
Space Elevators on Luna and Mars
Tentacle Nutrient System attached to hydrothermal ocean vents
Vacuum Energy Communicator
Vacuum Energy Concentrator

Weapons

Cosh
Fan
Glock 29

Jiujiebian, a Chinese nine section whip, segmented metal chain used in their martial arts

Kama, right handed or left handed (looks like a deadly sickle)

Katana (long sword)

Nanosite DNA-seeking Deconstructors

Nanosite IT code-seeking Deconstructors

Nunchaku (nunchuks) capable of delivering lethal or stunning blows, DNA-specific poisons and deconstructors, electric shock and vacuum energy via its Kontei; used by young female warrior monk—she calls her pair of nunchaku 'The Trods' short for freedom fighter in her language; its two handles are connected using a Himo (wire rope) instead of a chain—useful for garroting; performed in collaboration with Taekwondo

Sinofighter mindscanners

Tanto (knife)

Wakizashi (short sword)

Words/Phrases/Conventions

Cartesian Powers, sometimes referred to as the Cartesian Axis or just Cartesia

Persons therefrom are called, on occasion, Cartesians

Cartesia is the 1,000-year alliance of Imperial China and Germania (a renamed EU)

Germanian, Germanians, persons living in Germania of Germanian origin

Intricate, to involve someone in a scheme without their apparent volition

Jeld, join and meld two people during or after intercourse such that a mild electrical current passes between them

Media Wall, universal, two-way video and audio walls

Meteormorphologist, weather shaper on Mars or Luna

Mindlink, thought exchange between bonded QE and human or between two QEs sometimes denoted by hashtag (#) before each such thought or exchange

NSM mix, nanoscale mix, painted or sprayed on to make any surface a media wall
Paparrazzoid, unwanted photographer
Rogue, Republican Old Guard
Ukes, short for unmated QEs or uQE.

New Games/Toys/Sports

Bananas
Kids Sit Down Windsurfer
Snowboard Mini Hang Glider
Street Paddle Tennis
Superflyer XIV

...

List of Learning Outcomes*

B
Baby Boomer, 139
Back to the Future, 472
Bad faith, 412
Bakvissie, 491
Bananas, 128-129, 518-519
Bankruptcy, 409-410, 414, 419
Barton Creek Wilderness Park, 484
Bass, large mouth, 73-74
Battle of St. George's Caye, 153
Baymen, 153
Beachburg, 86
Bearings, true north, magnetic north, 164
Belize, xi, 70, 143-159, 184, 510, 524, 526
Belize City, 143-144, 147-149, 151, 156
Belizean crocodiles, 189
Belizean independence movement, 153
Belmopan, 151
Benjamin, Simeon, 369, 511
Benjamins, 491
Bernoulli Effect, 215
Big Media, Big Business and Big Government, 20
Big Smoke, xi, 69-70, 113, 189, 334, 402
BIG win for me-LITTLE win for you, 390
Binge drinking, 263
Bizzaro, 74
Biochemical oxygen demand (B.O.D.), 75

Bitterroot National Forest, 85
Black swan event, 130, 432
Blake, William, 5
Bloody Code, 357
Blue Heron, 72, 74-75, 404, 451
Bluff, 294, 421
Boise, xi, 81, 96, 108, 113
Bonaparte, Napoleon, 37
Borg, 172
Bouazizi, Mohamed, 521-522
Bounty hunter, 420
Bourgeois taste, 39
Boys, Tim, 145
Bradley Fighting Vehicle, 392
Brandeis Brief, 365
Bright Angel Trail, 77, 78, 163
British Honduras, 145, 153
Brownian motion, 71
Brownstone, 213, 219
Brujo, 470
Brukdown music, 166
Bucharest, 33, 227, 246, 262, 327, 416
Building orientation, 230, 236
Building permit, 241
Bulgakov, Mikhail, 53
Bulleit, Augustus, bourbon, 488-489
Bureau of Indian Affairs Police, 347
Burgess, Anthony, A , Clockwork Orange, 406
Business Model, 37-38, 113, 123, 135, 137, 193,

HST, 411
Human rights, 252, 291,
369, 371, 437
Hydraulic gradient, 87, 95
Hypothermia, 89, 91
Hydroxychloroquine, 262,
330

I
I DREAM OF JEANNIE, 528
I LOVE LUCY, 397
IBM Selectric (typewriter),
278
ICANN, 31-32, 124-125,
196, 257
Ice storms, 93
Idaho, 81, 84, 114, 275,
508
Ideas, infinite, 133
IFP (Independent Financial
Planner), 411
Ignorant, 224, 325-326
Illegal aliens, 370, 385, 496
IMG, 42
Immigrant, 56, 116, 146,
317, 443
Imprint, 97, 201, 208, 249,
376, 480
Income source deductions,
411
Individual Pension Plan
(IPP), 412
Inguinal creases, 105
INS, 385, 407, 420
Insight, Creativity, v, 177-
178, 285
Instructional sex video,
447
Insurance, 90, 151, 280,
408, 411-412, 528

Insurance, life, 412
Internal dialogue, 206, 499
Internal Rate of Return,
IRR, 200, 205
International
jurisprudence, 297
Intrapreneurs, 523, 529
Intricate, 314, 511
Investment Banker, 115,
118, 312
Investment House, 258-
259, 286
Inversion layer, 89
IP, 121-125, 182, 196, 286,
306, 416
iPhone, 1-2, 45, 53, 60, 65-
69, 81, 85, 96-99, 104, 118,
122, 137-138, 194, 198,
200, 203-204, 469, 512
IPO, 228, 244, 246-249,
255, 258, 265, 289, 291,
297, 302, 312
IQ, 272, 288
IRA, 413
Iron ring, 40
IRS, 377, 408
Island Expeditions, 148
ISPs, 223
It's the economy, stupid,
321, 347
iTunes, 137, 514

J
James, William, 359
Jaws, 17, 390
Jobs, Steve, 137, 512, 524
Joe jobs, 478
Johansson, Scarlett, 82
Joke, 47, 125, 215, 298,
370, 378, 410

* Please note that page numbers associated with the List of Learning Outcomes is approximate only. The number of editions and platforms in today's publishing world make it nearly impossible to have stable page numbers. In most e-editions, you can use ctl 'F' or a FIND function to locate a topic of interest to you.

www.ingramcontent.com/pod-product-compliance
Lightning Source LLC
Chambersburg PA
CBHW030921020726

47498CB00001B/51